BAREFOOT WITH Scorpions

A NEW LEG ZALIZO THRILLER

STEPHEN F. ROBINSON

Barefoot with Scorpions
Published by The Conrad Press Ltd. in the United Kingdom 2025

Tel: +44(0)1227 472 874
www.theconradpress.com
info@theconradpress.com

ISBN 978-1-917673-36-5

Typesetting and Cover Design by: James Sadlier, jamessadlier@me.com
The Conrad Press logo was designed by Maria Priestley.

Printed and bound in Great Britain by Clays Ltd, Elcograf S.p.A

For Bella and James...
...in absentia

SPIRITUS INVICTUS

Коли провидіння застерігає:
«Ти не зможеш поодинці перемогти Бурю».
Воїн відповідає: *«Сам . . . Я [стану] бурею».*

When providence cautions:
'Alone, you cannot prevail against the storm.'
The warrior replies: *'Alone . . . I [will] become the storm.'*

The before...

Prologue

DALLAS, TEXAS

The fact she's having a better than average day doesn't surprise Alicia Corazón one little bit. After all, her life is pretty darn good right now. And, with the results of the ultrasound scan she'd been handed less than an hour ago, nailed on to get a whole lot better.

She is thirty-one years old. With a law degree—*a damn good one*—from Texas A&M. And, until very recently, more than content to direct nearly all her waking hours toward developing her burgeoning private law practice. Steadily growing its reputation within the world of corporate governance. Almost exclusively in the specialist field of mergers and acquisitions; the fees she's now able to command for her expertise, nudging close to the top end of the scale.

An extraordinary metamorphosis that would occasionally catch her completely off guard, making her head spin.

For the majority of her life, she'd been guilty of viewing those imbued with pride and ambition with equal disdain. But the harder she pursued her dreams, the more she leaned towards moderating her judgement. Not just because she recognised how far both traits had driven her from the precarious start in life she'd endured. Far more because, when time allowed, it meant she was able to represent the occasional plaintiff *pro-bono*. A commitment she'd made to herself all the way back in college. Focussing her altruism solely in the direction of small shareholder, class-action lawsuits. Representing decent, everyday folk; your typical naïve victims of bad advice and unscrupulous practices. The kind of unglamorous litigation that rarely made the headlines. And no doubt the reason she'd been told—*on more than one occasion*—she was the kind of person who made a world of difference, in a world brim full of indifference.

And right now, it was all adding up to something she'd once thought far beyond her wildest aspirations. Certainly something her Salvadorian parents could never have imagined for their precocious *chica milagrosa*; a safe and prosperous foothold within a first-world diaspora. And nothing short of a miraculous transformation for an unaccompanied child immigrant who—*just like her impoverished and long-deceased parents*—had started out with little more than the clothes on her back.

Added to which, she'd only gone and found herself a man. Pulling her, suddenly and completely, into a maelstrom of passion she'd been totally unprepared for. A guy she'd literally stumbled into only ninety-five days, twenty-two hours and some-odd minutes ago.

Not that she'd openly admit to keeping a tally.

And when she thought about it now, it had been less like stumbling and more like veering head on into a brick wall. Recalling how she'd been peripherally aware he'd attempted to avoid their collision. Stepping to his right, just as she'd veered left. Because, despite the fact she'd been hurrying, head down, eyes glued to her cell phone, his imposing physique had cast a noticeably long shadow.

He'd caught her arm, to keep her from falling.

She'd caught her breath.

Then, for no reason she's been able to get straight in her head, she'd asked if he would consider letting her buy him a coffee for his trouble.

He'd said he liked—*it*, but—*it*—didn't like him.

Then he'd added, '*...go figure.*'

So, taking him at his word, that's precisely what she'd chosen to do. Figuring she would continue to stand right there, like some dewy-eyed juvenile, blocking the sidewalk. Gazing into a pair of shimmering blue-green eyes, until he gave in and spoke to her some more.

Eventually, he'd obliged by saying, '*...but I guess a cold beer would make for an agreeable substitute.*'

And, apart from the occasions when he'd put in a series of night shifts, working with Dallas PD's notoriously opaque organised crimes unit—*involving some kind of weird case he'd been called in to advise on, but couldn't really talk about*—they'd pretty much screwed themselves breathless ever since.

So, right now, she finds herself standing on the steps of the Earle Cabell Federal Building. Watching, with a dumb smile fixed on her face, as his 70s-vintage AMX eases away from the kerb. Back out into the rush-hour traffic. Its big-ass engine burbling a rich, deep note. Shiny paintwork and a whole bunch of polished chrome reflecting the mid-morning sun.

She'd told him her status conference would likely take no more than a couple of hours. And that she would give him a call in the event her meeting was curtailed to any significant degree. He'd said—*that suited him just fine*. Especially since they needed to talk. Because he'd made up his mind that same morning, he was thinking to quit his career in the military. So he would go find somewhere nearby to hang around. Then, just as her chest felt like it was set to burst, he'd leaned across the transmission tunnel and kissed her hard. Which was how he seemed to do pretty much everything. And by the time she makes it half-way across the federal building's vaulted concourse, that weightless feeling she gets every time he touches her—*dammit*—still hasn't faded.

Ahead of her, a majority of the figures in her field of view are funnelling toward a line of security desks, like iron filings to a magnet. Meanwhile, others in the growing throng were simply milling around. Some in small groups, talking intently in hushed tones. Others standing alone, eyes towards the entrance, checking out the steady stream of arrivals.

Just then, a lone figure glides by on her righthand side. Almost brushing her shoulder. Their focus fixed dead ahead. Towards the security desks. Wearing a grubby and ridiculously long khaki-coloured overcoat on what was, after all, a decently warm day.

She shortens her stride as the figure comes to an abrupt stop. Right in front of her. Sweeping his coat open. Like he's about to instigate some kind of flash-mob performance. And, for a brief moment, the series of loud spits she's hearing doesn't register as gunfire. The puffs of red mist she sees bursting from the figures in her line of sight, striking her as absurdly cartoonish. And, as bodies start to fall, she's unable to discern that some of the screams she's hearing are her own.

The gunman turns. Sets about re-loading a suppressed automatic assault weapon of some kind. Dropping a spent magazine onto the polished tiled floor.

She watches it bounce and spin.

For what seems like an eternity, the scrawny, lank-haired creature appears to be grinning straight at her. But when she looks—*real hard*—she sees his eyes are busy tracking targets.

The heavy veil of silence that descends upon her has an eery feel of unreality. But she knows it's likely coming to her aid. Giving her a moment of relief from the sensory overload violating her mind. So she can maybe think a little clearer. About the fact she'd carelessly dropped her legal binder. And how bizarre it looks as it lands, half-shredded, amid all the bullet casings. And how her hands—*now that they've instinctively dropped to clasp her belly*—feel strangely warm...

...and wet.

But mostly, she's struck by how unfair it is that she's yet to share her amazing news with the man she'd fallen head over heels for. How his decision to forsake his high-flying military career has completely blown her mind. And how, right now, all she wants to do is close her eyes...

...maybe rest awhile.

And, as she feels herself falling, she thinks it could be she's calling out his name. A name so unusual, yet so familiar; after only ninety-five days, twenty-two hours and those few extra precious minutes since she'd last tallied the time they'd spent together. A name consisting one simple, three-letter syllable. A name that, from the moment they'd shared their first beer together, has felt so comfortable on her tongue.

'Leg...'

Trouble was, the furnace pulsing through her abdomen has begun to consume what remains of her senses. So she's not at all sure she's managed to utter any distinguishable words.

Even so, regardless the mind-numbing carnage unfolding around her, she knows there's one thing she simply has to keep on believing. In spite of everything—*no matter the dark stain she's watching spread slowly away from her, out across the cold polished floor*—she's somehow managed to protect the brand new life they'd created together.

From nowhere, a moment of intense clarity washes over her. Like one of those warm Caribbean waves she recalls from her childhood. Helping soothe the wall of fire, now turning to ice, as it spreads through her core. Granting the fast-shrinking space in her mind the lucidity it's struggling to maintain. Because it occurs to her now—*in the seconds before she finally gives in to sleep*—if this inscrutable guy, with a body as hard as granite, is only half the man she's convinced he is...

...he will come for them.

Soon.

And after...

Day One

'The Itch...'

ALEXANDRIA, WASHINGTON DC

Carl Jordan Miller knows the mission he's been tasked is as simple as they come. Truth be told, barely more than rookie-level stuff compared to the kind of shit-storms he'd been deployed into during his close on two decades serving in one of the US military's most vaunted front-line units. Back when he'd been required to pit his combat skills against adversaries way more tenacious, and much harder to keep between the crosshairs, than the soft-bellied sap he's shadowing right now. And, for damn sure, in places way more hostile than Old Town, Alexandria.

After all, his objectives couldn't be more straightforward.

Track the target...

...wait instructions.

Nonetheless, as he begins making his way along Jefferson Street, the competing voices he'd woken to that morning continue their battle for supremacy inside his head. One demanding he man-up and stick with the program; insisting he ignore the tightening sensation he feels in his chest. The other, no less strident, pushing him to apply his customary instinct for caution and accept that maybe the time has come when he should seriously consider walking away.

Not that punching someone's lights is something that bothers him—*per se*. On the contrary. He'd made it through three ball-breaking active duty tours to the Middle East after all. Surviving more kill or be killed *fubars* than he cares to remember. Each and every one, he recalls with a bitterness that still burns inside him to this day, requiring strict adherence to bullshit rules of engagement.

And there it was. *The crux of his dilemma*. The disquiet lying at the heart of his growing unease. The reason he detects that all too familiar whiff of something turning sour. That same unpleasant odour every grunt he'd ever known registers whenever they suspect they're about to be hung out in the wind.

Even so, he'd still risen at 5 AM—*just like always*—sticking rigidly to his regular disciplined routine. A cold shower. Followed by a light work-out. Chugging down a bland protein shake and his usual intake of minerals and vitamins. Not forgetting the half an aspirin and canteen of water he takes religiously every day as part of his stringent health regimen. Because he knows, better than most, dehydration and thick blood slowed a man's reflexes and clouded the mind. And yet, despite all his physical and mental preparations, here he was, struggling to dispel this goddam debating society echoing around inside his skull—*driving him nuts*—blurring his critical thought processes. Disrupting the laser-like focus he'd come to rely on throughout the whole of his professional career; where an uncanny ability to clear his head of unwanted distractions had, more often than not, proved essential to his survival.

So, not for the first time that morning, he scolds himself to dial back his concerns. After all, if there was one thing he sure as hell doesn't lack, it's mental fortitude. Besides, with or without the turmoil going on between his ears, he'd long ago come to terms with a prevailing reality. When it all got boiled down to the bones—*especially for people in his line of work*—choices pretty much always turned out to be binary affairs. Certainly no different than the one he faces right now.

Either he keeps moving forward, much as he's done for the greater part of his adult life, one foot in front of the other, following orders—*without question, without hesitation*—or he bails out.

It's 9.48 AM, *Eastern Standard Time.*

Through force of will, he pushes the voices from his mind. Tugging the peak of his baseball cap a little lower as he approaches the intersection with South Washington Street. Targeting his thoughts back to the job at hand as he begins heading north along the broad, tree-lined thoroughfare, bisecting through the heart of Old Town's up-market business district. Passing by a whole bunch of tastefully-appointed commercial establishments devoid of homeless veterans huddled in doorways. Traversing street corners absent the usual pods of restless youths, wearing their ill-fitting pants hitched closer to their knees than their midriffs. A neighbourhood conspicuously free from the usual unsightly social stigmata plaguing other less-prosperous zip-codes of the nation's capital.

In point of fact, for the time of day, pedestrians and road traffic are both unusually light. Two more random anomalies thrown into the mix, just to piss him off—*or so it seems*. Because, as a basic rule, he considers busy streets and sidewalks an equal opportunity environment for someone in his profession.

Out of nowhere, he pictures himself back on Liberty Street, Ann Arbor. Where, back in the day—*during his post-grad year at Michigan State*—he'd spent an unhealthy amount of time gazing at the abundance of eye-candy promenading its equally leafy parades. So, at any other time, he might have considered this part of DC a place worth hanging around. More than pleasant enough to merit a leisurely stroll; indulging his penchant for drinking cortados, people watching, from beneath the canopy of some trendy kerbside café.

But not today.

Because, right now, he's putting most of his concentration into maintaining a relaxed, easy stride. Biting down hard on the resentment he feels brewing in the pit of his gut. Doing his best to push aside the fact that his part in the mission has been recklessly compromised. You could put it down to his years of combat training, or a highly-tuned instinct for self-preservation. Either way, his request to be in position and hunkered down well before sun-up had been ignored. That most basic surveillance doctrine, tossed aside for no good reason he's been able to fathom.

The subject he'd been tasked to shadow had been ordered to attend an urgent meeting—*10 AM sharp*—in the building opposite the one he's heading towards. And knowing, all too well, the menacing persona of the individual who'd issued the summons, there was zero chance the instruction would have been ignored. Which meant the order to tail his target that morning had been utterly pointless. Achieving nothing other than needlessly risking his personal exposure. *And that's what rankled most.* The one thing he'd hoped his move out of regular military service, into the lucrative world of private security contracting, would help him break free from.

Following bullshit orders.

As it is, he finds himself heading like some remotely operated drone, toward a six-storey, concrete and glass office condo. Making sure he sticks to using designated pedestrian crossings. Because, from the moment he'd been forced to park his rental two blocks from where he needed to be, his primary concern has been centred on getting off the street without attracting unwanted attention.

And for good reason.

He is a fraction over six-foot. Broad-shouldered. Narrow

at the waist. Muscular in all the right places. With a facial structure, while far from perfect, ranking plenty better than average—*in his humble opinion*. And then there was the neat scar clipping the outside edge of his right eyebrow. The result of walking into the business end of a sucker punch thrown from the shadows, in a down-beat strip bar outside Nashville, better than ten years back. Delivered by some local punk in a grubby jacket, baggy jeans and beat-up sneakers. A scrawny little prick, at least a head shorter and close to half his weight, with a set of chunky metal rings nestling south of his knuckles. Likely looking to elevate his standing in some local neighbourhood gang. Or perhaps just making good on a petty dare. Either way, not someone worth chasing down and beating senseless. And positively not if you happened to be a US Army Staff Sergeant at the time, looking to avoid an aggravated assault charge and a stint in Leavenworth; swiftly followed by a dishonourable discharge.

Even so, he remembers fretting for weeks while the gash had healed, only to discover it was a defect all manner of folk seemed to find alluring. Likely drawing their attention to his pale blue eyes. A combination of genetics and happenstance that tended to get him noticed.

A lot.

Which was why, as he makes his way across the avenue, he keeps his head down and his shoulders hunched forward to lessen his profile. Pulling the peak of his baseball cap lower still as he reaches the condo's tree-lined parking lot. Approaching an entrance he already knows is covered by a couple of one-eighty-degree security cameras. One either side of the doorway. And the reason he'd dressed, head-to-toe, in dark blue gear that morning. Because he knows it's one of those maybe colours your average, off-the-shelf, commercial CCTV set-up finds difficult to discern. Maybe blue. Maybe black. Perhaps even dark green, depending on the light.

He's wearing lightweight slacks and a zip-up sports jacket, sans corporate logos. Both one size bigger than he needs, to soften his physique still further. And, as a final touch, a pair of thick-rimmed, clear-lensed glasses; clear because, even on a bad day, his vision was better than twenty-twenty.

Added to which, for the time being at least, the weather has turned in his favour. The sky hanging low and leaden. With just enough unseasonably cold drizzle in the air to encourage everyday folk to keep their heads down, eyes fixed on sidewalks turning slicker by the minute. Plenty depressing enough to discourage any casual, passer-by curiosity. Nonetheless, as he raises his latex-gloved hand to the door's security keypad, he glances back towards the street. Confirming, one last time, his movements have not been closely observed.

It's 9.55 AM.

The building he's about to access is low occupancy. Sandwiched between a Capital One Bank and an up-market funeral home. Rising like an irreverent, glossy middle-finger amid the otherwise dignified, colonial-styled, low-rise architecture. But such offences to urban planning continuity does not register in his mind. Because, his focus is dialled in on remaining unseen. On looking and acting much the same as any one of the slow-to-rise office grunts he'd seen that morning. Maintaining an appearance of familiarity for his surroundings as he drifts across the unattended foyer. A large, dark-grey canvas sports bag, slung casually across his shoulder. Convinced he'll be taken for nothing more than just some out-of-shape business-exec type who regularly hits the gym before work; likely compensating for an otherwise sedentary nine-to-five existence.

All pretty mundane stuff for an operator with his unique talents. Not to mention the eye-watering active mission bonus he's due to be paid.

Which is why, against his better judgement, he'd elected to do precisely as commanded. Tailing his mark from their swanky, waterfront apartment, to a high-end foreign import dealership. Kicking his heels for over an hour while a brand new Mercedes G-Wagon had been picked up. Swinging in behind the high-riding, boxy German SUV. Tracking it unseen, two vehicles back, east along the Capital Beltway, toward the Potomac River. Waiting in his own drab airport rental until the remote camera-feed he has linked to his cell phone confirmed his target—*one Dillon Robert Buckley*—had made it to his workday office.

Within minutes he is in position. The peak of his baseball cap spun round. Spectacles set aside. Video-cam broken down and stowed. Water bottles and energy bars lined up within easy reach. Cell phone set to vibrate. Lying prone in the far corner of an unfurnished, open-plan office space; rented a month in advance from a letting agent more than happy to deal in cash. His position concealed internally by abandoned, shoulder-height desk dividers. Externally, by tinted glass and vertical fabric blinds. Second-floor elevation. Overlooking the broad, tree-lined avenue. Opposite the headquarters of Lexstone Security Corporation.

Two days earlier, on his one and only set-up visit, he'd cut a six-inch fire-hole from the base of the floor-to-ceiling window. Six inches because that was the diameter he'd judged adequate for the maximum sighting sweep he would need. Plenty big enough to accommodate the high-end SOCOM suppressor he's just about to fix to the barrel of his customised M14 rifle. And the exact size of the silicon plug he will fit into the cut-out, once his mission is accomplished. Supremely confident that, from any angle—*unless someone was searching specifically*—he'll be almost impossible to detect.

So now he is ready. Weapon assembled. Zeroed in. Waiting...

...*as instructed*.

HALE COUNTY, TEXAS

There had been a time when the main highway from Lubbock to Amarillo had run straight through the centre of Plainview. Back when the town had been able to offer its inhabitants just enough employment opportunities, at just about sufficient pay rates, to support a standard of living tolerable for those content to subsist with modest expectations. Back before a seemingly endless cycle of droughts had begun placing a withered boot onto the backs of a community already halfway to its knees.

These days, Highway 27 is little more than a remanent; running through the heart of a town whose population had shrunk below twenty-thousand souls. The arrival of the interstate, routed out to the west, ensuring more and more of an already dwindling populous continued to drift away in search of brighter prospects elsewhere.

Out on the southern edge of town, on the eastern side of the old highway, adjacent the county's municipal airport, the headquarters of Hale County Sheriff's Department sits in stark contrast. Fresh and neat as a Brooks Brothers suit. A modern complex of single storey buildings; consisting an angular, pale-grey concrete jail block, slotted between a beige, brick-built administration wing on one side and a decent-sized vehicle maintenance hangar on the other. Out back, there's a well-stocked vehicle compound, bounded by a ten-foot high chain-link fence; with an MRAV—*a mine-resistant armoured vehicle*—dwarfing the usual inventory of police cruisers and SUVs. All of which represented some serious paramilitary capability for a rural county shuffling its way into decline. And, unless the small, one-time cattle town—*with its minor-league status as the birthplace of Jimmy Dean*—had suddenly become the centre of some unreported crime epidemic, the entire set-up had the look of being conspicuously over-funded.

On the other hand, the one thing it most definitely wasn't, was welcoming. And even less so on a blisteringly hot day out on the Texas panhandle.

Leg Zalizo has been seated in the administration wing's glass-fronted foyer for over an hour. Stared at and ignored in equal measure by an in-and-out flow of deputies. Most looking over-nourished and under-employed. Some escorting a rag-tag assortment of the county's less savoury inhabitants. The odd few restrained. Most of them not. And, although the minutes had ticked by at a decent click, it had still been an amount of time he was unsure he could afford to lose.

'Okay, *Colonel*...'

Sheriff Clyde Jeramiah Tillings glances at the thin sheaf of notes he holds in his left hand as he speaks. Behind him, beyond the glass divide, a knot of deputies are craning their necks, like a ball-park crowd anticipating the season's first pitch.

'...or whoever the hell it is you're claiming to be today.'

It's a little before 9 AM, *Central Standard Time.* And much the same as anyone with a good amount of military service under their belt, Zalizo had long ago learned to relax whenever and wherever the opportunity presented itself. So, for the time being at least, he elects to remain seated.

'I appreciate the promotion, Sheriff... but it happens to be *Lieutenant*-Colonel.'

'Noted,' Tillings says. 'Though, as of right now... I really couldn't give a damn...'

The multiple-term department figurehead rests a fleshy hand on the grip of his holstered nickel-plated revolver.

'But, okay... since you'd have me believe you're some kinda stickler for details. Let's cut the horseshit, shall we. See if I've got things straight.'

As theatre went, Zalizo finds himself mildly entertained.

'Sure,' he says. 'Let's do that.'

Tillings spends a moment making like he's diligently re-scanning his notes. Although, for someone trained to recognise and react to the kind of small behavioural signals your average civilian routinely ignored, Zalizo judges the Sheriff's fixation on his wad of hand-written papers more likely to be a well-practiced affectation than a genuine cognitive deficiency.

'So... some time back, you saunter into *my* county with a Dallas PD captain in tow. Requesting I deputise you onto the county payroll, for an unspecified period, to keep your rear-end off-grid... while you get your head back together after that federal building ruckus a few years back.'

Zalizo waits for the explosion of cold fury flaring behind his eyes to subside.

'Not exactly how I would've framed it. But I guess that about covers it.'

Tillings ploughs on undeterred.

'And, like the proverbial country chump, I agreed. Partly because, back then, you identified as a Dallas PD detective... and because the captain said he was happy to write up the admin and cover the cost. But mostly because I was obliged to the captain for earning his Purple Heart, rescuing one of my *real* deputy's kids from a hole in the ground out there in I-raq, or Afghanistan... or whatever.'

'That would be... *wherever,'* Zalizo says. 'And it happened to be Syria. But I'm guessing you don't give a damn.'

Tillings curls his mouth into a sneer.

'Okay, *Colonel...* if that's how it's to be, I'm going to level with you, here and now. Because, frankly, I was never comfortable with your little charade right off the bat. Besides, it's one thing my agreeing to help a fellow brother-in-blue. But to be told, this far down the line, you're a goddam serving army officer...'

'That would be... *marines,*' Zalizo says.

'Marines... army... or the goddam coastguard. Wherever you happened to have blown in from, means less than nothing to me.'

'Well, like you said, Sheriff... I usually find it's the small details that sometimes matter most.'

'Oh, really...? The same as when you deceived everyone into believing you were a Dallas PD organised crimes detective.'

'I was under secondment,' Zalizo says. 'Assigned to advise the Captain's squad. So... technically, there was no deception involved.'

Tillings lets out a patience-exhausted sigh.

'Well, Colonel... that was then and this is now.'

He waves his papers for effect.

'Your file says you've been hold-up in a shack on Davidson for these past months. And, I don't mind telling you, around these parts, that street lies in a somewhat hinky neighbourhood. Leastways for someone of your lofty rank to reside in voluntarily...'

Tillings exaggerates an expression of curiosity.

'...care to explain, *Colonel?*'

Zalizo shrugs.

'The shack, as you call it, is a loaner from a guy the captain served with one time. I'm told he moved on a good while ago... though, for the life of me, I can't imagine why. But I'm reliably informed it's where he was born and raised. So I guess he's loathed to let the homestead go... no matter how modest. And it suits my purposes just fine.'

'Does it now...? Yet your file says you're hardly ever there.'

'Like I said, Sheriff... it suits my purposes.'

'Your file also says you almost always eat out. Usually at *Table on Tenth*... and always alone.'

'Happens I'm a sucker for any establishment offering better than average chow... and the company of folk who know how to respect a man's privacy. So... it's another place that suits my purposes.'

'Fascinating, I'm sure,' Tillings says. 'Yet you don't frequent bars... or any other single-guy places. Instead, you go for long runs... and always at night.'

Zalizo shifts forward in his seat.

'It might have escaped your notice, Sheriff... but it tends to get a little warm around here during daylight hours. Though I'm more curious why it is you folk have developed what some might consider an unhealthy interest in my daily routines.'

Tillings breathes out slowly.

'You don't entertain anyone, of any persuasion, as far as anyone can tell. And but for that one, solitary in and out... you've never once paid me, or any of my staff, the courtesy of making yourself known, before rolling up here today, unannounced.'

Zalizo holds his expression neutral.

'I'm pretty sure, *one* and *solitary* amount to the same thing.'

Tillings reddens, narrowing his eyes. Backs it up with a better than average attempt at a menacing glare.

'Not one offer to give this community even a single goddam day of voluntary service. You know... maybe as a little thank you to the good folk of Hale County for keeping your ungrateful ass... *off-grid*.'

'As far as I'm aware,' Zalizo says. 'That was never a stipulated part of the arrangement.'

Tillings shifts his ample girth and not inconsiderable weight, lowering the wad of papers to his side.

'As it happens, *Colonel*... I couldn't agree more. Which is why, applying the exact same principle, I'm inclined to deny you this latest unstipulated part of our... *arrangement*.'

Zalizo hauls himself up off the bolted-down plastic bench.

Seated, and with only a cursory glance, his stature would have been hard to discern. Standing, he's a whole different ball of wax. Closely resembling a six-three by forty-eight inch column of roughly hewn granite. Though tapered at the middle somewhat—*and a good deal more mobile*.

Tillings takes an involuntary step back.

'Okay, Sheriff... I guess that's your prerogative. But it may interest you to know who it was tracked your *real* deputy's kid down after his ambush and abduction. And who it was vectored in the Captain's extraction team. Provided the suppressing fire... and stayed behind to mop up after the kid's squad was medivac'd out.'

Zalizo jabs his thumb towards his own chest.

'Happens that was yours truly. So... think of this as a kind of butterfly effect. You were honouring the Captain... he was honouring me. And now, albeit a little way down the line, you get a chance to have a positive impact upon a yet to be determined outcome.'

Tillings opens his mouth to speak. Then seems to think better of it. Acquiring the expression of someone whose brain was struggling to reconcile a particularly stubborn paradigm that had somehow lodged itself inside his pumpkin-sized head.

'Oh... and, one last piece of information for you, *Sheriff*.'

Zalizo steps a little further into the space between them. As incursions went, it was pushing a decent way toward being overtly provocative. Not that such considerations bothered him one little bit.

And certainly not today.

'The Captain who risked his hide at the pointy end of the kid's rescue. He was awarded a Distinguished Service Cross. Which... putting aside your indifference to details, happens to be one down from the Medal of Honour. Therefore, a few points north of his Purple Heart. And it's one of the reasons his wife and kids persuaded him to exchange his desert camos for Dallas PD blue...'

He watches the sheriff's pallor turn a darker shade of crimson. Registers the man's hand tighten on the grip of his revolver. Only a fraction. But it was there. If you were paying attention.

And, as it happened, paying attention to his surroundings—*and the demeanour of the individuals he encountered*—was, unquestionably, one of his more deeply imbedded instincts.

'All I'm asking for is the loan of a badge and a cruiser... twenty-four hours max. Then I'll be out of your hair for good. Meantime, I'm pretty sure your world's not going to stop turning. Parish churches won't spontaneously combust. Local virgins, if you have any, are unlikely to become the victims of miraculous conception.'

Zalizo turns. Begins heading for the exit.

'I'll be waiting outside.'

Two oppressively hot minutes pass before a decent-sized tub of grease appears. Squeezed inside a uniform designed for a frame at least two sizes smaller. Wearing a wide-brimmed hat and a heart-felt scowl.

His name tag reads *D H Abbott*. His gold-coloured badge proclaiming him the department's senior deputy.

He comes to a stop a few strides from the entrance. Tosses over a shiny, five-pointed silver star, encased in a leather belt clip.

'CJ says... y'all better make sure it's returned in the condition you got it.'

Zalizo catches it smoothly.

'And the cruiser?'

'CJ says... y'all can whistle for the cruiser.'

Zalizo hooks the badge casually onto his belt, next to his double-stack .45 automatic. Checks his tactical watch as he turns towards his emissions-busting AMX.

It's a little after 9 AM, *Central Standard Time*.

'Much obliged,' he says.

ALEXANDRIA, WASHINGTON DC

Across the street from where Carl Jordan Miller lies prone, Dillon R. Buckley is seating himself toward one end of a long, faux marble conference table, stacked with bottles of some thinly-disguised, rip-off version of Perrier. Opposite two smooth-skinned Ivy Leaguers. Both lounging, bored but relaxed, in their open-necked linen shirts and cashmere suits. Thick-piled carpet beneath their equally expensive, handcrafted shoes. The seats they occupy, high-backed and over-padded. Pseudo Mondrian artwork adorning the adjacent wall, bathed by the thin glow of low-watt LED spots. No doubt someone's lazy interpretation of boardroom chic. B-movie Wall Street at best.

It's 10.05 AM, *Eastern Standard Time.*

Taking up the better part of a two-seat lounger, set against the wall beneath the artwork, the fourth man in the room sits equally at ease. Eyeing the three men seated at the table with passive contempt. Allowing the uncomfortable hiatus in play when Buckley had arrived to continue. Entirely content with this momentary impasse. After all, he's always judged himself a patient man. Intrinsically self-possessed. A man whose deeds have always far exceeded his words. A man familiar with the fear he triggers in other men's bones. Besides, the other three men in the room were here at his specific invitation. Certainly, one they had not been at liberty to refuse.

He is also, by a significant margin, the largest man in the room. A status accorded him from a time not long after he'd barrelled out of puberty. And he knows Buckley, at six-five, two-sixty pounds, will be unaccustomed to being the second biggest man at any gathering. Which likely explains why the former Georgetown University left guard is the first to break the impasse. Exactly as the fourth man in the room had anticipated he would.

'Okay, enough of all this moody silence bullshit... How about someone explains what the hell we're all doing here...? Because, seriously. I don't see the problem.'

The fourth man in the room straightens the sleeves on his Annapolis blazer. Taking a moment before answering. Resisting the temptation to knock this uppity, shiny-suited slob out of his seat.

‘The fact you didn’t see a problem, Mr. Buckley... is precisely why there is a problem...’

He glances at the iron-work skeletal clock on the wall opposite. Because, as of right now, his schedule is tight. So, to put it mildly, he’s loath to tolerate Buckley’s impudent tone.

‘What’s more, it’s a situation that has now required my direct intervention. And, quite frankly, that displeases me.’

‘Yeah, we get it... you’re pissed. What I can’t get my head around, is why this has turned into such a big deal...’

Buckley continues to speak with an irritating nasally whine.

‘He’s just some backwater County Deputy. Likely some hick dickwad, wearing a shiny star and a big hat. What’s he going to do? Take hostages...?’

As Buckley continues, the two younger, leaner men in the room sit mute. Out-of-season tanned. Identical foppish haircuts. Disengaged, and still looking way too self-satisfied.

‘He’s coming to witness an execution for crying out loud. And he’ll be unarmed. Inside the most secure facility we have... plus he’ll be alone.’

The fourth man in the room unfolds his mammoth frame from the lounger. Moving towards the table with surprising grace, considering his overwhelming mass. Seating himself next to Buckley. Making the otherwise heavy-set, one-time college football star look slight in comparison. Resting his elbows on the mirror surface of the table. Knowing full well the other three men in the room couldn’t fail to miss the strain he’s exerting on the seams of his blazer, now that his powerful arms are flexed.

‘Unfortunately for you, Mr. Buckley... your contention is flawed in a number of crucial respects. Because, believe me, if he were just some backwater flat-foot... I would have had no reason to fly all the way up here this morning to avail myself of your stunning intellect.’

The fourth man in the room allows a moment for the disdain in his voice to leach under their skin. And if they continued to harbour any doubt as to his superiority, it would soon be dispelled—one *way or another*. He might not be suitably dressed for violence. But that had never stopped him before.

'The *problem*, as you so crudely put it, is not the fact he's currently engaged playing county copper out on the Texas panhandle. No, gentlemen. The problem is his former reputation as one of Dallas PD's most efficient and... from what my sources tell me, ruthless organized crime detectives.'

The fourth man in the room eyes the other three men in turn.

'And... notwithstanding his current status, it appears the kind folk of Dallas PD are still happily paying him full salary. Curiously, they're also content to sit on his resignation after six... whole... goddam months.'

Despite his deep-seated loathing for the feckless, the fourth man in the room keeps his voice low and even.

'Now... I would suggest if you'd discovered nothing else, these facts alone should have been sufficient to raise a flag. Not least because... in my humble opinion, his request represents a deliberate deception.'

The fourth man in the room knows, from years spent scolding countless other vacuous jerks, that these three imbeciles were beginning to grasp the scale of their miscalculation.

'And he is someone you... with all your fancy security backgrounds. All your DC Beltway *bien informé*. Your years running Pentagon and State Department contracts. Not to mention your obligations *vis à vis* exercising an abundance of caution... did not think to run a thorough background check on. Didn't even think to ask how this hick... *dickwad*, came to know the execution has been rescheduled. Or maybe we should assume it was just some random feat of inspired deduction... given the governor's order to expedite proceedings won't make the news until after the event.'

Buckley sinks back in his chair, while the two younger men exchange glances. Their demeanour turning quickly from smug to something approaching wary.

'Precisely, gentlemen. And fortunately for you'all... I've continued running checks at my end. Call me compulsive. Though to be perfectly candid... your opinions are of no interest to me.'

The fourth man in the room waits for the depth of his rancour to bore through their thick skulls, to whatever grey matter that passed for brains. Though, on the evidence so far, he seriously doubts they possess any capacity for critical self-evaluation. Even so, he always derives a small amount of pleasure from moments like this. When he pointedly lapsed into silence. Daring anyone to challenge him. He'd had it described to him once, as akin to being gutted with a fillet knife.

'So... do any of you well-connected professionals want to know what my latest inquiries have brought to light?'

Buckley remains stone-faced.

The fourth man in the room eases himself from his seat. Had any of the other three men in the room been a keen observer, they may have noted he wore his pleated, loose-fitting chinos, belted high above the line of his broad hips. Might have figured this bygone era fashion quirk for the conceit it was. Might have deduced he used the ploy purely to disguise—*to his own ego at least*—his proportionally short, albeit immensely powerful legs.

'Okay... so let me enlighten you. Because it transpires our so-called deputy made it to his post with Dallas PD by way of MacDill Airbase.'

He pauses for a couple of beats.

'Now that might not strike you as odd. For me, however... it's highly significant. Especially when you consider he's flagging as an ex-Jarhead. With a somewhat heavily redacted service record.'

The other three men in the room appear to be putting most of their concentration into staring at nothing. Even now, seeming not to register the significance of the information they were being fed.

'And may go a long way to explain why he holds a reputation, among his former Dallas PD colleagues, for being one zipped-up... ball-breaking... hard-on.'

The fourth man in the room has always taken huge delight demonstrating he has the smarts to go with his stature. Revelling in the ease with which he could impose his will on those around him. The disquiet he caused whenever he slipped seamlessly from erudition to vulgarity.

He glides to the head of the table. Leans forward to rest his bulk on his fists.

'Now... I might have been inclined to cut you *ladies* some slack. Could be you're blissfully ignorant of MacDill's little-known status as the heavy-lift operations base to some of our nation's most secretive Black Ops units. And I can overlook the fact you've likely never heard any of the inalienable truths that particular cadre live by. US Special Forces mantras, if you will. Humans are more important than hardware... quality is better than quantity... competent operatives cannot be mass produced... and so on.'

Buckley spins his seat.

'Listen... I get it. We missed the superhero back story. And okay... we could, and maybe should, have dug a little deeper. But, damn it. His woman was slaughtered by your baby-faced monster. Lord knows, if I were him, I'd want to be there. Maybe get some kind of closure. Besides… the governor's office had final approval on his invitation. It was signed off.'

The fourth man in the room moves in one fluid motion. Closing the space between himself and Buckley in a single stride. Shooting a hand into the man's groin. Locking on and squeezing hard. His other hand lancing forward, clamping like a bear trap onto Buckley's throat, a fraction below the jawbone.

Buckley stiffens. Every muscle in his upper body going into spasm. He grips the arms of his seat as his eyes begin to pop. Clawing his feet in a futile attempt to gain purchase.

Both Ivy Leaguers look to each other in panic as the fourth man in the room leans in close to Buckley's ear. Squeezing a little harder with both hands as he speaks.

'You'd be well advised to think long and hard before interrupting me again. Because I'm nowhere near finished.'

He releases his hold. Jabs a Cuban cigar-sized forefinger hard against Buckley's forehead.

'What… I'm… not… prepared to overlook, is you sending through a last-minute request to attend the execution entirely unvetted. Or maybe you can remind me when it was I gave you permission to hand over our security to the governor's office.'

The fourth man in the room steps back a couple paces. Watching with an expression of undisguised malice as Buckley collapses forward, elbows on his knees. Holding a hand to his throat as he pukes.

'No, I didn't think so. And, if you're aiming to leave this room with all your motor functions, I strongly recommend you contemplate your future health before raising your voice again. Leastways while I'm still in the room.'

The fourth man stares long and hard at the top of Buckley's head. Then he turns away. Pulling a handkerchief from inside his blazer. Casually wiping his hands as he moves towards the door.

'The problem you people failed to recognize, is that this has nothing to do with what our supposed deputy wants. It's about who he really is... and what he represents. Something you Beltway types would never think to consider. The fact that when their time in Special Operations is done... you can push the man out of the train, but you will never push the training out of the man. Which means I'm inclined to consider our interloper a far greater security risk than your plainly limited insight has assumed. And it's the reason I'm here to inform you... his request to attend tonight's little event, should have been respectfully declined.'

The fourth man in the room is pushing the back end of middle age. Nudging six-foot nine inches. Tipping the scales north of three-hundred pounds. And, just from looking at them, he knows the other three men in the room are beginning to buckle under the gravitational anomaly that is his overwhelming physical presence.

'And it just so happens, I've kicked dust and shit in more holes in the ground than I care to remember... with individuals cast from the exact same mould as this so-called deputy. Which means... from here on in, I will be the one to decide whether or not he represents a *fucking* problem.'

He pauses as he reaches the heavy panel door.

'So, like I said...his military records are coming back a whole stack of redactions. And I need them filled in... *post haste*.'

He turns to face the three men stalled in their seats.

'Until I say otherwise, this will be your sole purpose in life. And, for all your sakes... I hope I've made myself crystal clear. I will not tolerate any further omissions, errors or assumptions. And, while you're acquiring the information I need... you will not risk raising any flags. My delta is twenty-two hundred.

That means, I require answers from you no later than twenty-hundred... my time-zone, not yours.'

He opens the door.

'And Buckley... a final heads up for you. Fail me again, I can promise you, aggressive terminal cancer will seem like your best and only friend.'

Victor Labette taps the solid gold Patek Philippe Calatrava he wears low on his wrist.

'Twenty-hundred... *gentlemen.*'

CAPITOL HILL, WASHINGTON DC

Martin Devlin is not in the best of moods. Far from happy he'd been summoned away from the hermetic refuge of his Bethesda apartment; not unlike a domestic pet required to heed his master's call. No prior notice. And with nothing resembling an agreed agenda.

All highly irregular.

It's approaching 10.30 AM, *Eastern Standard Time.*

Less than an hour before, he'd been preparing a breakfast of avocado salad, on freshly-baked Italian-herb *pane moddizzosu*. Listening to Beethoven's Pastoral on vinyl, with all its rich imperfections, performed by the Berlin Philharmonic, under the sublime baton of Herbert von Karajan. Blissfully isolated from the daily risk of infection. Because, as far as he's concerned, the world outside his personal sanctuary has become criminally complacent on all matters germane to bio-security. Utterly convinced the price humanity will pay for such wanton disregard towards deadly pathogens will be a heavy one. Sure, day-to-day, he is able to tolerate the marble halls of the Capitol

Building. Because there at least, sanitary standards were generally tolerable. So long as he avoids using the washroom facilities, or touching surfaces he hasn't personally cleansed. It went without saying, he keeps his own cubbyhole-sized office in the Russell Senate Building scrupulously sterile. And after close on thirty years, anyone who was anyone, inside the Beltway, had grown accustomed to respecting the extent of his personal hygiene exclusion zone. No longer bothering to offer their hand in greeting.

Regardless, his boss had demanded this unscheduled meeting be arranged, without delay, at a location away from the Capitol Building. Making it abundantly clear, the usual accommodations to his senior aide's life-long hygiene obsessions were to be set aside. Heedless of the fact he'd been relaxing on one of his rare days off.

So here he is. Sitting opposite the once celebrated, former District Attorney from Terrell Hills, San Antonio. Ironically, a man with his own widely-known reputation for fastidiousness. Although lately, the once bountiful charm and vigour that had set the multiple-term Texan Senator apart from his contemporaries seemed diminished somehow. Increasingly reliant, as it was, on the odd subtle nip and tuck; with eye-watering fees attached. Absurdly white dental veneers a given.

'I presume we're taking all necessary precautions?'

For the first time he could ever recall, Devlin detects an unfamiliar edge to the Senator's smooth, south-Texan drawl.

'Seriously, Senator... you really feel the need to ask?'

The Chairman of the Judiciary Committee was fully aware of his closest confidant's fondness for deploying electronic countermeasures. Nonetheless, there is visible tension etched across his chief's otherwise camera-ready persona. High-tech precautions aside, both men are well versed in the manipulation of language beyond the point where a clear subject, or opinion, could be readily discerned. By even the most determined eavesdropper.

They were veterans. They knew their game.

The Senator has bossed the field inside the Beltway for close on three decades. And throughout all that time, he hadn't ever questioned security arrangements. At any level. Because he'd never needed to. Not once.

Ever.

Which is why the fleeting tremor in the Senator's voice had resonated.

During all their years together, Devlin has always envied his boss's effortless eloquence. Stately and soothing to those in need of calm leadership. Unflappable, whatever the crisis. And Lord knows, Texas had endured its fair share of crises down the years. And, through it all, whenever he'd risen to speak, he had never once failed to command the Senate floor. An unwavering orator. Steadfast, no matter how strident the opposition. Buttressed by elegant, leading man looks. Athletic, even as he'd aged. A man for all times. And a straight-up certainty to blitz the Presidential primaries in 2012—*and 2016, come to that*—if only he could have been persuaded to run. The fact he'd consistently declined had been galling, to say the least. Whenever Devlin tallied the funds that had been channelled the Senator's way—*most of it untraceable, and nearly all of it for the express purpose of elevating him to the highest office*—his anger roiled. His ambitions to become White House Chief of Staff thwarted, time and again. And the reason he'd eventually sought his own path.

Right now, his boss sits immobile. Staring at his plate of food as if it were unrecognizable as something he might consider eating.

They are in a private members' club. Alone, in a reserved dining room. At a table set for one. Perfectly positioned beneath one of the establishment's signature ornate chandeliers. A large portrait of Ronald Reagan smiling down at them from its place on the wall, above an elaborate maplewood sideboard. Opposite two floor-to-ceiling sash windows, each framed by heavy floral drapes. A room designed to cater for a premier league demographic. Spawned in an era of excitement and rekindled national self-confidence. From a time when consideration and calculous had been rigorously applied when dealing with the big, bad world. Before all the purposeless conceit and sound-bite superficiality had gained a foothold inside the Beltway.

The Senator picks up a solid silver butter knife, in the manner of someone preparing to sign an accord. Begins idly pushing fussy little breakfast patisseries around his plate. As usual, Devlin had declined to order food. Resolute in his aversion to eating out. Even at a venue as renowned as The Capitol Club. The mere thought of anyone, other than himself, touching anything that might pass his lips, was enough to make him break out in a cold sweat. Of his many problematic disorders, this one in particular was not open to compromise. Under any circumstance.

'*J-e-s-u-s Christ*, Martin... we're not playing games here. I asked you a direct question. I expect a straight answer.'

Devlin holds up a pale, bony hand. Aware his irritation is now on full display. Something of a first for a man who's spent his entire adult life bonded to political servitude.

'Senator. With or without my equipment... we're good.'

He pats the Italian-leather carry bag, slung over the back of his seat.

'Neither of us would have agreed to this location otherwise.'

The Senator places the butter knife back beside his plate.

Begins tracing circles with his manicured fingers around the cuffs of his obscenely expensive, bespoke-tailored shirt.

'Very well, Martin... let's cut to the chase.'

The former District Attorney stiffens his back.

'If someone... anyone in fact, decides to paste a whole new chapter into the playbook. With or without my consent. The least I expect is to be kept informed.'

'Informed...?'

'Yes, damn it... *informed*. And, to be entirely candid... I consider it an outrage that I wasn't.'

The Senator's attention moves from his cuffs to his oversized napkin.

'For crying out loud, Martin. You of all people had to know, if they'd brought this madness to me beforehand, there's no way on God's green earth I would have signed off on it.'

'With all due respect, Senator. Throughout our years together, have I ever once allowed such specifics to reach your desk? Besides, since when have operational details... especially those of, let's just say, such a delicate nature... required your personal sign-off? And I'm bound to point out... I did recommend you not to speak with the governor. Strongly, as I recall.'

His boss looks visibly cowed.

A definite first.

'I couldn't stall her any longer.'

The senator's tone sounds almost apologetic.

Another first.

'Besides, despite the rumours, she still leads the most influential group in our caucus.'

Devlin scoffs.

'The polling data suggests otherwise.'

'Be that as it may. Here and now, she remains the duly elected head of this country's second most populous state. And we both know this operation has been her rodeo from the get-go. Besides... our families go way back. Heck, they're the reason I'm in this town at all. And everyone knows it.'

'Believe me,' Devlin says. 'No one remembers. And those who do are either long gone or no longer disposed to care.'

'Okay... so tell me, Martin. At what point in all this did loyalty stop counting for something?'

Devlin raises an eyebrow.

'From the moment it started to compromise an ability to proffer denial, without an accompanying risk of perjury.'

The Senator lowers his eyes, like he's searching the napkin for a thread to pick at.

'Well... it's beyond me how any right-thinking person could contrive, let alone sanction, such an outrageous deviation. The original plan had conventional parameters, for crying out loud. So, what the hell happened...? It was supposed to be quick and neat. *Jesus Christ...* this is. Actually, I can't even put a name to what this is.'

Devlin shrugs.

'Sadly, the nominated contractor has a reputation for being a tad over-zealous. With a giant-sized ego to match his over-sized stature.'

The Senator slumps back in his seat.

'Son-of-a-bitch.'

'That he is,' Devlin says. 'So, to a degree... I'll concede it's a little problematic. But here we are. And it's not like we're being asked to carry the ball. Our exposure remains as close to zero as makes no difference. Calculations were made and tallied. Insurance has been procured... at considerable expense. Not to mention the effort and risk to me personally, I might add. Even so... it is an indemnity I happen to trust... *implicitly*. As should you.'

His boss appears to be only half-listening.

'Regardless... I may have to consider calling time on this entire enterprise. To say it's gotten out of hand, is the understatement of this, or any other century.'

'Senator... I seriously doubt you believe that option is available to us at this late stage.'

The Senator visibly bristles.

'Last time I checked... it says judiciary committee chairman on my office door. So, if I say this utter lunacy stops as of right now... that's precisely what it means.'

'On The Hill, perhaps,' Devlin says. 'Elsewhere, however... the ball has been snapped. And it's inside the ten. Added to which, our patrons are unlikely to tolerate anything other than the outcome they invested in at the outset. And I guarantee, they aren't the ones losing their heads over the odd unsanctioned... *deviation*.'

The Senator's pallor turns ashen. He dabs at the corners of his mouth with the crisply-starched napkin. Perhaps to disguise the tremor in his hands. If so, his effort is in vain. After a moment, he lets the napkin fall onto his plate.

Devlin waits. Gives his boss the space to muster his dignity.

'Okay, Martin... since you appear to think yourself the lead authority in this matter. You'd better make sure this goddam dumpster fire stays a long way from my office.'

'I'll do my best.'

'You'll do your best...'

The Senator lets out an involuntary snort.

'Well you'd certainly better. Because your hands are closer to the flames than mine. And just so we're clear... any collateral damage from here on in. It'll be on your head.'

'Indeed... *Senator*.'

'I don't care how it's done. You fire break this. As of

yesterday.'

Clarence Hellermann III rises from his seat. Setting his jaw, just like he'd trained himself to do all those decades before. Whenever he'd stood before a wavering jury. Projecting the kind of calm authority his opponents had failed, time and again, to break down. Holding each juror's rapt attention. Beguiling to males and females alike with his subtle, unscripted humour and Latin flourishes. All but commanding them to accept the logic of his closing arguments. As if he'd discerned the outcome before they'd even begun their deliberations. Blessed with a God-given countenance that had afforded him an unnerving ability to captivate. To hold an entire courtroom in the palm of his hand.

He turns and strides from the table.

'Just do your goddam job, Martin...'

Delivers his parting words without a backward glance.

'...and from now on. Keep me the hell out of this.'

CORNUDAS, TEXAS

Leg Zalizo enters the west-Texas roadside diner, conscious he's gotten his timing out by quite a margin.

Truth was, he'd anticipated delays somewhere along the route. A diversion around some crumbling infrastructure or other. A bridge here. A culvert there. But he'd encountered nothing of the sort. Not so much as a slow-moving semi. Or any of the obstinate agricultural rigs he'd come to loathe during his self-imposed exile on the panhandle.

He'd driven the better part of three hundred miles since leaving the welcoming embrace of Hale County Sheriff's Department.

Through heat and dust. Over endless stretches of sun-bleached flat-top. Most of it devoid of any need to move the steering wheel off the arrow-straight centre line. All to witness the grinning creature who had ripped the core from his life take their last, miserable breath upon this earth. A worthless piece of flesh and bone cable news outlets and the full spectrum of social media had done their best to immortalize. Turning him into some kind of abomination to the cult of diabolical celebrity. A living demon. When in reality, like all his kind, he was nothing more than a pathetic, limp-dicked freak. A diseased husk. With barely enough meat on his bones to hold down the trigger that had brought so much senseless carnage and mind-numbing grief to so many unsuspecting lives. And, even though it wasn't the mission he'd set out on—*close on six months earlier*—Zalizo knows he would have journeyed twice the distance he had, to watch the scrawny prick writhe and scream and soil himself. To observe the fear of certain death writ plain as day across his once perpetually smirking face.

To revel in his final, agonizing minutes.

Or hours...

...h*opefully*.

The execution is scheduled for 10 PM, *Mountain Standard Time*. His pick-up two hours before that. Right now, it's a little after 5 PM. Which means he has a good few hours to kill...

...or be killed.

He steps from his commandeered, government-issue GMC, moving along the front of the diner. Hesitating every few strides, feigning indecision. Dipping his head, like he's checking inside the roadhouse before he makes up his mind to enter. Enough unpredictable movement, he figures, to hinder even the most competent marksman. His heart rate running a few beats north of its usual sub-sixty five. Genetics and training meant, absent physical exertion, he could have held it a good deal lower if needed. No matter the situation. Whatever the environment. But today, for the first time in quite a while—*since he'd last fought hand-to-hand, in point of fact*—he allows a spike of adrenalin to run free in his veins. And, if it transpires someone out there harbours any intentions to cause him harm, he'll welcome the weird sense of time dilation a sudden surge of adrenalin tended to induce. That out-of-body sensation, causing anyone without specialized training to experience some degree of paralysis. One of many impediments to elite physical performance he's long ago learned to harness.

The diner sits, squat and exposed, beside Highway 62; a meandering two-lane, running from Carlsbad through to El Paso. A low, quarried-stone affair, painted vivid yellow. With a slanted front elevation edged with thick, rough-finished pine logs. All capped off by a rusted corrugated iron roof. *Doug's Place*, perched atop a tapered concrete pillar that spears through the centre of the building. Looking like the establishment has been dropped onto it from altitude. An incongruous beacon, topped out with faded, weather-beaten neon script.

By some unspoken custom, the pot-holed parking lot appears to be off-limits to commercial vehicles. Instead, a long strip of rough ground flanking either side of the highway is semi-crowded with heavy rigs and an assortment of panel trucks. And the reason why *Doug's* customers pretty much comprised your standard trucker types. Mostly overweight. Mostly razor shy. Mostly modelling over-sized T-shirts, with the odd wife-beater vest thrown in.

There are a few gaunt, heavily-tattooed teenage couples dotted here and there. Scrawny standouts among the rest of the myocardial infractions waiting to happen; like hooded, under-nourished poppies pushing through the weeds. Heads bowed to their cell phones; together and alone in some mutually agreed, non-speaking world. A fragile cohort struggling to reconcile their digital existence. Buckling mentally under the pressure of social media content ranging from the banal all the way to malign, then on through perverse to the downright sinister.

The crush-depth generation.

Other than that, a single down-at-heal, bearded loner occupies the booth flanking the entrance. With what passes for his world jammed to bursting into a raggedy canvas duffle. Chuntering some unintelligible complaint to himself. The filth ingrained under his nails testament to his authenticity.

Zalizo lets the door swing closed behind him.

A quiet hum of low-level conversation pauses momentarily, before resuming its auditory battle with a row of broad-bladed ceiling fans, noisily stirring the humid air. Even so, compared to the thirty something seconds he'd just spent outside, inside it feels like a cool box.

As road houses go, the place appears to be a pretty standard, middle-of-nowhere dry stop. Stubbornly independent. Isolated from the world of franchise dominance. Tired, by-gone era décor. Insipid beige floor tiles, de-glazed from heavy-booted traffic. Wood-framed tables with blistered laminate tops. Faded, frameless photos of old-school Motown muscle, shaft-driven V-twin low riders and chrome-stacked big rigs, scattered—*haphazard*—across the stucco walls. Nonetheless, all the surfaces are freshly wiped. The menu pretty good; in a wholesome, take-it-or-leave-it way. Food piled to a good height on decent-sized plates. And likely the primary reason *Doug* appears to have no trouble keeping his *Place* better than half-full this late into the afternoon.

The kitchen lies behind a pair of battered swing doors. Kick-plates scarred and bruised from years of abuse. A long serving hatch opening off to the right. Order slips bull-pegged to a metal strip above the counter. The smell of seared meat and hot oil, pervasive.

He dumps the canvas jacket he doesn't need into the first vacant booth. Settling in, with his back to the wall—*an old habit, never forsaken*—having already clocked that the entrance doors hinge out toward the parking lot. He files it under something useful to know, in the event he needs a quick exit. The sort of small detail an average civilian would never think to consider. But, at thirty-eight years of age, Zalizo knows he's about as far from average as it's possible to get. *Spec Ops* trained. Combat-hardened. Former US Marines Raider head-to-toe. So, when it came to matters of survival—*especially in hostile situations*—and despite his elevated rank, his latent skill sets fall heavily on the side of specialist.

A door to *His* and *Hers* restrooms sits directly opposite his booth. Maybe a rear exit lay beyond. Despite his instincts urging him—*to go check it out*—he'd decides to wait and see how things play out. Mostly because he figures a busy diner is way too witness-heavy for anyone to attempt a direct assault. Unless he was up against complete amateurs, they will likely bide their time. And throughout the close on two years preceding his arrival at *Doug's Place*, nothing he'd learnt gave any indication he was dealing with amateurs.

Nonetheless, permission to attend the evening's coming event had been pinged, late the previous day, to the blind mailbox he'd provided the governor's office. Detailing where he had to be and the time he had to be there. Giving him a number to call, once he'd made it to this out-of-the-way rendezvous. Which was why he'd spent most of the journey south trying to figure why they'd agreed to his request. Because, if his current information were only half-way correct, the shadowy cabal he's intent on running to ground had already demonstrated their willingness to be all kinds of ruthless. In all likelihood responsible for the commissioning of at least four deadly attacks on clean energy facilities, in at least two states. Each currently recorded, euphemistically, as industrial incidents.

He's also aware the rescheduled execution date had been a closely guarded secret. Print media, cable news networks, local TV and talk-radio channels, all kept in the dark. He knows, because he'd checked. So, for sure, he would likely be the only person attending with even a passing connection to any of Perry Morgan Blake's twenty-three victims. All of which meant, whoever was running the show had to have figured he'd somehow gotten hold of insider information.

Ergo, he represents a potentially significant security breach.

So he'd tried to anticipate the threats he might face. The plans they could put in place in advance of his arrival. Running a dozen or more scenarios through in his head. None of which had ended well. He was going in alone. His cover likely blown. No back-up. No heavy calibre suppressing fire. No live comms. No satellite feed off surveillance drones circling above. No *A10 Warthog* top cover on call, if his situation turned sour. So, not for the first time since he'd forsaken conventional military deployment for this current domestic counter-terrorism gig, he'd had to face a single hard fact.

Every which way, he is out on a limb.

A waitress ghosts into view. Squaring up to his table with her order pad ready. Her eyes auto-scanning the line of booths. The expression on her face, fixed and weary.

She wears her flared jeans low on her hips. Frayed horizontal slits at mid-thigh. Tight-fitting white blouse tucked into a rolled-down black apron. And although his customary default was to avoid making rash judgements, with possibly one too many buttons undone. That said, considering the number of glances tracking her every move, the majority of *Doug's* customers appear anything but offended.

'What can I get'chuh there, hun?'

She stands with her head inclined, stubbornly working her gum.

He says, 'Eggs on rye would be good.'

As was his habit, he finds himself staring at her hands. Nails varnished black. Chipped and hard-bitten. A bunch of gothic rings. Skulls, tattooed in a band around heavily bruised wrists. He can't help but wonder if her bruises had been willingly acquired. On any other day than today, he might have been tempted to enquire.

'And how'd yuh like those eggs fixed?'

'Scrambled,' he says. 'Not too runny.'

'Get'chuh somethin' to drink with that...?'

From somewhere that seems only half remembered, she attempts an expression of apology.

'...though, thirst alert. We don't stretch to alcohol.'

She shrugs her narrow shoulders.

'Sorry, hun. It's kinda preachy round here.'

Zalizo part-raises his hand.

'Not a problem... iced water will be good. Pitcher if you have it.'

At that precise moment, he hopes the journey hasn't made him smell as sour as his mood. Hopes it isn't the reason she's breathing through her mouth while she chews. Though, judging by the heavy make-up around her eyes, his suspicions lie in the direction of a busted nose in the not-to-distant past.

The smile she offers doesn't reach her eyes.

'You bet'chuh, hun.'

He returns his own forced half-smile.

'Thank you... *ma'am.'*

He settles back to wait for his order. Wonders, idly, what impact the alternate vehicle he'd acquired earlier that day was having on the rest of *Doug's* clientele. United States Marshals Service in bold, block lettering on the forward doors, centred under an eagled star. As far as he could tell, no-one was paying it any heed. But he'd bet a month's salary some of the eyes, now stubbornly fixed on their meals, will have pegged its arrival. Averting their gaze the moment he'd made it through the door. Holding their petty secrets in close. Shrinking into their booths to avoid attracting unwanted attention from the badge-wearing intruder in their midst. Truth be told, not so different to any number of places he'd walked into over the years.

For sure, he'd found himself in plenty worse.

He rests his palms flat on the table. Takes in the scar tissue on his knuckles. The broad white streak across the back of his left hand. Acquired three weeks after he'd hit the deck at Bagram—*on his first deployment to that testosterone-soaked, Afghan sand pit*—on day two of his inaugural four-day patrol. From when a seven-point-six-two millimetre AK47 round, fired blindly from behind a low, dry-stone wall, had kissed his gloved hand. Serving as his permanent reminder, if one were needed, that any notion he might harbour of being in control, in any combat situation, was nothing more than a convenient delusion. A lesson swiftly learnt by every Spec Ops bonehead he'd ever met; and the reason his steel-framed, double-stack automatic—*loaded with the one-sixty-five grain high velocity round he favours*—sits holstered on his tactical belt. Grip angled toward his dominant left hand. Safety off from the moment he'd exited his vehicle.

Another old habit, not forsaken.

There had been a time, early in his military service, when a

Beretta M9 had been the only side-arm he'd been permitted to carry. But US Marine Corps standard issue hardware had been for a different life.

A different time.

That morning, he'd risen at five-thirty. Put on a pair of thick socks and thin boxers. Lightweight but sturdy, khaki-coloured field slacks. Heavy-soled desert boots. And a fresh, loose-fitting cotton polo; which now clings like a laundry vacuum pack to his combat-hardened frame. No fat. No excess muscle. Just broad, square shoulders. His father's iron-boned hands. And his mother's unyielding will to prevail. No matter the odds.

No matter the cost.

He'd picked up the hastily-arranged, aging four-by-four, in Lubbock. Courtesy, once again, of his favourite ex-Green Beret turned Dallas PD captain. Then set out in the direction of Odessa on Highway 62. Swinging west at Seminole. Crossing the state line into New Mexico, the other side of Hobbs. Blowing through Carlsbad, heading south-west. Steady pace all the way. Until he'd crossed back into Texas. Easing into the diner's parking lot, half-a-click west of a pin-hole in the map named Cornudas. The entire ride south, brutally hot. The miles laying down a thick coat of dirt and silica over the GMC's faded paintwork. The windshield tattooed opaque from six hours straight collecting bug gore.

He'd taken it easy. There had been no need to rush. The piece of garbage he'd come to watch breathe his last—*wasn't going anywhere*. Leastways, nowhere he couldn't get to him if, at any time during the previous two years, he'd decided to put his mind to it.

But he hadn't. For good reason. And that reason remained. His searing need to know who, and what, lay behind that one inexplicable decision to move the Lone Star State's most notorious death row inmate, from Huntsville, to a covert, out-of-state, private sector detention facility. And why a legal process that ordinarily crawled along for a decade or more had been bumped forward to a degree bordering on the unfathomable; especially when the perp's complexion hued toward the paler end of the pallet.

So after he'd pulled into the diner's parking lot, he'd sat a while. With the engine idling to keep the air-con pumping. Staring at a bank of dark-grey thunderheads, forming up like pyroclastic flows, somewhere north of Interstate 10. Barrelling in toward the Guadalupe Mountains. As if metrological confirmation were needed that he was headed into the eye of a storm.

But, given the way the evening's logistics had been set up—*and the bottomless pit of grief and ice-cold hate he carried in his gut*—he'd already figured the optics for the evening to come were not looking good. And as sure as sunrise followed sunset, he was someone who knew how to read the optics of the situation laid out before him.

From a time, way before his boots first hit the parade deck at Paris Island, for Marine Corps basic training, it had been the skill he'd grown to trust above all others. A primal instinct. One that had been with him from as far back as he could remember. Imprinted, somehow, into his DNA. The one that had never failed him—*but for that one time*—when it had mattered most. On that black day he'd driven the woman he'd fallen for, through Dallas's downtown, rush-hour traffic to the steps of the Earle Cabell Federal Building.

Which is why, when he'd pulled in next to the diner, he'd sat like a statue. Watching as the first drops of rain began hitting the windshield. Tracing slow streaks through the grime. Before he'd finally fetched his satellite phone from the centre console and made the call he'd been instructed to make. Forsaking all his years of strategic and tactical training. Driven to recklessness by base impulses barely held in check.

So, right now, all he can do is settle in and wait.

So many old habits unforsaken.

And, if anyone chose to come for him, he would do as he'd always done.

Shoot first. Shoot straight.

Deal with the consequences later.

TEXAS PANHANDLE

Anne-Marie Hollenbeck knows, down to the very last detail, what kind of image she needs. A little used two-lane. Somewhere isolated. Scarred from decades of neglect. With faded divider lines, leading nowhere. Eternally barren. Bordered by lop-sided telegraph poles, with wires that had long since surrendered their tension to time and wind. A stretch of broken-down fencing would be good.

But there is one must have above all others.

An abandoned fuel station. Preferably with ole-timey pumps. Weathered clapboard. Peeling, sun-bleached paint. Rusty advertising plaques. Maybe a workshop with double swing doors. And an old wreck or three. Auto or agricultural, she doesn't much mind.

She's been told the western side of the panhandle would be a good place to start. Maybe east New Mexico, if she has the time. And when she'd finally corralled enough courage to let him know what she was trying to achieve, her faculty head had encouraged her.

'Don't go searching hard and fast... start by asking around. Enquire, young lady, and ye shall find. Out-of-town folk, they just love to talk. Mostly about past times... how by-gone places used to be. They get a kick from sharing their history... the stories behind why things had gotten to be the way they are. You'll gain a deeper insight. They'll give you the meaning behind that special image you're after... help you to feel it before you see it.'

When he spoke, there were occasions when all she wanted to do was close her eyes. But he wouldn't have understood. And she couldn't have explained. Likely, he wouldn't even have noticed. She had just turned nineteen. With only the barest concept of the emotions she felt toward him. He was pushing late-forties, and seemingly oblivious of the soft-spoken appeal he held. And that was the point about the way she felt. The sentiment that sometimes made her mind sing.

Besides, she knows well enough, she is far from being the only young female on campus to harbour such feelings toward him. Truth was, some of the lurid desires other girls confided made her recoil from embracing her own unspoken infatuation to any meaningful degree. Even so, she wonders if it had been one of the reasons she'd let the boy from church—*who, as plain as the difference between night and day, wanted to be something more than just a friend*—ride along with her. A serious and sometimes solemn-looking kid she'd always gotten along with just fine. Long-limbed. Long-grain muscular. Tall as corn, as her grandpa would say.

To her own surprise, she'd said it was fine with her that he tag along. So long as he provided a better level of transport than she could muster. And, more importantly, so long as he promised no screwing around.

He'd said he was cool with that. And she'd known, instinctively, he'd be true to his word.

For the first time in a while, her grateful companion brakes the easy silence that had settled between them.

'Do you mind if I ask you something...?'

He is driving speed-limit safe. Eyes on the road. Contented half-smile. Dopey far-away look. Kinda cute she would have to admit—*if she'd felt the need to give it any thought*.

She says, 'Ask away.'

'Why all this effort...?'

He looks across at her. Shoots her a coy smile.

'This... *intensity*?'

She looks back at him, appraising his profile. Noticing, for the first time, the way his hair falls in soft waves, just below the nape of his neck.

'Like I told you... it's for a book cover.'

'I know... you said that already.'

He turns his eyes back to the road.

'It's just, well... there seems a little more to it than that.'

Out of nowhere, she feels drawn to his casual sincerity.

They are riding his RAM 1500 pick-up. Black, and shiny as a jewel. Engine the size of Rhode Island thrumming under the hood. Your typical Texan, semi-rich kid indulgence. Compensation, she hazards a guess, for time and attention—*or the lack thereof.*

'It'll be published,' she says.

'Yeah... you said that too.'

'It's for my grandfather.'

'Straight up... he's a writer?'

'Anthropologist, to be exact.'

'Not sure what that is,' he says. 'But it sounds academic.'

She says, 'How about social historian?'

'How about it?'

'It's what he does. Well... did, really. He says this will be his last offering to go to print. Said he needs me to be his eyes. Claims his hips have all but given up... *haulin' his saggy rear end*. Says he'll give me a really bold credit that might just open doors. Down the line, maybe. No promises, of course.'

'Straight up?'

'That's what he said... and Grandpa's never lied to anyone his entire life. Least ways, not that I'm aware of... and, for sure, never to me.'

'You're not kiddin'... that's pretty cool all by itself.'

'I guess. Anyway... getting the perfect cover shot was always going to be the hardest. Grandpa said it has to capture everything that lies within.'

She leans her head toward the frigid air streaming from the dash vent. He shifts his hands to the bottom of the steering wheel. For a moment or two, he seems content. Though, in truth, his doleful expression rarely changes, so she finds it a little hard to tell.

'So you gotta get something really special?'

She says, 'I surely hope so.'

'So... is your Grandpa some kind of professor?'

She lets out a giggle-come-snort.

'Mostly... no.'

'Mostly...?'

'He's long retired... so he's pretty much just my grandpa. The person I've always been able to go to when I need to get my head straight, I guess. Usually because he has this weird way of telling me the things I need to know, yet somehow make it seem like I came up with the solution all by myself...'

She feels a smile find its way to her lips.

'I still haven't figured how he does it... and I'm not sure I really want to.'

Kenton MacKendrick Junior doesn't say anything for a good long beat. The far-away look returning to his eyes.

'Well, my grandparents passed away before I made it to high school. Can't say I remember them being good or bad. Truth is... I never saw them a whole bunch.'

She sees his grip on the steering wheel tighten a fraction.

'My old man... well, he's kinda difficult to be around. But whenever they did come over, I can't honestly say I remember how they made me feel. For sure, nothing like you do for your grandpa. So he sure sounds pretty neat to me.'

Anne-Marie Hollenbeck eases herself back. Watching an endless vista of irrigation circles and flat earth drift by. Feels her smile return unbidden.

'He most certainly is.'

CORNUDAS, TEXAS

Zalizo checks the tactical watch he wears on his right wrist.

Twenty minutes and counting.

The storm is at full throttle now. Hammering the front of the diner in blast waves as it barrels through. Drum-rolling the diner's roof. Bands of rain pulsing in across the parking lot. Turning it into a shallow lake. Thunder rattling the windows. Off-the-scale loud. Curtains of sheet lightening—*bright as the sun*—illuminating dark mountain peaks to the north, as the sky rolls through cobalt to black.

Apocalyptic, almost.

Just over four hours earlier, when he'd made the call, a disembodied voice had given up precisely one instruction, and one detail.

He figures the trip out to the ultra-max facility will last forty-five minutes—*give or take.* Factoring in the mountain gradients. Thirty-something miles through forbidding terrain. On the one unsurfaced road leading in and out—*if it hadn't been washed away already.*

Satellite images had shown no construction anywhere within a thirty-mile radius of Devil's Den Canyon. Just a low resolution smudge between two mountain ranges. But, what suddenly felt like half a life-time ago, he'd hiked in. Scoping the area for three whole days. And two whole nights. During which he'd taken photos. Plotted routes to areas providing sightlines and suitable terrain for cover. Came to accept his surveillance options were all long range. But it meant he knew exactly where Coal Island ultra-secure detention facility was located. No matter the efforts someone high up, in some shadowy corner of the national security food chain, had taken to keep it digitally concealed.

As was his habit, he'd tagged the topographical data he'd assembled—*item one.*

Six weeks before, he'd received his latest feed. An encrypted file from his former unit's sergeant, back in DC. Revealing Coal Island to be little more than an elaborate conduit to funnel significant amounts of federally-funded, untaxed liquidity from the United States Treasury to the Cayman Islands. Through a holding company, Lexstone Security Corporation. Licensed under a fifty-year joint State Department-Pentagon contract to provide the facility's boots on the ground. No doubt something approaching a small army of guards. Plus a roster of security-cleared cooks, cleaners and maintenance crews. Not to mention the usual strata of management, likely skimming off their own decent-size cut from a network of other Lexstone-run detention facilities. All set up to a similar basic business model.

Turns out, the contract was huge. In the hundreds of millions across what appeared to be nothing more than some shadowy private-security franchise for rent.

He'd tagged this information—*item two.*

The holding company CEO was a one-time Georgetown wannabe left guard. Going by the name Dillon Robert Buckley. Someone his former unit in DC had been scoping for months. Mostly carding pretty lousy numbers at Congressional Golf and Country Club. Mostly in the company of two baby-faced Beltway lobbyists. One pushing for some nebulous equity group, operating out of the Cayman Islands. The other, a hot-shot venture capitalist, based in the Bahamas. Whose true sponsors were currently cloaked inside a labyrinth of corporate registrations. Likely little more than privileged dilettantes, whose sole purpose in life involved covert distribution of significant cash incentives to slack-skinned congressional incumbents, with a taste for striding marble halls and lining their pockets with untraceable campaign contributions. All those parasitic corporate lackeys, masquerading as the people's representatives, reliant on their constituent's perennial apathy. Hiding behind an endless stream of meaningless political soundbites. Beholden only to the peddlers in dark money.

Items three, four and *five.*

During the extended leave of absence, following his resignation, his former unit had continued to operate exactly as they'd been trained. Gather the data. Interrogate the data. Break it down into its constituent parts. Corroborate. Validate. Discount nothing. One of his best operators had put the current *DC* tag-teams together—*unofficially and without being asked*—working her contacts the way she'd been drilled. Higher echelon for access. Lower echelon for information. And, after what seemed like an eternity of necessarily cautious digging, between the two of them, they'd teased out that Coal Island was Lexstone Security's flagship house-and-hide facility. Out-of-sight to all but those with the highest security clearance. Reserved for the US government's most troubled offenders. Highly dangerous individuals the departments of State and Defense would rather not admit existed.

Fort Leavenworth for the in-and-outers. Coal Island for the in-and-keepers.

Item six.

All of which meant, the civilian responsible for ripping a jagged hole in his life was currently residing in a *de facto* military penal facility. In the middle of a broad, rock-strewn valley. Ten clicks beyond the northern boundary of Guadeloupe Mountains National Park.

The problem was, Perry Morgan Blake had never served. Not in the military. Certainly not in Langley.

All the same, there had been something unsettling about the security camera footage from that black day two years back. His progress tracked as he'd made his way through the building's concourse. The way he'd gone about his deadly business. Releasing and reloading magazines with callous efficiency. His movements precise. Firing in short bursts—*calm and unhurried*—in a manner at odds with his backwater bio. Could be he'd honed his murderous skills, armchair combat-gaming in some dingy bedroom with the curtains drawn, as had been the overwhelming consensus at the time. But, even though he'd had to concede it was plausible, Zalizo had never been entirely convinced. Because one thing was certain. Of all the people who'd spent countless hours analysing those sickening recordings—*frame by agonizing frame*—a former US Marine Raider knew better than most, one factor of combat held true.

Competency required training.

Item seven.

The itch he's been waiting to scratch.

Six months earlier, one of a handful of people whose opinion he valued, had told him straight.

> *'Look, Zalizo... I know you went through hell... But you need to let this one go, my friend... Word is, Huntsville can't guarantee his safety... Don't forget, even our criminal community lost people that day... Could be they've simply had it with policing all the demonstrations... Damn-it, I'm not sure I'd trust you not to bust in there yourself... Save the state some serious tax-payer dollars... Either way, the decision to transfer his ass came down from somewhere higher than the top floor at State Justice... I assume no-one wants him getting shanked before he burns... And, rumour has it, some big-wig in Senate Judiciary got involved... For damn sure, you don't want to start locking horns with folk pushing that level of influence... So take it from someone who's learnt when to poke the nest and when to let things ride... I mean, let's face it, ain't no-one around here lying awake at night fretting this decision... And it shouldn't be your focus right now either... But I know what you Slavs are like... Bone-headed doesn't cover it... So if you're hell bent on picking at this particular scab, feel free to let me know... Short of direct involvement, I'll make whatever arrangements you need... I owe you that, and probably more... Just promise me you'll think it through, is all I ask... Because you and I both know, it would have taken*

some serious heavy lifting to get a transfer like this signed-off... Besides, when all the dust settles, no matter the address, your boy's gonna fry.'

Captain Brett Marcellino—*United States Army SFOD: Retired*—had made a valid point; as he was want to do. The problem was, Zalizo can't remember a time in his life when he'd allowed base emotions to become a distraction. Not after the death of his parents. Not even during the endless hours and days of dark rage that followed Alicia's brutal slaying. To say he personified a proverbial dog with a bone, barely scratched the surface of the person he'd always been. And while he remembers his father had considered his unrelenting nature a blessing, he often suspected his mother had viewed it a curse. Although, had she still been alive—*and had anyone thought to ask*—Olga Magdalena Zalizo would have told them a truth he'd been holding in a vice-like grip for better than two years. It was deeply imprinted within his Slavic bloodline to avenge the ones he loved.

He had done it before. *More than once.*

And now, as he sits listening to the storm's banshee wail, he's pretty damn sure of one thing.

He was about to stride that path again.

There was no getting round it, Perry Morgan Blake's transfer to Coal Island had pushed a button he ordinarily kept locked off tight. Because, when all was said and done, the creep had been weighed and measured in Texas. So, given the resurgence in states' rights advocacy, and a notoriously inflexible local Department of Corrections, it was almost inconceivable anyone could have been persuaded to blithely hand him over to anybody—*threats to the freak's personal safety not withstanding*—let alone some federally appointed private enterprise goofers headquartered in Virginia.

So here he was, like a bug on fly-paper.

Stuck on—*item seven.*

The water jug stands empty in the middle of his table, *ditto* his second plate of eggs, when the shift-change waitress swings by.

She moves in relatively close. Maybe because the din from the storm is approaching the level of a marching band—*or possibly not*. Whatever the reason, up close, she smells better than relatively good. He feels a blunt-edged spike of shame that, as she'd drifted over, he'd also judged her better than good to look at.

'Can I get you something a little stronger than iced water?'

Despite his less than sociable mood, he finds it difficult to avoid her eyes.

'That would be limited to coffee, right?'

'Pretty much,' she says. 'You don't strike me as a lemonade kind of guy.'

Her accent is educated north-east. Her skin, close to flawless. Practically cosmetic-free. She is a little above medium height. Medium slim. Glossy, free-style dark brown hair. Track and field muscle tone. It strikes him as odd that she was here, in this nowhere place, forcing him to deal with the kind of visual inputs he'd never once registered over the preceding two years.

He offers what he hopes will pass for an apologetic smile.

'I like *it, it* doesn't like me... Go figure.'

The moment the words are out of his mouth, the memory of the first time he'd uttered them rises like acid bile in his throat.

He swallows hard. Hopes he's not pegging himself as some kind of socially inept halfwit.

She tilts her head, running her eyes over him for a few seconds longer than he'd been expecting. Her gaze lingering on the badge clipped on his belt.

'Sorry, *Deputy*... no time. Inclination pending.'

She pirouettes away from his booth. Rhythmic hips. Light on her feet. Faded denim pressing comfortably against her curves.

He finds himself pondering what she did to stay in shape this far from a gym. Struggling with the fact that something so carnal has even registered in his mind. Particularly now. At this moment. In this place. He wants to believe his curiosity is purely down to her pithy comeback. Nothing to do with the sway of her hips. Her confident, long-limbed stride. So he tries to persuade himself his interest is piqued by nothing more than idle speculation. After all, what kind of waitress uses a word like *inclination*, with that particular syntax, in a south-Texan roadside diner.

Not now, he scolds himself.

Besides, if the schedule held, he doesn't have much longer to wait. Enough time for a second trip to the men's room. Cupped palms face-wash, at most. Five finger comb-through. Back in time for the deluge outside to properly hose him down as he makes his way to whatever transport they were sending.

So he figures he can easily hold off processing the truth behind the unbidden longing he registers as she walks away.

Either way—*it feels like betrayal*.

As it is, the Coal Island transfer ploughs into the diner's swamped parking lot fifteen-minutes early. Main-beams blazing. Illuminating broad curtains of rain. Slewing to a halt in a slot indecently distant from the diner's entrance. Exactly as he'd anticipated it would. Sitting there, squat and threatening. Like an APC had up and mated with a school bus, then gotten itself spray-painted black.

He scoops up his jacket and slides out of the booth.

An SMS buzzes through to his cell phone as he makes his way to the counter. But he ignores it. Choosing, instead, to dump a twenty and the coins he doesn't want to carry into the glass tray sitting next to the cash register.

Then he turns and heads for the exit.

The lady without the time, or a buttoned-down inclination, transfers the cash without acknowledging his generous tip. Even so, he feels her gaze linger on him as he turns. Sees a hint of curiosity on her face, masquerading as a half-smile, reflecting in the glass as he makes ready to push through the door.

For no reason he'd be prepared to admit—*especially to himself*—he turns back to the counter. Moving in close. Keeping his voice low.

'I have a favour to ask.'

Her eyes lock onto his.

'Nothing ventured,' she says.

He feels a jolt of something run through him. Something palpable he'd prefer to deny. Something more than the cryptic inference contained in her reply. Because, once again, it was an intriguing riposte. Neither no, nor yes. Nor maybe. More like: *I'm listening, so you'd better make it count.*

'I'll be taking a trip in that Judge Dredd ride waiting out there.'

'You mean the one idling just far enough away to guarantee you're going to get soaked?'

Zalizo shrugs.

'Just as well I'm not made of sugar.'

'I'll bet,' she says.

Somewhere inside his head, he registers a fleeting sense he may be smiling—*though likely not*. After all, it had been a while.

'I could be gone a few hours... maybe longer.'

'And you want an eye kept on your vehicle?'

'I'd sure appreciate it.'

She leans in closer still. It has the feel of something bordering on intimacy—*but just as likely not*.

'Anything of particular value inside?'

Up close, she really did smell good.

'Not at this precise moment... it's more to do with it being a loaner. I feel obliged to make sure it's returned. Besides, it'll be a long walk home if it's not here when I get back.'

She pulls an expression that's hard to read.

'So... I take it home's not any place around here?'

He shakes his head. Figures her enquiry means she's pretty much guaranteed not to be from around here either.

She raises an eyebrow.

'We're not open twenty-four-seven.'

'For as long as you can, would be better than nothing.'

'I'm fairly sure a US Marshall four-by-four will be safe enough around these parts...'

She shrugs.

'...but I guess it costs me nothing to keep an eye out.'

'Much obliged,' he says.

She says, 'You're welcome... *Deputy*.'

He strides along the front of the diner to his GMC. Mostly under cover of the diner's overhanging roof. Mostly at a slow—*fuck you*—pace. Opens the driver door and slides behind the wheel. Turns the engine over, snagging reverse. Eases back the twenty-something yards. Slotting in next to the transfer. Its driver staring straight ahead.

Zalizo ducks out of the GMC, pulling his forty-five free of its holster. Grabs the handle on the transfer's sliding panel door. Pulls it rearward—*hard and fast*—staying parallel as it opens. For his trouble, all he gets is soaked to the skin. Other than six unoccupied seats, the rear is empty. Blacked out windows, encased on the outside by thick wire mesh. Lockable three-point seat harnesses. Shackle hoops fixed to the deck. No access to the driver.

He spots the miniature, rear-facing camera the moment he begins hauling himself aboard. Attached to the bulkhead, driver side, close to the frame of the door. Pencil thin and a decent attempt made at concealment. Nonetheless, looking like it's been fixed there in a hurry.

No matter.

Early in his life, he'd been taught a fundamental maxim. Every action, regardless how random or seemingly disconnected, signalled the moves to come. Something his parents had never ceased drilling into him—*over and over*. His mother, when she'd taught him the intricacies of chess. His father, from the moment he'd begun schooling him in the arcane Spetsnaz arts of endurance and self-preservation.

Decision made, he climbs fully aboard. Opting to take the forward-most seat on the driver's side. Which means, whoever was tasked with monitoring the camera feed would be lucky to catch anything more than the top of his head.

He closes his eyes as he settles in for the ride.

Yet one more habit not forsaken.

Unbidden, his mind flips back to the diner. To the mess of silky brown hair. To the denim-clad form he'd seen swaying below the maker's label. To the two things he'd thought, until moments ago, would never again find traction in his life.

Time.

And inclination.

COAL ISLAND, GUADALUPE MOUNTAINS

Just like always, it's the smells that come to him first. Drifting in ahead of sights and sounds. Salt water mingling with the reek of decay. That dense smell of atrophy peculiar to the Atchafalaya Delta. A kind of entropy, fuelled by the rhythm of endless tides washing in over deep, bug-laden silt and the rotting husks of fallen trees. Where isolated pockets of humanity toiled against the twin assaults of heat and deprivation. Unserved by even the most basic utilities. Abandoned by all but the most stubbornly resolved; and those condemned to remain imprisoned by the callous indifference of poverty.

Keeping up a steady rhythm, he propels the beat-up aluminum skiff with practiced ease. Bath-sized and acned with the scars of a thousand BB pellets. Navigating silently along the calm, brackish waters snaking ahead of him, smooth as glass. And, despite his skinny fingers and short, scrawny arms, his progress is driven by a burning hunger.

A fierce desire.

A determination born of guilt.

Gripping the oars with mounting fervour, he manoeuvres the diminutive craft along the narrow creek. Miles from anything resembling even a dirt track. Anticipation tingling under every inch of his pallid, freckled skin. Easing the skiff through clouds of mosquitos, shifting in veils. Bald Louisiana cypress rising dark and sentinel along the slick mudbanks on either side. Here and there, the ripple from a bluegill, rising to snag a strider.

It was a long pull for someone so young. His destination necessarily isolated. But he knows exactly how long it will take to arrive. Knows every inch of the arena that will be laid out before him. The smells that will greet him. The metallic tincture of blood. The acid tinge of sun-baked viscera. The smoky-sweet mix of burnt flesh and rotting fur. The relentless wall of white noise from the frenzied swarms of blowfly.

But, most of all, he yearns for the terror he'll see in his captives' eyes. The feral stench of fear that will greet him, even before he sets foot in the carefully prepared clearing. The way the creatures will sense his arrival. Straining against their chains. Cowering away from him as he approaches. Their flesh trembling. Eyes bulging. Nostrils flaring. The same pathetic ritual, each and every time he pays them a visit...

...to punish them—and keep on punishing them—for the wicked thing they had done. And, one day—he didn't yet know when—he would know their fear for himself. Share their torment as punishment for his own cowardice. For his failure to repay the debt of loyalty he owed. But most of all, for his betrayal of the only person who had ever shown him an ounce of kindness.

Which is why, even to his twelve-year-old mind, this feels like a journey he's be making for millennia. And, as he slips past the half-way point, he whispers the same words he always does.

'Not long now.'

Perry Morgan Blake registers the approach of heavy-booted footfalls. Listens as they shuffle to a stop beyond the bars of his ten-by-eight cell.

He lays completely still on his deliberately thin mattress. Hears the serving slot grate back. Waits as the compartmentalised feeding tray is pushed through onto the platform fixed to the door. Plastic and unbreakable. And way too flimsy for fashioning into any sort of instrument for attack—*or self-harm*.

As he leaves, the guard runs his high-voltage baton over the bars of his cell.

'Eat, Perry... next meal's gonna be your last.'

Perry waits, eyes closed, until the guard departs before rising off his back. Hinging at the waist. Swinging his legs slowly off the bunk. Planting his bare feet shoulder-width apart. Feeling the smooth, cool cement beneath his toes. Placing the tips of his fingers on his knees as he begins to rise. Staying bent at the hip. Then he pitches forward, landing smoothly on his hands. Press-up position.

For the whole of his existence before Coal Island he'd been little more than a stack of bones. *Nothin' but piss'n'skin*, as his drunken slob of a father had often slurred. Now he is something else entirely. Sinew and muscle. Latent strong. Durable, in the extreme. So much so, he'll push out one-twenty reps in a little over two minutes. Short and sweet. Just enough to get his blood flowing. Enough to aid his digestion. After which he will return to his bunk. Allow his mind to drift into the cruel embrace of his more recent sleepless dream...

...re-living the intimacy of fear he'd brought to the wide open concourse of the Earle Cabell Federal Building. Re-implanting himself in the chaos. The screams. The wide-eyed, disbelieving stares. The snivelling. The pleading. The involuntary soiling, in anticipation of the pain to come. The sharp spit of bullets exiting the suppressor. The hiss of soft alloy passing through flesh. The dull thud of high velocity rounds shattering bone. Indifferent to all those murmured prayers that would forever go unanswered...

...savouring, once again, each and every last breath his victims had taken. The sensuous thrill of detachment he always has. The heady sensation he was soaring above the blood-art he created.

He'd never known the year of his birth. So, best guess, he is somewhere close to mid-twenties. And for all the years he can remember, since the mother he could no longer picture in his mind had walked out of his life—*disappearing in her pale blue, Sunday dress, like some ambivalent spectre down the rutted mud track leading from their shack in the woods*—all he's ever yearned for was a violent death. To live it. Breathe it. Taste for himself the gut-freezing terror. To be hunted and to know, just like his own victims had known, that for every second of every minute stretching forward, there would be no escape.

But ever-present in the dark recesses inside his head. The one's he reserves for his deepest needs—*those most secret of all his many desires*—he knows the possibility remains they may simply choose to deceive him. Knows the close-on six months of waiting, since his sudden transfer out of Huntsville, might have all been for nothing. The secretive and brutal training program he'd so readily agreed to endure, all just some elaborate ruse to keep him distracted. Or worse. Turned into little more than a pathetic, deluded lab rat, trapped inside some kind of perverted experiment. Motivated to excel. Ultimately, destined to perish without so much as a whimper.

Could be they'd intended, all along, to go back on their promises. Humiliate him by easing him into chemical sleep, in the manner his death sentence had decreed. Either way...

...not long now.

COAL ISLAND, GUADALUPE MOUNTAINS

Fifty-one years ago, he'd been christened Jacque Victor Labette. Tipping the scales at fifteen pounds and change at birth, he'd dropped the *'Jacque'* before he'd made it to junior high. His Louisiana drawl neutralized by the time he'd felt those soft, manicured lawns under his brogues at Ithaca, upon his arrival at Cornell University. And if his whore mother had cared one iota about either of these pivotal transformations, when he'd first set out to shed the carapace of poverty and customer abuse he'd been born into, he might have been inclined to go back once he'd made good. Help her stop cooking that pale-brown, frothy shit in her tarnished spoons. Help her stop flicking her fucking needles. Applying the tourniquets. Maybe suture her blistered lips shut; to keep the cheap liquor from hitting her stomach ulcers. Had he been able to think of her as a human being at all, he might have considered trying to help her crawl from the gutter—*just like he had*.

As it was, he'd left her sprawled unconscious. Eyes glazed and vacant. Walked out of their wood and corrugated-iron, two-room shack. Hopped a bus to the first place that wasn't Gulfport, Louisiana.

Covington had turned out to be the first place that wasn't Gulfport. The place where he'd spent the night, sleeping on a drug store roof, out of sight from the cops patrolling in their bull-barred cruisers. Scavenging through trash cans. Anything that meant he wouldn't have to take the risk of getting caught stealing food. Or spending the whoring cash he'd lifted from its ill-conceived hiding place. Catching the first bus out and pushing on through. With no inkling that, from the moment he landed in New Orleans, he'd find it all too easy to get noticed by one elderly, well-heeled southern gentleman after another.

Up to the point in his life when he'd started shaving, he had nonetheless always credited Audrey Jacqueline Labette for his most singular defining attribute; his freakish ability to master languages.

French had been a given. Spanish and Italian a gentle walk in the park. And when his German became technically proficient, with a minimum of effort, thanks to an art dealer who'd welcomed his visits to that grand apartment abutting Lafayette

Square, he'd known for sure he possessed a preternatural gift to go with his immense size and strength. And when he'd begun to learn Arabic, it had been like discovering the world of fine wines. Like licking *Chateau Lafite* from a virgin's nipple, the last of his many delicate and appreciative, loose-skinned patrons had extolled. And—*even though it had gone unspoken at the time*—he'd known well enough, the unsullied recipient of said champagne would more than likely be entirely limited to a lower than voting age, compliant male of the species.

He'd been three years off voting age. And the notion hadn't disgusted him—*not in the least.*

Truth be told, it was just as likely he'd acquired his linguistic chromosome from some sweaty, foul-mouthed deckhand, fresh off the pier in Gulfport. Either way, Russian, Japanese and Hindu had followed during his four years at Cornell. Portuguese within a month, for a bet, halfway up the Amazon. Hebrew, it had to be said, had taken somewhat longer, during a two-year long, back and forth Agency cluster-fuck in Beirut.

And, as things turned out, his gift had gone on to become the driving force behind his pre-eminence in the field of private security recruitment.

For the better part of two decades—*following his sudden and somewhat ignominious fall from grace in the murky world of CIA covert operations*—his sole pursuit in life had been working with, or acquiring, specialist human assets. Those suddenly displaced, deeply resentful refugees. Lethal discards from the finest Black Ops units across the globe. Something akin to childhood abandonment for men who had nothing resembling a social structure to fall back on. No families. No friends outside their former units. No purpose in life, other than to seek and destroy.

He put his undeniable success down to the fact that he'd

been able to offer them something few others could. Something more than pay checks commensurate to their unique abilities. Because, more often than not, he'd been able to speak to them in their own language. Offer himself as some kind of benevolent surrogate. Providing them the opportunity to recapture their sense of belonging. And over the years, he'd honed this particular specialism into a fine-tuned process that rarely failed. Entice. Mentor. Manipulate. And there were, of course, those rare occasions, when his mission in life had brought with it a more tangible reward. A visceral expression of gratitude from a solidly-toned, like-minded warrior.

To say the least, his life since Gulfport had been gratifying.

His cell phone issues an impatient buzz.

It's 8.50 PM, *Mountain Standard Time*, which means the call is close to an hour late. However, his attention has been fixed on the grainy image of this curious visitor from Plainview, Texas, so he's going to let the caller's tardiness slide.

'*Erov tov*, Mr. Buckley.'

'I'm sorry...what?'

'In Hebrew, it means... *good evening*. But according to my reckoning, you're exactly fifty-one minutes late. Which means you now have my rapt attention for precisely five-hundred-and-forty seconds.'

'Okay... so, it turns out you were right. Our deputy from the panhandle would appear to be a singular individual.'

Victor laces his voice with malice.

'At this precise moment, I neither require... nor am I inclined to solicit, your personal endorsement.'

There's a pause on the other end of the line. And a sound like someone trying to swallow something they know will make them gag. He suspects pride. Though, after their previous encounter, bone-deep fear is just as likely.

'Okay... so our subject was born Oleg Constantine Zalizo, in Albuquerque, in eighty-one. The family moving to Lubbock in ninety-seven. Graduated magna cum laude, from Texas Tech. Majored in physics and chemical engineering. Remembered to this day as some kind of wonder kid, by all accounts. Excelled academically... even more so in sport. Heavily into athletics... swimming... boxing... wrestling... fencing. And contemporary dance, can you believe?'

'Yes, Mr. Buckley... as a matter of fact, I can. But I'm not inclined to enlighten you as to why.'

'Uh-huh... anyway. He up and joined the Marine Corps shortly after he quits academia aged twenty-six. Both parents long deceased. Fugitives who'd escaped Ukraine and Belarus... back before the wall came down. Brutally murdered, apparently... not long after they'd moved from New Mexico to Texas, or so the story goes. Though the exact manner of their death is unconfirmed. But, by all accounts, it made the local headlines in a big way at the time. Plus we've established a bunch of other interesting facts, like him turning down West Point. And that, from day one at Parris Island, he blew through everything they could throw at him. Off-the-chart in marksmanship... especially with a side-arm. Chewed up weapons and tactics. Spat out his unarmed combat instructors. Had his choice of commissions, but opted to stay in camo. At which point, he gets whisked to Camp Lejeune... where he earns his Marine Raider patch. Swiftly followed by a series of in-theatre promotions all the way to Captain... call-sign ITEM-One.'

'I see. So like you said... *impressive*.'

There's another nervous pause.

'Uh-huh... and our intel is saying his posting to MacDill was a short-term thing, early in his career... definitely nothing recent. So your information he moved from there to Dallas PD, appears to be bogus.'

'Is that so...? Well, Mr. Buckley... I'm all ears.'

'Okay... So he's embedded into MARSOC by age thirty. Fast-tracked up to JSOC by thirty-one. Postings to MacDill, like you said... and some place out in California I can't recall the name of.'

'Coronado?'

'Yeah... something like that. Anyway, he goes on to make Major before he turns thirty-three.'

'Major...? Who makes an O-4 in under seven years?'

'I wouldn't know. But what we do know is... close on three years ago, he ships out of JSOC. Then, to all intents and purposes... vanishes.'

'Define... *vanishes.*'

'Just up and drops off every Spec Ops command grid... Delta said, never went through our pipeline... SEAL teams said, likewise... ISA said, not one of ours... Raiders said, he didn't come back to us.'

'CIA...?'

'Langley said... who?'

'Did they indeed. And no one said... *who's asking?*'

'The way we framed it... we gave no-one any reason to inquire.'

'And how, exactly... did we frame it?'

'A solid contact we have in State, pushed a Ukraine angle. Along the lines of a distant relative, searching for kin known to have made it stateside. Looking to pass on an ancestral plot of mud.'

'And, are there any such... long-lost ancestors?'

'Yes. We're not idiots... Plus it helps that he has a decidedly uncommon family name, even for a Ukrainian second gen immigrant. And it turns out there's an uncle, on his father's side.'

'And what's the likelihood this uncle could become aware of your enquiry?'

'Highly unlikely. But not impossible... I guess.'

Victor calculates the risk. He figures, worst case, he has at least one asset from that neck of the woods he can deploy to re-sanitize, if the need arose.

'Very well, Mr. Buckley. Little of anything I can use right now. But, if nothing else, it should serve as a reminder never to under-estimate. And I appreciate time was limited.'

'True... but then we played a hunch.'

'What sort of... *hunch*?'

'We stopped searching active-duty rosters and came across a mini-legend at Defense Clandestine Services... Turns out our friend had been pulled out of his beloved camo, following some sort of ruckus out in the hills someplace in Oregon, to head up an off-the-books special unit within DCS.'

'What type of *unit*, exactly?'

'Whatever it is... it's classified beyond our reach. Much like the ruckus in Oregon.'

'Now that is interesting. And do we know if he's autonomous?'

'No... no-one seems to know. Or, if they do... it's one more thing they're not telling.'

'You don't say?'

'Uh-huh... But, apart from the fact he's now a Lieutenant-Colonel, that's all she wrote here in DC...'

There's another pause.

'Do you want to go over the Dallas angle?'

Buckley's words explode inside Victor's head.

THE DALLAS ANGLE.

He performs a quick recalculation. Factors in some cause and effect as a hole opens up in his gut. Questions and self-recrimination exploding somewhere between his temples.

How the hell had he missed it; how had he failed to make such a simple connection?

Close on six months ago, he'd lost a three-man squad,

at a solar farm in Ellis County, not far south of Dallas. An above average team. Almost impossible to replace. Specially selected. Combat-proven operators—*with numerous successful demolition operations under their belts*—made to look like boy scouts.

He finds himself staring blankly at the monitor, as a wave of fury roars through his skull. For a moment, he considers dropping the cell phone and stomping it under his thick-soled boots.

He thinks about the operation as it stands right now. The private security organisation he'd created to support it. So meticulously put together. The potential it represents. Naturally, he accepts that elements of his product development were still somewhat experimental. And that, statistically, every system has a failure rate commensurate to its complexity. But, when all was said and done, he trusts his processes. The finesse encapsulated within his training and deployment protocols. The behaviour control conventions. The retrieve and dispose resources he has put in place. Sanctioned beyond civil authority countermand.

The potential for his creation is incalculable. A lucrative market—*both foreign and domestic*—for a level of confidentiality and exclusivity his security force was specifically designed to cater for. Servicing a customer base he'd worked assiduously to nurture. The kind of premium packages he'd spent half a lifetime refining. Ideally suited for a cadre of wealth and influence with a predilection for keeping their hands clean and their *raison d'être* cloaked in the deepest shadows.

Now, seemingly out of nowhere, there's a prospect of interference he'd convinced himself had been factored out.

A familiar voice in his head cajoles him to stay calm. An anxious voice, he doesn't recognize, demands—*you have to pause, you need more time*. Time he knows the schedule he'd committed to could not accommodate.

Even though he knows the answer, he hears himself saying, 'Is there a Dallas angle I haven't covered?'

'Uh-huh...'

'Buckley... *uh-huh* is not in any reputable lexicon I know of. So please refrain from using it within my auditory range. It's starting to really piss me off.'

'O-k-a-y... so, yes. It appears there is.'

'So spit it out. Clock's ticking this end.'

Yet another pause creeps its way down the line.

'Well, it seems the organized crime detective line you were fed is nothing more than a construct. Seems Dallas PD was having sleepless nights over some elusive domestic terrorist perps... suspected hard-core ex-military. So our one-time Spec Ops Major rocks up from out of nowhere to lend a hand... embeds into Dallas PD's Organised Crimes Unit, under a strict need-to-know. Then lady love crashes the scene. Even so, he pushes his case with brutal efficiency, that much was true. A number of prior-to-arrest fatalities eventually ensued. Then fate came knocking a second time. The federal building massacre. His squeeze... some high-end corporate lawyer, working her off days pro bono, is in the wrong place on the wrong day... at the wrong time. And worse, the autopsy found she was pregnant. A couple of months at most, but confirmed. No DNA check was done for paternity. But, hey... why wouldn't it be his?'

'I see... and is that everything?'

'It is... apart from one last detail.'

'Buckley... you're really starting to test my patience.'

'Okay... okay. His Dallas PD resignation letter is more than likely just another hoax... because he was never officially on their pay-roll. However, one does actually exist... received and processed

through regular channels at his real home back at DCS. Which pretty much confirms he's been freelancing for close on six months. So, as I suggested... looks like our guy's a lone wolf.'

'Well, haven't you been the astute one? Excellent work, I must say.'

Despite his broiling rage, he is genuinely impressed. But he's still loathe to accept the lone wolf status. Because he knows, only too well, once men like Zalizo networked, they stayed networked. In the same way Dillon Buckley's circle of Beltway contacts has been able to reach deeper into the haystack than his own, not insignificant, intelligence web has managed. Added to which, he'd spent a considerable budget infiltrating Dallas PD and been fed a line of bullshit for his trouble. And it doesn't soothe his rage one bit that the contact he'd engaged had most likely given his intel in good faith. Bottom line, he is operating in the middle strata at best. And all because Cornell University wasn't Princeton, Yale or Harvard. Or even Georgetown, it would appear. His decade in the Agency, performing wet-work operations all over the globe, ultimately counting for nothing.

A fact of life that, to this day, really boils his piss.

'Well, it may interest you to learn that since we last had the pleasure of each other's company, so to speak... I've experienced an epiphany all of my own.'

'Uh-huh... I mean... you have?'

'Indeed, I have. You see, it occurs to me that our mysterious marine, or whatever the hell he is, has unwittingly revealed at least some of his cards.'

'How so...?'

'Because the timing of his move out to the panhandle never did hang together.'

'I'm not sure I follow...'

'The point is, our antagonist made his request to join Hale

County Sheriff's Department precisely three days after our inmate was transferred out of Huntsville.'

'I still don't follow...'

'Then it transpires your elevation to the ranks of the astute has been lamentably short-lived, Mr. Buckley... *C'est la vie.*'

Victor feels a portion of his usual composure return.

'So, let's consider the synergy of timeline and behaviour for a moment... Our friend, by every confirmed account, is as mentally tough as he is brutally efficient. Yet what we're being asked to swallow, is that this supreme being is able to chomp down hard on his deepest emotions all through our subject's arraignment. All throughout his lengthy, high-profile trial. And on through his appeal... somehow, our shadowy friend copes with it all without so much as a sniffle. Then suddenly, six months ago, this anvil-made-flesh can't take anymore and heads off to Plainview, Texas. For what exactly? To soothe his bleeding heart? Not on the day his beloved was gunned down, mind you. Not a week later. Or a month. Nor when the last-ditch insanity plea is thrown out and the death sentence upheld. No, Mr. Buckley... his breakdown occurs at the exact same time our subject is transferred into our custody. Do you seriously buy that?'

'PTSD affects people in different ways, I guess.'

'Well... I'm not buying it. For one thing... from what you've discovered about his uncompromising arrest record, I'd bet heavily this has nothing to do with post-traumatic stress disorder. In fact, I'd wager our mysterious friend's coping mechanisms are at a level way above that pseudo-psychological, man-made mountain of bullshit.'

'Okay... could be you're right. But I'm still convinced, one way or another, he's flying solo... on indefinite compassionate leave, possibly. Maybe even AWOL. And you're discounting the fact

we've confirmed his resignation. Which means, whatever Deep State access to intel he may have had, and any official cover he was operating under... it's pretty much a given that's denied to him now. So, I'll grant you he's capable. But I still wouldn't sweat it... because, like I said, my take is that he's one man, with an itch he's been waiting to scratch.'

'The fact you continue to think this way, Mr. Buckley, is precisely why I am here... and you are not.'

Victor cuts the connection abruptly. Ponders idly whether Buckley is even curious why he'd been alone for the call. Then he forces his eyes away from the monitor. Selects another entry in his cell phone's contacts.

The pick-up is almost instantaneous.

'Yes...'

'I trust you're still in position?'

'Sure... but, right now, it's fitness central out there. Goddam joggers everywhere.'

'How's our window?'

'Wait one...'

Victor glances back to the figure on the screen. Feels an alien tightness spreading across his chest.

'I'd say our window's just about to close fast. The target is on his cell phone... approaching his vehicle as we speak.'

'Okay... so switch to Plan B.'

'Plan B...?'

'Yes, Miller... short of a record-breaking onset of Alzheimer's, I believe that's what I said.'

'What about the new guy, Abelman? Doesn't he have two targets?'

'Carl... you need to remember you are not employed to ask me questions. Nasi has his orders... and now you have yours.

Let me know when it's done.'

Carl Jordan Miller says, *'Roger that...'*

Victor ends the call. Re-focuses his attention back to the grainy image on the monitor. Attempts to clear his mind of pointless self-reproach.

'So, Oleg Constantine,' he mutters to himself. *'You want to engage me in a game of chicken.'*

From what he observes, this Major, or Colonel—*or whatever the fuck he was*—has not made the camera feed. Right now, he's just sitting there. Passively. On the driver side. Forward-most seat. Which is somewhat inconvenient, as it affords the least favourable camera angle. But then, he'd only ordered the device installed on a whim. Hoping to study his unwanted guest during the transfer. To get some kind of feel for this individual before he arrived.

'So be it,' he says to himself.

He swipes through his cell phone contacts a second time. Pictures the ghoulish individual who would answer. Sets himself to keep disdain from his voice for as long as he can manage, given his dark mood.

This time, it takes a good deal longer for the call to hook up.

'It's a little on the late side, Victor...'

The voice is reedy. Disembodied almost. As if digitally generated.

'I might have chosen not to answer.'

'I need a sanction,' Victor says.

'Who and when?'

'Our so called Deputy from the panhandle... imminently.'

'Out of the question.'

'Well... since it now appears our unwanted guest might not be what he's led us to believe. I deem it imperative.'

'And since I assume you are back on Mountain Standard Time... maybe you didn't hear me. Your request is denied.'

'*No,* Martin... it's because you're not listening.'

Above all others, there are two traits Victor despises in a man. And, without even trying, Martin Devlin represented both.

'So... maybe I need to speak to the homeowner.'

'At this hour... that's also out of the question. Besides, the Senator is not in the habit of keeping a dog and barking himself.'

'That's your call. But you need to be aware... I may be forced into making an autonomous decision.'

'Likewise, that will be your call. But I can assure you, any such action, tonight of all nights... will risk severe consequences for you personally.'

'For your sake, Martin... I hope that's not a threat?'

'Take it however you want, Victor... my decision holds. Meantime, I suggest you prep any one of your numerous... assets. And wait instructions.'

The line goes dead.

Prep your assets. Wait instructions.

The fact a pretentious prick like Martin Devlin actually thought he needed to be told makes Victor smile.

He returns his attention to the camera feed. Considers his options. Struggling to hold down the resentment he feels at having to run anything through a jumped-up political dick-wipe.

So he waits for his thoughts to settle.

After a moment, he raises a couple fingers to his lips. Then presses them to the figure on the screen.

'Alors, mon ami...

...le temps est venu pour toi et moi danser.'

ALEXANDRIA, WASHINGTON DC

Dillon Robert Buckley leans on the door-frame of his delivery-mileage-only Mercedes G-Wagon—*a Brabus 900 Edition*—with its new ride aroma and showroom shine. Customised with a whole bunch of bells and whistles. Top-end infotainment, with enough speakers and sub-woofers to rock Carnegie Hall. Replete with beaucoup carbon fibre and quilted leather. Not to mention the pearlescent blue livery, with the faintest hint of turquoise iridescence shimmering across the quasi-satin paintwork. A fifteen-thousand dollar option that really pushes his buttons.

He's cradling his gold-plated cell phone tight to his right ear, waiting for the money guys to finally pick up...

...across the street, a seven-point-six-two match grade round explodes from its hand-loaded brass casing. Beginning it's micro-second surrender to angular momentum, imparted by twenty-two inches of precision-machined rifling, on its passage down the well-oiled barrel. Streaking toward the bottom left quarter of his skull—a couple of inches above his top-most vertebrae. One-hundred and eighty-one grams of high-end copper-zinc alloy. Eight-hundred meters per second at the muzzle—near as dammit. Maybe take a little off for the SOCOM suppressor it passes through on its way to its target. Twenty-seven hundred pound foot of energy. Twenty-six hundred foot per second at impact—give or take. Minimal elevation. Air temperature, six-degrees Celsius. Next to no crosswind. Range less than one hundred yards, to a stationary target. Nothing too taxing for the individual who had just applied precisely three-and-a-half pounds of pressure to a perfectly balanced trigger...

...because all three of them had agreed they would meet at 7.30 PM. Yet both miserable little weaners have no-showed. And it wasn't like he'd asked them to contribute anything worth a damn. After all, when everything was said and done, they were just funders. He understands that. So all they'd had to do was turn up once they'd finished the round of golf he'd been forced to miss. Show a little *fucking* solidarity...

...the round impacts with a dull thud. Punching a neat hole through the back of his skull. Exiting the lower right quarter of his face with a short, low-resonance buzz. Removing his entire cheekbone and greater portion of his jaw. A spray of blood, bone fragments and gore adding a little more iridescence to the SUVs hood...

...Buckley doesn't feel himself pitch forward at the hip. Right knee hyper-extending. Torso half-spinning. Doesn't register what was left of his head impact the side-view mirror of the vehicle he's only ever driven twice.

Carl Jordan Miller removes his baseball cap. Lays it on the floor beside him. Wipes the sweat from his hairline. Locates the still warm brass casing. Then settles back, turning his Aimpoint scope on the jogger with the dog, who'd suddenly materialized out of thin air. Two dark shapes. Coming to a dead stop, just inside his sightline.

The jogger is wearing a dark beanie hat, pulled down low against the unseasonable cold. A dark neck-warmer, tugged up beneath their nose. A dark, lightweight sports jacket, zipped tight under their chin. Dark running pants. Dark sneakers. No designer labels. Body shape suggesting an adult female. Athletic build, and on the tall side—*for a woman*. Not far short of six-foot, if he had to guess. Appearing distracted and confused.

As they move within his sighting arc, he makes sure to keep the sweep of the red dot away from the jogger's body mass.

Spends a few seconds recalculating. Weighing the risk. To what degree another corpse will complicate matters.

After all, collaterals had not been sanctioned.

It's been a long day. He is stiff, sweaty and tired. The competing voices inside his head have fallen silent hours ago. But now a familiar voice speaks to him. Telling him there was something off-script about this female jogger. Something he can't quite put his finger on.

So he judges it better to watch...

...and wait.

The jogger makes a barely audible clicking noise with her tongue. Moko, a four-year-old Belgian *Malinois,* pulls up instantly at her side. Ears canted toward the tree-lined parking lot. Nostrils flared. Dark, streamlined snout raised a little above horizontal.

'E-a-s-y there, boy...'

She stops abruptly, swinging her head this way and that. Just like any startled civilian would. As sure as she can be her reactions are plausible. Turning points of the compass. Indicating, to anyone scoping, she's witnessed the victim go down and is now standing confused. Unsure what she's just seen. Unwilling or unable to make up her mind what to do next.

In point of fact, she's about to gamble. Her initial instinct had been to keep jogging. But she'd seen subject *Georgetown's* cell phone fall from his hand. Knows the value of the data it might hold.

There's a waste-high, red-brick stone wall enclosing the barriered parking lot. Edged by an evenly-spaced boundary of trees. So she quickly calculates line of sight. Figures the shooter has minimal elevation—*likely maxed at second-floor—*

on account of the height of the canopy. Registers most of the parking slots are occupied with your typical, up-market SUV dick extensions. Most with conveniently high roof lines. So she figures there's a decent level of cover for a low-moving target.

All things considered, she judges it worth the risk.

She's been slow-jogging for the past forty minutes. Ever since Dillan Robert Buckley had parked up and exited his vehicle. Keeping up a lazy holding pattern at less than half her normal pace. Moko glued to her side. Blending in easily with all the other die-hard suburban fitness freaks, braving the late-evening chill.

She sees a red dot splutter across a spread of foliage, off to her left. Watches it arc back. Stuttering across branches and leaves. It might have been anything. A trick of the light—*perhaps*. A taillight reflecting back off a window—*maybe.*

But it wasn't.

She pulls her cell phone. Makes like she's calling *Nine-One-One*. Holds it low, as she fakes punching the screen, so she won't fail to see the red dot, should it reappear—*centre mass*. Maintaining an outward appearance of being bewildered. Keeping her movements panicky. Making herself hard to scope.

The shooter will have to calculate. Time to sirens and flashing blue lights.

Risk versus reward.

She vaults the wall. Quick-walks to the big Merc. Bending low every few seconds. Making like she's soothing her companion. Ensuring she'll be harder to fix.

The shooter will have to decide.

She'd seen subject *Georgetown* spin. Seen his head jerk down. Forward and to the right. Seen the puff of gore-spray. So she calculates the direction of fire...

...duck and soothe.

Because she knows ballistics...

...duck and soothe.

Making sure she presents little more than a couple of inches above vehicle roof lines...

...duck and soothe.

She makes it to the G-Wagon. Drops down to the body. Stays down. Locates Buckley's cell phone beneath an adjacent vehicle. Quickly stows it. Stays low for an eight count. Moving, still crouched, to a position a few vehicles over.

The shooter will have to anticipate.

She is at full sprint before she makes it to upright. Maintaining the tight, zig-zagging pattern of a slalom skier. Still has a reserve of speed that had informed her active-duty call-sign. Her solid yet lithe physique giving her an uncommon ability to compete successfully at both the four-hundred sprint and cross-country at college. So she determines she'll be a real pain in the rear to sight. Just some random female fleeing in panic. Some hapless busy-body who'd nosed her way into something she had no stomach for.

Untethered, Moko keeps up with an effortless lope.

By the time the shooter makes his decision, US Army Sergeant Eleanor Rundell, calculates she'll be long gone.

Miller curses under his breath. Pulls his baseball cap back on. Stows his brass and begins quickly breaking down his piece.

He'd watched the jogger make a call. Scoped her once she'd vaulted into the parking lot. Ducking and shimmying to where Buckley had fallen. Kept his crosshairs planted squarely on the G-Wagon waiting for a figure to reappear. Caught a glimpse of one fleeing a little outside his sight line. Dressed head-to-foot in dark-coloured clothing. Maybe blue. Maybe black. Perhaps even dark green—*considering the orange glow of streetlight*. Zig-zagging hard and fast and impossible to scope. As a person might, if they'd taken time to familiarise themselves with the terrain they were working.

Just like a professional would.

'FUCK.'

So, now he has no choice. He will have to get to Buckley's corpse pronto. Work fast. Set up a random attack scene. He figures he'll have just enough time until the first DC Metro cruisers show. Though he now has serious doubts the cops had been called. Either way, he'll be making adjustments to his planned route out. After which he'll meet with this new Israeli guy—*Benjamen Nasi Abelman*—per his orders. In the meantime, he knows he'll have to report in. Omit the fact his judgment had fallen foul of his innate misogyny. That he'd left it way too late to deal with what he now knows for certain had been a well-trained operator. Brace himself for the inevitable shit-storm headed his way.

All he can do now is hope—*pray even*—that his boss will be in a forgiving mood. That, with a little luck, the personal intimacy they had shared—*that one time*—will spare him.

Sergeant Eleanor Rundell has called in a favour. Arranging to drop her companion off at the dog pound in Fort McNair. After which she'd headed back to Marks Centre. Home to the Department of Defense Clandestine Service. The place where she'd first encountered another steel-boned, hard-to-read attack dog, who'd gone on to become her XO. A man she would crawl over broken glass to help. No matter when. No matter why. No matter what.

For the better part of two years, their investigation—*into whatever crazy shit was going on in Texas*—had moved at a glacial pace. Shifting from one stall-point to another with monotonous regularity. Hampered by a long-standing directive from the Lieutenant-Colonel.

Wherever possible, avoid showing your hand.

Now, it appears, someone had added accelerant to some previously buried fuse. Because she'd also been notified, by SMS, of two other take-downs that evening. And that could mean only one thing.

Someone, somewhere was sweeping tracks.

So she begins keying her own SMS report...

...SUBJECT GEORGETOWN DOWN

Hopes her alert is not already too late.

She hits—**SEND.**

It's 20.35 hours, *Eastern Standard Time.*

CLOVIS, NEW MEXICO

Anne-Marie and Kenton have chosen pretty much the first bar they'd hit. Seating themselves by a window with a view out onto a street running parallel to the main highway. The glass still radiating heat from a full day of direct sunlight. Part of a thin, mid-evening crowd.

Background noise is muted. Old-school soft-rock ballads, from the sixties and seventies, subtly filling the occasional lulls in conversation.

A couple of plaid shirts are aimlessly shooting pool, off to the side of a small dance floor abutting a raised platform that juts out from the wall at the back of the room. A few thirty-something couples, cradling beers, looking on. Enough weather-beaten elderlies propping up the bar to make Anne-Marie think it worthwhile sticking around. Perfectly matching the old-timer description her faculty head had evoked in her mind.

The bar clings on to the end of a well-lit, lively strip which leads into town from the east. Luckily, Kenton has turned twenty-one.

In any event, the bartender chooses not to ask for IDs.

They are twenty minutes inside the New Mexico state line, having travelled way further than she'd intended. But there'd been nothing resembling what she was looking for out on the panhandle. It had all been too agricultural. Too featureless. And way too sterile. Nothing but irrigated crop circles and low, fabricated warehouses as far as the eye could see. She is searching for something that had once been. So they'd kept on driving. Steady pace. Comfortable silences.

Truth was, turns out Kenton's pretty cool to be around. Quietly contented. Strong-jawed. Easy on the eye.

They'd agreed to share stints behind the wheel sometime after Guthrie. On their way through to Lubbock. Where they'd spontaneously started singing Buddy Holly songs. Kenton had a good voice. She'd had plenty of enthusiasm.

They'd crossed the state line in the late afternoon. Found a motel a little further up the strip. Nothing too pricey. Booked separate rooms, with bedding and floors that passed for clean.

Ten minutes later, they were back on the sidewalk. Out front of the motel. Walking side-by-side—*a little closer together than ordinarily she'd be comfortable with*—heading towards the strip, where they found the bar and settled in.

'So... you're one-hundred percent okay with me taking your truck tomorrow?'

'Sure,' he says. 'Not a problem. Like I told you, it's insured for any driver.'

'I know... but what are you going to do while I'm gone?'

'I was hoping to see some sexy stuff flying out of Cannon.'

'Cannon...?'

'Air Force Base... I Googled it. Some of what they do out there sounds pretty neat. Least ways, a darn sight cooler than a dawn search for abandoned fuel stations. Apparently, there's Special Forces stuff going on. Hopefully, I'll find somewhere to hang around without gettin' myself arrested.'

'Okay... so long as you're sure.'

'For sure...'

Kenton takes a sip from his beer.

'What were you and that old guy at the bar laughing about anyway?'

'Oh, that...'

Anne-Marie giggle-snorts.

'He said he could tell I was going to hit on him as soon as he saw me walk through the door.'

'You bein' serious?'

'Honestly... that's what he said. Word for word.'

'Pretty neat pick-up line, if you ask me.'

'Yes, it was. And when I told him what I was searching for, he suggested heading a little further west, toward Vaughn. He said there used to be a fuel stop on a spur, just off the highway. Someplace between Fort Sumner and a... *nowhere scrape in the ground,* called Yeso. He said he recalled, twenty-years back, when a... *leather-skinned dude, with no use for money,* did nothing but.. *sell a few drops of fuel and the odd Hershey bar, then sit cussin' his dogs 'till the sun went down*. He said, he doubted it would still be a going concern. Said... *the dude would have to be at least a-hundred-and-twenty, if he was still drawing breath*. Reckons even the spur may be blocked off by now... on account of it... *leading nowhere anyone wanted to go*.'

'You think you'll be able to find it?'

'Oh... I don't know, Kenton. But, like I told you, my faculty head said I would get to meet folk just like that. And he was right. The old guy also said the highway stayed pretty much deserted until the early-morning rush. That's when he started laughing. Said he was only... *yankin' my chain*. He reckons I'll more likely see a UFO than something on wheels.'

'Hey... you shouldn't joke, Anne-Marie. You do know Roswell's around here someplace?'

They settle back in their seats. Staring through the window at the strip coming to life. Plenty of straight-backed, military types sporting buzz-cuts. Plenty of bob-tails eyeing the buzz-cuts. A good number of older folk waddling back and forth. Middle-age locals trailing kids. All coming out to eat now the heat has dropped from brutal to just plain hot.

The bar is a throw-back all of its own. Hidden in plain sight. No doubt through a lack of franchise neon. Or maybe, just like everywhere else, the good folk of Clovis, New Mexico were blind to any enterprise that couldn't afford to take out radio commercials—*every hour, on the hour.*

Anne-Marie turns her eyes back to Kenton's profile. Aware, suddenly, it was a pretty neat place for them to rest.

'How you aiming on getting to the airfield...? I was thinking to head out kinda early.'

'How early... is early?'

She could have sworn she'd detected a trace of concern in his voice.

'Well... it's pretty much an east-west highway. Guess I'd like the option of catching sunrise.'

'So darn early then...?'

'I guess so.'

'Well... I figure an airbase is pretty much guaranteed to be on a bus route.'

'But what if it's not?'

Kenton takes another sip of beer.

'It'll be fine,' he says. 'It's the military, after all. Those type of guys gotta get into town at night. Then get back in time to raise the flag at reveille.'

She feels herself being drawn to the odd mix of hometown and formal in the way he speaks. To the way it makes him sound a little goofy. Like he's yet to figure what kind of man he truly wanted to be.

Something unfamiliar tingles through her chest. Odd, in a way she wouldn't be able to explain. Certainly different to anything she's felt before. Something with a deeper intensity than she'd been expecting to feel at that moment—*and a good deal less fleeting.*

Out of nowhere, she comes to the conclusion that if everything about him remained exactly as it is right now, she certainly wouldn't complain. Quietly reassuring somehow. And it's the reason there had been moments, during the ride, when certain of his traits had reminded her of her dad. Laid back and purposeful, coexisting in perfect tandem.

And, for sure, she knows her mom would approve.

They resume their easy silence. Relaxing back in the worn-out, soft-leather armchairs. Making like they aren't eyeing one another as they sip their beers.

GUADALUPE MOUNTAINS

They're barrelling down what still feels like a decently steep gradient. Though nowhere near as switch-back and certainly far less perilous than he'd endured over the preceding forty minutes. Descending fast, along an unsurfaced road, toward an unseen valley plain. Coal Island looming spectral through heavily-tinted glass. Bathed in the glow of powerful halogen floodlights, shimmering diffuse—*like a pulsating aurora*—through the bands of driving rain.

Zalizo judges they are heading north-east. His best guess is they're still a couple miles out.

He recalls well enough the layout he'd spent better than thirty-six hours studying. The main complex spread out like a concrete swastika toward the southern end of a rock-strewn valley. All single level. Modular layout. Blocks of medium-sized, reinforced concrete units banded together by what he'd guessed were narrow, enclosed walkways. Easy to isolate. Quick to secure. Surrounded by a vast expanse of flat terrain, offering clear sight lines and expansive kill zones. A large helipad prominent between a continuous ring of two imposing, minimum five-metre high perimeter fences, set three metres apart and canted out from each other in the shape of a *V;* the void between them filled top to bottom with dense coils of razor wire. There was no denying, it was a damned impressive set up all round. And pretty much impenetrable without employing a considerable amount of high explosive.

On the eastern side of the complex, a well maintained, mid-length, north-to-south airstrip was serviced by a compact two-story terminal. Its roof cluttered with an array of comms antenna and a golf ball-shaped radar dome. All sandwiched between a couple of strategically placed tarpaulin-covered box frames. Even from distance, something about their placement had shouted mini-guns. It seemed plausible. But he couldn't be sure.

One thing he knows for certain; there would be other security paraphernalia in play. A whole bunch of embedded high-tech systems he'd been too far out to scope. Cameras covering the entirety of the main compound. Vibration sensors. Heat detectors. Off-road chase vehicles, no doubt equipped with machine guns and search lights. Attack dogs a distinct possibility. Or maybe Lexstone Security Corporation had looked to save themselves a good pile of bucks and had the entire valley floor laid with anti-personnel ordinance. Added to which, there was little doubt in his mind that the perimeter would be electrified. More than likely to a lethal degree, or something close.

He puts their current speed at fifty plus. And he knows they won't be slowing down for any barriers. He recalls scoping a thirty-meter high, steel pylon at the southern end of the runway terminal. With camera pods arranged at ten-meter intervals. Positioned to cover a three-sixty degree sweep; ensuring all angles of approach were covered. And, given their elevation, out a substantial distance. Plenty far enough to detect any unauthorised approach, without the need for wasting manpower on isolated checkpoints.

Six weeks before, on his second trip in, he'd lain in a narrow ravine. Scoping two flights using the runway. Citation XLS on both occasions. Same number on the tail fin both times. He'd been on the wrong sight-line to ID passengers. And likely too far out in any event.

No matter.

He is here now.

The transfer comes to a halt between two flat-roofed, three-storey box towers—*silhouetted black against the floodlights*—either side of a single vehicle width, heavy gauge, steel-slatted roller door. Both structures topped off by their own stand of antennas, bent almost horizontal by the storm.

As the noise of the barrier closing reaches his ears, he pictures again the desolate valley plain out there in the blackness. Unfolding for miles in every direction. With no possibility for escape and evade. Not that his original plan had ever envisaged a fire-fight. Nonetheless, his new plan is reliant on nothing more than whoever he might encounter inside not knowing what resources he can bring to bear. Because fear of the unknown is a weapon he has used before. At a time in his past, when he'd also found himself out numbered. And out-gunned. And the fact he is here, and his enemies back then are not, is all the encouragement he needs that it has the potential to be a viable plan. And, right now—*regardless his preference for details*—he can do little more than trust it's a strategy that will serve him again.

The transfer's panel door slides back, revealing a defensive-end sized neanderthal sporting a caveman beard, dressed in a heavy long-coat and leather stetson, proudly toting his stubby Sig Sauer MCX carbine.

Zalizo elects not to wait for an invitation to disembark. Stepping into a narrow, brightly lit space he estimates to be half-a-dozen paces wide by thirty long. With a second steel roller door at the opposite end.

The gap between the towers is covered. So at least he was going to avoid getting soaked a second time as he's ushered toward a door marked **VISITOR TRANSFER.**

He pauses at a point along the wall with no overhead cameras. Finger-prints his cell phone's screen to life. Brakes down the SMS he'd received during the transfer.

SUBJECTS NASSAU/CAYMAN DOWN.
CG & CC.
REPORT PENDING.
PRESUME DOA.

He'd chosen to ignore the message when his cell's notification had chirped. Because, even though he'd made one camera, he might have missed another. And, for sure, he hadn't wanted to be seen performing a thorough sweep.

Ahead of him, the caveman reaches the tower's entrance. Buzzes the intercom. Waits for the lock to release. Pulls the door open with his free hand, holding it ajar with his foot.

'You there... I'm gonna need you to keep movin'.'

Zalizo continues to stall while he reads the message he'd received back at the diner. It was much the same as the one he's just deleted.

SUBJECT GEORGETOWN DOWN.
REPORT PENDING.

Despite the time lapse between messages, he figures, even if the rounds were recovered, the rifling will be different at each scene. One shooter covering two locations, that far apart, in a city the size of DC, would have been tactically naive.

Curious. But no matter.

Sit-reps were pending, so any speculation was pretty much futile. All the same, it has the feel of a coordinated sanitizing operation.

Off to his right, the caveman sets his mouth into a snarl.

'I said, keep movin'... y'all won't be getting another warning.'

Zalizo hits delete a second time. Moves to follow the less than happy primate. And, truth be told, he's a little pissed himself. He'd been working this itch for close on two years. So, if the pace was going to step up suddenly, he'd hoped to be the one forcing the change.

At that moment, a thought occurs to him.

Maybe he was.

Once inside, he's directed to a glass-fronted counter, where he's ordered to surrender his few belongings by a bug-eyed, cut-down version of the *Alpha*-specimens he's encountered so far. Barking his instructions in the manner of someone desperate to elevate their rudimentary function to something approaching relevant.

And, in his experience, all pretty standard machismo bullshit where private security outfits were concerned.

He pushes his cell phone into the well beneath the security glass. Followed by his holstered side-arm and spare mags. Just for the hell of it, he decides he'll keep a hold of his badge.

Right on queue, a jacked-up no-neck clone steps in from the side. Thumbs jammed into his utility belt. Elbows out. Shoulders back. Chest thrust forward.

He jabs a finger at the five-pointed silver star clipped to Zalizo's belt.

'We'll be needing that to.'

'And why might that be?'

'Because I said so.'

'Is that a fact?'

'First off,' the no-neck sneers. 'I'm saying it is. Second... it's company policy.'

'Well... it's my *policy* not to comply with your company's policy.'

'You can either hand it over... or I can take it off you.'

'You'd fail.'

'You reckon?'

Zalizo eyes the no-neck up and down.

'Let's just say, my level of certainty involves a one and two zeros.'

'I don't know who or what you think you are, mister... but I'm tellin' you... this ain't the place to run your mouth.'

‘Who I am, is not your concern. What I am... is a guest of Governor Brandt. Here at her specific invitation. So... if you’re still upset with your momma for pulling you off her tit too early, I suggest you ask her who your daddy was and take it up with him. Meantime... suck it up and go about your business without involving me in your personal inadequacies.’

He hears the caveman in the long-coat move in closer from behind. And that was the problem when you chose to wear too much clothing, just because there was a little extra moisture in the air.

Then again, could be the guy was made of sugar.

Zalizo relaxes his knees and shoulders. Sets himself. Ready to crouch and pivot. Because there were times, no matter the situation, when some folk needed to be reminded of their limitations.

As it is, the no-neck standing in front of him decides now was an ideal time to jab a gloved finger at his chest. As a prelude, he resets his mouth into an even bigger snarl.

‘You need to...’

Zalizo shoots out his dominant hand. Seizes the guy’s finger. Pushes back hard, like he’s opening a refrigerator door. Angles himself against any retaliatory strike. Using his free hand to hold the guys gun-arm by the wrist. Pinning it to his side in an iron grip. Increasing pressure as he walks Mr. Pointy and his dislocated digit back against the wall.

The guard fails in his attempt to stifle a yelp.

‘Tell your colleague at my six... he takes one more step, he’ll be responsible for you not being able to pick your nose for the rest of your life. Because right now, it’s only bent a little out of shape. But I can assure you... I hear one more squeak from either of you. I’ll rip it the whole way off.’

The guard begins breathing hard and fast between gritted

teeth.

Zalizo decides whatever the guy lacked in situational judgement, he more than made up for in attention to oral health. His dental work was stunning. With two rows of bared, chalk-white teeth that look to be his own.

At that moment, someone up the food chain bursts through the door to the side of the booth. Same basic gene pool denoted by his similar physical mould. Though with a decidedly more conciliatory tone of voice.

'I'd be obliged if you leave my over-zealous colleague be... *Deputy*.'

Zalizo eyes the newcomer. Eases the pressure he's been steadily increasing off a fraction. Turns his gaze back to Mr. Pointy.

'You going to behave?'

The guard nods his head. Gets his finger handed back.

The new silverback shoots his subordinate a warning with his eyes.

'Go get yourself checked out,' he says, his tone radiating disgust. 'Come see me when you're done.'

There's another rustle of clothing from behind. The crew chief turns. Glowers beyond Zalizo's shoulder.

'Scoot... same goes for you. We have everything we need from our... *guest*.'

He waves Zalizo forward.

'Lucky for you, I'm in a good mood.'

Zalizo says, 'Unlucky for you... I don't care.'

He's ushered forward for mug-shots and digital fingerprinting. Then on through pat-down and body scans.

It is 9.40 PM, *Mountain Standard Time*.

He is the only witness passing through **VISITOR TRANSFER.**

The only occupant for the waiting sedan, idling out in the

open. Just far enough forward of the inner roller door to ensure he was going to pay for pissing off a bunch of boneheads.

Zalizo smiles to himself.

Gets soaked through a second time.

As they drive across the kill-zone, he tags three birds on the flood-lit heli-pad. One-hundred yards distant. An ancient Bell UH-1, with patchwork panels. Its orange and black tipped rotors bucking in the storm; looking like a Da Nang lost and found. The other two birds are Agustas. Identical executive spec. Sleek and expensive—*though the model escapes him*—which means there will likely be a bunch of VIP rubber-necks at the party.

No matter—*he can make like he wasn't there in a crowd of any size.*

After all, he'd had plenty of practice.

CORNUDAS, TEXAS

The shift change waitress is standing in Doug's kitchen. Mostly to keep Doug company, now the crowd has thinned.

She's leaning on the serving hatch. Looking out to the parking lot. Eyes fixed on the US Marshals Service GMC. Her mind—*as it often did*—pondering the rationale lying at the heart of both her dubious taste in men, and her less than traditional *modus operandi* when hunger gnawed through her self-imposed restraint on an otherwise wholesome libido. At one time, she'd wondered if it was a simple case of subliminal rebellion. Against a mother who'd endlessly advocated for the supremacy of financial security and emotional subordinance on all matters germane to intimacy. For sure, something lay behind her pre-disposition to flout normal conventions when it came to evaluating the opposite sex. Not to mention disregarding all those misogynistic evocations linking women's personal safety to supposedly reckless behaviour.

Screw that.

Besides, there had been something quietly brutal about the way the guy moved. Ramrod straight, minus any strutting machismo. The kind of unconscious power and fluidity that made her bones tingle. That and the scars on his hands. But, most of all, it was the pain she'd seen behind his eyes. Something that felt like grief, veiling an intensity of spirit. She'd been willingly drawn into their shimmering blue-green depths. Speculating how immersive they would be close up. Wondering how deep the dive into them would be.

And how dangerous.

'Hey, Ness...'

'Hey, Doug...'

'I'm guessing we'll be shutting up late?'

'If it were down to me, that would certainly be my *Plan A*.'

'And, *Plan B?*'

'If we run out of customers early, or you need to make tracks. I could always lay on his hood until he comes back.'

'In this weather...?'

Doug appears next to her at the serving counter. His expression implacable, as it usually was, beneath an unruly dark brown beard flecked with grey.

'Not much of a Plan B, if you ask me.'

'*Oh*... I don't know. I've got a feeling he'd be worth the wait.'

'Worth getting soaked like a stray dog for?'

'Well... I promised to keep an eye on his ride.'

'Ness... it's got US Marshall's Service plastered all over.

There ain't no-one goin' anywhere near it.'

'I know that.'

'Don't tell me,' he says. 'You figured he did to?'

She smiles to herself.

'You know my motto, Doug... nothing ventured.'

'Well... I can tell you right off. He ain't no deputy like his badge said. Which means he likely ain't no United States Marshal neither.'

She continues to smile. Surprised that Doug had somehow also spotted the jurisdictional discrepancy between badge and vehicle. But then, she'd known for some time that Doug had his own unnerving way of discovering the truth of things. And to date, despite her many attempts, she still hasn't worked out how the heck he did it.

'Yeah,' she says. 'He claims it's a loaner.'

'And that doesn't bother you none?'

'I refer you to my motto...'

Without turning, she knows Doug would be shaking his head. And she knows, with equal certainty, he'll stay with her until she gives up on her prize.

COAL ISLAND, GUADALUPE MOUNTAINS

Zalizo ignores the maybe two-dozen or so chairs arranged in three rows at the front of the death chamber. Choosing instead to stand alone at the rear of the gallery. Partly on account of being sat on his rear end for the better part of eighteen hours straight. Added to which, his eyesight was plenty good enough to see from one end of a room to the other. But, mostly because he has no particular desire to rub shoulders with a herd of VIP ghouls.

Give or take, he estimates the witness gallery at roughly twenty-by-twenty, its reinforced concrete walls painted a bland light beige.

Up front, there's a floor-to-ceiling view of the chamber, through a practically invisible barrier of thick plexiglass. A less than subtle, frameless two-way occupying the centre of the wall he'd chosen to back up against. No reason for a large, rectangular mirror to be in a witness gallery otherwise.

Out of nowhere, he feels an acute sense of unease. For damn sure, nothing approaching compassion. Certainly not forgiveness, or anything close. All the same, something unsettling. A feeling that regardless the class of psychopath Coal Island was charged with keeping securely locked away—*out of sight and out of mind*—abdicating responsibility for extinguishing a life—*any life, including that of one Perry Morgan Blake*—suddenly feels like an ultimate demonstration of the insidiousness of market forces-driven ideologies. And, in so many ways, antithetical to anything approaching standard democratic norms.

With an effort, he pushes the thought to the back of his mind.

Other than himself, there are four guards in the room. Each packing Heckler & Koch nine-mils, judging by the grips. Lexstone Security Corporation patches embroidered on their arms. No name-tags on their chests. Standing like statues. One occupying each corner of the gallery, beneath security cameras angled toward the array of seats. All of which strikes him as somewhat excessive. Leastways for a space supposedly designed to accommodate invited guests.

No matter. *For now at least.*

Besides, the fact this heavy-handed honour guard are carrying weapons is to his advantage. The primates just don't know it yet.

Up front, the death chamber spans the entire width of the gallery. White-washed and garishly lit a halogen blue-white. Raised a couple feet above the level of the gallery floor. Looking like a low-budget TV studio mock-up. As if someone thought it a grand idea to elevate the already macabre up onto a stage.

The gurney, with an olive vinyl-covered mattress, sits front and centre. Heavy-duty wrist and ankle straps. Pump peddle for height adjust. A video camera set-up, off to the right, angled across the chamber. A low, metal cabinet facing sideways on, set a couple paces back from the head of the gurney, with three tubes slung beneath. Terminating at a single line running up to the gurney. Three digital readout displays on its forward side. Three spigots protruding above. An ECG monitor and cables, cluttered atop a separate chrome trolley.

It's 9.47 PM, *Mountain Standard Time*.

Zalizo waits for the order to—*go take a seat*. A little surprised he hasn't been instructed to do so already. Could be their protocols weren't buttoned down. Could be word has filtered through from **VISITOR TRANSFER**.

Stand well clear of the nuke with the badge.

Truth be told, he doesn't much care either way.

The VIP guests have begun filing in. Susan Meridith Brandt, Texas's notoriously urbane governor, front and centre. Impeccable, in her dark blue trouser suit and mid-height heels. Not a single hair out of place. High-collared, crisp white blouse, open conservatively at the neck.

That, at least, explained the Agusta executive birds.

As the witnesses slowly troop in, the majority keep their attention fixed on the glamourous, three-term politician. A few eyes drifting around the brightly-lit gallery. None lingering on him. Not even half a glance. Exactly as he prefers.

The crowd begin occupying the arranged seats. Huddling toward the centre of the room; like there would be safety in numbers. The odd murmur breaking through the self-imposed silence. A good deal of unconscious fidgeting. Shared tension building. Morbid excitement leaching out.

The door at the rear of the death chamber opens at 9.50 PM—*almost to the second*. A pudgy-faced, head-honcho type—*garbed in an ill-fitting grey suit*—waddling through first. Two guards striding in close behind. Followed by two other suits wearing over-sized lab coats.

Then the coward—*responsible for rendering his dreams to ash*—leg-iron shuffles through, ahead of a third guard. No hesitation. No reaction to the gurney. Eyes on the crowd. Thin-lipped grin. Shackled hands raised to his chest. Wearing a loose-fitting, orange jump suit. Unbuttoned at the neck. Sleeve rolled up high on his right arm. A single cannula taped just below his elbow joint.

And still the order doesn't come for him to park his rear end.

Perry Morgan Blake's appearance hasn't changed anything worth a damn. Five-ten. Five-eleven at a push. Greasy light brown hair hanging limp over his eyes. A little less slight, for sure, but still wiry; in the manner of farm labourers and miners from times gone by. Or folk unused to three square meals a day. Wearing the same dim-witted half-smirk he'd worn throughout his trial.

He penguin-hobbles over to the gurney. Hauling himself on without assistance. Raising his face to the ceiling.

Guards one-through-three step forward. Guard number three fixing ankle straps. Pulling them tight. Checking the buckles twice. Guard number two folding a loose-fitting hood over Blake's up-turned head. Guard number one placing both hands on the condemned man's shoulders, easing him flat. Leaning down to hinge a ratcheted U-shaped metal restraining frame up over the creep's head. Clamping it down hard across his chest. Guards one and two ditto-strap his wrists on either side. Ditto-checking the buckles, before retreating to the rear of the chamber.

At precisely 9.55 PM, the head-honcho nods to the shorter of the lab-coats, who moves forward to hook up the line.

Zalizo leans back and folds his arms. Considers the protocols playing out on the other side of the glass. Assumes the order to take a seat isn't coming.

At the rear of the death chamber, a figure the size of a mountain emerges through the door-frame. Wearing a tight-fitting lab coat over expensive-looking outdoor casuals. A pair of loose-fitting pleated slacks belted high above his redwood hips. And despite his proportionally short, but no doubt powerful legs, he has to be six-eight—*minimum*. At a guess, pushing a good way past three-hundred pounds. Slick, news anchor hair, with no hint of grey. Clean-shaven, even at this hour. Shiny skin of a narcissist. Chest like he has a bath tub strapped under his shirt. Ducking unconsciously as he steps across the threshold. Incongruously light on his feet. Hands like catcher mitts; one of them holding a tray.

For a moment, *The Mountain* just stands, staring blankly back through the Plexiglass out into the witness gallery. A full ten seconds of frozen time stretching out, until he appears to remember where he is. Or what he's there for. He hands the tray to the taller of the lab-coats, then pivots on the heels of a pair of thick-soled hiking boots—*shining like they've never seen a grain of trail dust since the day they'd been carried out of whatever over-priced store they'd been purchased at*—backing out of the chamber as abruptly as he'd arrived.

The lab-coat sets the tray aside.

Behind his eyes, Zalizo runs through the anomalies he's seeing on the other side of the glass. Struggling to focus on the figure lying stock-still on the gurney—*like he's already lapsed into some kind of coma*. And, because he'd majored in chemical engineering, he knows the effect the cocktail of lethal compounds were designed to induce as they pump through a victim's bloodstream. He's also aware there was a notoriously high, first-time failure rate. And that, even with the best protocols in place, it could take as much as two hours before *subject deceased* could be declared. It was far from a subtle process after all. A bullet through the head, a good deal more humane. Added to which, there'd been a catalogue of screw-ups over the years. Failures to sedate. Lethal agents administered in the wrong order. Morbid tales of inmates dying in agony...

...sodium thiopental, followed by vecuronium bromide, followed by potassium chloride...

...a holy trinity of chemical pain he'd hoped would be eternal.

Zalizo is the first of the honoured guests to leave the viewing gallery. Replaying what he's just witnessed over in his mind. Sure of one thing. Whatever had just gone down—*it was all wrong*. All just a little too—*neat*. A little too—*performed*. Or maybe the people running the show were straight-up lazy. Entirely convinced their audience would be easily deceived.

Or maybe, just like every other Dunning Kruger specimen he'd ever encountered, they'd over-estimated the limit of their competency.

Truth was, he couldn't care less either way. Because, in the here and now, all he needed to focus on was controlling his rage...

...and getting the hell out of Dodge.

Because, as he always did, he'd zeroed in on the condemned man's hands. In particular, when the ECG pads had been taped to his chest—*and there hadn't been so much as a twitch*. And when they'd hooked up the tube to the cannular—*still not a tremor*. And that simply couldn't be.

At least not with this particular freak.

And, sure enough, the illusion fell apart completely from the moment they made like they were pumping chemicals. The digital displays running through their elaborate countdown sequence.

It had been like one of those glitches in the fabric of time you saw portrayed in the movies.

The—*blink and you'll miss it*—moment.

But he hadn't blinked...

...so he didn't miss it.

Because he was fully aware that even the most basic protocols demanded a carefully orchestrated, three-stage process. *Sedation. Induced paralysis. Catastrophic cardiac arrest.* Yet no-one had even bothered to check if Perry Morgan Blake had been rendered unconscious.

So, what he'd just witnessed had been theatrics at best. Bordering on comedic. Because three tubes into one, running to a single cannula, simply didn't work. Dosage control would have been all over the place, regardless the fancy digital displays. And chemical cross contamination inevitable.

As far as he knows, it had been the first execution by lethal injection outside a state or federal system. Anywhere. *Ever.* And while, on the surface, the spectacle had looked exactly as it needed to look. Everything in the place it needed to be. Everyone playing the role they'd been assigned to play. When, in reality, it had been nothing more than a charade. A collection of lavish props and a bit of fancy choreography, with a cast who'd carefully rehearsed their roles.

Which likely explained *glitch* number two.

The fact they'd left the video-cam switched off.

Zalizo recalls the single image he'd never fully shaken from his mind. How Perry Morgan Blake had behaved all through his trial proceedings. From beginning to end, there had never been a moment when he wasn't flexing his bony fingers. One picking the skin of the other until they'd bled. Entering the courtroom, as he had, each morning. Sitting, hand-cuffed, beside his media-savvy attorney. Being led away in the late afternoon. Constantly worrying his calloused, murderous hands. Because, deep down Zalizo had known, no matter his outward bravado, Perry Morgan Blake had spent his entire life living in fear of what was to come. Paradoxically, the kind of fear that gave certain men purpose. Driving them to act out their perverted desires. Because he'd met Blake's type before—*more than once*. And, on occasion, he'd taken an unhealthy pleasure making them realise that fear could be driven from their black hearts. Re-educating them; making them understand, fear amounted to nothing once it was replaced by bone-freezing terror.

And therein lay the problem. Because tonight the freak's hands had been completely blemish free. Manicured almost. So, for damn sure, something had changed. *Something fundamental*. Enough that a murderous rodent like Perry Morgan Blake had given up the habits of a lifetime.

Fanciful—*perhaps*. Speculation—*maybe*. But Zalizo knew from personal experience, there were times when intuition played the best hand. So, no matter what anyone else might think, it had been all the evidence he needed that the piece of shit lying on the gurney had known—*one-hundred percent*—he had nothing to fear. And the reason a mantra his mother had instilled, over and over throughout his childhood, buzzed its way to the front of his mind...

...consider every move... the ones you can see and the ones you cannot... especially the ones you cannot.

So here he was, hemmed in on four sides by more beige concrete. Staring at the man mountain. Regretting that he hadn't first taken a trip to the Navajo Nation. Cursing he hadn't assembled a bigger team. Hoping his sergeant, back there in *DC*, would pick up the trail if things went south. And knowing, deep in his gut, that hope was a pastime reserved for those who set out without a buttoned-down plan.

The man mountain had been waiting as he'd entered the anti-chamber. Minus the tight-fitting lab coat. Standing with his feet planted wide apart. Arms crossed behind his back. Expression implacable. Weighing Zalizo through thin-lidded, soulless grey eyes.

He pushes a bear-sized hand forward.

'Detective Zalizo... I've been very much looking forward to making your acquaintance.'

Zalizo keeps his own hands loose by his side. Waits for *The Mountain* to withdraw his. Given his size and obvious strength, he obliges faster than anticipated.

It strikes Zalizo, this was going to be an option one, option two gig. Play weak or play strong. Play weak and they might consider he presented no immediate threat. More likely, they would convince themselves he is isolated. That they were free to make their move. Play strong, he might force them to consider he has his position covered.

As is his nature, he opts to play strong.

'That was a careless assumption... whoever you are.'

'*Oh*... I'm just the greeter. But I'm curious why you would say that.'

'Well... *Mr. Greeter*. You said detective. Whereas, my badge is silver and says deputy. As does my invitation.'

'*Ah*, yes... unfortunately, my eyesight's not what it once was.'

'That may be... but, if I'm not mistaken, optometry has

become widely available in the meantime.'

'*Touché*... Deputy.'

Zalizo remains motionless. Relaxed. Casually balanced. Owing to his freakish bulk, he suspects The Greeter is someone entirely unfazed by imminent physical threats. But he knows that, no matter the disparity in shear body mass, he also gives off his own—**DO NOT FUCK WITH ME**—aura. Something intangible that very few people fail to miss. Something he'd carried even before he'd started wearing long pants. Then on throughout his high school years. Only allowing it free reign in the weeks and months following the death of his parents. Then buttoned it back down tight during the remainder of his time at Texas Tech. Mostly to avoid the attention of the football coaches. But, from boot camp on, he'd honed it to the exact degree required for the situations he found himself in.

Right now, he has four walls and three doors occupying his attention. He knows where two of the doors lead. What lay beyond the third was an unknown. A situation he doesn't much care for.

The Greeter offers a plausibly hospitable expression.

'Anyway... the Director has asked me to extend a personal invitation.'

Without missing a beat, Zalizo says, 'Invitation declined.'

'Might I ask why?'

'You might... but I'm not in the habit of indulging idle curiosity.'

'*Oh,* come, come now... Deputy Zalizo. Why the hostility?'

'Because even your Pitbulls got themselves enough schooling to read a badge. But mostly because you keep using my name without offering yours. And, in my book... that pegs you as either a sociopath or a fuckwit. Or it could be you lack the breeding necessary to employ common courtesy.'

The Greeter raises an eyebrow. Feigns ambivalence. Almost succeeds. But he can't quite keep a sudden wave of fury from leaching into his otherwise dead eyes.

Zalizo registers the man's—*now I'm really pissed*—button is all lit up like a flare. So he decides—*nothing ventured*. Because, as sure as hell is hot, he's not going to allow a man this size free reign to dominate the space.

'And to be completely candid. Right now... I could care less which one of those assessments is factually accurate.'

'Very forthright of you...'

'I aim to please, but often miss.'

'I seriously doubt that... *Deputy*.'

Zalizo hears the VIPs start to form up back in the witness gallery. He spots a guard appear in the frame of door Number Two, from the reflection in the glass of door Number One.

Windowless door Number Three silently cracks an inch.

Without shifting his gaze, The Greeter gives a barely perceptible shake of his head.

Zalizo turns to face door Number Three. Unclips his badge. Holds it at arm's length, then pushes it back onto his belt.

The Greeter creases a smile.

'So... I'll wish you good day. *Oleg*...'

The hum of conversation grows louder as the rest of the VIPs begin filing in from behind. So Zalizo moves casually sideways to head their ranks.

'...be careful how you go.'

Zalizo says, 'I appreciate your concern...'

Allows a smile of his own to edge the corner of his mouth.

'I'll be sure to wipe my feet on the way out.'

The Greeter re-fixes his dead-pan gaze. Unfolds his massive arms. Reaches over to open door Number One.

'Be seeing you around... *Deputy*.'

COAL ISLAND, GUADALUPE MOUNTAINS

'Do you mind telling me what the hell that was all about?'

Victor allows Director Ray's question to wash over him. Keeping his focus out toward the heli-pad, shimmering like a giant mirror now the storm has blown through. The Huey squatting, like some prehistoric insect, between the two ultra-sleek Augustas. The rotors on all three aircraft, slowly rising and dipping. An emerging moon bathing the two guard towers in an eerie glow as the VIP shuttle trundles its way back to visitor transfer.

Right now, he's busy running everything through again in his head, convinced he's just been played. Pretty sure this Zalizo character had been pushing a double blind. He's also sure he'll never know for certain. Because, even without the kill-ban, he would have had to let this asshole go. Because, whoever or whatever the fuck he is, the guy had played it ice cool. Like he'd amassed an army out there somewhere beyond the hills. And there'd been no way to confirm if he had. But there's one thing Victor knows for certain, one way or another, he'll find a way to make this cock-sucker pay for the slight on his breeding. Because no-one has ever spoken to him like that. Even before he'd hauled himself from the gutter. And for good reason.

He'd slit throats for lesser insults.

On the plus side, any lingering doubts he might have had regarding his decision to clean house in DC, they were now completely dispelled. Because no-one, no matter who they were, would have picked that fight—*not on this night, and for sure not at this event*—without a very strong and very personal agenda.

'Victor... are you even listening?'

'It would appear, I have little choice.'

Coal Island's director leans forward. Elbows resting on his desk. Hands clasped. Fingers steepled, tapping his lips.

'And...?'

'That was about a request to attend tonight's little *soirée* that should have been declined. But wasn't. As a result... we may have some unwanted interest in our affairs, from an unwelcome party, with unknown resources at their disposal.'

'Fuck.'

'Succinctly put, Mr. Ray.'

'So... what are we doing about it?'

'I can't speak for... *we*. But, for my part, I've organized an escort home for our visitor. Fortunately for us, Highway 62 is his only route back to Texas. I'm told he's driving a US Marshall SUV, so he'll be hard to miss. We'll be on his tail before he reaches Carlsbad. After that... who knows what misfortune might befall a tired and overly-emotional witness driving home on an unlit road, in the dead of night... Meantime, *you* are going to keep to the schedule.'

'That's all very well, Victor. But you need to be aware that I'm not prepared to have this facility compromised beyond what's already been agreed...'

Director Ray leans back in his chair. Begins drumming his stubby fingers on his overly ornate desk.

'I hope I'm making myself clear.'

Victor barely manages to stop himself from laughing out loud.

'Well, Mr. Ray... for your sake, I hope only two things.'

Victor turns away from the window. Moves across the room in a couple of easy strides. Leaning forward. Placing both hands on the director's desk. Aligning one foot half-a-stride behind the other.

'Number *one*... you're not making some kind of inept attempt to pull rank on me.'

He pushes hard and fast against the heavy wooden desk. A couple hundred pounds of mature oak no longer at rest. Better than three-hundred pounds of muscle and bone in full motion. Newtonian laws ensuring Montgomery Edgar Ray slides backwards on his wheeled, executive chair into an equally solid cabinet of unread, trophy books. The blunt edge of the desk lodging squarely under his ribcage.

Victor keeps right on pushing. Venting all his built-up frustration. Leaning in harder each time Montgomery Ray makes a feeble attempt to resist. Steadily increasing an unyielding force each time the jumped-up little jerk gasps.

'Number *two*... you are never again foolish enough to issue a threat, of any kind, toward me, while I'm still in the room.'

Coal Island's director is close to passing out. His eyes wide with panic. His grip on the desk surrendered. Unable to gain any purchase with his feet. Paying a heavy price for the vanity of having set the height of his seat a little too far off the ground.

'Let me hear you say, you understand, Mr. Ray.'

The pressure is unrelenting.

'If that's too difficult right now... just nod your head.'

The badly out-of-shape director passes the point where he won't black out. His eyes rolling in their sockets. His vision no doubt edging from fogged to black. Diaphragm crushed. Even so, Victor keeps on pushing.

The Director's chin slumps to his chest.

'Excellent, Mr. Ray... I'll take that as a yes.'

COAL ISLAND, GUADALUPE MOUNTAINS

Zalizo has made sure to stay tight with the rubber-necks. Ignoring the waved instruction to ride in the sedan. Opting, instead, to board the VIP shuttle uninvited. At least until they make it back to visitor transfer, where he anticipates he'll be kept waiting until the last of the voyeurs are processed and begin heading out for the helipad to board their executive birds.

And, sure enough, he is not disappointed.

After repeat pat-downs and re-scans, Zalizo finds himself back at the glass-fronted counter, where the same sour-faced wannabe-*Alpha* shoves his holstered pistol back through the slot, followed by his cell phone.

Without taking his eyes off the gofer, he ejects the bullet he habitually keeps chambered. Proceeds to field-strip his gun. Dropping the mag and breaking it down. Sighting through the length of the barrel. Reassembling it. Working the hammer. The ambi-safety. Racking the slide a couple times. The entire routine taking less than a minute. An amount of time not even approaching his record. Which was fine, because he hadn't intended it to be.

Next, he gathers his spare mags and cell phone. When he'd handed it over, he'd made sure to wipe its screen on the leg of his pants. The gofer had placed it into a zip-lock bag, wearing surgical gloves, like he was handling a bio-hazard. So he decides to angle the screen to the fluorescent tube above his head. Knowing, full well, he's likely being observed via the multiple camera feeds covering every angle.

The screen is a mess of prints.

No matter.

By design, DCS comms devices hold no retrievable data.

He turns to leave. Then turns back, standing the ejected bullet on the counter. Dead-panning the gofer with his eyes.

'Something to remember me by.'

After which, apart from a few cold stares—*which, to keep up appearances, he returns with interest*—he makes it back to the ride they'd fetched him in without further drama. Grateful not to get soaked a third time, now the storm has blown through.

For the entire ride back, he sits with his gun resting in his lap. Left index finger pressed to the trigger guard. The nineteen-round, double-stack magazine short one bullet. Though, in truth, he figures they'd be more likely to employ gas than weapons. And, since there's no wire mesh protecting the windows on the inside, he has it ready to break out the glass. And the primary reason he favours steel-framed pistols over polymer. For sure, it made them a good deal heavier. But that meant a softer felt recoil. Plus a good deal less muzzle-climb during rapid fire. Besides, as his instructors at Paris Island could personally attest, he'd inherited hands and forearms that could easily cope with pretty much any impediment.

CORNUDAS, TEXAS

Doug's Place is still all lit up. So he waits until the transfer clears the parking lot. If there was someone in place to scope him—*red dot, centre mass*—he accepts his immediate future will likely be nothing more than a game of chance.

He gives it a short minute, then holsters his gun. Pulls his keys from his pants pocket. Flips the central locking a couple strides out. Sneaking a look over to the diner as he reaches for the door handle.

Apart from a lone figure, occupying a booth just back from where the drifter with the duffle had sat, the place looks pretty much empty. A little further in, he can see the shift-change waitress, leaning against the serving-hatch counter. Her head angled down. Hair covering her face. Eyes on her cell phone maybe. More than likely checking in with some significant other in her life.

He feels something in his chest ping loose just looking at her. Something he knows he should ignore. Something he'd felt only once before in his past. Something undeniable—*back then as now*. So, in the moment, he faces a dilemma he certainly hadn't anticipated when he'd set out that morning.

Hang around or move right along.

Once again, a sense of guilt flares from under his ribs. Pushing him to expel this idle nonsense from his mind. This unbidden yearning he feels. This longing sprung somehow, fully formed, out of nowhere.

He lets his fingers fall from the GMC's door handle. Flips the locks back closed as he returns his keys to his pocket. Allows his feet to carry him towards the diner.

The sign on the door reads: **OPEN 'TILL WE CLOSE**. So he anticipates the door might be locked. To keep out any unwanted stragglers.

It's 11.02 PM, *Mountain Standard Time*.

But for a solitary UPS panel truck, pitched at an angle on the hard shoulder, the highway is deserted.

But, when he pulls on the door, it opens.

So he steps inside.

She raises her head as he walks in. Smiles with her eyes as he heads for the same booth he'd occupied earlier. Only this time he keeps his jacket on. Partly because it was at least fifteen degrees cooler. Mostly because there was no telling how things were going to go.

After a moment or two, she sashays over to his booth. Brushing a straggle of hair behind her ear. Pulling an order pad from her apron.

'Well, hello again... *Deputy*.'

'Hello... *ma'am*.'

She lets out a small chuckle. Strokes a second straggle of hair behind her other ear.

'It's way past any watershed' she says. 'So Vanessa is fine with me. Or Ness... or Nessa. Your choice.'

'Okay... *Vanessa*. Is there any chance it's not too far past the watershed to order steak?'

'It might not be.'

He leans back into his seat, forcing his eyes not to wander from her face.

'So, medium rare. Eggs however they come... and whatever vegetables you've got, not shaped like fries.'

'To drink...?'

She holds up her hand.

'Don't tell me... Iced water. Pitcher if we have it.'

He can't help but smile.

The one remaining diner gives a polite wave. Fetching his UPS-logoed jacket from the back of his seat. Slinging it over his shoulder.

'Don't go anywhere,' she says. 'I'll be right back.'

'Sure,' he says. 'I'll be right here.'

She turns her Levi's and makes toward the trucker. Takes the guy's money, offering a few friendly nods. A couple take it steady out there smiles. Sneaks a quick glance back toward his booth as she moves across to the cash register.

The trucker raises an arm in farewell as he pushes through the door. So now, apart from the two of them—*and whoever was responsible for preparing steak, medium rare*—the place is empty.

She pegs his order to a bull-clip above the serving hatch. Flips the open sign to closed. Locks the door and re-sashays back to his booth, taking a seat on the opposite side of the table. Facing him square on. Elbows firmly planted. Fingers interlaced, supporting her chin. Breathing slow and shallow. Regarding him with peaceful, caramel-brown eyes.

The diner's external lights blink out.

'So... Deputy. Since you're not sporting a name tag or badge number... what do I call you?'

'Zalizo.'

'Z-a-l-i-z-o...'

She pronounces his name slowly. Like she's weighing something of value.

'That seems a little formal.'

'Fair enough,' he says. 'Leg Zalizo.'

'Leg Zalizo...'

She pulls an expression that's hard to read.

'Italian...?'

'Ukrainian.'

She sits back. Lips slightly parted. Placing her hands flat on the table. Spreading her fingers apart. No tell-tale tan line or depression where a wedding band would have left its mark.

She says, 'Now, that is unexpected... what with your skin-tone and all.'

'Zalizo is Ukrainian for iron... and not all Slavs are pale-skinned. Or blond for that matter.'

'No, I suppose not,' she says. 'Besides, desert postings are apt to fix a tan pretty deep, I guess.'

'Whatever gives you that idea? Let's face it... but for industrial-scale irrigation, I'd wager half the state would pretty much qualify as a desert these days.'

'You could be right. But I don't see you as someone who started out as a county flatfoot who never moved on.'

'Is that so...? And how exactly do you figure that?'

'Oh, I don't know,' she says. 'I guess there's something about the way you carry yourself. It kinda pegs you as a little more... *capable*.'

'Capable...?'

'Sure... I mean, what are you? Six-three?'

'Thereabouts...' he says, mimicking the expression she'd pulled only moments before. 'Perhaps a tad more with my boots on.'

She shrugs in the same casual manner he'd often seen southern-Europeans pull. The kind of off-beat body language he'd always struggled to read.

'Weight,' she says. 'Two-ten... two-twenty, at a push. Annoyingly stable BMI, I'll hazard a guess.'

He raises his eyebrows slightly.

'I've never felt the need to check on a regular basis.'

'Good for you, *Leg Zalizo*. But, either way... you don't look or move like someone who spends the majority of their day sitting behind the wheel of a cruiser, eating doughnuts.'

'A not unreasonable supposition.'

'And... despite the badge, I'm not one-hundred per cent convinced you're a county deputy at all.'

'Is that so?'

'Yes, it is... and I'd know for sure if I can take a look at your hands.'

He thinks for a short moment, then holds them up. Palms facing forward. She leans in close, running her eyes left to right. Then up and down.

'And you didn't answer my question... about what brings

you all the way out here.'

'No... I didn't.'

He sets his privacy filter to ninety percent.

'Let's just say... I was searching for an answer to a long-standing riddle.'

She raises her hands to his. Begins forcing his fingers apart with her own. Casual and unabashed. Like they were just two people—*come together after some long-standing separation*—totally relaxed with displays of public intimacy.

'So... Deputy Leg Zalizo. Who just happens to ride around in a US marshal four-by-four, way outside his jurisdiction. Did you find what you were searching for?'

Considering the weather, her skin is remarkably cool to the touch. Her movements sensual and unhurried. Her grip surprisingly strong. Neat, unvarnished nails. And somewhat incompatible with hours spent humping crockery.

'Not exactly,' he says.

For a moment, her gaze is steady and unblinking.

'Interesting...' she says.

She forces his palms flat to the table. Begins tracing the scar on the back of his left hand. Her brow furrowing, as she moves to tracing his knuckles.

'...so, does that mean you could be spending any amount of time nearby?'

'Right now... that would be hard to call.'

She brings their palms back together. Like she was judging the difference in size.

'Well now... *deputy*. One thing's for damn sure. These are hands that have done their work someplace other than Hale County, Texas... Of that, I'm certain.'

'How so...?' Zalizo says.

'Happens my Pop was an army JAG back in the day. From

when I was a babe-in-arms, I've been held by military hands. I know how they feel. I know how they don't feel. And yours, *Leg Zalizo...* have seen and served.'

'So how does the daughter of an Army lawyer end up taking steak orders, in a truck stop, stuck between nowhere and someplace else?'

'*Oh,* that's an easy story to tell...'

She leans back, resting her fingers on the edge of the table.

'...my Pop ran out his time at Fort Bliss. Decided to stick around the area. For one thing, he got to keep his non-com golfing buddies. That and he'd gotten used to the climate. He likes the dry air. Says it's good for his bones. Plus, he had no trouble getting picked up by a local law firm... For sure, I thought about going back to Albany a couple times after I graduated. But I didn't ever hit it off with Mom's new tow. Guess that's why I ended up hitching with the cranky old dog in the first place. Plus, I also knew how lucky I was, what with there never being a time when he wasn't happy to have me around.'

'Well... for what it's worth. Cranky or not, I'd say he must be an impressive old dog to have raised such a perceptive young lady.'

'That he is. And, if nudging mid-thirties still counts as youthful these days. Then yes... I guess young and perceptive is what I am.'

'Enough to go get my steak? Looks like it's ready back there.'

She tilts her head.

'Reckon so, *Leg Zalizo...* but don't go anywhere when you're done.'

She holds her thumb to her fore-finger a quarter-inch apart.

'I may have found a tiny bit of... *inclination.* Plus you'd be saving poor old Doug a detour.'

'Which way will we be headed?'

'El Paso,' she says. 'If that's doable.'

For a moment, he makes like he's giving the idea plenty of thought.

Then he says, 'Happens El Paso's okay for me.'

'That's good to hear, *Leg Zalizo*... very good to hear.'

COAL ISLAND, GUADALUPE MOUNTAINS

Victor lights up his cell phone for the third time in as many hours.

Though he doubts it would have changed the dynamic of the evening's events, he regrets ignoring the earlier call. Knows it represents another error of judgement.

Which was why, deep down, he's still cursing his *'detective'* slip. Allowing slights to his ego to drive his mouth, instead of relying on his intellect to temper his innate aggression. Ordinarily, something he would never do. Because, until an hour ago, he'd never met anyone who'd come close to provoking him into such a careless blunder.

Still, what's done was done.

He forces his attention to the voice on the other end of the line. Registers stress the moment his man begins to speak.

'I've been trying to call...'

'I know you have. But, what with one thing and another, I've been a little... *preoccupied*.'

'Well... we might have a problem.'

'Go on...'

'A jogger witnessed our man go down.'

'And...?'

'It looked like they were calling it in. Before they began snooping around.'

'They...?'

'She had a dog.'

'Miller... what, exactly, are you telling me?'

'I'm saying, first-off, it all seemed pretty random. Mainly because she looked nervous... panicked even. So when she used her cell, I assumed she was calling the cops... but they never showed. And, considering how weird things were playing out, I came damn close to removing her from the field. I guess it was lucky for her you didn't answer my call. Because, by the time I got in close, jogger and dog had bolted.'

'What breed of dog?'

A pause nudges its way down the line.

'Could have been a Malinois. Short-haired, so not an Alsatian. Could just as easily have been a cross-breed... it's not my area of expertise.'

'How did it behave?'

'The dog...?'

'Yes, Miller... the *fucking* dog.'

'Alert, I guess... from what I could see. Well-trained, for sure.'

'Interesting.'

'Anyway... first off, I figured her for some sort of opportunist, prepared to take a chance for a quick score.'

'So, I take it she wasn't?'

'Hard to know for sure. But now I'm thinking... maybe not.'

'Define... *maybe*.'

'I saw our man drop his cell phone. But, when I get there... the phone's gone.'

'I see.'

'I finished a standard robbery set-up. Took our man's wallet... jewellery... Rolex.'

'What was in the wallet?'

'A bunch of cards. Maybe a couple hundred in cash.'

'So you're telling me our mystery jogger takes a traceable cell phone, likely damaged... and leaves a wallet and a ten-thousand-dollar Rolex. I don't fucking think so.'

'Maybe she doesn't know horology like you do. Maybe she got spooked.'

'Horology be damned... you idiot. Even a petty criminal, female or otherwise, would recognize a Rolex. And no-one was *spooked.* Christ, Miller. Any bitch brazen enough to roust a gunshot victim on the fly, is not going to miss out on a wallet full of ready cash. Added to which, any bona fide resident of that neighbourhood would have no need to steal a cell phone. Think about it... you moron. You were in Alexandria... not east Baltimore.'

There's a brief silence.

'I guess I messed up.'

Victor lets his own pause hang for a moment longer than strictly necessary. Partly to quell his growing rage. Mostly to send a message. One he knows Miller is savvy enough to receive—*loud and clear.*

'Have you picked up Abelman?'

'Affirmative...'

'Okay... the pair of you meet me in Austin. I'll let you know when and where. And, Miller... I've a strong hunch we'll be going up against someone soon. With a skill-set and resources at least equal to our own.'

'Understood.'

'Maybe... all the same, I'm going to spell it out. You will leave your B-game in DC. Because, believe me... where this party is concerned, even your A-game may not be enough.'

'Roger that.'

'And one more thing.'

'Yes...'

'From now on... Nasi will be my lead.'

Victor cuts the call.

DULLES INTERNATIONAL, WASHINGTON DC

Carl Jordan Miller stows his cell phone.

He's standing next to Benjamen Nasi Abelman. Across from Starbucks, in Terminal B—*having dropped off their rentals within ten minutes of each other*—the concourse a chaotic melee of passenger traffic churning in every direction.

So, regardless their casual demeanour, they are both alert. Changing their sightlines at regular intervals. Scanning for anyone whose attention lingers on their position longer than it should.

Nasi hands over a *latte*-to-go. His first act of comradery since the two of them had been paired together. And while, ordinarily, Miller would never turn down the offer of a free coffee, *lattes* have never been his bag. He much prefers *cortados*. Or the bitter kick of a double *espresso* on occasion.

So he dumps the take-out cup, untouched, into an adjacent trash can. Then he turns to face the Israeli.

'He says we're to meet him in Austin.'

Nasi stares back. Expression inscrutable. Seeming not to have taken the slightest offence at the coffee being tossed. Though it was hard to be sure since the man's eyes give nothing away. Irises so dark, they look like they've been surgically removed and replaced with coal.

'And... is that all he said?'

Nasi is unremarkable to look at. In all likelihood, deliberately so. Six-two at a guess. High cheek bones. Olive-skinned. Close-cropped dark hair. Permanent five o'clock shadow. With what might typically be classed as a rangy physique. And when he spoke, his words were usually sharp and intense. His accent clipped. No nonsense. No distractions. No possibility of intimacy—*or anything close*. Not even casual friendship. He is fire and forget. And once locked on, better to get out the way.

'He said... from now on you are his lead.'

'Good,' Nasi says. 'So now we can go.'

Miller feels his heckles rise a little further.

'So, that's it... that's all you got to say?'

Nasi cocks his head.

'You need to get something straight, Miller...'

'And what might that be?'

'You and I... we are not friends.'

'You don't say.'

'*Oh...* but I do say. And you need to listen. Because I'm assuming I'm the new lead on account of you screwing up somehow. Which means I don't want you around. Because I don't want to be near you when you screw up again... which you almost certainly will. Because failure is a habit. It makes a man smell a certain way. And I can smell failure on you, Miller... just so you know.'

Miller feels his stomach tighten.

'You can think what you like. But, as my old XO used to say... a man should keep from running his mouth until the battle's good and won.'

Nasi lifts his nose to the air, moving his head forward in Miller's direction. Sniffs twice.

Then he turns and walks away.

COAL ISLAND, GUADALUPE MOUNTAINS

Victor has left Director Ray in the medical unit. Under observation for a suspected seizure. The bruising on his chest assumed to have resulted from his collapse against his big old trophy desk.

His twin engine XLS sits refuelled at the southern end of the runway. Flight-plan no doubt submitted. Pre-flight checks complete and ready to go. He'd been advised to expect a twenty-minute turnaround, start to finish, despite the late notification. A result of the crew being hand-picked and well compensated. And a good few rungs up from reliable.

The call he's been anticipating for at least an hour, rings through as he makes to leave for the terminal.

'Speak.'

'Your Deputy was a no show,' the voice says.

Victor grinds his teeth.

'We waited way longer than scheduled.'

'And did what?'

'Kept our eyes peeled...'

The voice sounds aggrieved.

'But nothing fitting the description you gave passed our way.'

'So, what did... pass your way?'

'A couple of fuel tankers, a UPS truck and a beat-up estate.'

'Humour me, Mr. Turner... What's an estate?'

'Shit... yeah. I guess you'd call it a station wagon.'

'Okay... then what?'

'We gave it a while... Then headed back to the diner.'

'And...?'

'We're here now, and it's closed... Nothing's moving... Not even tumbleweed.'

'I see...'

'We didn't miss him... Those were the only vehicles to pass by.'

'I believe you.'

'So what now?'

Victor feels the alien tightness return to his chest. Only now it's cranked up a notch.

'Head up to Plainview... I'll message you the address we have for him. That, at least, has checked out as real. Then the pair of you will rotate. No gaps. Not even to take a leak... Do I make myself clear?'

'Which way is Plainview?' the voice says.

'Has *Google* maps not reached your little island?'

'Yes... sir.'

'Okay, so get going... Call me when you're in position.'

He stares through the window at the dark spread of hills rising in the distance, topped out by a blanket of stars now the storm has blown through. Certain another cyclone is building out there somewhere. The path it will take, unclear. Its terminal strength as yet unknown. But, at its heart, Victor has little doubt Leg Zalizo will be the next relentless force of nature with which he'll have to contend.

And soon enough.

Day Two

'Little Old Crow...'

EL PASO, TEXAS

They are sitting outside her three-story apartment block. Fronted with a serious amount of floor to ceiling glass. Well-tended balcony flora. Well-lit sidewalks. Expensive foreign imports on weed-free drives. The silence between them, comfortable. Like it had been most of the way since they'd left Doug locking up.

He says, 'Nice place.'

She keeps her eyes fixed straight ahead.

'Not what you expected, I'm guessing.'

'It might surprise you... but it's a habit of mine never to pre-judge.'

She says, 'That's good to know.'

'Still... now I'm thinking it's not a neighbourhood I would assume is within reach of many waitresses. And a Tesla for a ride.'

She smiles.

'Even allowing for tips?'

'From truckers... You're kidding me, right?'

'Okay, *Leg Zalizo.* You explain *Leg*. Then maybe I'll explain how I get to afford this neighbourhood... and my ride.'

He turns to face her.

'Only *maybe*...?'

She turns to look his way.

'That's the deal... for now.'

He rests his hands on the steering wheel. Takes a moment to re-set his filters. Opting for seventy percent. Seventy-five at a push.

'I started using it the day I enrolled at Texas Tech. Before that it had been *Oleg*... For a while, abandoning my given name felt... *disrespectful.* To my parents, that is. But it had caused no end of problems growing up... Not so much for me fundamentally. Mostly for those dumb enough to express an opinion on the merits of having Slavic ancestry... I guess I grew tired of standing out. Tired of knocking bone-heads on their ass, no matter how easy it had been... Besides, I was fully committed to my mission by then. My parents weren't what anyone would classify as wealthy folk. They'd had me late... a short while after they'd managed to escape their previous lives.'

'Previous...?'

'They'd fled the Soviet regime a good while before the Berlin Wall came down. Made it out of Ukraine via Belarus and Riga.'

'*Riga*...?'

'Capitol of Latvia.'

'*Oh*... I see.'

'Some of the old eastern bloc countries were just beginning to show signs of open discontent, long before anyone had heard of *perestroika*. But they were both well educated... and as sharp as they come. So they decided to get ahead of any purges or reprisals that might ensue. They made it out via Sweden. Worked hard at making a go of their new life. Mom used her brain. Pop used his muscle... mostly because he had a lot of muscle. Though we were always pretty comfortable, I guess I decided early on to respect what they gave me by staying focused. Strictly study and sport... Then they up and died. Not long after we'd moved to Texas so we could keep our little unit together while I studied. As far as I recall, they never actually heard the name spoken out loud... Funny how things turn out.'

'They sound amazing...'

'My mother made it clear, very early in my education, the

only truly amazing thing in life is childbirth. But, I'll give you they were... *steadfast.*'

She goes back to staring through the windshield. Seems to come to her own decision. He wonders to what level she'll be setting her own privacy filters.

'Okay... I get to live in Mission Hills because, for my day job, I head up the clinical psychology unit at Las Palmas Medical Centre. I also hold a doctorate and teaching post at U-Tex... and I'm on a retainer with the VA. Just so happens I choose to donate that part of my earnings back to its source... much like my tips.'

'Impressive résumé.'

'Much like yours, I'm guessing...'

Zalizo shrugs.

'...though something tells me, since I'm not security-cleared, I'm not going to get to hear much about it.'

'Like I said... perceptive lady. Which makes taking steak and egg orders on Highway 62, kinda *Nancy Drew*... wouldn't you say?'

She sucks in a deep breath. Holds it for a few seconds before slowly breathing out.

'I guess... you could call it a factory reset thing. Once in a while I like to bail out of my everyday life. Go somewhere to be the woman I'm not otherwise able to be. Put myself some place where I just might see a guy who piques my interest... so to speak.'

She settles further into her seat.

'Truth is... I've never been into standard dating. I find it all too... *conventional.* A little too predictable, you could say. For one... my work wouldn't allow me to be hemmed in anyway. Also, I'm not that interested in dating standard guys. I guess you could blame my Pop for always encouraging me to set the trend rather than follow it...'

She turns to face him.

'I met Doug at a VA session a few years back. Strange thing was, he said he saw the need in my eyes before I felt it in my soul. And I was supposed to be there helping people like him... He said he'd been a medic. Said he'd always had a talent for reading certain runes. And that mine were all lit up like neon. He told me, if I let him lend me a hand, I'd be helping him... So I agreed. And remember, I've been immersed in military speak long enough to decipher what a certain class of veteran means when they claim to have been... *just a medic.* Plus it's always been in my nature to know who I can trust...'

She drops her head a little.

'I guess it wouldn't make a whole lot of sense to regular folk. I suspect there's plenty who might judge me unfavourably... Anyway, it's only an occasional thing. And tonight's shift was just a straight-up favour to stand-in for one of his regular girls who called in sick... Happens it's in Doug's nature to hire waitresses who find themselves trying to escape what you might call unfavourable domestic situations. Excepting yours truly, of course... Come to think of it, I pity the guy responsible for making Lucy miss her shift. Anyway... that's a whole other story...'

She stalls for a moment.

'I usually work at places he recommends through the people he knows here in town... restaurants and bars mostly. I get to indulge my desires. My preference for strangers. My need to feel alive, with some degree of anonymity. And only he knows how important it is for my sanity... and now you.'

After a moment, Zalizo says, 'I'm honoured... seriously.'

She says, 'The good thing is... I believe you.'

'Isn't it a little risky though...? Or maybe that's part of the appeal.'

'A little, I guess... but not as much as you'd think. Plenty of creeps masquerade as professionals. Hold down high-paying jobs. Work in fancy offices. Wear shiny suits and pointy shoes. Besides... most psychopaths live pretty ordinary lives.'

'That hadn't occurred to me,' he says.

'And, for the record, I don't just parade around waiting for guys to pick me up. Who I choose, or don't choose, is my privilege to exercise. Besides, you can tell a lot about a person from the way they treat the hired help. And, like I said... I trust my instincts. Besides... when I stand in at his place, Doug insists on picking me up and dropping me off. Claims folk who trust vehicles that don't pump gas into cylinders need their heads examining.'

Zalizo begins to think this Doug fella might be the kind of guy he'd like to meet—*one day maybe.*

She goes back to staring out through the windshield. To breathing slow and steady. He decides he really likes the way her chest rises and falls.

'Zalizo...?'

'Yes, Vanessa.'

'Are you sure there's not just a little bit of you that's going to judge me?'

'Where I hail from... Miss...?'

'Clarke,' she says. 'Vanessa Jean...'

'Well, Miss Clarke... nothing you've told me comes anywhere close to being a crime. So, *yeah*... I'm sure.'

She continues to stare towards her apartment.

'*Okay*... in that case, my place is a decent enough size. And I have a spare room, in case I scare you. Spare towels. Eggs for breakfast. And I'm *inclined* to think you qualify as a stranger.'

He stays silent.

'I won't ask you where you're heading... I know you

probably couldn't tell me, even if you were inclined.'

'I can tell you, I'll be heading out early.'

'Well, there are convenient places to stay around here for sure. But I guarantee my floors are cleaner... sheets too. And I promise I don't bite.'

Before he can stop himself, he says, 'That's disappointing.'

By the time they make it to her door, it's 1.15 PM.

By 1.45 AM, they're showered and under the sheets.

Still damp. Naked and nowhere close to settling down to sleep. And, even though she'd showered hot—*to purge the smell of cooked meat, she'd insisted*—her hands are still the comfortable side of cool.

That only leaves his rising sense of guilt.

But he'd already decided, even before they'd made it halfway back to El Paso, the time had come to work on that.

COAL ISLAND, GUADALUPE MOUNTAINS

Victor is carrying a standard-size, steel-framed folding chair; looking absurdly small in his enormous hands. Like he's pulled it straight out of a Junior High equipment closet. Even so, as he enters the cell, he snaps it open, spinning it round so its back is facing square-on to the half-naked form lying on the bunk.

He waits a few seconds before sitting, draping his arms over the back of the chair.

'Okay, Perry... let's go over the rules and restrictions, one more time.'

He's returned on a whim. Or so he tells himself. The

unfamiliar voice in his head still admonishing him to—*back away*. Let the program stall. At least until all the facts were known. And fully assessed. But that would mean dancing to someone else's tune. An outcome that was entirely unthinkable.

And, of course, there was always the added security of a little known reality. One that insulated him from having to face any accountability. A fact of life that would undoubtedly cause the general populus to freak out, if they were ever to become aware...

...when it came to breaking the law and avoiding serious consequences, the more outrageous and despicable the crime, the more inevitable it was an officially-sanctioned cover-up would follow...

...and for damn sure, right from the outset, this entire operation had been off-the-scale in all its many aspects. Conceived by individuals operating far beyond the reach of any mere civilian authority.

He leans forward, stressing the chair's puny steel frame to the max, staring at the individual lounging with his orange jump suit rolled down to his waist. Pale skinned. Lean and muscular. Appealing enough, in his born-to-be-abused sort of way.

Perry Morgan Blake is lying on his back—*grinning to himself.*

He'd just pictured his old man desperately flailing his flabby arms. Trying to keep his head above water. Recalling how he'd paddled the flat-bottomed skiff in a series of lazy circles. Just out of reach of the bloated old ghoul. The rods and bait gone. Along with the salt beef and sourdough bread. A half-empty bottle of sugar cane vodka, bobbing in the wake of all the thrashing. The yelling and screaming going unheard. The murky waters of the Little Tensas Bayou swallowing up all the ruckus. Far away from anywhere it might have been heard. And the reason his own screams for help had gone unanswered, on all those dark nights that vile excuse for a man had loomed like a shadow monster at the foot of his bed.

Perry says, 'Have the rules changed?'

'No... but I'd appreciate some additional reassurance that you're committed to the program. Exactly as it's been designed.'

'And if'un I manage to reassure you?'

'I am here to personally guarantee the finale you seek. In addition to the assurances you've already been given.'

'I was denied once before, remember.'

'That was Dallas PD, Perry... and I can promise you, I'm nothing like Dallas PD.'

Perry rolls onto his side, resting his head on his hand.

'Where you from... originally, I mean?'

'Why do you ask?' Victor says.

'I guess I've always been a little curious.'

'And why are you all of a sudden looking to satisfy your curiosity?'

'Well... you don't have no accent that I could ever place.'

'That's because, I'm from somewhere I put behind me. Much like yourself.'

'I chose Texas for a reason.'

'Let me guess. You were sure that when they caught up with you, they would gun you down.'

'That's what I figured. Plus a better chance to make the headlines. Least ways, more likely than being shot in the woods by some pudgy deputy from Shit County, Louisiana. Maybe make the national news from one of them TV chopper live-feeds.'

'Well... your reasoning was a little off. If it was extra-judicial execution you were seeking, you should have considered getting yourself a darker skin-tone. And, if it had to be Texas, you should have chosen somewhere like Houston. Their fatalities during arrest statistics are somewhat more impressive than Dallas.'

'I guess policin' stats were never gonna be my strong point.'

'Clearly not,' Victor says. 'But let's get back to the matter at hand, shall we?'

'Yeah,' Perry says. 'Let's do that.'

'Okay... your target is scheduled to be in Lubbock three days from now. My people will be on campus. They will see to it you are transferred to my property once you've completed your task. I will allow you a couple of days to set up... before your new trial begins. Once this operation is in motion... there will be no going back. That much I can guarantee. You will be on my territory. And... when it's over, you will be buried next to your mother, as agreed.

'I know all that...'

Perry rolls onto his back, hands behind his head, eyes fixed on this weird benefactor.

'...but tell me, one more time, how hard am I allowed to play in the meantime?'

'My people have assured me they've been over this with you.'

'So remind me. I enjoy a hard-on as much as the next guy.'

Victor regards him with what passes for indifference. His pale grey eyes devoid of emotion. Perry figures the freak was still hoping to be feared. And, if he was, Perry wondered how pissed he'd be to know he was failing. Because, until he was living through those final few seconds—*when he would know with absolute certainty the end was close*—he dares not imagine if his own fear will be greater than he'd seen in his father's eyes, during those last few seconds before the dark bayou waters had swallowed him whole. Dallas had been intoxicating. Absent the pain he'd waited all his life to feel. And one, without the other, was like those snuff movies he used to be hooked on, minus the blood—*and the suffering.*

'Outside of wanton genocide... *à la* your previous exploits that brought you here to me... you're free to take whatever actions you deem necessary to avoid exposure... Other than that, I expect you to lay lower than a rattlesnakes ass.'

'Well I'll be... I didn't figure you for the earthy type.'

Perry shifts his weight a little.

'I remember back when I was a kid. When y'all first took me in. Saying it was okay to hang around that big-ole fancy place of yorn. When all those tough guys you had around the place started training me. I know you used to watch me bathin'... before y'all got bored and dropped me like a stone. But I sure don't recall no cussin'.'

Victor stares into Perry's eyes, long and hard.

'And you stay low. If you try to play games with me, you lose all your privileges. You are not autonomous, Perry. There are multiple fail-safes built into this operation. Consequently, the only way this goes down the way you want it to, is if you play by the rules.'

'Mister... you gotta change the way you speak to me. Better than half the words you use, I have no idea what they mean. But I'm guessin' you've always known that... haven't you?'

Victor rises from his chair.

'Just stick to the plan, Perry. Is that plain enough for you?'

Perry smiles. Resumes staring at the ceiling.

'Whatever you say... *Boss man.*'

EL PASO, TEXAS

There are small sounds escaping her mouth. Some short and soft. Some a little louder and a little longer.

Her back is arched. Her hips keeping up a steady—*back-and-forth*—rhythm. Strands of hair clinging to the sheen of perspiration glinting across her neck and shoulders. The neat strip of hair between her thighs appearing and disappearing. Captivating his gaze.

His eyes drift to her breasts. To her mouth as she bites her bottom lip. To her arms, taut and stretched behind her back. Her nails digging hard into his thighs.

For sure, she'll likely be leaving her mark on his flesh.

Then she stops abruptly. Pressing down hard. Giving a small shudder. Like someone has just walked over her grave.

He reaches up. Runs his fingers through her hair. Down over her shoulders. His hands coming to rest, tight on her hips. She throws her head back, breathing out what he hopes is a contented sigh.

She leans forward—*slowly*—hair shimmering as it cascades. Kissing him hard. Pressing her weight onto him. Biting his bottom lip. Renewing her slow, rhythmic grind.

Again, she stops abruptly. Pulling herself closer. Holding him tighter. Encouraging him to take over the lead in their dance.

He spins her over without warning.

She closes her eyes. Parting her lips. Hands reaching out behind her head. Pressing her palms hard against the headboard. Wrapping her legs around his back.

Matching his rhythm. His strength. His passion...

...his need.

'I don't care how early it is... if you're hitting the road, I'm making you something to eat.'

He says, 'I'd like that.'

'Eggs on rye,' she says. 'Scrambled. Not too runny. I'm sure I've got a pitcher around here someplace... leastways, I know I have ice.'

He says, 'How did you know I'd come back.'

She tilts her head.

'You left your ride in the lot.'

'How could you be sure I wouldn't just hop in and drive away? I might not have been hungry.'

'Oh... you were hungry, Leg Zalizo. I'm a psychologist, remember. I *saw* it in your eyes before you felt it in your soul.'

'Seems to me, that medic friend of yours has got a lot to answer for.'

'*Yes*, he does...' she says, turning and heading for the kitchen. 'I must remember to thank him.'

MARKS CENTRE, WASHINGTON DC

Sergeant First Class Eleanor Rundell—*'Runellie' to her small circle of Ranger brethren*—is thirty-two years old. Atlanta born and bred. And fiercely proud of it.

She stands a little over six-foot tall with her boots on. Maybe a little less when she slept. Tonight, however, she suspects she'll likely remain at her combat-ready height all the way through to sun up.

To date, she'd given eight of her adult years to Airborne Rangers *LRSD*, the United States Army's specialist long-range surveillance detachment, and become the first female ever to wear both sniper and airborne insignia on her dress uniform into the bargain. Sure, she'd had to endure the inevitable media attention and a good dose of peer resentment—*not to mention the oft and none-to-subtle enquiries regarding her sexual preferences*—until she'd proven her detractors wrong during two messy active duty deployments to Iraq, at the outset of *Operation Inherent Resolve*.

On the upside—*no matter she'd had to acquire the hide of a rhino*—her efforts had gotten her transferred to Defense Clandestine Services. A highly coveted assignment for those in the know. Though, for damn sure, no less perilous or stressful than the time she'd spent in the middle east. Mainly because her former boss had recruited her early into his team; when the newly-formed unit's operational doctrines and rules of engagement had been in their infancy. And certainly no less demanding than any counter-ISIS engagements she'd endured. And she'd learned, pretty damn quick, the recently promoted Lieutenant-Colonel was the kind of commander who, if something needed to be done—*it got done.* Heads needed to roll—*they rolled.* Their missions, anything but routine. Adversaries, a long way from your run-of-the-mill embezzlers. Far from your average bone-heads, selling knock-off ammo and truck parts to your typical sweaty, black-market grease-monkeys pushing over-the-fence military surplus.

More often than not, they went after mob boss equivalents wearing their starched dress uniforms. The kind of individuals who'd earned their fancy epaulettes then, for one reason or another, had turned against their brothers. The kind of people happy to risk filling body bags in exchange for a pallet of bucks. Or dangerous ideologues at home and overseas. Supremacist sympathizers, with delusional plans to sink the republic from within. A mission brief predicated on an irrefutable truth few would ever admit publicly. The stark reality that, once corrupted, the US military could easily—*and swiftly*—become the most powerful criminal organisation on earth.

Most investigations had only lasted weeks. Very few more than a couple months. Because the Colonel was nothing if not efficient. Regardless, it had been wall-to-wall intense.

Lately, she'd found herself musing if her life in DCS would ever go back to how it had been before the Colonel's resignation. During the past couple months, she'd felt like there was a possibility he might reverse his decision. Only for something to change suddenly. Because the last time they'd spoken, he'd seemed determined to keep her distant. A scarily unfamiliar state of affairs, truth be told.

Unbidden, her system throws in another shot of adrenalin.

She's been awake sixty-hours straight. Her body-clock now so far out of sync it's long since switched to applying zealous amounts of pressure somewhere behind her eyes.

Georgetown's phone has given up little of anything useful. Numerous lurid text messages, to a lady who went by the name Hannah. Graphic shots of former or current conquests saved to his cloud account. Seedy and compromising, to be sure. But nothing vile. No accompanying threats to expose. A good number of calls to New York that turned out to be Wall Street broker types, no doubt the source of numerous installed dark-web trading apps. Half-a-dozen recent unanswered calls to *Nassau* and *Cayman*. Nothing new. Certainly nothing useful. Little they didn't already know. Apart, that is, for a couple of calls that had bounced off a tower in southern New Mexico. The first, close on six months before. The second, little more than six hours ago. She guesses Coal Island. But the call's recipient remains a mystery, resisting all her efforts to trace.

Beyond that, however, she knows there's still something she's missing amid all the cryptography and human intelligence clutter. A small thing in all likelihood. Because, in her experience, that's the way things often played out. Whatever it might be, it was something the fog in her head seemed determined to keep shrouded.

A source inside DC Metro had advised they were calling robbery on the victim in Alexandria. Staying open minded for the Congressional Country Club hits. Leastways until bullets or cartridges could be found. So she knows there's a chance something might turn up where *Georgetown's* lights had been punched. But much thinner odds against finding anything useful where *Nassau* and *Cayman* had fallen.

And there's one more fact she has to consider.

Just like she had, the surveillance team she'd assigned to *Nassau* and *Cayman* had witnessed their marks go down. Which meant she'd been able to run the scene through in her head; exactly as it had been described. Which put the shooter at Congressional Country Club in the exceptional category. Because, despite what you saw in the movies, two kills within seconds of each other—*at distance, against moving targets*—was pushing towards the top end of the talent curve. And she should know. She'd been assessed as possessing a God-given ability when it came to hunting, by every instructor she'd ever been assigned. Yet, throughout two messy tours in Asia, she'd pulled off a double-strike like that on a couple of occasions at most.

So now she knows for sure. At a minimum, she's looking for two shooters. Not just because of the timeline involved. Much more because, somewhere at her core, she knows she would be face-down in a parking lot right now, but for the fact she'd been in the company of a lesser talent the previous evening. Which means, all things considered, she judges the time has come when escalation was fully justified.

First off, she'll start by warning the Colonel. Then she'll begin her search for operators with standout reputations. Because, in her current line of work, next-level marksmanship never went unnoticed. So she's fairly confident, sooner or later, she'll find her candidates. *Sooner, hopefully*. Because, when it came to ferreting out buried information, her record for interrogating digital intel is on a par with her hard-earned reputation as a former Recon sniper.

EL PASO, TEXAS

She'd prepared his food wearing nothing but a sports bra and high-riding briefs. Plus the barest hint of a smile. The eggs done perfectly. Iced water fetched straight from the dispenser centred on her refrigerator.

'You promised a pitcher,' Zalizo says. 'And that you wouldn't bite...'

She offers him a diffident shrug as she drifts past.

'So... care to explain the teeth marks, at least?'

She shouts her answer from the bathroom.

'Think of them as a badge of honour.'

'Is there honour in pain?'

'Sure,' she calls out. 'Especially when the recipient's in a position to complain and chooses not to. A kind of unspoken mutual contract, wouldn't you say?'

'Not always,' he calls back. 'At least not in my experience.'

'Well, *Leg Zalizo*... I'm not talking combat rules of engagement. I was thinking purely in terms of passion.'

'You sure about that?'

'Absolutely,' she says. 'If you apply a simple axiom.'

'And that would be?'

'Always avoid setting out to cause harm. Because it usually ends up destroying your own soul. Therefore somewhat masochistic... wouldn't you say?'

'I'm not sure we always have a choice.'

'Confusing choice with preference, Leg Zalizo... is the first refuge of a disordered mind.'

'Isn't that a little Freudian for this early in the day?'

'I came up with that back when I was unbearably precocious and keen to impress. Eighth grade, I think it was.'

'Eighth Grade... I'm not sure if I should be impressed, or terrified.'

'I was on the debating squad.'

'What were the chances,' he says.

He hears her laugh.

'I was pretty overbearing... I can't deny. A twelve-year-old advocating *choice* as the single most corrosive agent in the human psyche. Eating away at the value of evidence. And truth. Distorting our, so called, moral compass. A cognitive convenience store. Where folk are always able to pull obligations... or genuine beliefs... or deeply held faith... off the reduced to clear, lame excuses shelf, to justify their actions whenever doing the right thing becomes inconvenient.'

He suddenly feels a layer of the cold-hearted organism he's become slowly being peeled away. Like the thick dermis that had allowed him to do all the brutal things he's done—*and still fall asleep at night*—is being surgically removed. The hiss of a protective seal he'd kept in place since the death of his parents, abruptly ruptured.

'And... best you know,' she continues. 'I haven't changed my mind since...'

He considers his own favourite maxim. *If you're not ready for the answer, better to avoid asking the question.*

'And speaking of people leaving their mark...'

Her voice sounds oddly distant. As if she's somehow forming her words from a moment yet to be lived.

'Given you've left an impression of your own... is there a chance you'll make it back this way anytime soon?'

He doesn't answer.

'Anytime... *Ever?*'

At length, he says, 'Hard to tell.'

'*Hard to tell*... does not sound promising.'

'That's because the world I operate in has inherent uncertainties.'

She appears at the edge of the dining area. Her hair wet and tangled. Held in an unruly scrunch by an oversized hairgrip. A tube of toothpaste in one hand. Toothbrush in the other.

'So I don't scare you off completely. Let me rephrase...'

For a moment, she seems hesitant.

'If you were inclined not to employ choice. And the uncertainties were not, let's say... *terminal*. Would you think about coming back this way?'

'Under those circumstances... I'm sure I would.'

It surprises him that he'd given his answer so freely.

She says, 'You're sure... you're sure?'

He says, 'Yes.'

'Sure enough, I could think about quitting my forays as a waitress?'

'Wouldn't that mean you'd have to make a number of your own aforementioned choices?'

'Such as...?'

'To wait, or not wait... for one. And doesn't coming back carry with it the inevitability of me losing the status of being a stranger.'

'*Umm*... so I guess some mindset adjustments might have to be made. Though, by standard model measurements, I'm not sure anyone would describe us as well acquainted.'

'When someone knows how you like your eggs prepared, I'd say that's a few steps down the road to being familiar.'

She offers him a shrug. Then disappears from view.

'Well... I did cheat a little on that front, I guess. But, like I said... I'm not asking for any kind of up-front obligation.'

'Just a pending inclination,' he says.

She calls back, 'Exactly...'

'So... all things considered, I'm sure I'd be a little bit inclined.'

She re-appears, towelling her hair.

'And you can say this because?'

From nowhere, he makes a decision. Choosing to re-set his filters as close to zero as makes no difference.

'Because, the instant I saw you, you reignited my appetite for something I'd convinced myself was lost to me. I guess I'd like to know how come that's even possible.'

He'd spoken as if his words would only be heard inside his head.

She stops towelling. Brushes back her hair with her free hand. Offers him a broad smile. Then she turns, heading toward the kitchen.

As she moves away, he hears her say, 'That's good to know, *Leg Zalizo*... very good to know.'

MARKS CENTRE, WASHINGTON DC

Runellie watches as the clock on the wall nudges its way towards 02.00 hours. Registers the fact her blood sugars are critically low. Her concentration levels impeded. But she knows a call has to be made. To someone whose identity is currently unknown to her. And likely to remain so, even after the call. Because all she has to go on were the Colonel's long-standing and explicit instructions.

'You only call this number if I'm out of commission... and you're one-hundred per cent sure the threat is at Category Five. And imminent. Understood?'

She'd said, she understood. Because, above all things, she is a person who's always prided herself on rarely—*if ever*—agreeing to anything she couldn't hold to.

So when the realization—*the insight she'd been unable to dial into focus during the preceding hours*—had broken through the fog billowing inside her head, she'd begun interrogating every intel system she could access. Doing her best to confirm locations for the list of elite freelance shooter she'd identified.

She'd been in her element. Because, other than hunting, this is what she did best. And, by the time she'd finished, there was one thing she knew for sure.

The only class of people with access to—*and more importantly, control over*—the individuals she'd identified, were unquestionably at the level of Category Five. Because every operator in DCS was fully briefed on the unit's category ratings. One-through-five—*unlike hurricanes or tornadoes*—the categories were not created to define any specific level of danger. Real or perceived. Instead, they existed solely to classify the true level of influence of those being investigated. The position they held within the nation's power structure.

More specifically, their power to corrupt.

So she thinks it over one more time. No longer harbouring any doubt the previous evening's events had been part of a *Cat-Five* operation. Everything she's been trained to recognize screamed that her instincts were solid. The victims had all come from wealthy families. Ivy League educated—*or near as dammit was to cursing*. Undoubtedly, they were well-connected scions of the donor class, masquerading as harmless Beltway flunkies. Shadow-government operators, hiding in plain sight. Hoovering up secretive State and Defence department contracts—*likely running into the billions*—in exchange for a few tens of millions in secretive political donations. The kind of victims whose termination could only be sanctioned by someone with extraordinary authority or influence.

Or possibly both.

Even so, she knows once she's made the call, all she can do is wait—*for however long*—for someone to confirm her reasoning is sound. On the other hand, if her judgement was considered in any way flawed, she knows she'll likely be clearing her desk by sun up. Either way, she's intent on hitting the sack. Maybe she'll sleep for a week.

She pulls the receiver from its cradle.

Issues a silent prayer to herself.

Then, as she often did at times like this, she puts a quiet voice to the deeply-held belief she's harboured since completing her basic training.

'Rangers lead the way...'

EL PASO, TEXAS

Sun-up is still an hour west of the Organ Mountains when a call buzzes Zalizo's satellite phone to life.

He is running a good bit behind schedule, so he's been pushing the GMC hard; its big engine thrumming a dull counterpoint to the steady drone of off-road treads on concrete. The high-beams cutting an anaemic furrow along Highway 54.

He is thirty minutes into his journey. Albuquerque still lies a minimum three hours hard sprint north. The Navajo Nation an hour further west. For reasons he'd had no time to discover, the Interstate on-ramp had been closed. Ditto on his second attempt to join the freeway. As a result, he's routed a lot further east than he'd originally intended.

He glances at the caller ID. Despite his ever-tightening schedule, he's persuaded to pull over.

He tugs the steering wheel hard right. Sliding to a stop on a triangle of rough ground splitting the intersection with Highway 70. Killing the engine. Placing the call on speaker phone.

'Colonel...'

The voice is monotone and gravelly.

'...are you free to talk?'

'Yes, General.'

'Okay... then I'll keep this brief.'

'Sir.'

'You're still receiving your Government paycheques, are you not?'

'Yes, sir... I am.'

'And using your official ID?'

'Occasionally... as the need demands. Are you intending to pull it?'

'Let's just say... for the time being, I'm prepared to keep that option under review.'

'Thank you, General... I appreciate it.'

'I imagine you do. On the other hand, the Government... if asked, would declare you an ex-employee. Would it not?'

'If asked... I anticipate it would.'

'Well, Colonel... as of yesterday, we have been asked. In the

form of a somewhat spurious enquiry on behalf of a distant relative. Do you have any such relatives?'

'It's possible. On my father's side, at least. But it's extremely unlikely they'd be capable of making contact after all this time.'

'That was my guess also. Be that as it may... I've also received a call from one of your dedicated subordinates that further persuades me the enquiry was bogus.'

'I see... Can I ask who you spoke to?'

The General holds a pause before answering.

'Your somewhat enigmatic sergeant.'

'Runellie,' Zalizo says. 'Okay... makes sense.'

'And just in case you're wondering... she was right to invoke our protocol.'

'That's good to know.'

'You pick good people, Colonel... It's why I picked you.'

'Yes, sir... and the upshot is?'

'Of course... I keep forgetting you're not one for small talk.'

'In my experience, General... it's unlike you to forget much of anything.'

'That may be so. However... the upshot, as you put it, is you will need to cover your back and dust your tracks from here on in. I've given you extraordinary latitude in this little recuperation exercise of yours, Colonel. And we both know, it's fast approaching the time when I'll have to act on that letter you submitted. What is it... close on six months ago now.'

'I believe so.'

'Whatever... as of two hours ago, a Cat-Five has been flagged. And I've determined it has merit. That means this unit can no longer remain in this unofficial stasis you've forced it into. So... to put it bluntly... this little private enterprise gig you're currently embroiled in, has just become an option one, option two engagement.'

'Another one so soon...'

'Come again?'

'Nothing, General... option one, being?'

There is a slight hesitation before the caller continues.

'Option one... is that, going forward, you withdraw your dumb-ass request to quit on me, and get back to running this unit with some semblance of normalcy. In return for resumption of accountability, I will ensure standard services are resumed... Full cover and back-up... Full logistics... and a better than average chance of you crawling out of this meat-grinder you've jumped into.'

'And option two...?'

'I sit back and wait for you to go completely rogue on me, and hope you can stay alive and out of jail.'

'And, if I choose option two?'

'I think you already know the answer to that question.'

'True... but I'd still prefer to hear you say it.'

'Very well, Colonel... In short order, I will have no choice but to disavow. Permanently. At which point, your offer of resignation becomes somewhat moot... Is that clear and concise enough for you?'

'Perfectly... but I have my own caveat.'

Zalizo knows he has to choose his next words carefully. The voice on the other end of the line belongs to a White House appointee, answering only to the nation's commander-in-chief. An appointment carried over from multiple administrations; regardless the prevailing party affiliation. Something close to remarkable in a landscape plagued by rampant, partisan politics. A man charged with two singular functions. Pre-empt and protect the nation's armed forces from any and all operational risks. Both foreign and domestic. Predict and interdict—*if need be, with extreme prejudice*—all potential rogue elements within said organisation.

'So let's have it... I don't have all day to shovel sawdust.'

'Okay, General. No matter the option... I'm pretty sure I'll eventually be forced to employ unsanctionable tactics.'

'As well you know... where this unit's concerned, nothing is unsanctionable. Besides, I'd anticipated as much.'

Zalizo stays silent.

'Your sergeant has been particularly innovative in pursuing her lines of inquiry. Not to mention... somewhat forthright with her attitude toward this unit's command structure.'

'She's Regimental Recon. And I've never met a Ranger who didn't speak their mind.'

'It's certainly a common point of view, Colonel. Regardless... considering her background, she still seems somewhat out of the ordinary.'

'I make it...'

'...a habit never to judge. Yes, Zalizo... I am well aware of your standards.'

'Most people make the mistake of focussing on only two things when they meet her. First... she made it through 82nd Airborne's AAT to earn her wings. Second... she went from being a company sharp-shooter, all the way through full sniper school on her first cycle, then into the Spec Ops training and active duty deployment. For me, I figured pretty quickly that deep down she'd always been a geek. Add in a singlemindedness that's second to none... it persuaded me to look beyond her housing project, Baptist Church-going roots and recognize talent whatever its origins.'

'Point taken, Colonel. And, as a matter of idle curiosity, the MIKE-One call-sign comes from what, exactly? I know some of you Spec Ops types can be prissy about such things.'

'I believe her hero was Michael Johnson... the sprinter. Something to do with her being from Atlanta... and being there as a kid to see him tear up the track in ninety-six.'

'Okay... so getting back on point.'

'General...?'

'It's just possible, your closet cyber-junkie may have uncovered some high-roller connections to some recent tragic events here in DC. As such, I would advise you tread cautiously.'

'I'm aware of the take-downs.'

'Why does that come as no surprise?'

'So, what level of... *connections*, are we talking?'

There's another pause.

'Upper echelon Beltway, unsurprisingly... A senate incumbent for certain... Nine-fifty Pennsylvania Avenue and State Department are also looking probable... Possibly even a certain state governor with a questionable moral compass. However, at this precise moment, your sergeant has only unearthed some dubious dark money support for characters who may, or may not, be associated with your current area of focus. And... bearing in mind a standing Supreme Court ruling on the supremacy of privacy regarding political contributions... nothing anyone, including you, Colonel, could hang their hat on.'

'So, what are you saying exactly?'

'Good question. Because, from where I sit, this situation has become a good deal less straight forward than you might appreciate.'

Zalizo gives the General time to complete his answer.

'Put simply, my dilemma can be distilled as follows... I let you run free, I'll have no option other than to cut our one-to-one umbilical from this moment on. That said, I gave MIKE-One the same choice and she said she'd choose whichever option you did. Which, I must confess, I found disappointing on one level... and admirable on another.'

'I wouldn't allow her to follow through on that commitment. You, of all people, should know...'

'Don't worry, Colonel... I'm fully aware of your integrity when it comes to your people. It's one of the reasons we became acquainted.'

'Good to know... General.'

'That said... if you're tempted, even a little bit, to recruit from the network of dubious contacts you no doubt have access to... I strongly advise you reconsider. Because, I shouldn't have to remind you... there are no circumstances under which I'll allow any direct threat to this country's national security, or the interests of my unit, as a result of your current... freelance activities.'

'That's always been fully understood.'

'And, as a matter of interest... were exactly are you?'

'*Sir*... I'd rather not say.'

'Okay, Colonel... given your answer, I take it you intend selecting option two?'

'I think it's best.'

'Very well... then it only remains for me to wish you good luck.'

'With all due respects, General... if I thought I'd be reliant on luck to play a significant part in this, I would have selected option one.'

'Your reverence, is duly noted... though I would remind you of Napoleon's attitude towards luck and senior officers. I would also caution that I'm the one person who knows all about your true lineage. Including just how ruthless your parents, and their associates, used to be... and what it cost you all in the end. Just because you claim to have stowed those indiscretions away some time ago, soldier... I would strongly advise you not to cross that particular Rubicon again. Because, there may be no route back for you this time. And, if you choose to ignore my counsel in the here and now... don't doubt, for one minute, my resolve to track you down.'

Zalizo buttons down an unfamiliar urge to ask questions for which he hasn't already acquired answers—*even if only in part.*

Choosing, instead, to let his commander's explosive revelation slide.

'General... it was good speaking with you.'

'Likewise... Colonel.'

YESO, NEW MEXICO

One thing was for sure, the old guy in the bar certainly hadn't let her down. The location he'd pointed her toward turned out to be way more than she'd hoped for. So much so, as she'd pulled off the highway—*squeezing Kenton's truck between a set of concrete barriers, through onto the abandoned spur*—Anne-Marie Hollenbeck had felt butterflies rising in her chest.

As always, she carries two cameras. A slimline Canon digital for the set-ups. And for its superior quality lens, a thirty-five mil Leica M6 for the money shots.

And—*boy-oh-boy*—was she ever getting her shots.

The promise of a burnt-orange sunrise, exploding over distant low ochre hills rising above an otherwise flat landscape. The perfect, narrow strip of long-since deserted highway. And the kind of derelict fuel stop she'd prayed for, silhouetted against the expanding dawn. Back-lit with a blazing sunrise and the promise of another day of blistering heat.

So, right now, she has everything she needs—*and then some*. More importantly, she knows her grandpa will be thrilled with the images she's capturing.

Less than fifteen minutes into her shoot, away in the distance, somewhere to the south, the unmistakable beat of rotor blades begins to penetrate the still morning air. Just like she'd experienced on that field trip a couple years back, standing in the middle of a wind farm. Only these have a signature resonance she recognises instantly. Just like in that famous scene from *Apocalypse Now*. Because, for as long as she can remember, Grandpa John had been a Vietnam movie addict.

Instinctively, she gets the feeling the craft will be coming in low, its nose pitched down.

She looks up, scanning the southern horizon. Acquiring what sure looks like a Huey in the mid-distance. Rising up over a shallow crest. Instantly turning her day into a two-for-one shoot.

She can't believe her luck.

The craft's nose pitches up about a hundred yards out, blasting a corona of dust and grit out into the dry vegetation either side of the road.

She shouts out loud.

'*Y-E-S*... I love you, old timer... Thank you... *thank you*.'

The Huey barely touches down when a figure emerges through the hatch behind the pilot, balanced nonchalantly on the ski rail, tossing a canvas bag out onto the road. Half-stooping as he jumps a couple of feet to the ground. Staying crouched against the downwash. Keeping his head bowed, as the aircraft engines throttle back up.

Then the figure rises and begins moving forward.

She swings the Canon behind her shoulder, where it nestles in its usual place, half-way down her spine. Then she brings the Leica up—*smooth and steady*—centring the viewer on the figure. The Huey thundering away in the background. Barrelling over. Suspended for a magical moment, like it was just about to fall from the cloudless sky.

She kneels down next to the fuel pumps. Gets off close on

twenty shots before the dust begins to settle. Of course, she will ask the guy if he's okay with her using the photos with him in frame. Because she knows they'll be amazing. Good enough, she's certain, to use for some future project.

And, if the guy objects, she'll promise to edit him out.

The figure walks, slow and relaxed, up to within twenty or so yards. Right arm tucked behind his back. Then he stops. Dropping the bag at his side. He has a mountain-man beard, bald head and John Lennon shades. Medium height. Lean and angular like Kenton. Though somewhat shorter in stature. Still, he cuts an imposing presence amid the settling cloud of dirt, in his urban combats and tight-fitting black T-shirt.

She notices tiny motes of silica, drifting behind his head. Glittering like gold dust in the fast rising sun.

She continues taking her shots.

Then the figure swings his arm slowly from behind his back.

Perry Morgan Blake had seen the glint of a windshield from better than a mile out. So he'd patted the pilot's shoulder. Tapped his finger to his headphones.

'Down there...'

They had come in low from the south-east. Settling a hundred yards out from the abandoned fuel stop. A glossy pick-up sitting fifty yards back from what was little more than an over-sized shack. A mass of gloss-black paintwork and polished chrome, sitting with its driver-side door slung open, juxtaposed against a carpet of dried tuffs of weeds and the skeletal remains of a rusted-out forecourt canopy.

He'd stepped from the Huey's ski rail. Landing in a crouch next to his carry bag. Pulling his Smith & Wesson ACP. Holding it behind his back. Feeling its familiar bulk in his hand.

Up ahead, the lone figure he'd seen as they'd swept in,

sinks to their haunches, next to a set of decaying, hose-less fuel pumps. A young-looking female. Gripping the body of a camera with her left hand. Rotating its lens with her right as he moves forward.

Even from distance, he can see that she is unconcerned. Snapping away like the world would just have to stop and wait until she'd gotten her fill of stealing someone else's God-given right to privacy. Oblivious to the fact he might choose to be seen only when he wanted to be seen.

So he comes to a stop. Swings his arm forward. Plants his feet a little ways apart.

Raises the big-ass revolver.

Shoots her through the sternum from twenty yards out.

For a frozen moment, her shoulders pitch in. Her hands still gripping the camera. Then kinetics go to work. Lifting her—*as if she's decided to rise of her own accord*. Heaving her backwards, like a crash-test dummy. Slamming her onto the earth amid a fine cloud of dust. Her pretty little head settling last of all. Like she'd up and decided to take a nap.

He moves up close to her body. Intending to tap her through the skull. But when he looks down, the spray of blood from the exit wound has made a perfect fan-tail above her head. Looking like a Native Indian headdress has been freshly painted in the dirt.

She looks amazing. Just lying there. Frozen in her moment of submission. All her mild curiosity surrendered now, to the brutal and overwhelming power of his creativity.

The notion juices through him. But nowhere near as much as it usually did. More than likely, because he's a changed man. An asset with a purpose...

...and a yearning for reward.

Perry picks up the bitch's camera. It looks real expensive. So he stows it in his bag. Then he reaches around, pulling his big-ass knife from the sheath centred in the small of his back.

He needs a fuse—*and knows just how to make it.*

Then he kneels down at her side. Begins cutting through her jeans. Making sure he drives the blade deep into her flesh. Drawing it across her groin. Then down each leg, from thigh to ankle. Ripping off a strip of bloodied material with one hard pull. Though, truth be told, there is less blood than he'd expected—*which spoiled things a little.*

He ambles to her pick-up. Tosses his bag onto the passenger seat. Next he moves to the fuel cap. And—*just like that*—a couple of paces off to the right, he spots a length of rusted wire. Like the entire set-up has been laid out that morning for his convenience...

...and his alone.

He forces one end of the denim fuse into the pick-up's fuel tank. Pushing the wire as far as it would go. Waiting until the material turns darker still as it soaks with gas.

Bingo!

He pulls the makeshift fuse, then retraces his steps. Back past the girl's body. For a moment, he gazes at her wounds. Both curious and confused at how she's able to look at peace. But he figures that's okay by him. Because he's on his way back down now. The buzz in his veins fading fast. As it always does, once there's no more pain to inflict.

The cover to an underground fuel tank lies ten or so paces off; road-side of the pumps. He kicks at the heavily-rusted, circular lid, making a hole the size of his heel. Kneels down to feed one end of his fuse into the void, now leaking gasoline vapours out into the morning air. Laying the dry end on the dirt away from the fumes. Setting it ablaze with the storm-proof lighter he'd demanded—*along with the carton of Marlboro reds*—as part of his provision of going away presents.

He turns and runs full tilt, back to the pick-up. Clambers aboard. Turning the key that's been conveniently left in the ignition. Stomping hard on the throttle.

The tank blows before he makes it fully off the dirt. The pressure wave rocking the two-and-a-half ton truck as he accelerates away.

AUSTIN, TEXAS

Susan Brandt opens her eyes with a start. Her cell phone all lit up and vibrating hard. Displaying caller withheld on the screen.

She glances at the digital clock she keeps on the intricately inlaid rosewood cabinet beside her bed.

It's just turned 5.25 AM.

Reluctantly, she taps the green pick-up icon.

'Who is this...?'

'Governor... we need to meet.'

She forces herself fully awake.

'Why...? Do we have a problem?'

'In my considered opinion... yes, we do.'

'At my end, or yours?'

'External.'

'Is it being fixed?'

'That status is currently pending.'

She pauses, calculating her next response. Knowing—*with this particular caller*—she needs to demonstrate control.

'Has a threat level been determined?'

'It's being assessed.'

'And do you have an action plan?'

'Let's just say... it's in the process of being formulated.'

'Then... regardless how you acquired this number, it's not obvious to me why we need to meet.'

'And, I would suggest, it's in your best interests to...'

'*NO*... Victor. It is in *your* best interests not to play *Godzilla* with me. Who the hell do you think I am? You think you can call me at this ungodly hour with a pile of nothing? We've got a problem... can't say what... can't say why... can't say how serious... can't say what the fuck you're going to do about it. *Jesus Christ*. What's in that fat head of yours? You imagine I exist just so you've got a chain to rattle? If so, you can think again... So you are correct, Mr. Labette. I am not suggesting... I'm telling you. You can consider contacting me... through agreed channels... when, and only when, you get your shit together. Until such time... please feed at the appropriate level in the food chain.'

She cuts the call.

Mutters, 'Goddam mutant.'

Within a minute, her cell phone buzzes a message through.

For a moment, she simply stares at the screen. Feels a sheen of sweat forming on the fine hair above her lip.

The message is typed in all-caps.

YOU HAVE A LEAK AT YOUR END.

I'M SENDING SOMEONE TO FIX IT.

WITH OR WITHOUT YOUR CONSENT.

YOUR LACK OF COOPERATION IS REGRETABLE.

MY PEOPLE... THE ONES MONITORING YOUR CAMPAIGN... WILL INFORM YOU WHEN AND WHERE WE WILL MEET.

SLEEP WELL... SUSAN.

She throws her cell phone on the bed.

'Fucking freak,' she screams.

GUADALUPE COUNTY, NEW MEXICO

Traffic is light to nothing at all when Zalizo hits the intersection, two clicks west of Vaughn. And it's the reason he figures the flashing high-beams he sees, as he slows at the intersection, are likely directed at him.

A battered Ford Taurus, being driven by a figure barely visible above the steering wheel, pulls sedately over to the shoulder. Fifty or so yards ahead. Its hood pointing east along Highway 60.

He is headed west.

Regardless, he hangs a right. Nudging in behind the ancient government-issue sedan. Pops his holster clip. Checks his pistol's safety and gets out of his GMC. He keeps the motor running. Leaves the driver door open. Closes the gap to the Taurus. Stopping to rest his fingers on the trunk. Hooking the thumb of his right hand into his belt next to his badge. Figuring he'll attract less scrutiny if he adopts a routine common to civilian law enforcement.

Not unlike a larva emerging from a chrysalis, a small, slim figure eases from the ancient sedan. Legs first. Feet clamped together. Clad in leather hiking boots. Oddly contrasted against a loose-fitting, grey linen trouser suit. After which, a sharp-faced, elderly woman turns to face him square on.

The first words out of her mouth are nothing if not direct.

'So... now I'm just straight-up confused.'

He says, 'Is there a problem, *ma'am*?'

'I'm hoping not,' she replies. 'But I'll have to insist on an explanation for the disconnect between your vehicle and your badge.'

'Well, *ma'am*... first off, I'll have to insist you give me your status. My decision on how intimate we can be will come after.'

From there on in, it's more or less plain sailing between the two of them.

Not too long ago, the Honourable Elizabeth Holt had retired from her lifetime judicial appointments. The last of which had been to the Tenth-Circuit appellant court. Sometime after that, she'd temporarily taken over as medical examiner for Guadalupe County—*on account of her starting out life as a forensic pathology graduate at Yale School of Medicine*—and something she'd agreed to as a favour for a life-long friend; who happened to be the soon-to-retire county sheriff. Who'd subsequently up and died. Leaving her holding the baby, so to speak, until the new electee had gotten his size-twelves all the way under his newly installed desk.

She is seventy-nine years old, five-foot-two, and tough as boot leather. Sharp nosed. With eyes as bright and focused as a hawk. Radiating a lifetime's curiosity. And the upright stance of a school mistress well used to dealing with young men twice her size.

That morning, she'd gotten a dawn-call from Stan Mullen. A retired mechanic, who'd called her about an abandoned fuel stop that had somehow blown its buried fuel tank.

Now, poor old Stan was in a pickle. He'd had to cancel his fishing trip to Lake Sumner. On account of him finding a body in the wreckage.

Zalizo holds out his official ID.

She accepts the offer and, after a quick scan, seems satisfied.

'Well now,' she says. 'You may not be what I expected, given your pony, but I've never had any issue with the military. So... if you don't mind helping out, I'd appreciate some company until the cavalry arrives.'

She turns and begins heading to her vehicle, visibly

preparing for the ordeal of negotiating her way back in behind the steering wheel. But not before her eyes momentarily drift to the GMC's license plate.

Zalizo feels a rare smile crease his mouth as they ease, one behind the other, back onto the highway. Making for an abandoned spur, lying—*if the wily old Judge's memory served*—somewhere close to a scratch in the dirt named Yeso.

Now they are standing next to a dusty but evidently well-kept seventies Ford Courier flatbed, waiting for Stan Mullen to stop shaking his head.

'I gotta tell you, Beth... it's none too pleasant over there.'

She makes a short clucking noise with her throat.

'Did you call anyone else?'

'No... just you. I have your number up here.'

Stan Mullen taps a meaty finger to his temple.

'Okay, Stan... we'll be fine from here on in. This young man is a Government Agent, in a manner of speaking. It's a little complicated... but he was passing by and kindly offered his help.'

She places a diminutive hand on Stan's upper arm.

'You can go fishing now. That's if you're still up for it, of course. I'll get Cummins to send someone over to see you later. They'll take a statement.'

'I don't know, Beth... someone's done a terrible thing...'

He shoots Zalizo a sideways glance.

'...you sure you'll be okay.'

When they'd arrived, Beth had advised he stow his Hale County badge. Making it clear that, hereabouts, folk were sluggish when it came to accepting outsiders. But sharp as a razor when it came to spotting anything out of place. It hadn't been a hard sell. His time as a Hale County deputy had pretty much served its purpose in any event.

He flashes his official ID in Stan's direction.

Then offers his hand.

'Leg Zalizo.'

The old guy thrusts out a large, fleshy palm in return. His grip plenty firm, minus any pointless attempt to dominate.

'Stan Mullen... I'm guessing you're not from around here?'

'I was heading for Albuquerque. But the Interstate was shut off when I set out from El Paso. Found myself passing through Vaughn when this young lady flagged me down.'

Elizabeth Holt issues a dry chuckle. Nods her agreement that he's on the level.

'Okay... I guess I'll catch you later, Beth.'

She offers her friend a doleful smile.

'Bye, Stan... later today, no matter what, I promise I'll come see you.'

Stan hauls himself into his truck.

The two of them stand and watch as he heads back to the highway.

'Poor old Stan,' she says. 'I've known him since he was a kid. What you'd call a real good sort... and nothing like as slow as he acts.'

'Agreed,' Zalizo says. 'And it's clear he knows who his friends are.'

'That's the way of things around these parts.'

She sounds momentarily wistful.

'Okay, Colonel... let's go take a look.'

The victim is lying face up.

A young female. Late teens at a guess. Although, *post mortem*, it was hard to be sure. Dressed in a khaki jacket, a thin cotton blouse, bleached denim jeans—*or what was left of them*—and DM sneakers. Lying on the dirt, with the repose of someone who'd lain down for a while to gaze at the stars.

There's an entry wound mid-sternum. Blood splatter fanning the dirt above her head. And one thing was certain, whoever had hacked the jeans from her legs had done so sometime after they'd put a hole through her chest. The wounds are savagely deep. Had she been conscious when they were carved, there would have been a spray of arterial blood spreading out across the dry earth.

And there wasn't.

Elizabeth Holt makes a short clucking noise with her throat.

'Do you think whoever did this reckoned they'd cover their tracks by blowing the place up?'

He says, 'I'm not sure they gave it any serious thought.'

'What makes you say that?'

Zalizo re-scans the scene.

'The tank looks like it was buried pretty deep. So the blast was only ever going up... never out. And, judging by the hole in the ground, too far away to take out the pumps. Also, by the looks of this place, I'm betting it was mostly fumes. No napalm scenario. No chain reaction. No secondaries... all pop and fizzle.'

'I'll take your word for it, Colonel. And it looks like Stan did a war dance round her before he called it in...'

She stoops over the kid's body.

'Is that some kind of ligature?'

He joins her, leaning in close.

'I'd say it's a little loose for that... and there's no obvious signs of abrasion. My guess is, it's a strap of some kind.'

He crouches down.

'How do you feel about moving her?'

'Honestly... I think we've pretty much lost any evidence of

who visited with us today. What do you have in mind?'

'We could take a look to see if there's anything on the other end.'

For a moment or two, she seems conflicted. And he couldn't really blame her. To disturb the scene further would be reckless. Particularly the corpse.

'And if there is...?'

He says, 'Then we'll know.'

She makes a clucking noise with her throat.

'What reasons would I give for my incompetent handling of a murder scene?'

'The way I look at things, time is usually your closest ally. Trails that start out hot can go cold very quickly. We could put some of the blame on Stan... but it's your call, Judge.'

'These days, I much prefer Beth.'

'Okay, Beth... I'm going to level with you. The kind of unit I command rarely debates shall we, shan't we. We gather data... Plot scenarios... Agree a worst case and whether it demands a rapid response. If the answer is yes... we go in heavy and disrupt. And we rarely concern ourselves with who's going to be pissed. Often times, we don't worry about who gets in the way. We don't do due diligence. We do cost benefit, solely as it relates to national security.'

'And, your point is...?'

It's at that exact moment, Zalizo decides he really likes the Honourable Elizabeth Holt.

'Sometimes, you've got to strike while the iron's hot.'

An expression ghosts across her face. Like she's contemplating an unpalatable dilemma. So, he decides not to push.

'Okay... I'm not sure why you couldn't just say that in the first place. But try not to change her position too much. I don't want to have to tell a big lie. And Stan never caused anyone an ounce of harm his entire life. For sure, I won't be putting any blame on him.'

Zalizo figures there will be less disturbance if he rolls the kid, rather than lift. Either way, her body doesn't weigh a whole bunch. And by the time he has her at forty-five degrees, a compact and relatively slim camera comes into view.

Beth is looking down. He looks up. Sees the pain—*swimming in a lake of fury*—flash momentarily behind her eyes.

He says, 'So... what now?'

She makes a clucking noise with her throat.

After a moment, she says, 'I'll have to call State in on this... I know it's a digital model, but we can't touch it before we get some expert forensic help out here... This is a poor county... We simply don't have the resources.'

'Okay... then what?'

'I'll handle the forensics comedy hour. Tell it like it was. Generally, I try to avoid subterfuge. Mostly because, I don't like it a whole lot when it's used on me.'

He says, 'Fair enough.'

'Please... be gentle when you lay her down. I can't tell you how much I hate it when kids are involved.'

He cradles the girl's head. Eases her slowly back onto the dusty earth.

'Who's going to come?'

She shrugs.

'First off... locals from Vaughn get primary jurisdiction. But Cummins will likely call in back-up from Santa Rosa. They have a couple detectives up there. And, if he's got any sense, he'll take my advice and check in with State in Albuquerque... just in case this ties in with any other recent incidents of a similar nature.'

'So... Cummins. I take it he's the new County Sheriff?'

'The very same.'

'Any reason I should know why Stan called you, rather than him.'

She hesitates a fraction before answering.

'Trust is a hard earned currency around here, Colonel. Cummins is relatively unknown by local standards... and the first thing he did was get a bigger, fancier desk. Things like that tend not to go unnoticed by a guy like Stan.'

'Will I be able to stick around?'

'That's some seriously fancy ID your carrying, Colonel... Don't you get to choose?'

'I'm military intervention, Beth. I don't do *protect* and *serve*. And the kind of people I bring to heel operate way outside standard civilian jurisdictions. Federal or otherwise. So, it's my guess... eventually, someone's going to give my ID a little more scrutiny than Stan did.'

He watches her think it through.

'Okay... I'll stick with you for as long as you need. More than likely, if I hold your hand and do the talking, you won't even need to show your ID. Let's just say, there was a time when I was a notable fixture in Albuquerque. If I refer to you as Marshal... assumptions will be made. Besides, your pony will help.'

'And your distain for subterfuge?'

Elizabeth Holt's eyes fall back to the girl's body.

'Momentarily subordinate to irons striking while they're hot.'

'I appreciate it, Beth... I'm not sure why right now, but I'd be keen to know if she snapped anything out of the ordinary.'

'Me to, *Colonel*... or should I say, Marshal?'

He rises. Checks his G-Shock.

'For now, I'm happy with... *Leg*.'

It's approaching 8.30 AM, and he knows, if he's to hang

around for any length of time, he'll need to get a message out to the Navajo Nation soon. Notify his delay.

She turns to him, raising her head to meet his eyes.

'Speaking of iron. Do you know why I mentioned I used to be a fixture in Albuquerque?'

'Can't say I do.'

'Well... happens I'm an old crow with good faculties. And that means I remember names. Unusual family names especially. I was a Tenth Circuit judge for twenty-five years. Albuquerque was on my roster. And you, Leg Zalizo, have a memorable ancestral name... wouldn't you say?'

Even from the better part of twelve inches down, Elizabeth Holts eyes bore into him.

Zalizo turns and starts walking. Begins typing a short message—*notifying his delay*—into his cell phone. Because he knows, if he uses too many words, the recipient will likely ignore it entirely.

After maybe a hundred or so paces, he comes to a spot on the road where a thin dusting of dirt lies in a shallow arc across the derelict highway. Another fifty strides, and a repeat arc of dirt lay in a similar width band.

He back-tracks, counting out twenty-five paces in his head. Spins in a slow three-sixty. Contemplates the wide circle of scrubbed earth on both sides of the road, devoid of loose vegetation.

Out of nowhere, he pictures orange and black rotor tips. Patchwork panels. Hears rotors beating the air. Feels the buffeting from the down-wash. Recalls the taste of foreign dirt in his mouth. The sting of sand in his eyes. From when he used to rock out of 160th Night Stalker birds, back in the day.

He ambles back to where the old judge had remained—*head bowed*—staring down at the kid, as if in prayer.

'I guess, that was real slow of me,' he says. 'Small world.'

Elizabeth Holt issues a short clucking noise from her throat.

'Yes, it was,' she says. 'And yes it is... and, if you don't mind me asking. How were things for you after your parents' passing?'

He fixes his gaze on a line of low hills in the distance.

'I got by.'

AUSTIN, TEXAS

'Let's get one thing straight, *Mr. Labette*... here and now.'

Victor can't help but admire her balls. Because, despite her undeniable femininity, she has a curious kind of machismo about her that—*for some strange reason*—really makes him twitch.

For a moment, he wonders if she knows just how special that makes her.

As always, she is immaculately presented. With just the right amount of cosmetics. A hint of eye-liner. A subtle wash of blusher adding definition to her already striking features. Not a hair out of place. Camera ready, in her mid-thigh, dark blue power suit and crisp white blouse. Signature two buttons undone. Delicate crucifix on a barely visible chain. Displaying not a trace of apprehension.

Without doubt, Governor Susan Brandt is a singular piece of work.

'I will not be intimidated by you,' she continues. 'I don't give a fuck how big you are... I don't give a fuck how strong you are... I don't care how many of your former CIA whack-jobs shit themselves whenever you walked into the room... I can assure you, I've seen off plenty bigger fish than you, throughout a life spent swimming with sharks... So, if it's in your head that your past reputation somehow makes me nervous, believe me... you are sorely mistaken.'

The governor keeps her eyes facing forward.

'As a matter of fact, all you ex-Langley types make my skin crawl. And, in my experience, a good number of you are full of piss and wind. So you can take it from me... We are not in bed together... We are in *cahoots*.'

Victor smiles.

'Well now... that was informative.'

'Whatever it is you want, *Victor*... either spit it out, or get out.'

They are seated in a large, executive spec'd, unmarked sedan. None too shabby, but not in the same league as her official stretched Lincoln. As a consequence, there isn't a whole lot of space between them. Which is fine by him, because she smells pretty good. In a freshly showered whore sort of way. And if he could ever imagine getting hard for a woman, this would undoubtedly be the one.

'I must say, your scent is particularly... *appealing* today, Susan.'

'*Fuck you*, Victor.'

'Okay... I'm only playing with you, in a manner of speaking.'

The governor rolls her eyes.

They are on the third level of Parking Lot A, at the north terminal of Austin-Bergstrom International airport. In a corner of the level she knows is blind-spotted from security cameras. Because it's a location she's used before. *More than once, as it happens*. And, right now, her recently-engaged executive driver is standing outside the limo. Hips resting against the hood. Eyes front. Arms folded.

‘In all seriousness, Susan... I need to ask you the sort of question I assume we’d both prefer went unheard.’

‘Okay... now we’ve both finished waving our dicks. I’m happy to hear your question.’

Victor smiles to himself.

‘Do we have any latitude for delay?’

Texas’s notoriously tough-talking governor turns to face him for the first time since he’d shoe-horned himself aboard.

‘You’ve got to be kidding me.’

‘Try not to soil your underwear. I’m not asking because it’s absolutely necessary. I’m simply asking because it may be prudent.’

‘Well, either way, the answer is *no* ... we do not have latitude.’

‘Okay... that’s fine.’

‘So why couldn’t you ask me this yesterday? I flew in early, at your specific request. And... apart from a thirty-second cameo behind the glass, you no-showed. I had VIP guests, Mr. Labette... and they had expectations. It wasn’t fifteen-thousand dollars a head for an evening at Caesars Palace. It was an execution for crying out loud. Pure evil paying the ultimate price... Justice striking with vengeance...’

She raises her hand. Snaps her fingers for effect.

‘It was supposed to be dramatic. Something memorable. A bucket-list occasion... I expected someone with a modicum of gravitas to provide an impressive build-up to the main event. Up front and personal. With a sordid back-story they couldn’t get from press clippings... And what did I get? A ten-minute, dull-as-dirt glad-hand with Director fucking Ray. I had people I needed to impress... They wanted gruesome... they got Grey’s Anatomy.’

‘I know... but, as I tried to explain. You’re campaign team is not watertight. As a result, I had to entertain an unwanted visitor. Which meant, I had to make adjustments.'

'If what you say is true. Will plugging any leak, I may or may not have, help you fix the problem?'

'As of right now... possibly not. However, you need to appreciate it's not a good time for either of us to tolerate, how shall I put it... *indiscipline.*'

She spends a moment chewing the inside of her lip.

'I guess I have no choice but to grant you that.'

'Look, Susan... we both know the stakes here. I know your fund-raising is dependent on keeping your fossil fuel brethren kneeling in your church. I'm also aware our troublesome energy commissioner continues to lobby smarter than your supporters. But, in my humble opinion, that has more to do with them being dinosaurs than him being an asteroid.'

'*Oh...* very droll, Victor.'

'Quite so... but I had to ask. Now I have my answer, I'll proceed as scheduled.'

'Please do exactly that... if it's not too much to ask.'

He cracks the rear passenger door.

'Indeed not, Susan... indeed not.'

'As you probably know... right now, I'm behind close to double digits in the polls. Even the most optimistic margin of error is nowhere near enough to cover my rear end.'

'I know,' Victor says. 'I have access to your polling data before you do.'

Susan Brandt doesn't react—*not even a little*. Even so, he can just make out a faint sheen of perspiration breaking out above her lip.

'However... I still have capital in this town. And enough Senate votes to get this thing across the line. So... what I need right now, is for the Commissioner to be re-purposed. Permanently and with immediate effect... as per the plan. And, to be entirely candid, I think I've indulged your fondness for complexities about as far as I'm prepared to...'

She turns away. Resumes staring through the windshield.

'I need this thing over with.'

'Well, of course you do, Susan.'

'Don't smart-mouth me, Mr. Labette.'

'I wouldn't dream of it,' he says, half-grinning.

She gives him her version of a—*just remember who you're dealing with*—side-eye. Unconsciously raising her chin. Only a fraction—*but it was there*. The subliminal petulance of the monied elite, ill-prepared to cope when things weren't going their way. So, despite all her outward bravado, Victor knows she's more than a little rattled. Knows she's battling hard against her inevitable decline. And knows she's fully aware her demise is likely terminal.

'*Oh*... and one more thing.'

'Yes, Susan.'

'It's *Governor* to you, Mr. Labette... So let me assure you... we won't be meeting again.'

'As you wish, *Governor*... as you wish.'

ALBUQUERQUE, NEW MEXICO

Elizabeth Holt was true to her word. No-one had asked to check his ID. Right now, they're alone in the Superintendent's office. Central Precinct. At her request, not his.

She's seated on a low-backed swivel chair, staring out over Civic Plaza, the tips of her boots not quite reaching the carpet tiles. He's settled on the edge of a long, rectangular conference table, criss-crossed with a bunch of cables and a parade of landline phones that have the look of a job-lot purchased from a garage sale back in the eighties.

After a moment of silence, she turns away from the window. Eyes focussed. Voice laced with steely determination.

'So what gives, Colonel?'

They'd just finished viewing the two-dozen plus digital stills retrieved from the victim's camera. Seven of them, gathered together around a table in an interview cell. Everyone arriving within a couple hours of her making her calls, like drones to their queen. A lean, bespectacled ATF veteran up from El Paso; who looked like he ran desert marathons for kicks. A stern-faced local FBI field agent, with a passion for busting sex trafficking gangs; all business in her ubiquitous black trouser suit and loose-fitting blouse. A silver-haired city coroner; every bit as sharp as the judge herself. A sheepish-looking Jedidiah Cummins, Vaughn County's recently appointed sheriff; on the off-chance the perp turned out to be local. And APD's chief of forensics; Elizabeth Holt's carbon copy, but for the fact—*despite his outward appearance*—he was more than likely twenty years her junior.

Beth had quickly sold them all on their perp being from out-of-state. That a female victim this young was unlikely to have travelled alone. That it was equally implausible she'd been abandoned. Or brought to *Yeso* to be murdered. Given the fact she'd taken a whole bunch of professionally-framed photos of the abandoned fuel station, back-lit by the rising dawn. Not to mention shots of an unmarked Huey dropping off the individual who'd gone on to blow a hole through her spine. Then there was her shiny SUV ride, replete with its high-end off-road options, which turned out to be registered to someone else. And a driver's license, recovered from the pocket, hand-sewn into her jacket.

They'd finished off debating when to make a call to the kid's family. Finally agreeing to keep the lid on tight, until the picture was a little clearer on how and why she'd ended up out there on her own. And, improbable as it seemed, whether she'd had any connection with the perp. So, for the time being at least, there would be no interviews. No statements. No press releases. And, if news of the incident should happen to leak out, any questions would be met with a flat—*no comment.*

She turns, fixing him with a penetrating gaze.

Right there and then, there was no escaping the focus in her eyes. Zalizo suspects a polygraph would come a poor second best.

So he opts to set his filters at a little over fifty percent.

'I saw a bald, bearded white male. Indeterminate height and age. Though my guess would be somewhere short of six-foot. Maybe twenty-five to thirty. Lean. Angular. Cold and ruthless. So... pretty much the same things you saw, I'm guessing.'

'Really, Colonel? Because that's pretty darn specific... considering there's little in the way of markers.'

'Happens I have other reference points.'

'By which you mean... you've seen him someplace before.'

'I believe so, yes. Wearing somewhat different attire and with a totally different appearance, for sure. But I'm convinced they're one and the same individual.'

'Am I permitted to know where and when?'

He hesitates. Chooses not to answer.

'Recently...?' she pushes.

'Yes.'

'A person of prior interest?'

'Very much so.'

'To whom?... Department of Defense?... Langley?'

He says, 'It's complicated.'

'You mean... classified?'

'Strictly speaking... No.'

She says, 'Very well... what else?'

'I've seen the bird too.'

'Also recently?'

'Yes.'

'In spite of the fact it had no markings?'

He finds himself thinking—*boy you're a sharp one.*

'There were features that make it uniquely identifiable... and I'm no fan of coincidences.'

Elizabeth Holt makes a clucking noise with her throat.

'And is this a situation that's going to continue playing out anywhere near my county?'

He says, 'I suspect not.'

'Can you give that to me in quantitative terms?'

He says, 'Ninety-nine percent.'

'Okay, since we're talking percentages... what's the likelihood he's the shooter?'

'Given he had his arm in an unnatural position behind his back, I'd say better than ninety-nine point nine.'

'Do you suspect any other parties were involved... *post mortem*, or otherwise?'

'Indirectly, there's no question. Although... at this particular crime scene, other than the pilots, almost certainly not.'

She makes a clucking noise with her throat.

'Okay, Colonel... since you seem determined to hold out on me. Give me one good reason why I shouldn't throw you under the bus... and let things take their course.'

'Because, you make that call, there's a good chance some very bad people, in very high places, get to walk away with their hands clean. And because there's more in play here than I'm authorized to let you know.'

She turns to resume looking out the window.

'Okay... let's say I'm prepared to take that on faith. It still doesn't account for everything I've observed since I flagged you down this morning. And, while I may not be far from my grave young man, as I've already demonstrated... my faculties are in fine fettle. Plus, I'm sensing there's something personal in this for you. And don't bother coming back with '*...it was you who flagged me down*'.'

'You said you had a question, Beth.'

He watches her shoulders reset. Only a fraction—*but enough if you were paying attention.*

'What are your intentions, Colonel... from here on in, so to speak?'

'Seek... and destroy.'

'And would that be in an official, or unofficial capacity?'

'That's a whole other question, Elizabeth. And... like I said, it's complicated.'

'Even if I were buying that... I still figure you owe me at least one *quid pro quo*.'

He moves over to the window. Seats himself on the low sill. Offers her his least hostile face.

'Sorry, Beth... you're just going to have to trust me. Because, right now, my read is... certain things are better left unsaid.'

She makes a clucking noise with her throat.

'As a matter of interest... how old are you now?'

'I was born in eighty-one,' he says.

She tilts her head. 'So, thirty-eight?'

'That's what the math says.'

'And what year did your parents... pass away?'

'Where's this going, Beth?'

'It's going back to an incident in... let me think. Sometime around September of ninety-seven. Involving a number of highly questionable Russian immigrants... who turned out to be Ukrainians. Who somehow met an unfortunate... strike that. Grizzly end. In a meth lab... south of Farmington.'

'Like I said, Beth... where's this going?'

'I was wondering how old you would have been back then. Sixteen, going on seventeen... sound about right?'

He says, 'Close enough.'

'You'd moved to Texas with your parents by then... correct?'

'Sounds about right.'

'I don't suppose you would know if it was an expensive move?'

'That would also be accurate.'

'Still... a post-grad education at Texas Tech. We're not exactly talking five-and-dime.'

'I don't recall the specifics.'

'No... but you could hazard a guess.'

'Then, I guess not.'

'And... if I remember correctly, your mother was a pharmacist.'

'She was a scientist before they emigrated. A molecular chemist.'

'And your father... a cab driver, yes?'

'Yeah... for a time, at least.'

'So not what anyone would call... well healed.'

'Not compared to Jeff Bezos, or the Koch brothers. But they did alright. By any metric... we certainly weren't poor.'

'Yes. And as I recall... there were a number of Russian, or rather Ukrainian, cabbies in this town back then. Though, strangely, none after ninety-seven. But maybe, just like with your family, that could be down to the vagaries of shifting demographics.'

He could have sworn she was feigning whimsey.

'Could be,' he says.

She rises suddenly.

'Well, that's all in the past...'

As she walks briskly to the door, she drops her head, like she's seen something of particular interest at her feet.

'So here are my final questions, Colonel.'

He says, 'Fire away.'

'What are the chances you'll find this creature and put him in the ground?'

'In percentage terms?'

'At this precise moment... percentage terms will do just fine.'

'As close to one hundred as makes no difference.'

'And, what are the future risks for the general populous?'

He says, 'That's a little more difficult to quantify.'

She turns suddenly, her face pinched. Her expression straddling a line between troubled and malevolent.

'Young man, that's a very long way from being a response I'm prepared to accept. In fact, it's something I would expect our visitor out there in the scrublands to say. So, not only is it callously flippant... it's totally crass. No-one, with any degree of moral integrity, should set out to do anything dangerous, or controversial, and not consider the harm they may cause others along the way. The proposition is as axiomatic as it is self-defeating...'

He feels the intensity of her rebuke like a hard kick to his groin.

'Nor should they live out their life simply seeking authorization. Cost benefit does not cover what may happen from here on in, Oleg Constantine Zalizo. This is not Farmington.'

Inside, the shock of hearing someone other than his mother speaking his given names stings like acid. The direct association with Farmington—*a whole different crap-pile.*

'I guess not,' he says.

'So, allow me to be direct... just so we're clear. In the past, was the collateral damage you speak of so casually limited to military personnel?'

'I'd settle for... government-trained.'

'Entirely...?'

He doesn't answer.

'What about wives, or girlfriends? Siblings. Dependents. And how about our burgeoning weekend-warrior class... running around out there in our sparsely populated states? Persuaded they're the righteous defenders of their pseudo-marginalized, mono-cultural faith. Are they not increasingly likely to be designated as combatants?'

'That's not for me to determine.'

'Maybe so... but did you ever consider it?'

'Not as far as I recall... No.'

'And why might that be?'

'People are free to make their life choices, I guess... mixed with a little cognitive dissonance on my part. Besides, generally speaking, I take a position... I stick to it.'

She pulls an expression that seems to say—*is that really the best you can do?*

'Well... I put it to you, it's a short hop from ambivalence to callous indifference.'

She folds her arms.

'So, *Lieutenant*-Colonel... you have a decision to make. Here and now. No equivocation. No more... *complexities*. No more... *ambiguities*. Are you prepared for that?'

He says, 'I'm listening.'

'All of us are weak by degrees, Leg Zalizo. You... Me... *Everyone*. And all consciously inflicted cruelty is predicated on weakness... mental or moral. To debate which holds supremacy, or prevalence, is little more than semantics. And as hard as it may be for someone like you to stomach... those who follow do not share the same culpability as those who lead. And those who just happen to be in the way have no culpability at all. For damn sure, they should never be sacrificed in the name of expediency... *Never.*'

'Do I get a moment to decide?'

'No, Colonel... you do not. I should think it's a simple enough proposition to buy into. Maybe you get caught in the middle of a fire-fight, you get to set aside societal norms... like whether you have the right to be so goddam ruthless. But that's nothing like the situation I'm seeing here. So no, you don't get... *a moment to decide*. Because you shouldn't need one. You're an intelligent man. Besides, I would have thought you had ample time to decide if innocence, and the innocent, deserve protection, while you were out there, holding that poor child in your arms. And... before you give me your answer, you better believe I'll know the truth when I hear it. Especially from you.'

He meets her eyes, square on.

'So, I agree...'

'Good for you,' she says.

'But only to the extent it doesn't fatally compromise my oath to protect the constitution.'

She pauses for a moment.

'It's *uphold*, Colonel... but that, I can tolerate.'

She turns to open the door.

'Come, young man... we need to find you a new badge. Then I'll let you strike out while the iron still holds some heat... so to speak.'

He makes it to Albuquerque Police Department's rear exit. Moments ahead of two uniforms. Both heading in as he's heading out. Escorting a red-faced long-beard, huffing and shifting his weight against a double-team arm-lock.

He holds back for the incoming trio. Tipping his head to Elizabeth Holt as he stands aside.

The ample-sized threesome side-shuffle through the double swing doors. The uniforms visibly relaxing the moment they make it across the threshold.

Long-beard does the exact opposite.

Zalizo sees it in the way his shoulders square up an inch or two. It's subtle. But it telegraphs his intentions nonetheless—*if you were watching*.

The guy gives it ten, or so, strides before making his move. Yanking his arms down hard. Pirouetting through one-eighty degrees. Using his steel-capped lugger boots to kick the legs from under one uniformed dough-boy. Ramming his knee into the midriff of the other.

All-and-all, a pretty neat move for a barrel of lard.

Long-beard pivots for the exit. Driven by substance-induced bravado, or latent training, was anyone's guess.

Zalizo decides to reserve judgement. Knows it will take a matter of seconds to get a definitive answer. Because, in his experience, it rarely takes grown men—*especially those with any level of training*—very long to agree a result.

One way or another.

He moves to the centre of the lobby. Blocking Long-beard's line-of-sight to the doors.

In the proper sense of the term, the man now charging toward him is large. Six-five if he's an inch. Broad as a grain silo. Two-eighty pounds if he's an ounce.

He slows a fraction. Eyeing Zalizo without concern.

Squinting and grinning. Squaring up as best he can, given his momentum—*mistake number one*. Like a lot of guys impressed by their own bulk, more than likely figuring the opposition is no physical match. Battleship versus light cruiser—*mistake number two.*

Through all the huffing and puffing, this lump has either missed or dismissed all the critical details on display. His opponent's total lack of concern. Speed and agility *versus* unfocussed bulk. Conditioning over volume—*mistakes three to five*. Because Zalizo possesses all of these attributes in spades. Added to which, beyond arms reach, he'd spent close on three decades disguising his explosive physicality. His unrelenting ferocity. And, generally speaking, that has always suited his purposes just fine.

Long-beard aims his best two-handed round-arm where Zalizo allows his face to dwell unconcerned. Whereupon, a meaty pair of fists arc through thin air. And, throughout the entirety of his swing, a broad, toothless grin never leaves the guy's face.

Zalizo had stalled his retreat in the same manner he'd begun it. *Imperceptibly*. Dropping into a low crouch in one seamless movement. Laterally balanced. Left foot and left palm planted. Sending the heel of his right foot through Long-beard's right knee. Pitching him forward, like he'd run up against a low wall. Cartilage, tendons and ligaments, all surrendering to a sledge-hammer impact. And the reason larger, stronger than average athletes routinely suffer career-ending lower joint injuries. All that weight, with only a couple of pounds of soft tissue and gristle holding everything together.

Long-beard lets out a high-pitched yelp.

Zalizo pushes off the deck. Rising, hard and fast, directly in line with Long-beard's unintended forward pitch. Exposed sternum versus rock-hard shoulder. More than enough kinetics to buck the big guy backwards like he'd hit a tree. His shattered knee whiplashing forward as his head snaps in the opposite direction.

He falls like a sack of corn. Shackled hands rising to his throat. Trying to scream, but failing. Managing only strangled grunting, as he lies there, gulping for air. His face turning through crimson, on its way to purple.

The second phase of contact has brought with it an unintended mis-match between forehead and windpipe. If Long-beard's colour palette makes it all the way to blue, Zalizo knows he'll likely have to lend a hand. Maybe punch a hole below the larynx. Feed in a length of tube. Or the tapered end of a ball-point would do at a push. Not everywhere carried paramedic kits with surgical instruments in their inventory.

He looks over to where Elizabeth Holt has stalled on the stairwell. Considers the promise he'd made only moments ago. So he kneels to check the man's breathing and pulse. Decides he'll live and function, given a decent period of hospital rest.

Meanwhile, the two uniformed dough-boys have made it back to their feet. Grimacing and rubbing their bruises. Hefting their utility belts back above their shapeless hips.

Zalizo shrugs. Shoots them a quizzical—*the fuck, guys*—stare.

Dough-boy *One* focuses in on Zalizo's newly acquired US marshal's badge. Dough-boy *Two* kneels, rolling Long-beard onto his side. Uncuffing and re-cuffing his wrists. This time behind his back.

Zalizo says, 'Better late than never.'

Dough-boy *One* is breathing hard.

'*Oh*... yuh'think?'

'As a general rule,' Zalizo says. 'You, on the other hand... I'm guessing not so much.'

'Yeah, well. Marshal or no... I don't recognize you. So you'll be leaving a name.'

'Only if I thought you could spell it.'

'Yuh'think you can just haul out? You may have done some serious damage here.'

'Caused...' Zalizo says.

'Pardon me...?'

'I may have...*caused*...some serious damage.'

'So... yuh'think you're some kind of smart-ass?'

'There's a long, hard trail between thinking and knowing, fellas. And I'm a lot farther down that track than you appear to be.'

He turns, pushing through the doors.

'Your man starts turning blue... be sure to look up tracheostomy in your training manual.'

The last glimpse he gets of Elizabeth Holt, she's in the process of turning away. Slowly shaking her head.

CLOVIS, NEW MEXICO

Anne-Marie hadn't called. And she'd promised him she would.

He'd started out thinking he'd gotten lucky. Mostly because they'd let him into the base's visitor centre early. But straight away he'd been informed, he couldn't have picked a worse day to pay them a visit. Nothing more than one or two Northrop T38 slots around mid-morning. Then *zip* scheduled, in or out of the airbase, for the rest of the day.

Either way, it hadn't mattered any. Because Anne-Marie hadn't checked in.

And worse, by mid-morning she still hadn't answered any of his calls. Each one going straight to voicemail. Which meant her cell had been switched off. And he'd known, right there and then, the girl he'd fallen for was in deep trouble. Because turning off her cell phone was something she would never have done voluntarily.

For hours now, it's been eating him up inside that he hadn't stayed with her. Even more that he hadn't called the cops when his gut had demanded, over and over, he should.

Now he is sat in a stuffy room, empty but for a couple of bolted-down metal chairs and matching steel table, somewhere in the bowels of Clovis Police Department headquarters. His knees bouncing up and down. His sweaty hands trembling. Unable to get her face—*smiling back at him*—out from behind his eyes. Not knowing what the hell was going on.

Because no one was telling him squat.

And, as if things weren't bad enough, he doesn't know how his father is going to react. He hasn't been on the receiving end of a hard beating since he'd pushed past six-foot; close on four merciful years ago. But he has a strong feeling, all that was about to change. Mostly because the folk in his congregation were a close knit bunch. And because the Hollenbecks were especially well regarded. Mrs. Hollenbeck in particular.

Anne-Marie, even more so.

He screws his eyes shut. Rubbing them until his sockets begin to ache. Over and over, four simple words keep hammering inside his head.

'What have I done...?'

MARKS CENTRE, WASHINGTON DC

'I take it you want to help the Lieutenant-Colonel?'

Runellie has woken at her desk. The inside of her head pounding across her temple, somewhere deep behind her eyes. She looks from the clock on the wall to the figure stood before her. The one with a narrow bar, adorned with three small gold stars, fixed to the collar of his plain white shirt.

She says, 'I guess so... depending on who you are exactly.'

The figure says, 'You can address me as, General.'

'Okay, so yes... *General.*'

For someone pushing an O-9 pay-grade, the man standing beside her is pretty unremarkable. Neither big nor small. Spikey salt-and-pepper hair, cropped tight above his ears and cut square over the rest of his head. Narrow eyes, a boxer's nose and a knot of old scar tissue above his left eyebrow, suggesting he'd likely been a southpaw sometime back in the day. He's dressed in civilian clothing. Dark grey, loose-fitting suit. Thin tie. Tight collar squeezing the slack skin around his neck. West Point ring resting against the pinkie-knuckle of his left hand.

'So... go get your coat, *Sergeant*. I take it you're trained to walk and talk at the same time?'

'I give it my best shot most days, General.'

'And how long has it been since you last caught some shut-eye?'

Runellie shrugs.

'Discounting the last ten minutes. Around sixty hours... give or take.'

'Okay... so belay that last order. Go home. Get some rest. And I recommend you get some carbs in your belly.'

'Yes, sir... *General.*'

As he turns to leave, he says, 'I'll come get you in four hours.'

She says, 'But, sir... I live...'

'Don't worry, Sergeant,' the general says. 'I know where you live.'

THE NAVAJO NATION
STANDING ROCK, NEW MEXICO

Zalizo makes it to Standing Rock by 6.30 PM *Mountain Standard Time*, a good haul west of Crownpoint, along Service Route 9. A steady wind blowing across the Navajo Nation, lifting fine motes of dirt ankle-high above the deck. Nothing but dry lake beds and bare, eroded bluffs as far as the eye can see. Remnants of an ancient prehistoric oceanic floor, raised to a high plateau by countless millennia of subduction a thousand miles to the west.

Right now, he's crouching at the edge of a dried out water hole, watching a dust cloud burst over a shallow crest, no more than two clicks out.

Moments later a black Camaro, with a large scorpion motif on its roof—*emblazoned in blood red*—swings in next to his GMC. Wallowing on its suspension as it slews to a stop.

The man behind the wheel is bare chested. Blowing smoke from his cheroot through the driver-side window. For a moment, he seems focused on the glowing tip. Twisting it this way and that. Drawing deeply.

Rinse and repeat.

After a full two minutes, the muscle car's occupant cracks the door open.

The figure that emerges is an inch or two taller than Zalizo's height, and at least thirty pounds heavier. Standing barefoot. Dark-eyed. Quasi-focused. Loose-limbed. Muscled without being muscular. In the manner of someone with beaucoup reserves of stamina. Above all, Leg remembers him as the meanest fighter any man could wish to encounter. Utterly fearless. And likely still was. So, if they were going to bang heads, he knew from memory, it would likely be a bruising affair.

He flicks his smoke into the air as he moves forward, casually rolling his shoulders.

'You're standing on Navajo land... *bilagáana*.'

Zalizo chooses not to rise. If they were going to lock horns, low-to-high is his favoured ploy.

'I may well be.'

'And, if I recall,' the big Indian says. 'The last time we breathed the same wind, you did not offer gratitude for services rendered.'

'Whereas,' Zalizo says, 'I recall, minimal services were required.'

'That may well be... *ak'is*. But, had they been required... they were available.'

'Then I'll gladly offer my thanks when they're used.'

'Umm... So I guess things can remain good between us. Though I'm guessing you're still wasting your life taking Uncle Sam's greenbacks?'

'That I am,' Zalizo says. 'And I take it, you're still wasting yours breeding those stumpy mules no-one wants to buy.'

'Could be... white boy. Either way, it's been a long time since you walked with my people.'

'Indeed, it has,' Zalizo says.

'Still... the Navajo remember you well enough.'

'Well enough that I'm still welcome on your land?'

The big Indian scans the landscape in a slow one-eighty.

'You dared to walk barefoot with us once before, man of iron.'

'That, I did,' Zalizo says.

'So take off those Yankee boots... and hand over your weapon. We will see how it goes with us.'

Zalizo rises. Unholsters his gun. Places it in the big Indian's outstretched hand.

'A question for you, Seigo.'

'Ask what you wish.'

'Did you ever speak native shit like this when you ran with Task Force Green? You know... just to freak the humpers out.'

Seigo lets out a belly laugh loud enough to raise more dust.

'You gotta be fuckin' kiddin' me... Jarhead.'

Zalizo says, 'Yeah... pretty much as I thought.'

WASHINGTON DC

They are standing halfway down a slipway. On the western shore of the Georgetown Reservoir. As far away from people and vehicles as it's possible to get. Enough of a wind blowing to keep a set of shin-high waves breaking against the gravel shoreline. The only sounds disturbing the silence coming from a melee of gulls, patrolling raucously overhead. And the low hum of distant traffic from across the Potomac.

'So, Sergeant... I need to know what you aren't telling me.'

'With respect, *sir*... this is not the place.'

'And why might that be?'

'I don't like wide open spaces, is all. In my experience... they're rarely as private as they appear. Especially where directional mics are concerned.'

'And I have a deep mistrust of information converted to zeros and ones, Sergeant... and, trust me, there are sufficient precautions in place to prevent us being overheard.'

Runellie sticks out her chin. It's an unconscious thing she's had since forever, and something she wishes she could control, well aware it pegs her as petulant.

'I still haven't spoken to the Colonel.'

'Well, *Sergeant*... I have.'

'Am I permitted to ask what he said?'

'Let's just say... I offered him the same two options I've just offered you, and he chose the one I would not have recommended.'

'Then you already know my position.'

'Fortunately for you, Sergeant Rundell... the Lieutenant-Colonel and I both advocate strongly against you taking that path. And you should also know... I'm not extending the same latitude to you as your commander enjoys.'

'I fully appreciate that, General. But... here and now, you're expecting me to just accept your word.'

'I'd be extremely disappointed if you choose not to.'

'Again... with respect, *sir*. Feel free to be disappointed.'

The General stiffens. Takes a stride towards the lake, shaking his head. Visibly bristling.

'Tell me, Sergeant... is this only a matter of trust?'

'Yes, *sir*... you could say that. I mean, I understand you may not like it but, right now, you're a guy in a suit and overcoat who just happened to turn up after I made my call. You've offered no ID... No formal introduction... No order papers... Nothing. And, while it may turn out the stars on your collar trump the stripes on my arm, until I speak with the Colonel... No matter what trouble it brings. I'm gonna need something more than... *'you can call me, General'*.'

The General continues to stare out over the choppy water.

'Okay, Sergeant... let me ask you a question.'

'Sir...?'

'Did the Lieutenant-Colonel trust you with his validation code?'

'Yes, *sir*... he did.'

The General looks back over his shoulder. He seems a little surprised—*but it's difficult to tell.*

'And he explained what it means when it's offered by a third party.'

'Yes... *sir.*'

'And?'

'He said... I could trust that party beyond the beachhead.'

'Does the word we're not speaking have anything to do with a certain order of arachnids... with a curly thorax?'

'Yes, *sir*... it does.'

'So, are you going to make me speak that word, given your stated mistrust of open spaces... or are we going to talk?'

At that moment, Runellie knows she's backed up hard against a wall. It's obvious the General could have spoken the word if he'd chosen to. She also knows the individual, standing one stride ahead, has no obligation to show the degree of patience he already had.

She'd started out as nothing more than an 82nd Airborne sharp-shooter, turned Recon Sergeant. And, despite what she'd led the General to believe, she'd run her checks and made inquiries. Had it confirmed she was facing a genuine three deuce hand; albeit he was flagging as retired.

So, time to stop screwing around.

'I could bore you with the long version, General. But I'm guessing you're not that guy.'

'Very shrewd, Sergeant.'

'The semi-short version then...'

Runellie softens her posture, dropping her chin.

'Two years ago... when the Colonel made it back from his little stint down in Texas. He tasked me to find out as much as I could about who was footing the bill for the lawyer engaged to defend the federal building shooter. The Colonel was a little concerned that the suit appeared to be far from your typical overworked public defender. Turned out his suspicions were bang on the mark... and it seemed inconceivable a Louisiana swamp-rat could engage the services of what turned out to be some fancy five-hundred-dollar-an-hour Austin-based corporate attorney.'

'And...?'

'Well, it's taken what seems like forever, but we've uncovered links between said attorney and a private security outfit running a black-on-black ultra-max detention facility, hiding north of the Guadeloupe Mountains. Back-channel sanctioned. Next, we find that the initial outlay for this private sector outfit was linked directly to Texas oil money. Then Governor Brandt's and Senator Hellermann's names get fingered for pushing the Pentagon to engage Lexstone Security Corporation. A previously little-known contractor headquartered in Alexandria. Then we discover two off-shore big-money hitters are spending hard and fast. Lobbying here in DC and covering a truckload of legal battles on behalf of Lexstone, tying up the Renewable Energy Commission in protracted litigation in the process. Stalling a giant wind-farm development on the high ground, north of a pin in the map called Dell City, New Mexico. Which happens to neighbour our ultra-max at Coal Island. In isolation, nothing unusual... but for the fact things quickly turn into a concerted disinformation campaign against all forms of renewables. Both in New Mexico and all across Texas. The money being spent is staggering. Running into the tens of millions. It's a war fund, General... with physical attacks being reported, against every kind of clean-energy installation out there... But the battle is being lost.'

'Enlighten me.'

'The Energy Commission is led by a well-connected eco-poster boy, Sommerhays Holberton...'

'Sommerhays is a first name?'

'Apparently so. Anyway... this guy is smart. Not to mention federally-appointed. He also has considerable personal wealth. Old money. Heir to the Holberton Investment Holdings empire. Huge tech-stock portfolio. Incorruptible, supposedly, and heavily into sustainable energy... no matter the sector. Unsurprisingly, he's also highly tech savvy. Smiley-media groomed. A social media dilettante, currently making carbon a dirty word in the Lone Star State of all places. He's pushing hard for off-shore and on-shore wind farms. Lobbying for a huge carbon capture program... and a Clean Water Bill he's selling to Congress, not to mention the wider agri-lobby, that he claims will cost them nothing. Because he has a plan to...'

'I'm sure the details are fascinating, Sergeant...'

'Yes... *sir.*'

'And...?'

'So, like I said... starting three years ago, there's a spate of attacks on renewable energy facilities all across the region. Solar... wind... and a battery plant under construction outside Dallas. Military style operations. Eco-terrorism in reverse, it seems. State Police ask Dallas PD Organized Crime for a little muscle. A Dallas PD captain, who'd served with the Colonel in JSOC, called in a favour, because of the suspected para-military footprint. Then the Colonel had the idea of leaking a report to the media, suggesting the battery plant had only suffered superficial damage. And sure enough, there was a repeat attack on the same facility. Only this time the Colonel was waiting... and I'm guessing, you can pretty much work out the rest.'

The General continues to stare out across the lake.

'Okay... let's go back a chapter, shall we.'

'Back... *sir?*'

'Yes, Sergeant... to the grain missing from this particular silo. The part you glossed over a little too quickly.'

'Sir...?'

'Whatever your loyalties, Sergeant... right now it's the Government who's paying your salary. That means you are not permitted to work for me and hold out on me at the same time.'

Runellie feels herself being skewered. The steel in the General's voice every bit as cold as the lake—*and slicing just as deep.*

'Yes... *General.*'

'So... enlighten me further.'

She takes a breath.

'The mercs the colonel bagged were never identified. Sterile, pretty much. No IDs... No print records... Nothing Homeland could link to entry visas. But they were presumed to be foreign nationals. Something about their dental work. And an item of jewellery. Whatever... they went down fighting. And, right now... they're still on ice in Dallas.'

'Interesting,' the general says.

He thrusts his hands deep into the pockets of his overcoat.

'Okay... go on.'

'So we now move up to close on six months ago. The perp who gunned down the Colonel's lady gets transferred from Huntsville to Coal Island... our private sector ultra-max facility. By order direct from Governor Brandt.'

'I don't suppose the Colonel ever considered simply asking the governor's office for an explanation.'

'He felt if he was going to get an answer, the transfer would have made the evening news. Besides... nothing about the prisoner transfer made sense to the Colonel. He said the optics just didn't play right.'

'*Ah,* yes... that would certainly present the Colonel with an insurmountable problem. Although I have to agree. Especially considering this ultra-max of yours appears to lie over a state line. In my experience, Texans are none too keen relinquishing jurisdiction at the best of times.'

'That's more or less what the Colonel said. And now... on top of everything, we've uncovered a DoD-slash-State connection with these three shootings here in DC. And, like I told you, NSA have offered up a pretty solid list of foreign talent for these kinds of hits. Which I've narrowed down from potentials to probables. A South African... A Filipino... An Israeli... and a Ukrainian. All currently off grid... All being actively sought by their own governments... All with a last known location here in the US. Mossad came close to bagging their man three months ago. Word is they dead-ended in Cuba when, for one reason or another, they had to bug out of Havana in a hurry. Even so... all four are now confirmed to have entered the US through Florida.'

'And, they're all known to have gone corporate?'

'According to current intel... yes.'

'Confirmed by whom?'

'CIA stations in Tel Aviv, Kiev, Manila and Pretoria. And you agreed with my evaluation that operators with their capability and reputation... not to mention their own government's current status assessments, are more often than not employed in a political theatre. Or, I'm guessing, we wouldn't be here.'

The General seems content to let the mild insubordination slide.

He turns, his expression a little less abrasive. Somewhere behind his eyes, a question of mutual trust appears to have been resolved.

'Do we have mug shots?'

'We do now.'

'Does the Colonel have them?'

'I sent them through to Albuquerque, like he asked.'

'*Albuquerque*... He's back in Albuquerque?'

'That's what I heard. Though I wasn't aware he'd ever been there before.'

'Believe me, Sergeant... the Lieutenant-Colonel has most definitely been to Albuquerque before.'

'Sorry, General... I don't know what you mean by that.'

'I fear it means, he's not just planning an isolated skirmish...'

The General turns abruptly. Begins heading back to his 90's-era Plymouth sedan.

It takes Runellie a few strides to catch up.

'In fact... I strongly suspect he's intending to recruit for an all-out war.'

STANDING ROCK, NEW MEXICO

'Where'd you get your shiny badge, Leg?'

Zalizo creases a hint of a smile.

'Off a little old crow, who thought I needed a better match for my ride than the Hale County Deputy badge I started out with.'

'So who's this... little old crow?'

'A retired Tenth Circuit judge.'

'So... the badge is legit?'

'Yes, it is.'

'And the marshal's pony?'

'Borrowed... like the badge.'

'I get the feeling you're holding out on me again, *ak'is*... so what, exactly, is the play here?'

'First... I need to ask you something.'

Seigo says, 'Fire away.'

'Do you recall if any of your boys were ever questioned after Farmington?'

The big Indian stares off into the distance.

'You were sixteen, Leg. After you burned those fuckers for what they did to your folks, you high-tailed it back to Texas. I was two years older and could handle myself well enough. Even so... I figured I needed to be some place where vengeful types would struggle to find me. So I ran to the nearest Army recruitment centre. Let's face it... neither of us knew if they'd import some heavier heavies. *J-e-s-u-s,* man... that thing you did. I ain't kiddin' you. Even now... if I stood still long enough, I swear, I'd still hear those screams today.'

Zalizo slows to a stop. Looks down at his bare feet, now properly caked with dust.

Seigo says, 'Why are you asking?'

'Because, the little old crow knew about my involvement... and I'm wondering how she managed to put the whole thing together. Maybe there's security footage out there somewhere. Strikes me it's a distinct possibility.'

'I dunno,' Seigo says. 'Sounds cuckoo to me? I mean... why the hell would anyone sit on shit like that? Especially a federal circuit judge. Makes no sense.'

'You could be right... but I'm inclined to take her at her word. Let's face it, paranoia among drug gangs is nothing unusual. They're naturally incentivised to keep a close eye on anything or anyone who comes into contact with their product. And we know that particular crew made damn sure there were no middlemen operating in their territory. And, no matter how much I revered him, there's no getting away from the fact my old man was associated with them, giving them direct access to mom's highly specialised expertise. Which, no doubt, made for an even more lucrative operation. So it should come as no surprise they would have kept a twenty-four-seven eye on their investment.'

'*Yeah*... I guess so,' Seigo says. 'And not something either of us would have thought to check out at the time.'

'*Oh*... I thought about it. I just figured any camera set-up would likely get destroyed in the blaze.'

'You always were a few dimes smarter than the average pocket of change.'

'Apparently not,' Zalizo says.

They were most of the way back to the water hole. The sun behind them, low in the sky and sinking fast. They'd walked and talked and kicked the last embers of their active duty history from the firepit. What had happened south of Farmington was never going to be a subject for fond reminiscing. Most of the *Scorpions* had gone in for a look see before the gas burners were set under the gutted and fuel-doused tough guys, who moments before their entirely unforeseen re-education had thought themselves unassailable. Some of the tougher juvey gang members had come out shaking their heads. Most of the wannabes had puked and run away. Seigo had been the only volunteer to keep watch outside the warehouse until the fire got properly seated.

It had been a slaughterhouse.

Despite his tender age he'd decided—*one way or another*—he was going to make someone identify the individual who'd wielded the axe on his father—*after forcing him to watch his wife suffer unspeakable violations on their kitchen table until she bled out*. But it was only later he'd figured exactly what had freaked that pack of animals into submission. Why such heavy-boned men had shit themselves like babies. Pissed in their own mouths as they'd hung naked by their feet. It was because they'd known, despite his height and athletic physique, they were suffering at the hands of the kid they had allowed to survive. More boy than man; and likely the reason they'd spared him on that treacherous morning. Waiting until he'd set out for college before butchering his parents. Choosing not to come for him during the weeks that followed. Even so, he remembers sensing them watching. Waiting to see how he would react. So he'd waited to. Long enough for them to get bored. Satisfied it was safe to let him be.

Which had been their first mistake.

And their last.

'Okay, Leg. Let's get back to the top of the hill, shall we...'

They are within sight of their vehicles. And though the ground under their feet still held the last of the day's heat, the wind had turned chill. Up ahead, the Camaro's windshield bursts into flames as the sun dips into the line of high ridges of the Navajo Nation proper.

'What else is not being said here.'

Zalizo turns to his friend.

'I found a woman... Or, closer to the truth. She found me.'

Seigo tilts his head.

'I'm happy for you, Leg...'

'She was gunned down a couple years back.'

The big Indian stops dead.

'*J-e-s-u-s*, man... you gotta be cursed. I mean... what is it with you? You gonna lose everything you touch, for the whole of your goddam life? And why the fuck didn't you come get me?'

'I had to work things through, I guess. Plus, like you said, I'm still drawing a hefty government salary. I needed to carry on doing what I was paid to do.'

Seigo starts back walking.

'So... how deep were you in to her?'

'Deep as it gets. But I had this weird gig I needed to tie up. Though I'd already made up my mind. When I'd finished... I wasn't going back. Turns out there was a kid on the way... and Dallas PD would have been thrilled to keep me around.'

'J-e-s-u-s...'

Seigo whistles and shakes his head.

'And what about your chain of command?'

'That's a single tier arrangement,' Zalizo says.

Seigo shoots him a quizzical look.

'Well that's novel... but even so.'

'I figured my CO would have let me go. I'd given him a more than decent legacy team. Besides... turns out he likely also knows all about Farmington.'

'Is that a fact?' Seigo says.

'He only recently let it slip... but, thinking about it now, it's not too hard to figure out. Mom was a molecular chemist from Belarus. The old man was an ex-Spetsnaz hunk of steel from Ukraine. They both got out a good while before the wall came down. They had to have been tagged. I also suspect all our Farmington friends were ex-Ukrainian military. My guess is, they'd been tagged to. Now this thing with the judge.'

'Well I'll be damned...' Seigo says.

For a brief moment, the big Indian stares off into the distance.

'So what is it exactly you need from me, my friend. After Farmington... it's surely not funds.'

'No... I'm still squared away on that front.'

Seigo lands a meaty slap on Zalizo's shoulder.

'You and me both, *ánaaí*.'

After a ten-minute slow walk, they make it back to their vehicles.

Seigo levels Leg's forty-five, flicking the safety, shooting off three quick rounds—*one-handed*—at a hunk of rock fifty yards distant. Scores two hits and a graze, then holds the gun up level with his eyes. Twisting it back and forth. Dropping the mag and racking the slide a couple times. Checking the chamber was clear.

Old habits never forgotten.

He nods his approval.

'I can see why you hairy Raider types prefer longer pistols. What with you'all having small peckers an'all.'

'How come,' Zalizo says, 'All you *Teir-One,* Ray-Ban model types never learn. It ain't the length of the barrel... it's the size of the load. And... while we're speaking of *dicks*. I'm after deploying reliable forward observation.'

Seigo asks, 'When and where?'

'Plainview, Texas,' Zalizo says. 'A little ways north of Lubbock. You'd be going in ahead of me. Scoping for humpers. Maybe encourage whoever you flush out to re-evaluate their employment choices.'

Zalizo can almost hear his friend's mind mashing through its gears. Something he usually did in his own good time. Besides, he knows he's asking a lot. After all, off-reservation, someone Seigo's size had a tendency to stand out some.

The big Indian re-sights the gun. Chambers a round and fires off another couple shots—*two handed*. Scores two hits.

'This really is a nice piece. If I had money to waste at gun stores... I might just get me one.'

'For the time being,' Zalizo says. 'I don't purchase my hardware retail. Besides, it's a customised model. With higher-grade steel... and a twenty-round capacity. Though I rarely fire more than seven-round bursts. Which usually fools all but the very brightest I'm running single-stack.'

'Sneaky,' Seigo says. 'Meantime... exactly what level of encouragement are we talking?'

'The way I see it... whoever they send after me, bare minimum, they need persuading to choose a different line of work. One that can be done from a wheelchair. Or carrying a white stick. Or using sign language. I really don't give a rat's ass, Seigo. Whoever got themselves involved, they did so voluntarily. So they're going to have to pay.'

'So, same as it ever was.'

Zalizo says, 'You and I both know, you can't cross the river...'

'Without paying a fair price,' Seigo says.

He gives the pistol one last look before handing it back.

'Meantime... where are you going to be?'

Zalizo performs a press-check and holsters his gun. Then crouches and begins tying his laces.

'Looking for the owner of a Citation XLS. Unless plans change.'

'Plans always change, my friend.'

Seigo props his elbows on the roof of his Camaro.

'Speaking of which... you gonna tell me where you got that little smudge on your forehead?'

Zalizo rises. Begins heading over to his GMC.

'I ran into someone... back in Albuquerque.'

'And, how did that go?' Seigo says.

Zalizo says, 'Breathtaking.'

AUSTIN, TEXAS

They are out in the open. Because Nasi had insisted. On account of his unbreakable rules. No enclosed spaces. No bars, restaurants, or hotel lounges. Or anything of the kind. And, if they took issue with his level of caution, he would not be joining them—*simple as.* They'd been free to decide.

As it was, no-one had felt any need to raise objections.

So they'd agreed to meet at Wooldridge Square. A compact, undulating plot of grass and mid-height trees in the heart of downtown. An ornate public gazebo off-centred towards the intersection of West 9th and Guadalupe Street.

Victor seats himself on the gazebo's white-washed steps next to Nasi. The sound of traffic rising all around the park. Rush hour steadily building. Though pedestrian foot-fall is still relatively light in their isolated corner of Texas's capital city public real estate.

A few paces away, Miller is nursing his pride.

Meanwhile, Nasi sets to activating his audio jammer. An ultra-high frequency model. Available only to those with access to certain specialist, non-commercial markets. Compact and black. The size of a hardback novel. Eight-hour battery life. With an effective range out to better than one hundred yards.

The device sits in his backpack. Which rests against his knee.

Victor senses Nasi's disapproval that he'd been the only one who thought it necessary to take precautions.

'This *problem's* name... remind me again.'

If there's one thing Victor admires about the Israeli, it's his uncompromising directness. No preamble. No words wasted. Not an ounce of sycophancy. Always straight down to business.

'Lieutenant-Colonel Leg Zalizo. Leg being short for Oleg...

A Slavic derivative of an Old Norse word, Helgi... or Holy, so I've learnt. Zalizo, on the other hand, is Ukrainian for iron. So... intentionally, or not, the late Mr. and Mrs. Z christened their only progeny Holy Iron. A somewhat aspirational soubriquet for anyone to live up to... don't you think?'

'I have no opinion either way,' Nasi says. 'Where is he now?'

Miller takes a step forward.

'We don't know. But we have eyeballs on his last known address.'

Nasi says, 'Who is... *we?*'

'Hatton and Turner,' Miller says.

'The Brits.'

Nasi doesn't bother to disguise his contempt.

Miller doesn't bother to hide his irritation.

'They're white... They're on the panhandle... They fit in.'

Nasi says, 'They have accents.'

'As do you,' Miller says.

'Yes... but I'd wager I don't talk as much as they do.'

Victor raises his hand, bored with the direction the conversation is heading. Because if there's one more thing guaranteed to boil his piss, it's grown men acting like frat boys measuring their dicks.

'Nasi... is there some kind of point you're trying to make here.'

'My point... Okay... You say this Lieutenant-Colonel is a Marine Raider, right?'

'Correct.'

'Except he isn't... at least not now. Not if he moved through your *Special Operations* command structure the way you were told. Because, if it's as you say... he's a spook. Fatigues and former unit patches mean nothing. Someone flies that high... that fast, says only one thing to me. It works the same in our Defense Force. Someone starts out in uniform. Makes his cohorts look like amateurs. They get shipped out. They're the zero-point-two percent of the top two percent. The Brits pull them from their SAS and SBS. Incorporate them into the field elements of their Secret Intelligence Service. The Poles borrow them from GROM. Push them into Wywiadu. We recruit them straight from Shayetet 13 into Mossad. You Americans pluck them from everywhere and stick them into your, so-called...'

Nasi makes *quote* signs with his fingers.

'Black Ops programs.'

Miller huffs.

'You said you had a point,' he says.

Nasi's expression remains implacable.

'From what little you've told me, Hatton and Turner are ex-paratroopers... so they're proficient at best. Which means they're not coming back. You can't pull them. Because then you're guaranteed to have no eyes. Leave them in the field and they bump up against someone like this... take my word. They will fall. Or maybe they get unlucky and learn to eat through a tube in their neck.'

Miller says, 'How come you're so sure?'

Nasi ignores him. Turns to address Victor.

'So... he just walked into your impregnable facility, correct?'

'Unfortunately... he was invited,' Victor says. 'You could call it a clerical error.'

'Whatever you choose to call it... it was you who let him walk out.'

'Indeed... it was.'

'Why?'

'Because a no-kill order was issued.'

'*No,* Victor... you let him go because he scared you. He lit you up, and you froze...'

Nasi pushes himself upright.

'I didn't assess you as someone who would compromise his own security, just because the soft-skins won't take their share of the risks. So... I'm sorry, Victor. In such matters, your money does not counteract my autonomy.'

Nasi holds up a crooked trigger finger.

'This is what it buys. And even then... only when I approve. If it's not the same for you... like we agreed. I'm afraid, we're done.'

Miller moves in closer.

'Okay, Abelman. I think you need to...'

Victor says, 'Shut up, Carl. In fact... go wait in the car.'

Miller looks from Victor to Nasi and back again. Walks away, slowly shaking his head.

'He's a cretin.'

'Thank you, Nasi... but I'd appreciate it if you left staff psych-appraisals to me.'

Nasi shrugs.

'So tell me... what really happened in New Mexico?'

'I made a mistake,' Victor says. 'But not only then.'

'When else?'

'Awhile back... six months maybe. Outside Dallas. I didn't figure some unexpected losses for what they were. I thought it was just a case of us pushing our luck. Or bad timing... or both. And assuming my guys had made an error of judgement, thinking themselves invincible, and finding themselves heavily outnumbered. When it turns out, they were taken out... surgically, you might say.'

'By this Colonel?'

'It certainly seems that way now.'

'So... what was he like?'

Victor feels the rage he's been supressing spike back up to the top of the dial.

'At a guess... pushing six-three or four. No power-lifter, but...'

'I didn't ask what he looks like... and I don't care.'

Although he appears oblivious just how close to the wind he's sailing, Victor has to concede, his newest lead operator has a point.

'Very well, Nasi... First off... I'd say supremely focused. And definitely not short on confidence. Sharp-tongued and a provocateur for sure... as I discovered. And some of his extra-curricular studies at Texas Tech were interesting... to say the least.'

'In what way?'

'Fencing... Chess... Contemporary dance.'

Nasi says, 'So, it's likely he's a fan of Brazilian martial arts.'

'*Capoeira*... sure,' Victor says. 'And *krav maga,* I'd wager.'

'And your reasoning?' Nasi says.

'I can't say for sure... but there was something more than mere physicality about the way he moved. He had this weird kind of fluidity. Hard to explain but, trust me... I'm more than a capable judge in such matters.'

'Is this the reason he scared you, Victor?'

'He didn't scare me... and no-one ever has.'

'So, what then?'

'Somehow, he knew which button to push to get under my skin. He didn't know who I was. And it wasn't a pretence... I'm certain of it... Yet, somehow, he managed to light my fuse.'

Nasi picks up his backpack.

'Okay... if what you say is true, and he really doesn't know who you are, it's possible he doesn't know the force you can bring to bear. That means we retain an advantage. One we'll need to make use of sooner rather than later. And from now on... keep your pet, Mr. Miller, away from me.'

Victor rises to his feet. Grips Nasi's shoulder and squeezes hard.

'We have more than one advantage, my friend. And don't worry... it's not in my nature to keep a lap-dog once they start pissing on my rugs.'

'Glad to hear it,' Nasi says. 'So, tell me of this other advantage we have.'

Victor releases his hold.

'If I choose to heed your advice, I have another option I can turn around to point in the Colonel's direction.'

'Sending Miller in solo would be the biggest miss-match since Yom Kippur.'

'I'm not proposing to send Miller on his own.'

'So, who else?'

Victor smiles.

'I have someone in mind I can use as bait.'

'Fine,' Nasi says. 'But I don't see how we set it up. We have no intel on this Colonel's position... which means, right now, he could be anywhere. We don't know his tactics... or his force strength. So, as far as I can tell, we're blind.'

'And I might agree. But there's always a chance Buckley's take on this whole thing could have been right all along.'

'Which was...?'

'We're dealing with nothing more than a lone wolf with some kind of bug up his rear end. However, for the time being at least, I'm reluctant to go all-in on that possibility. For one thing... we can't ignore the fact that DCS has considerable reach into this country's intelligence networks. And our late lamented Lexstone colleague confirmed this Zalizo character used to head up an eyes-only unit within what is already a pretty opaque branch of the national security apparatus.'

'So, what is this DCS exactly?'

'Defense Clandestine Services.'

'As naming conventions go,' Nasi says. 'That's not particularly subtle.'

'Maybe not,' Victor says. 'But their remit certainly is. They're pretty much the Defense Intelligence Agency's Tier One HUMINT outfit. Tasked with boots-on-the-ground intelligence operations that are either too deep or too hazardous for your average DIA desk jockey. And, if Buckley's information was only half way legit... we're almost certainly outmatched when it comes to access to intelligence data. I would also hazard a guess, our guy doesn't suffer from restraint or self-recrimination. I know ruthless when I see it. And you can take it from me... he qualifies.'

'In which case it would be unsafe to assume he hasn't acquired your ID.'

'We were face-to-face... and I'm telling you, he didn't know who I was. But you're correct. He'll likely find out soon enough. And that's exactly what I'm counting on. If I could tip the scales to ensure he does... I would. But I've a feeling he'd smell entrapment like a jackal scents carrion.'

Again, Victor smiles.

'*No*... we let him find me in his own good time. Allow him to think himself the hunter.'

'And we get to prepare the ground,' Nasi says.

Victor holds out Zalizo's Coal Island security mug-shot.

'Precisely...'

Downtown Austin is emptying it's low-wage earner pens. Washers and cleaners and restaurant workers. All the service-sector have-nots, merging with those who plainly had more than enough to get by. A co-mingling of daily drudgery, notwithstanding the pay-scale differentials. Those sporting fancy suits and hundred dollar haircuts, all striding to their glossy town cars and over-priced SUVs. Those wearing t-shirts with company logos and the back-bending weight of the low-status economy, all shuffling to over-crowded bus stops and low-cost taxi ranks.

Victor can see Carl sat inside their rental. Slumped behind the steering wheel. Staring through the windshield. Blind to the hum-drum swirling around him. All his hard won bravado blown away by the stark truth lying behind the command *'...go sit in the car.'*.

He finds himself pondering if Miller has come to represent a *truth* hiding in plain sight. A sign that he's losing his touch. After all, up to now he's never had to concern himself with the capability of his stock. It had always been the natural order of things that his teams were in the ascendance. The opposition inevitably inferior. Poorly trained. Hopelessly mismatched. Wannabees whose hardware gave them a fatal mix of swollen dicks and bluster. In the past, his need to recruit had been purely down to voluntary retirement. Not attrition. Never MIAs. Now, it appears his kingdom is under direct attack. He'd lost three of his best. And may lose more before this episode was over—*whatever threat level it turned out to be.* So, not for the first time in his life, he knows he's going to have to adapt.

The rental's driver-side window is rolled down.

Victor opens the off-side door and slowly shoehorns himself into the passenger seat.

'Stop sulking, Carl... I have a new task for you.'

ALBUQUERQUE, NEW MEXICO

Zalizo had showered short and hot. Then long and cold. Partly to soak away the stiffness from all the driving. Partly because, whenever he got together with Seigo, he always came away with the feeling he'd gotten fine Navajo earth baked into his pores. Foreign somehow. Dry and invasive. A far cry from the soil his ancestors were bound to. That dark and heavy mud that spent half its existence frozen solid. Most of the rest, unrelentingly wet and clawing. As difficult to work and traverse as a long Ukrainian winter was to endure. And, right now, for no reason in particular, he feels the pull of his Slavic origins at a cellular level.

He'd booked himself into The Hyatt. Spitting distance east of the CanAm Highway. Half-a-click from Albuquerque International Sunport. The room clean and functional. Struggling to imitate utilitarian chic. And, like most places he's been required to spend his waking hours in since his parent's slaughter, it feels a very long way from where he wants to be.

Her apartment lies two-hundred and fifty miles and change due south. The GMC has a siren and a bank of dash-mounted strobe lights. If he pushes hard, he can make it back to El Paso in under three hours. Though, chances are, she'd be working late. But he could always sit outside her apartment and wait for her to get home. He figures they might not get a whole lot of sleep—*especially if it turned out they were both hungry*—and that would leave him with a killer drive back to the Texas panhandle in the morning.

But worth it, for damn sure.

He starts playing back some of the things she'd said. Re-immersing himself in the way she'd made him feel. And, in that moment, Seigo's words stab home—*loud and deep.*

'You gonna lose everything you touch... for the whole of your life?'

He finishes towelling off. Seats himself on the edge of the king-sized bed. Stares at his laundered clothes, folded on the chair beside the vanity table. Knowing, regardless the thoughts racing around inside his head, he can't go back to her.

Least ways, not yet.

What he really needs is a distraction. But nothing comes to mind. He's already eaten. In a mid-town 66 Diner, off Central Avenue. Where the food had been decent enough. From a broad enough menu. With jukebox music from the eighties and nineties. Power ballads mostly. Service provided by staff wearing smiles that passed for genuine. A nice enough place for a guy used to eating alone.

He hauls himself upright. Dresses in two minutes flat. Decides he'll go buy a razor. Figures there has to be a 7-eleven somewhere close by.

At that moment, his satellite phone buzzes its screen alive.

He hits connect.

'Yes...'

'Checking you got the mug shots, Colonel.'

'Affirmative... thank you, Sergeant.'

There's a pause before the call continues.

'I met with the General.'

'He came to see you?'

'Yeah... said we needed to walk and talk.'

'Well, that's a first. You should be honoured.'

'I felt... skewered.'

'I can imagine. He's one of a kind.'

There's another pause.

'Colonel... he seemed concerned you were in Albuquerque.'

'I was hoping he wouldn't find out.'

A longer pause.

'Have I screwed something up?'

'No, Sergeant... you serve a chain of command. I don't expect, nor would I ever ask anyone to disrespect that covenant.'

'That's good to know, Colonel.'

'So what else have you got... or did you call so I could sing you to sleep?'

'The Citation XLS tail number you sent over. It's registered, under lease, to JVL Executive Security. Home port at Lafayette Regional. It's a relatively recent upgrade on a lease that's been running for over ten years. Unsurprisingly, JVL is mailbox only. No website... No e-mail... No phone. It feels like a dead drop... but at the same time not. A shell company, more than likely. Especially since invoices are sent to our Lexstone Security outfit. Either way, they get paid on time, in full... so the leasing company say they're content. I get the impression, if we want any more information out of them, we're going to need a grand jury subpoena.'

Zalizo puts his phone onto speaker. Seats himself back on the corner of the bed. Begins massaging the itch that's just kicked off under the scar on his left hand.

'Okay, sergeant... I think it's time we cast our hook a little further out from the shoreline.'

'I'm listening.'

'Well... there's little doubt our DC take-downs are connected. So let's get our *NSA* friends to make a list of all the locations for suspected long-range hits, corporate and political, over the past eighteen months. Then get whoever we normally speak with in Homeland to look for any corresponding flights, to relevant locations, logged to this JVL outfit. Let's see if we can't get a face from a security archive anywhere this *XLS* bird has landed during the same period.'

'Sounds reasonable... I'll start with Lafayette.'

'The more confirmed sighting points you get, the better. We're not going to miss this guy. He's a goddam mountain.'

'So you said.'

'And, Runellie...'

'Sir...?'

'Do the same for the shooters.'

'All of them?'

'Yes... but start with the Israeli. He's the one we have the most reliable intel on. And, I get the feeling we don't have time for a multi-axis investigation. Besides, we've been chasing too many angles recently. It's starting to feel like Oregon all over again.'

There was a final pause.

'And... speaking of Oregon. Do I need to check the sights on my piece are dialled in good?'

'Affirmative, Sergeant. I've a feeling that would be wise.'

HOUSTON, TEXAS

The lights inside the executive jet-sized hanger are stadium bright. The flight crew huddled into a small glass-sided cabin, set off to one side of an open quad roller-door; the structure occupying a remote corner of William P. Hobby Airport, sitting well back from the apron. Unmarked and unremarkable. Leased through a shell company, headquartered at a mailbox.

Miller has pulled point duty. Right now, he's power-suited. Sporting a Secret Service-style earpiece. Projecting his best nothing-to-see-here pose. This far out on the apron, there was no need for anyone to pass by. And, as it happened, nobody had.

During the short flight over from Austin, Victor has gone over everything a dozen times in his head. Knows he could—*and possibly should*—consider making a cut and run. But only if he cared nothing for his reputation being fatally compromised—*so to hell with that.* No way he would allow this Marine Raider-turned-spook to bluff him into abandoning all his ambitions, just because of one little insult.

Besides, Miller had been placated and re-purposed. Which would resolve at least one of his current irritations. And, should he survive the encounter, Perry Morgan Blake will soon be re-vectored to solve another. So, right now, he's confident this raft of unforeseen complications would take care of themselves soon enough.

And, if push came to shove, he could always deploy back into the field himself, as he'd done on numerous occasions in the past. At times when his mere presence had been plenty sufficient to ensure a far swifter outcome than had otherwise seemed possible.

Just like it had in Beirut.

Added to which—*he has Nasi.*

A shiny black Cadillac swings into the hanger moments after the LED on Victor's two-way radio flashes red. The angular sports sedan's tires chirping to a halt.

The driver-side rear door opens. Martin Devlin climbs out. Thin as a twig. Frameless oval glasses pinched high and tight on the bridge of his pencil-slim nose. Next to no meat on his bones. Head smooth and white as a billiard ball. Hands like a concert pianist. Stick-out ears that look like they've been pulled from a photo-fit kit no-one had any use for. Walking his bony frame, like a heron stalking its catch.

Just the sight of him sets Victor's blood boiling again.

He carries a small, expensive-looking leather shoulder bag. Barely big enough for a hard-back novel. Which makes Victor chuckle to himself. Nasi, on the other hand, would have approved of this pompous stick insect's penchant for taking precautions.

'Victor...'

Without waiting for an invitation, Devlin proceeds to climb aboard. Like he owned the goddam plane.

Victor mouths—*cock-sucker*—under his breath. Seething that this jumped-up lackey viewed himself as some kind of Machiavelli within the DC beltway. A self-proclaimed maestro in the art of manipulation. Consummately cunning. When nothing could be further from the truth. Because, in reality, the bony little prick's rise to prominence was purely down to his long-time master's legendary charisma. A man who'd now become little more than a pale imitation of the kind of men Texan senators used to be. Someone who could no longer hold a candle to all those pugnacious individuals endowed with reserves of tenacity and resolve. Men of fierce independence. Tough individuals who would have never allowed themselves to be influenced in any direction they didn't want to go.

And most assuredly not by the likes of Martin—*fucking*—Devlin.

Senator Clarence Hellermann III is little more than a shadow of such men. Nothing but a fancy suit and pearly-white teeth.

Victor stows his disdain as he follows Devlin aboard. Seating himself in the second of two over-sized swivel loungers. Swinging to face this repulsive ventriloquist dummy. Not bothering to offer his hand. Or any other form of welcome.

'The Senator said he would come in person.'

Devlin emits a stupid little snort.

'Well, he's a busy man... as well you know.'

'Then our discussions will be somewhat limited.'

'That's a choice I'll leave entirely up to you, Mr. Labette.'

'I would much prefer we stick to first names... *Martin.*'

'Fine by me,' Devlin says. 'But I'm not here to exchange pleasantries. I'm only here for the update on our troublesome energy commissioner you've so far failed to provide.'

Victor leans back in his seat.

'Let's just say... adjustments have had to be made.'

Devlin scowls.

'Adjustments...?'

He lifts his leather satchel. Places it nonchalantly on the low, oval table positioned between the two seats, like the pathetic little weasel he was.

'Yes, Martin... *adjustments.*'

'Perhaps you'd care to be a little more explicit.'

'As a precaution,' Victor says. 'Against the continued possibility of outside interference, for one... which I now hold you directly responsible for. And as a consequence of the latest polling data, for another... for which others may also consider you liable.'

Devlin slides back in his seat, staring at his shoulder bag.

'Let's face facts, Martin... the governor is in denial. She is outside her margin of error. Significantly outside.'

'Granted,' Devlin says.

'I also think it highly likely, your state legislature will choose to seize upon this weakness. Possibly rendering our plans moot. Maybe they'll view this opportunity for what it is.'

'And what might that be?'

'A chance to... *re-align.*'

'With all due respect, Victor, I recommend you tread very carefully. I'm sure, if the Senator were here... he would advise that such considerations lie a little outside your remit.'

'Duly noted,' Victor says. 'Nonetheless... it's my intention to take a more hands-on approach with some policy decisions. Because I'm no longer prepared to play the chips as they lie.'

'And I would point out,' Devlin says. 'There's still ample opportunity in the calendar to appoint our preferred Energy Commission nominee a good while before November.'

'From your point of view, that may well be true. But I only have the word of a notoriously fickle lady that she has her people under control.'

'I can vouch...'

'*No*, Martin... you can't vouch for anything. Because neither you nor the Senator have taken the trouble to visit your benefactors... let alone your constituents, in person, in months.'

'Need I remind you, Victor... there are a number of commercially available digital platforms that afford effective communication over extended distances.'

'And I might remind you, Martin... that no matter who, or what you think you are... to me you're just a jumped-up little pin prick, who has singularly failed to appreciate there's no substitute for pressing flesh... and looking your supporters in the eye when you issue your reassurances.'

Victor towers forward.

Martin Devlin shrinks back an equal distance.

'You'd do well to ask the losing presidential candidate in twenty-sixteen. I think you'll find she would agree.'

Devlin examines his finger nails.

'Are you attempting to re-negotiate?'

Victor says, 'I would prefer to call it... *re-positioning*.'

'I'm going to need you to be a little more specific?'

'Fine,' Victor says. 'So let's just say, I'm not into three-ways anymore. Besides, Susan is just not my type. And, over time, I've become dissatisfied with the forecast on future benefits with our current arrangement. And you'd do well to consider that if the landscape shifts to, shall we say, a more *liberal* outlook... chances are any new commissioner, with a declared fondness for carbon fuels, will become an outlier in a new world order. Because, as it stands, you people seem incapable of anything other than containment... even when change is inevitable. And the sector you currently advocate for, needs strong encouragement to broaden its horizons. Think of it as diversification. Your new man will need to *control* not *impede*. In my opinion... your thinking has become far too narrow-sighted. The tracks you people ride are old and rusty. Laid down at a time when change was incremental. Glacial even. You now find yourselves running up against the mountains... and you can't see the route through.'

'That's very eloquent, Victor.'

'I'm not the least bit interested in your appreciation of my metaphorical prowess. You are here to receive a message.'

'That being...?'

'The horse Susan's backing is lame. Her long-term strategy, flawed. So you can tell your boss I strongly recommend he consider a new runner, once my end of the bargain is complete. One with some grounding in technology and innovation... One who understands how to make old dogs learn new tricks... One with enough subtlety, and courage, to marginalize the current big hitters in favour of some new market entrants. Someone with a presence and force of will to dominate said new marketplace.'

'Okay, Victor. I'll be sure to pass on your message.'

'Excellent... and my staff will insist on a thorough search of your person before you leave this building. Call me old fashioned. But I'm a stickler for private conversations remaining private.'

'As you wish.'

Devlin starts to rise.

'Wait a minute. Surely you're not suggesting that you...'

'That's correct, Martin... I'm not suggesting.'

Victor settles back in his seat.

Devlin removes his spectacles. Pulls a silk handkerchief from his waistcoat pocket. Begins leisurely cleaning the lenses—*first one then the other*—an air of confidence returning to his demeanour.

'You need to understand, you're calling a play you cannot execute. Because you're not privy to the rules of the game. In fact, you are entirely ignorant to the game being played. And the reason you're in the dark, Victor...'

He creases a thin smile.

'It's because, despite what you think, you're not even on the team. Be under no illusion... you couldn't make the draft in this league if you trained for another hundred years. So, in spite of offences to your ego, in this arena... you are not the apex predator. Not even close...'

Devlin pushes his spectacles back onto the bridge of his nose.

'In fact, you don't even qualify to carry the water. You're equivalent to the guy who throws hotdogs into the crowd. That's why you'll never get to see the game being played. Never mind step on the field...'

He lifts his satchel from the table.

'And there's one more piece of information you'd do well to consider before you embark on this little shakedown of yours.'

'Rather like yourself, Martin... I'm all ears.'

Devlin ignores the jibe, pulling the sleeves of his jacket straight.

'Senator Hellermann is not the quarterback in this

enterprise. And certainly not the head coach. Sure, he's called a few defensive plays here and there. But he didn't author this particular playbook.'

Victor says, 'Is that so...?'

'Indeed, it is. You see... that's the thing about well-conceived deceptions, Victor. They're like a dynasty with an extended lineage. And like all things dynastic, there are branches you can see and follow... and there are roots you cannot. You look at this enterprise as some kind of corporate power struggle. But on that, you are sadly mistaken. It's simply an impression you were supposed to form. A hall of mirrors, in which you're convinced you see reflections of your own inflated image. Greed... Ego... Self-aggrandizement. And that tantalising opportunity to fulfil the one desire you cherish most.'

'And what might that be?'

Devlin brushes imaginary debris from his sleeves.

'Why elevation, of course. The chance to move up a rung on the social ladder. To sit at a higher table. Join the ranks of the truly advantaged. Gain access to that strata of privilege you've both envied and despised your entire life. So, go ahead... *Jacque.* Throw your hail Mary. You'll find out, soon enough, who authored this particular playbook.'

Victor sits for a moment in silence. Keeps the shock of hearing his given name—*after all these years*—from forming any visible expression. Then he bursts out laughing.

'So be it,' he says. '*Laissez-nous danser*, this mysterious scribe and I...'

He springs from his seat. Grabbing a fistful of Devlin's collar. Hauling his bony frame from the seat like a rag doll.

Devlin scrambles to retain his balance.

'But, whereas I may perish attempting to become my own master. You, my dear Martin, because you lack fortitude, or any understanding of the courage it takes to defy all the disadvantages of low birth... will be forever content with the indignity of sycophancy and servitude.'

Victor shoves him bodily down the length of the fuselage, toward the hatch.

'Now get the fuck off my plane.'

Day Three

'The hell you say...'

PLAINVIEW, TEXAS

Simon Hatton and Mark Turner are both thirty-four years old.

Five years previously, they'd rocked up in the English county town of Hereford together. Two testosterone-fuelled hopefuls in a twelve-man intake. Withstood the months of brutality together. Yomped across the exposed Welsh mountains. Endured weeks shivering in the bone-chilling rain and biting winds. Alone and in their four-man squads. Passed through escape and evasion. Waltzed through weapons and tactics. Suffered sleep deprivation during countless hours of simulated interrogations—*so real they seemed to stretch into days*. But, in the end, they'd both failed to make it through final psych-evaluation. No reasons given. Nothing more than a terse injunction, one morning, to return to their regiment. The British Army having deemed them unworthy of admission into the Special Air Service. Not for them the honour of wearing the coveted winged-dagger insignia, proclaiming *'Who Dares Wins'*.

Which had been complete and utter bullshit.

They were Gulf War veterans. Deployed to lie in shit-filled ditches south of Basrah. Watching the teenage rag-heads laying their IEDs. They'd still been the ones tasked to vector in the drones and follow the insurgents home. The ones ordered out on overwatch as the grunts had swarmed in to clear and detain. Lasering in smart-munitions strikes on the booby-trapped bomb factories.

They'd melted into crevasses and wadis in Afghanistan. Eaten the same food. Shared aqua-tabs to purify their water. Sometimes they'd shit in the same plastic bag. And they'd been screwing their way through the bars and clubs of Tangiers when a man mountain had walked up to them, blocking out the sun.

Neither had thought twice about accepting the private sector offer he'd proposed. British Army pay had never engendered undying loyalty. And *3 Para* work was all graft and no glamour. Not unlike the Foreign Legion nut-job they'd signed on with. So, if some dumb shit had reckoned they weren't good enough for entry into the SAS, private enterprise would just have to take its place.

Right now, they are in position. Sat in a beat-up beige Bronco. In the middle of a beat-up beige neighbourhood. Parked at a kink in the road between two run-down streets. One called El Camino. The other El Barrio. Slotted between a row of serviceable wrecks. Hatton facing north-east. Turner facing south-west. Between them, they have eyes on both ends of the street called Davidson—*their target's declared place of residence*—pleased with themselves at how well they'd blended in.

It's been brutally hot since 07.30. So they're holed-up with the windows down. Soaked through with sweat. Half a dozen piss-filled water bottles littering the rear footwell. A dozen more, unopened, piled on the rear seat. Suppressed Heckler & Koch MP5s nestled in their laps.

Twenty minutes earlier, they'd shared a laugh as a big bundle of bones had passed by their position. Knotted-off handkerchief covering his head. Chin bouncing up and down on his smooth, bare chest. Mumbling to himself, about who knew what. Shuffling barefoot—*like some kind of zombie on*

Netflix—behind a battered and rusted-up shopping trolley, half-full of junk.

Now the dumb fuck is back.

Hatton says, '*Eh-up*... here he comes again.'

Turner snickers.

'*Yeah*... looks like he's been to get his liquid lunch.'

The object of their derision has light brown skin. Despite his obvious size, he has the posture of an octogenarian. Utterly reliant on his makeshift walking frame. Right hand pushing the trolley. Left hand cradling a brown paper bag like a sacred relic.

'Oh, *Christ*,' Hatton says, 'He's comin' over for a chat.'

Turner says, 'What the hell's that on his back?'

'Cardboard... I think,' Hatton says. 'Maybe it's part of his house.'

Turner snorts like a hog.

'*Yeah*... and I bet you a tenner he stinks of piss.'

Seigo says, 'You gringos got a dollar you can spare for a burger?'

The one facing north-east says, 'Fuck off...'

When he doesn't move, the one facing south-west says, 'Didn't you hear 'im, mate?'

Their accents are British. Their attitude rank with contempt. Seigo's accent is thick pseudo-Mex. His breath stinks of whiskey.

'Hey gringos... I can do you a good exchange.'

The one facing north-east waves the liquor fumes from his face.

'Which part of *fuck off*, don't you get? The *fuck*... or the *off*?'

Seigo swaps the brown paper bag over to his right hand. Thrusting it part way through the open window.

The one facing north-east turns to grab his arm—*a fraction too late.*

The bag falls into the Bronco's littered passenger footwell.

The one facing south-west says, 'For... *fuck*... sake...'

Seigo pulls his arm from the Bronco's open window, turning his back. He has a quarter-inch thick rusted steel plate hanging off his shoulders. Held in place by a thick leather strap running from around his neck. Over that he's hung a broken-down cardboard box.

He opens his mouth, like he's yawning, pressing his fingers tight into his ears.

The blast punches him forward a half-step.

He turns, leaning in through the open window. Pepper-sprays the occupants for being so uppity. Then he cuts the metal plate free with his knife. Skips around the hood and opens up the driver-side door.

He muscles his way into the driver seat as the smoke clears. Heaving the nearest body over the transmission tunnel into the passenger side footwell. It's a tight fit, and they're bleeding plenty. But nowhere near enough for him to care. He zip-ties them both, then starts the motor. It labours like an old dog, until it settles into an uneven rattle. He stares at the stick shift, cursing under his breath. It's been years since he's driven one.

So he guesses, he'll just have to see how it goes.

PALO DURO HILLS, TEXAS

Zalizo slept for a little over four hours. Showered a second time. Dry-shaved for the first time in days, with the disposable razor he'd picked up the previous evening. Hitting the interstate on ramp sometime around 4.30 AM. Stopping to take on gas on the eastern edge of Santa Rosa, New Mexico. Ordering chow from a taco joint a little further up the road.

He'd taken a call from Elizabeth Holt at around 6.30 AM.

Turns out the victim had been christened with a real sweet name. Anne-Marie Hollenbeck. Late of Denton, Texas. The owner of the RAM 1500 going by the name John Henry MacKendrick. Although it was junior who'd made the missing persons call.

Clovis PD had done a quick two-plus-two and patched through to Albuquerque. Confirming MacKendrick junior had been on a road trip with the deceased and was currently under the supervision of Clovis PD family liaison. Least ways, until MacKendrick senior showed up.

Zalizo was pretty sure the MacKendrick's pick-up would be a burned-out shell by now. All the same, a tri-state APB had gone out.

Right now, the GMC's chassis is bucking like a bull. Trail-dust spiralling in the rear-view mirror. The steep, knife-edge ridges of the Palo Duro filling the windshield.

It's 10.30 AM *Central Standard Time*.

He pulls up close behind a beat-up Bronco. Front windshield cracked and splattered with blood. He climbs from the GMC. Walks to the head of the bluff. Taking in the clear line of sight for fifty clicks in a one-eighty degree sweep.

The big Indian stands bare-chested. Hands loose by his side. Though it was undeniably hot, Zalizo figures his pose is mostly for effect. His captives lie, hog-tied with zip-chords, close to the edge of a steep drop off. One has little more than a mangle of flesh where his right hand used to be. Both have multiple lacerations to their face and arms.

Seigo is standing with his eyes closed.

Zalizo says, 'Have they got their hearing back?'

Seigo opens his eyes and says, 'There's a good chance... I

used a low-grade popper. But I guess there's only one way to find out.'

They both move to where the mercenaries lie bound. Their expressions long on doubt and short on optimism. One of them looking like he'd lost the use of his left eye.

Zalizo barks his opening question.

'Names...'

Neither man answers, but their eyes fail to disguise the fact his question has been heard. So he figures this was going one of two ways. For them, a game of cat and mouse to begin with, if they're even half-way trained. For him, technique versus available time. A less than subtle application of finesse over brutality—*like a club-rooted tooth resisting extraction*. Unfortunately for the two men lying at his feet, he was short on time and long on technique. Added to which, he had a strong stomach.

'I won't ask so politely a second time.'

The one with the injured eye mumbles, 'Hatton.'

The one with the mangled hand says, 'Turner.'

'My friend here tells me you're carrying fake IDs. Good ones, in his opinion... and I happen to know he's a fair judge. And since federal IDs, authentic or otherwise, suggests a good amount of planning and a decent amount of funding... I'm more than a little curious how and when they came into your possession.'

Both men remain mute.

Zalizo extends his hand. Palm facing up. Seigo passes over his Gerber infantry knife. He turns back to the mercenaries. Thrusts the four-inch blade, two inches into Hatton's thigh.

Hatton lets out a loud grunt that fades to a long-drawn-out moan.

'You both need to come to terms with your situation... No amount of prior training is going to get you through this. I know because I helped re-write the manual. I don't know what you *Brits* call it. For us it's Hell Week. But let me be clear... this will be like no simulation you've ever endured... Out here, with us, you won't last an hour, never mind a week. You decide you're going to try and tough it out... I start twisting the blade. And it's a wide blade... so I predict it's going to smart some.'

Turner snarls, *'Screw you.'*

Zalizo pulls the knife from Hatton's thigh, turns through one-eighty and hacks off Turner's left ear.

Turner issues a full-throated scream. Followed by a long, ragged choke. Hatton starts breathing hard and fast through gritted teeth, bubbles of spit forming at the corners of his mouth.

'I'm guessing they're contractors?'

Seigo says, 'I didn't ask. We blew over formal introductions... in a manner of speaking.'

Zalizo tosses Turner's ear.

'What happened to this one's hand?'

'He thought it was a good idea to pick up an unidentified discarded package. I'm guessing he's already figured it wasn't the best decision he's ever made.'

Zalizo reaches up. Pulls a knotted handkerchief from Seigo's back pocket. Begins cleaning the knife.

'Okay fellas... here's the good news. If this stops right now, you're in good enough shape to make it home. The bad news... my friend and I have been here before. Some time ago, I'll grant you. But, I can promise you both one thing. Back then, just like now... it didn't end at all well for a bunch of guys, not unlike yourselves. And they were every bit as tough as you two think you are... maybe tougher. So, I'm going to deal you the only hand on offer.'

Zalizo leans forward. Cuts the ankle ties from both men. Drags the one named Hatton over to the Bronco. Sits him upright against the front fender. Uses the man's own belt to strap the wound on his thigh.

Seigo says, 'The hell you doin', soldier?'

Zalizo performs a rinse and repeat with the one called Turner. Ditto strapping the man's belt to hold the blood-soaked kerchief in place over the jagged remains of his ear.

'I'm going to give our guests one last chance at redemption.'

Seigo says, 'Well that's novel.'

'They get ten minutes of my good nature,' Zalizo says. 'After which I'll resort to type.'

'Your call *ak'is,*' Seigo says.

'Okay fellas... questions. Am I right to assume, since you allowed yourselves to get suckered by this has-been, you're not SAS?'

Both men shake their heads.

'What then?'

Turner says, 'Ex-Paras.'

'And what's with the federal IDs?'

'We were dual tasked. You were priority one. Second involved claiming a body on behalf of the US government.'

'With those accents?' Seigo says.

Turner says, 'When we have to... we do passable Bostonian.'

Zalizo says. 'Who's body?'

The one going by the name Hatton makes like he's going to speak. Then his one good eye glazes over.

The one calling himself Turner continues.

'We haven't been told.'

'When and where?'

Turner looks at Hatton, but his companion has gone lights out. His head, slack-jawed, slumped on his chest.

'Two days from now... in Lubbock. The university campus Memorial Circle.'

Seigo glances at Zalizo and shrugs.

Zalizo says, 'How do you know for sure the body will be there?'

'Because we've been tasked to put it there. Our mission was to drop our target from distance. Then arrive, as if by magic, to pick it up.'

'So next question. Why will your target be there?'

Turner says, 'Because he has a target of his own… who he has to drop up close. After which, we hit him.'

Seigo asks, 'Why up close?'

'It's a televised event,' Turner says, 'I imagine someone's looking for maximum impact.'

Zalizo says, 'So who's your target's target?'

'We don't know. You were the only one we had with a name.'

Seigo lets out a low whistle.

'Well, if that'all don't make your head spin.'

'Okay,' Zalizo says. 'So… pivotal question. Who's paying the bill?'

Turner looks at his unconscious partner, colleague, comrade, friend—*whatever*. Spirit broken, he turns to stare out over the bluff.

Zalizo holds Seigo's knife at arm's length, re-inspecting the blade.

'We haven't been told,' Turner says. 'All our taskings are delivered encrypted to our mobiles… equipment and IDs via dead drops.'

Seigo says, 'Mobiles . . .?'

'Cell phones,' Turner says.

Zalizo says, 'So who recruited you?'

'A guy… in Tangier… a while back.'

'And does this guy have a name?'

'Not that we were given. Just the codename… *Invictus*.'

'Okay... I'll buy that for now,' Zalizo says. 'So let's go with what he looked like.'

The one called Turner drops his head.

'Like a fucking mountain,' he mutters.

Zalizo hands Seigo his knife. Then walks back over to the edge of the bluff. Stands for a moment, staring at a view stretching out to the western horizon. Across a landscape of countless irrigated crop circles fading to dots beneath ranks of grey-bottom clouds migrating north.

'Choice is the refuge of a disordered mind.'

Truth was, he finds it something more than unsettling that he can hear the words of a woman he barely knows, as clearly as if she were standing next to him. As if she were on her toes, speaking into his ear. Yet he could no longer hear the soft voice of the woman torn from his life little more than two years before.

Right then and there, he feels like he's going to puke.

For two whole years, whenever he'd closed his eyes, Alicia Corazón had been the one to whisper inside his head. Pleading for answers to the questions she never got to speak.

'Why were you not able to see?'

Calling his name from behind a heavy black veil.

'Leg... Why didn't you come?'

Her voice wracked with pain. Blood-soaked hands pressed to her belly.

'Why did you leave us there to die?'

And now, suddenly, she's fallen silent in his mind. Or perhaps—*just maybe*—he'd pushed her away.

Choices.

He turns back to the Bronco.

Seigo is sitting in the passenger seat. One of the MP5s gripped in his right hand. Its barrel resting on his left forearm.

Zalizo stares at the two men propped against the Bronco's fender.

'Okay... here are the new mission rules. You agree to follow them, maybe you get to go home. You deviate the thickness of a single strand of hair, you die alone in these hills... in ways you can't even begin to imagine.'

Turner regards his companion's inert form. Gives it a couple of beats. Then nods his head.

'Fair enough,' he says.

HOBBY AIRPORT, HOUSTON

Carl Jordan Miller is seated in Economy. United Airlines flight 307. Grateful to feel the thrust of jet engines in his back. Content not to be face-down in a ditch with his brains seeping through a jagged exit wound in his forehead.

For the time being at least.

Instead, he's been re-tasked. Twice to be exact. The first, menial. The second, an obvious set-up. So when the first task is done, he's going to follow his own plan. Which involves the other airline tickets he'd purchased that morning—*paid for in cash.*

Lubbock to DFW. DFW to Atlanta. Atlanta to Des Moines.

All through his time at college, his mom had constantly pushed him to follow in his old man's footsteps. Insisting he should return home. Carve out a career for himself in insurance. Just because he'd been better than fair at math. But he'd seen his father become little more than a dried out, bitter husk by aged fifty something. Endlessly lashing out with his tongue. With little or no regard for the occasion—*or anyone's feelings for that matter.* So no way was he ever going to let that happen to him. Fortunately, the government had provided him with a set of sought-after skills. Ones he felt confident private security companies would be willing to offer a decent monthly pay cheque to acquire. After all, Des Moines was a pretty big place these days. And getting bigger every year. For sure, the old man would still have his corporate connections.

So he will go out on the panhandle and do this one last thing.

Then he was gone.

HOUSTON SOUTH WEST AIRPORT

Hatton and Turner had reported in.

Or, to be completely accurate, Turner had. Because Hatton was out on patrol. Because the target was still a no-show. Which, Victor decides, is not unexpected. As a result, his mood remains upbeat. So instead of wallowing in pointless self-recrimination, he'll apply the doctrines he's spent a lifetime following. Command the space. Control the environment. Whenever and wherever possible, apply swift and overwhelming force.

He punches in the number for Perry's burner.

It's answered on the third ring.

'You were supposed to check in.'

'The agreement was I had to call each day. By my reckonin', and the position of the sun... it's still today.'

'Well, I thought you might be interested. I'm sending something to keep you entertained...'

Victor hears only breathing.

'...they should be with you later this evening.'

'Will I find it challenging?'

'It's an adult male. At a guess... you'll be giving him at least a couple inches, and close on a hundred pounds.'

'I guess that might be interestin'.'

Victor says, 'Think of it as stress relief. An additional challenge to keep you on your toes. You prevail... you get to execute the original plan. You fall... my assets will complete your task. So now we both get two bites of the cherry.'

'Could be you're the father figure I always craved.'

'You and I both know... that's highly improbable. Keep in touch, Perry. And remember... your dot moves somewhere on my screen I don't approve of, our agreement is null.'

'I have no idea what that means,' Perry says. *'But whatever you say... Boss Man.'*

PLAINVIEW, TEXAS

Seigo had agreed to sit with Hatton and Turner in the hills. So Zalizo had ferried in food, medical supplies and a cell phone charger pack. After which they'd played medic for close on an hour. Tended the two men's injuries as best they could. If infections took hold, that's the way the dice would roll.

Turner's right hand was past saving. His ear little more than a shapeless knot of flesh. Apart from the deep wound in his thigh, Hatton had almost certainly lost his left eye to shrapnel. The direction his physiology persuaded it to travel was in the lap of the gods. As it was, he'd lain unconscious throughout their efforts at treating his injuries. At a guess, odds on psychological recovery for either of them was sitting at slim to none at all.

Zalizo pushes Elizabeth Holt's compliance checks to

the back of his mind. Partly because neither man had been bystanders. Mostly because they sure as hell qualified as active combatants. Mercenaries who'd made their employment choices long before they'd had the misfortune of making his acquaintance. Prostitutes to the peddlers in fear and tyranny. They'd chosen to play dice at the table of risk and reward and come up short.

The inevitability of cause and consequence.

At that precise moment, Zalizo is leaning against the half-glass wall separating Hale County Sheriff's office from the day-to-day scrimmage of its deputies. Although all activity behind the divide had pretty much stalled from the moment he'd walked past their desks.

'We appreciate you returning the badge. But you surely realize how unorthodox this all sounds, Colonel...'

Sheriff Clyde Jerimiah Tillings sits behind a plain wooden desk. Pressed forward. His elbows resting on a spread of paperwork.

'Though, I see it's marshal today... So, once again, it's kinda hard to keep up.'

Deputy Sheriff Dale Abbott is bookending a row of filing cabinets. A half-dozen framed citations arranged along the wall above his head.

Both men are heavy-set, sporting salt and pepper spike cuts. Both pot-bellied, barrel-chested sacks of cholesterol. Tillings a twelve-year Hale County fixture. Abbott, a thick-skinned Oklahoman, who—*according to Runellie's cursory inquiries*—had been booted from his former employment for one-too-many financial irregularities. And, although it might represent the kind of tittle-tattle that likely didn't amount to much, it was often the small details that mattered most.

Zalizo settles himself next to a tall water dispenser.

'It will be a case of passing on information acquired... Credible intelligence from a creditable piece of police work... I'm not asking you to hang your necks out. You need a number at Homeland... I can let you have one.'

Tillings leans back, folding his arms.

'And how do I explain how we came by this credible information?'

Zalizo holds up one of the iPhones recovered from the Bronco.

'You found a cell phone in a recovered stolen vehicle. No arrests made. But you uncovered worrying messages... detailing a specific threat. Which you consider to be of imminent concern.'

'Okay,' Tillings says. 'For the sake of argument, let's say we agree. We'd still like to know what's with all the smoke and mirrors.'

Zalizo says, 'Because there's an active classified operation in play. Involving multiple threats... with national security implications.'

Tillings glances over to Abbott.

Abbott looks over to Zalizo and sneers.

'We're gonna need a little more than that... *soldier*.'

Zalizo's patience snaps like a bull-whip.

'You start flapping your lips at me... fat boy. The only thing you'll get will be my boot in your rear and a federal obstruction charge.'

Tillings pushes himself away from his desk.

'Okay, Colonel... that's way out of line. So, we either keep things civil here, or I'll have to insist you leave.'

'Sheriff... unlike the last time we met, you either do as I ask. When and how I require. Or the next time our paths cross, you'll find speed and combat training trumps tin badges and shovelling doughnuts. You got anything more to say. Keep it stowed 'til I'm gone.'

Abbott stares down at his shoes. Tillings goes back to shuffling paperwork.

Zalizo leaves without closing the door.

DENTON, TEXAS

As far as Glennis Hollenbeck is concerned, Denton had always been as good a place as any to raise a kid. Far enough from big city life to feel separated from all the crazy stuff you heard about on the news channels. Close enough for access to choice and opportunity. Decent schools and a good university. At least, one they'd known they could budget for—*if her Lord chose to bless them*.

They'd made the decision to move out to Denton when David had gotten his mall manager post in ninety-eight. Two years after her father had retired from SMU. So they'd agreed to sell their properties and pool their resources into a single residence. One that had suited all their needs. Something modern, spacious and easy to maintain. Her, David and Grandpa John.

A two-for-one upgrade that had benefitted everyone.

And from the moment her precious baby had issued forth a first startled wail, everything in her life had suddenly made complete sense. Because she'd known—*with unwavering certainty*—it was the will of the *God* she'd always believed watched over her. David, of course, and proffered his usual '*phooey*'. Meanwhile, Grandpa John had just gotten on with falling head-over-heels for his only grandchild; and a new purpose to the remainder of his life into the bargain. Grateful, beyond measure, for the chance to be around the beautiful gift he'd prayed so long and hard for. The only thing—*throughout an otherwise long and rewarding life*—he'd come close to giving up on, after so many years of waiting and hoping. Years spent bearing witness to the maternal yearning in his daughter's eyes.

Even so, there had been occasions when Glennis had felt sympathy for her husband. Playing second fiddle to her widowed father was a hard place to sit in their family ensemble. Third, if she included herself. But Dave Hollenbeck had always been something more than just a good man. Not one ounce of envy or malice in his atheistic bones. Which is why she'd always believed that it was her merciful *God* who had pushed her undying love his way. To try and prove her unbeliever wrong. But she'd never forgotten the words her father had spoken. To quell her shredded nerves the night before she'd uttered her one and only—*I do.*

'Listen, honey... There are folk all over this world of ours... worshiping deities and following doctrines we don't believe in... So, I guess you could look at it this way... Your young man only believes in one less Heavenly Father than you.'

Right now, Grandpa John sits immobile—*and pale as a ghost*—in their dried-out husk of a yard. Despite the unrelenting heat, he hasn't moved an inch in over four hours. The love for his only grandchild weighing like a hill of rocks on his frail shoulders.

Glennis had watched his face age a thousand years when his beloved Poppy had missed her morning check-in. Seen it age a thousand more when their only child failed to answer their repeated calls. Witnesses the light in his eyes dim to almost nothing as she leaves his side to answer the call they hear ringing at them from the silence of their home.

Less than a minute later, she returns.

Dazed and barely functioning.

'Honey... what did they say?'

She kneels before him, on the bone-hard earth, resting her head on his hands. Struggling to speak through her rising nausea. A vice-like pressure pounding through her skull. Crushing her prayers, for all this to be nothing more than some kind of silly misunderstanding, to dust.

'They said they couldn't tell me over the phone,' she hears herself say. 'Said they had to come see us in person.'

When she finally raises her head, her father's words spill from his mouth in a hoarse whisper.

'Oh, dear Lord... this is all my fault. I asked her to go.'

Glennis Hollenbeck has removed herself from the oppressive heat. Finds herself standing at the kitchen sink. Staring out through the window—*beyond the sunflower-patterned drapes, made from the left-over material she'd used back when she could still get her baby girl into a dress*—watching a Denton PD cruiser pull up to the front of her home; moments ahead of her husband.

From somewhere outside herself, she sees the man who had been her immutable rock scramble from the family station wagon. Watches him chase the officers down as they begin heading up the driveway. Hears him call out. Pleading for them to '*...WAIT UP*'. Grabbing at their shoulders to get them to stop.

She watches as the officers bow their heads. Watches them turn. Feels an icy chill spreading in tendrils across her flesh as they slowly remove their caps.

Then she witnesses the blood drain from the face of the man she has loved for the whole of her adult life. Sees him double over. Hands on his knees. Like he's been sucker-punched in the gut. Staggering backwards. The male officer reaching out to keep her man from collapsing.

And, from that moment on, all she registers is the unearthly sound escaping her throat. A long drawn out, suffocating wail that starts somewhere deep down—*from a place she'd never known existed*—thick and clawing and black as tar.

She reaches out blindly for something to hold onto.

But her bones refuse to carry her weight.

So she surrenders. Sliding to her knees. Burying her head in her hands, as the first raw stab of grief rips through every fibre of her being. And there, on her kitchen floor, she knows she is going to die. Her heart ripped apart by the knowledge that she will never see her precious baby again. The adrenalin that had kept her functioning throughout the preceding hours suddenly drained away. The mind-numbing dread she'd been holding at bay sweeping in, crushing the light and conviction that had guided every moment of her existence to darkness.

She begins rocking—*backwards and forwards*—between each choking sob. All the while praying, harder than she's ever prayed throughout her well-lived and faithful life. Pleading with her *Lord* to come take her...

...before the officers make it to the door.

AUSTIN, TEXAS

Susan Brandt enters her inner sanctuary, throwing her vanity purse onto her bed. Her mood darker than she could ever recall. Thankful the drapes were all but fully drawn. Welcoming the darkness. The comfort of shadows. The feeling it gives her that she's safe, for the time being at least, in the womb she's created within the east wing of the governor's mansion.

She's survived twenty-seven years in the game. Which, by any measure, was nothing short of extraordinary. Especially in Texas politics. Particularly as a woman. And—*for damn sure*—a good deal longer than she'd ever imagined.

Of course, it had helped that her father had been CEO of the state's fourth largest oil producer. Even more so that she'd been raised by a mother—*with steel wire for blood, running through her veins*—who'd entered into her union with Clint H. Morrison in possession of information every bit as valuable as the oil he spent his days chiding itinerant roughnecks to draw from the dry Texan earth. A woman way ahead of her time. With a level of intelligence far in advance of her tender years. A woman born in an age when looking good in a swimsuit and shoulder sash pushed a working-class girl further and faster than she could otherwise ever hope to achieve. When going down on your knees in front of a succession of baggy suits got you further still. And grinding your tits and pussy into old men's faces got you whatever else you wanted. If you knew what to ask for. And who to ask.

But Rosalynn Banks had been a special breed of woman. Fiercely intelligent. A woman who'd always known exactly what she wanted from life. Certainly nothing as mundane as sparkly baubles or fancy gowns. So, all through her crazy ride during Texas's post-war expansion, she'd selected her conquests carefully. Guaranteeing she would always be the sharpest mind between the sheets. To his credit, old man Clint had paid close attention when his rivals' exploits with the high breasted Lolita—*with an ass sweeter than a Georgia peach*—had been boasted about all through the summer of '55. And by the time she'd put her warm hand down the front of his pleated pants, he'd known exactly what she could offer him. Priceless insights into the minds of his rivals—*in addition to their envy*—if he could snare her for his own. And she'd quickly discerned the limited nature of his desires.

From that day forward, she'd lain beneath the old roughneck-made-good but a few times. Just enough to give him the heir he'd demanded; though not the son he'd longed for.

Unfiltered Marlboros and a life-long aversion to exercise had ensured their union was brief. And throughout all the years she'd gone on to head Morrco Oil, the legacy of cunning and tenacity Lady Rosalynn—*as she'd gone on to be known*—had bestowed on her only daughter was beyond calculation.

But now here she is, the scion of that imposing, pioneering business woman. Kicking off her thousand dollar shoes. Stripping off her three-hundred dollar blouse. Cursing the vultures who had seen through her performance.

Telling her, *'Susan... the polls don't lie.'*

Like she didn't fucking know that already.

The large sash window is open a fraction, at the top. The sound of late-night Austin traffic drifting through. Muted and strangely comforting.

The heavy drapes billow suddenly. The movement drawing her eyes to a figure sat cross-legged in one of her beloved Hepplewhite chairs. His outline as dark as the shadows that had kept him concealed. Close cropped hair. Dark coloured suit. *Maybe blue. Maybe black.* His shirt open at the neck. Silenced automatic pistol of some kind in his right hand. Something onyx-black balanced on the long fingers of his upturned left hand.

A cigarette lighter, perhaps.

'I'm guessing you must have some kind of death wish?'

'Why would you assume that, Ms Brandt?'

'Because, you disturb one hair on my head... you'll never make it out of here.'

'I got in... I can get out. Besides, I would advise against calling for help.'

'What makes you think I need help?'

The figure gestures dismissively with his gun hand. It strikes her as odd that what concerns her most, is that he doesn't smoke while he's sat in her chair.

'I am on the clock, Ms Brandt. Idle threats are of no interest to me.'

'So state your business and...'

'Don't presume to instruct me, Governor.'

The figure sits motionless. Accent hard to place. The lack of menace in his voice makes the skin on her scalp tighten and her throat turn dry. Her tongue suddenly feeling as fat as a side of ham.

'How did you...?'

'Get in here? You have a number of recent appointments to your security staff whose salary we enhance.'

'I'd like to put my blouse back on.'

He gestures with his head.

'Tomorrow, if all goes well, you are going to announce a change of energy commissioner nominee.'

Despite herself, she scoffs.

'Unless you have access to a sovereign wealth fund, you couldn't come close to making that happen. And even then, you would still be pissing in the wind. So I can assure you, or whoever you represent. No, wait... I've a pretty good notion who you represent. And he should know, I have never in my life entered into any bargain which offered no clear advantage. Besides, there are a lot of elected representatives and commercial interests who have invested heavily in the current candidate.

And once the incumbent is no longer an issue, their payments come due. So... no matter what happens here. No way the horse I assume you're suggesting is going to make it to the stalls.'

'Your compliance has nothing to do with what happens *here*, Governor.'

'Whoever you are. Your boss should have briefed you that I don't scare easily. And he forgets, I still have a lot of powerful allies. Especially inside the beltway. What other leverage is there?'

'Not the smartest question a woman ever asked an opponent.'

'How so?'

'Because you people instinctively think of leverage in terms of power and influence. So binary... shame on you. I would have thought your first concern would have been for your *Pequeño.*'

The governor feels the floor give way. Like she's riding an elevator with the cables cut. Suddenly in free-fall. Acid bile rising as the meagre contents of her stomach travel to her throat.

Her hands begin shaking. The buttons on her blouse impossible to manipulate. So she gives up trying. Letting her hands fall limp at her side.

Through nothing more than muscle memory, she manages to keep her chin high. But, for the first time since she was a child, there's no strength she can muster to hold back her tears.

The figure rises from her precious armchair, moving towards her, stopping as he draws level with her shoulder. She feels her blouse being stroked away from her breasts with the silencer screwed to the end of his gun. Feels a jolt of terror lance through her, all the way to the floor.

'So will you do as we say? A simple yes will suffice.'

She hears herself say, *'Yes...'*

He raises the lighter to her ear. When the click comes, she

flinches. Paralysed, as she waits for the heat and smell of hair burning. Instead, all she hears is her own voice speaking her own words from moments before.

'...access to a sovereign wealth fund.'

'Thank you... Susan.'

She screws her eyes shut as cold metal begins tracing a path to her cleavage. But she registers no humiliation. Just one simple word crushing her mind.

Pequeño.

Her little one.

It had been the affectionate pet name Maria Rodriguez had given her precocious charge from the moment she'd started as a maid. And the only meaningful gift, apart from her wedded name, her no-good, drunken bore of a husband had bestowed on their short-lived marriage.

'An edited recording goes out two days after the incumbent *vacates* his post... so to speak. You need to appreciate that the only way you can stop us applying our leverage is if you comply. You will not be able to protect your progeny. If you even think to try... our offer will be withdrawn. We have people in places you have never even heard of. You won't be able to shield her... or your grandchildren.'

The door behind her closes with barely a sound. She hasn't even registered the fact he'd moved away. All she can hear, as her room settles back to its familiar silence, is a bone-crushing terror roaring in her ears.

LUBBOCK , TEXAS

'I must confess, Colonel. I hadn't anticipated I would hear from you again...'

As always, the General's voice is baseball-coach gruff. Even more so through his cell phone's speakers.

'leastways, not in person.'

'If you mean to prevail in the face of uncertainty, never make a plan you can't adapt... I recall being told that once.'

Zalizo is sitting in his GMC. One block over from the Overton Hotel. Parked on the eastern side of Jones AT&T Stadium. Facing University Avenue. A fast sinking sun drawing down the worst of the day's heat. Painting the sky with a *Dantean* glow. The storms of the previous day having clung exclusively to high elevations, far to the west. Shunning a city that had barely seen a cloud, let alone anything approaching rain, in over a month.

He's been waiting on a call from Tillings, who'd been confident he could access his old network and acquire the energy commissioner's itinerary. In the meantime, he'd decided to make his own enquiries. Confirming Sommerhays Holberton was booked into Suite 1401. His entourage of acolytes booked to occupy the two rooms on either side.

'So let's crack the eggs here, Colonel. This omelette isn't going to make itself.'

'I've been using MIKE-*One* to ferret out some further information.'

'So I gather... and I appreciate you telling her to seek my approval.'

Zalizo smiles to himself.

'In point of fact, I didn't.'

'In that case, your Sergeant has risen further in my estimation.'

'Yes, sir... mine too.'

'So, I imagine you're thinking to offer the commissioner an elevated level of protection?'

'I intend persuading him to remain in his hotel suite.'

'That would be good advice.'

'I also need your authority to move MIKE-*One* beyond the beachhead.'

'You know that's not possible under the option you chose. Way too many complications. As is usual with you, there's getting to be too many broken links in the chain of command.'

'That's why I called.'

'I guessed as much. So say your piece, Colonel.'

'If I go any further forward with option two... the collateral risks are likely to rise above acceptable levels.'

'And, all of a sudden, that bothers you... why?'

'Because it's avoidable.'

'If memory serves, it's not something that's particularly concerned you in the past.'

'Well, it just so happens I've promised someone I would reconsider some personal... *deficiencies*.'

'The hell you say... May I ask who?'

'A little old crow who used to be a Tenth Circuit judge.'

'Well I'll be. You've met the Honourable Elizabeth Holt?'

Zalizo feels an alien chill run through him. Something ill-defined. Something primitive—*a primordial, fight or flight, thing*.

'Our paths crossed recently... *yes*. So, am I to take it you're acquainted?'

'As you say... our paths have crossed.'

'Am I permitted to know when and where?'

'No, Colonel... you are not.'

Silence spools its way down the line, during which pieces of the puzzle that informed his rapid promotions arrange themselves, then begin slotting together.

He is back in the town where he'd studied and excelled for close on ten years. A place where he'd felt safe. Where he'd been left alone to soak up knowledge. Honing his body to a level that matched his Slavic name. The substantial haul of cash he'd split with Seigo, after their Farmington exploits, lying practically untouched in a City Bank safety deposit on 13th Street. Conveniently added to his parent's modest estate twenty-two years before. He'd worked part-time and cash rented throughout his eight years at Texas Tech. The only withdrawals he'd made throughout the intervening years, for college fees and that one flight to Paris Island, South Carolina.

'So... given the tenor of our last communication. I'm going to need to hear you say it.'

Zalizo grits his teeth.

'Could be I need to re-evaluate my options.'

'Indeed, you do, Colonel. And now we've stowed that little indiscretion... what is it you need from me?'

'I have a number of concerns. Mainly about snakes finding shelter among the crevasses in DC and Austin. Also a sizeable sack of manure I ran into at Coal Island.'

'So same question as yesterday. Where, exactly, are you?'

'Lubbock.'

'And your excursion to Albuquerque?

'Possibly unrelated,' Zalizo says. 'Possibly not... Involving a kid getting herself killed north of Roswell and photo evidence that a he-lo, which I happened to ID during my visit to Coal Island, was somehow involved.'

'All very cryptic, Colonel. But let's move on... for now.'

'Yes, General... let's do that.'

'So, when do you meet with the energy commissioner?'

'As soon as a new Sheriff buddy of mine from Hale County makes a call to tell him I'm coming. Then I'll focus on poking the nest here in Texas. Make like I'm stumbling around blind... You go after any Pentagon and State Department big hitters in DC, before they start sweeping their tracks. The ones Runellie would struggle to gain access to.'

'Okay... agreed. What else?'

'I'm still working on that. Truth is, I can't figure why they needed to bring Perry Morgan Blake into this. And, having done so... why they let me attend his execution. I can't figure a lot of things right now. But I have a feeling, sooner or later, I'm going to need access to Runellie's magic in the field. Plus I'll need layouts for Coal Island. See if they're running an incinerator. I scoped a smoke stack on a separated unit. More than likely it's for waste disposal. But there's a chance it's doubling as a crematorium. It's what I would claim if I were them and I was missing DNA evidence of his demise.'

'And, if that's the case... how can you be one-hundred per cent sure they set your man free.'

'I just am. Like I said... it's hard to explain.'

'That's equally vague, Colonel. But I take it... you suspect he's somehow involved in whatever wider scheme's in play here?'

Zalizo hesitates. Wrestling with the lack of cohesion in his own mind. Struggling for the words he needs to attempt an explanation. Because what does he really have? A succession of gut feelings—*was that it?* An unusual prisoner transfer six months earlier—*so what?* The take-downs in DC—*told them nothing*. An execution that his instincts insisted was staged somehow—*beyond absurd*. And more likely at a level most people would consider close to the ravings of a lunatic.

Gut feelings. Instinct. Speculation.

Less than a handful of dirt.

'Truthfully... all I've got is a photo of a man on a murder victim's camera. Who looks nothing like the person who slaughtered the woman I fell for. And nothing like the freak I saw in the execution chamber. But I know it's him. Right now... I'll concede it reads like a B-movie script. We've got three John Doe mercs, on ice, in a *Dallas* morgue. We've got three fresh bodies in DC which has the stink of a sanitizing operation. We've got two contractors with pulses, on slow burn in the here and now... who say they were sent to fix me for a hole in the desert. And admitted they were booked to clean up after a hit in Lubbock, the day after tomorrow. But they don't know who. And they don't know why. Their instructions are to plug the shooter. Then claim the body. Meanwhile... we have a truck load of dark money being funnelled into fighting off clean energy development all across New Mexico and Texas. But, for sure, there isn't a DA in the country who wouldn't bust their gut laughing if we took it to them the way it hangs right now. So what I've got is no Canaletto... more like a poor man's Jackson Pollock. That said, I know what I saw. And it wasn't like any execution I've ever heard of. Added to which... I'm pretty sure a grizzly-sized hard-on, with a massive superiority complex, tried to slow walk me into a trap. But again, that's just me knowing. And, as you're fond of saying...'

'...nothing to hang our hats on.'

'Exactly,' Zalizo says. 'Added to which... I've got it in my head, I may be over-thinking this.'

'Surely the answers reside in Coal Island.'

'Some of them, maybe. But, if we go busting in, everyone else involved is going to know we're coming. Which is something we need to avoid.'

'It may be a bigger risk not to.'

'Could be you're right, General... but I'm convinced we need to keep all the pawns on the board. There's something shitty going on here in Texas. Something I only scratched the surface of six months ago. The people taken down back then were specialists. Imports, most likely. Unidentified to this day. Contractors for certain. Three individuals hell bent on going down fighting is unusual. Runellie and me, we both smell something more than plain old corporate greed in play here. We can feel it in our bones. We just don't know how deep all this goes right now. And we both know we're still some way behind the eightball... feeding off scraps. Making assumptions based on questionable probabilities. Though we've been able to run some basic modelling. It's how we were able to hit on Holberton as our probable target... what with his links to all those clean energy installations hit by military-grade gigs. Tens, if not hundreds, of millions of dollars blown to hell. All in less than nine months. And the governor never lifted a finger. If anything she put her foot on the break. Denying funds for the authorities trying to investigate. It was the reason Brett got called in... and the reason he called me. Construction crews pulled off projects in New Mexico because of death threats. Civilian transfers to DoD detention facilities. An aide to the Senate Judiciary chairman making an unscheduled visit to Huntsville. Claiming it was an on-the-fly social call. The Warden being a long-time supporter of the Senator. So, General, it's a jigsaw for sure. But that doesn't mean the picture can't be seen before all the pieces are snapped together.'

'It would be useful to know who Brett is.'

'He's an ex-Snake Eater. Ran with Delta out of Qa'im for a spell... up near the Syrian border. I played in the sand with him for a stint... rescuing a squad of Rangers... a little while before he hung up his Green Beret. He's Dallas PD now. Made captain in short order... organized crime division. Which came as no surprise. He was a standout, among a really sharp bunch of guys. And plenty solid enough, we made a pact to contact each other should we ever find ourselves backed into a corner. His was the request for help I responded to. He'd been called in by a number of County Sheriff's worried they were dealing with something way over their heads. Commando-style demolition jobs on solar, wind and battery production plants. All around the Dallas-Fort Worth area. And on out as far as Lubbock. With the same MO as some incidents over in New Mexico. It was Brett who help me set up in Plainview.'

'So why wasn't the Bureau called in... or Homeland?'

'This is Texas, General... since Waco, local law enforcement would have to be a good way beyond desperate to call for federal help. Especially if there's an available alternative.'

'Fair enough... but I'm not going to lie. With that many pieces in the puzzle, if you had clued me in earlier, we would have had a clearer picture by now.'

'Possibly... but I didn't have enough to go on back then.'

'As we say in Wyoming... you must think I came down with the last gully washer, Colonel. Because, you and I both know, this has nothing to do with what you had or didn't have. You simply wanted time to brood. Room to plan your own personal vendetta... using this unit's raison d'être as cover.'

Zalizo says, 'It's a point of view.'

'Yes, it is... and I'm not going to sanction you using our little corner of CDS to wage a personal war. As I recall, the first time we became acquainted, you'd gone freelance. I also recall it required a lot of body bags to clear up the mess. And, this time, you won't be wreaking havoc somewhere out of sight, like the backwoods of Oregon. This time you are under my direct command... and once we let the Commissioner know we've got his back, there's a

good chance we're going to be in plain sight. And, as fanciful as it sounds... if this Blake character has been let loose, no way we can risk a Dallas re-run.'

'Not going to happen. We know the when and where. I know what my man looks like. And, right now, my guess is... they don't know I know.'

'That sounds like a whole field of ifs, buts and maybes.'

'To a degree... but I need you to trust my instincts on this. And, don't worry, I made a promise to the judge that I'd be a little more circumspect.'

An extended pause filters own the line.

'Very well... I'll make like a heavyweight. Bounce around inside the ropes at this end for a while longer. For how long, exactly, will be at my sole discretion.'

'I appreciate it, General.'

'As you should, Colonel. And , from now on... make sure you keep in touch.'

Zalizo stows his phone. Decides he'll book into the Overton. Re-launder his clothes and order room service. Use the time to get a few things straight in his head. Button down the nagging thoughts crowding his mind during the call. Foremost of which was a notion he was searching for complexity where none existed. The product of a life spent dealing with data that had always demanded logical analysis. Of training himself to always search for a root cause. To always pursue a permanent corrective action. Data-heavy inputs that, more often than not, mandated the spilling of blood as validation.

After which he would check in with Seigo.

Front and centre, he needs to figure why this situation feels different to anything he's faced in the past. Why a part of it feels predicated on something more than pure greed. Why he senses something more than the naked arrogance of a privileged elite lay at the heart of it all. Something other than the usual supremacist clique deciding they'd like to play *Monopoly* with other people's lives. Just because they could. Because that's what they'd always done. Because they had some God-given right to do as they pleased. Strutting around with impunity. Devoid of anything approaching a prevailing social philosophy. Nothing but a cabal of callously indifferent hedonists, hell bent on preserving the neocon economic status quo. No matter the outcome. No matter the cost to society. Manipulate to accumulate. And screw anyone who gets in the way of their endless lust for personal wealth and keeping their hands on the reins of power. It was hard to fathom where such stochastic terrorism came from. And where they thought it would take them—*what twisted version of Nirvana they envisaged it would offer.*

But he remembers only too clearly, it had been more or less the same in Oregon. The conceit and vanity he'd rendered null in those cold mountains, against a legion of blind adherents to a warped ideology. So easily persuaded to commit acts of depravity and violence. Ignorant of their sponsors' true motives. Persuaded to nihilism by nothing more than their bone-deep hatred of anything they deemed as other. So easily manipulated by one simple delusion; an unwavering belief in the superiority of their birth. He recalls their rancid odour in the back of his throat. The animal fury it provoked in him. The satisfaction he felt when he'd spilt their blood.

The problem was, this gig has always felt different. Right off the bat. Because, for damn sure, no state Attorney General—*with even the slightest ambition to be re-elected*—would have given up the likes of Perry Morgan Blake to contractors. Even if they'd been ordered to do so. Especially if that person happened to be way behind in the polls.

He feels a chill settling in his gut. The kind he used to feel whenever he suspected his superiors weren't levelling with him. Back when he'd been forced to face them down. Soaking up the hatred he would see in their eyes. Daring them to take over the operational lead. Informing them—*in no uncertain terms and no matter the consequence*—no way he would take his men into the field based on bogus data. And quietly assuring them, if they were tempted to remove him from command, and he subsequently learnt of even the slightest hint of betrayal, no matter how long it took, he would hunt them down and slice out their hearts. Equally, it could be the General was right. Maybe he'd always been driven by nothing more than some genetic impulse to forever seek vengeance—*back then as now*—for the honour of his friends. His parents. His lover. All ripped from his life by murderous freaks. Supremacist ideologues. Pseudo zealots. Wanton psychopaths. For over twenty years he'd been propelled to face such people down. With an arctic chill in his heart. At home or overseas, it made no difference. He had either stood his ground, or he'd gone hunting. Driven by an equivalent zeal. Making them pay for their sickening conceit.

But what of the scars to his soul. The slow descent into his own personal abyss. Devoid of compassion. No quarter asked and none given. No capacity for pity or contextual contemplation. No room for regret. Blind to consequence. Operating like he'd been ordained some kind of divine proxy for undelivered justice. Striking out mercilessly, whenever life had visited pain on him.

Yet here he is, for some inexplicable reason, battling to hold down the growing emptiness he's felt from the moment he'd left El Paso. Ashamed he feels an aching need to touch her skin. To run his fingers through her hair. To watch her lips move when she spoke his name. Feel again, the comfort she swaddled around his frigid soul in those few hours they'd shared. A crazy mix of fizzing energy and mind-cleansing peace he still hasn't come close to figuring out. A yearning he'd thought someone could only ever feel once in a lifetime. A desire he'd not so long ago reserved for Alicia—*and her alone.* Consummated, as it had been, by the creation of a new life, with a woman who had literally stumbled into his arms.

The recollection coils like razor wire in his gut. Once again, raising a bitter taste of betrayal in his throat. A feeling that he's forsaken any right he'd earned to treasure her love.

Her memory...

...her life.

CAPITOL HILL, WASHINGTON DC

One of the four cell phones, arranged in an obsessively neat row on his desk, buzzes and lights up its screen. They are all low-budget, button operated models, acquired for less than a hundred bucks a piece. From four separate outlets. Four individual colours. Four individual ringtones. All intended to be used just once. Then subjected to ten seconds in a microwave. Followed by lighter fuel, matches and a thick gauge steel trash can.

Burners, in the truest sense of the word.

Martin Devlin is sitting in his shoe box-sized office in the Russell Senate Building. For a second or two, he does nothing but stare at the device. The blue one; freshly sanitized that morning. When it keeps on ringing, he hits the green hand-set symbol, slowly bringing the device to his ear.

'This had better be something I want to hear.'

'Yes... and no,' the voice says.

Devlin has met with the caller, face-to-face, just once. On an isolated, private beach. On the one-and-only visit he'd ever made in his life to south Florida. On a sultry day, despite the strength of a steady onshore breeze.

He'd flown into Fort Myers on a private charter, enduring the low-budget amenities and shoddy customer service. Not to mention the oppressive humidity and unrelenting sound of the ocean. Mostly, he remembers his irritation at having to spend time, once he'd gotten back home, removing stubborn fine white sand from his shoes.

'Okay... so I'm listening.'

'I'm still clean,' the voice says. *'But there are developments I am uncomfortable with.'*

'You don't say,' Devlin says. 'Who the hell does he think he is, pulling a stunt like this? It's preposterous. Where's his goddam oversized head at? How in God's name does he think he's going to get the legislature to work with him? They haven't got a clue who the hell he is... or who the fuck he represents. It's total madness.'

Devlin instantly regrets he'd resorted to cussing. Because, ordinarily, he despises foul language; thinking it beneath him, holding those who routinely indulge in such intellectual indolence in utter contempt. However, on this occasion, he's going to forgive himself. After all, the situation he's been put in is nothing short of intolerable. Forcing him to fend off a whole bunch of irate calls throughout the night. Placating people he barely knew. And cared about even less.

'I am not referring to our antagonist's castling manoeuvre on the governor.'

'What then...?'

'It has nothing to do with the... what,' the voice says. *'It is now*

all about the... who.'

'The who?'

'Precisely.'

'Are we discussing the individual who paid a recent visit to our New Mexico facility... on some spurious, last-minute invitation?'

'Correct.'

'What about him? Last I heard... he'd been confirmed as some angst-ridden Dallas cop. Boyfriend to one of the unfortunate deceased.'

'That information is not only out of date... it was far from being accurate to begin with.'

Devlin hears Victor Labette's contemptuous voice in his head. Hears himself refusing the man's request to nullify the intruder. Recalling the intense satisfaction he'd felt denying the over-bearing neanderthal's demand; albeit he understands well enough the capricious nature of hubris.

'By what margin is the information out of date?'

'Again... you are using the wrong calculus.'

'Okay... so how about you educate me.'

'It is not a case of margins. It is a matter of factors. And the factor hear is nudging the top of the scale.'

'I'd much prefer it if you stopped speaking in riddles.'

'Because he's a DoD spook... that's how.'

Devlin is only too aware of the reputation Mossad operatives hold inside the world of clandestine security services. Renowned as proficient as any covert force anywhere in the world. Or, more accurately, revered. Conditioned to be fearless, resourceful and tough as hide. And, without exception, skilfully multi-lingual. But, for the first time since they'd met, Devlin fails to catch the Israeli's clipped accent.

'Say again...'

'I said, he's a Department of Defense... SPOOK. In command of some off-the-books intelligence unit. Certainly not some knuckle-dragging Dallas cop. An ex-Special Forces major promoted to Lieutenant-Colonel, no less. And he's the reason the decision was made to begin our house-keeping in Washington. Initially, we were tasked to watch and wait. Then... out of nowhere, a call comes through to sweep clean in DC. Then rendezvous in Austin.'

'I see.'

'Yeah... but do you really?' the voice says. *'Because, the way things stand, I would say you people are currently running blind. In fact, it's only due to an in-field promotion that I'm able to deliver this information at all. Had the previous lead operator been half-way competent, I would never have gained our antagonist's confidence this quickly.'*

'Nonetheless... it would appear you have. And, let's face it... you're being rewarded at well above market rates to do exactly that.'

'That doesn't alter the fact, this entire operation is likely compromised.'

'As a standard operating procedure, I usually avoid jumping to rash conclusions.'

'And, as *a clown, in one of your previous administrations, was famous for saying... there are known unknowns. And I calculate they are in play, here and now. You need to remember... you employed me to infiltrate and advise. I have accomplished one... and I'm delivering the other to you now.'*

'Okay... so I'm listening.'

'Close this operation down.'

Devlin feels his heart rate spike.

'I'm afraid that's something far easier said than done.'

'Not for me,' the voice says.

Martin Devlin pictures Benjamin Nasi Abelman in his mind.

From the impression implanted during that one-time meeting. The man's angular intensity, and the cold disdain he'd seen in his eyes. The effortless athleticism. Silently contemptuous. In the manner of a physically superior alien.

'I can assure you... not everyone's options are that simple.'

'Well... my professional advice is, they should be. Our antagonist is no pussy, as you Americans like to say. But when this Colonel turned up, he made a very large and supremely self-assured Alpha blink first. And, by his own admission... with words alone.'

'With words,' Devlin says. 'What words, exactly?'

'He chose not to confide. Besides I didn't care... and I still don't. All you need to know is, as of right now, this Colonel is your known unknown. You try and marshal a defence against an unidentified force, with Yahweh knows what level of support, you might as well spit into a sandstorm. '

'Does this colonel have a name?'

'Zalizo.'

'Z-a-l-i-z-o?'

'Yes... Leg Zalizo. Leg being short for Oleg.'

'That is a particularly uncommon name.'

'Such things are of no concern to me,' Nasi says. *'What disturbs me is that your sponsors were unable to identify his current employment status or location. But we know he's out there. Because he disappeared from under the noses of two experienced spotters... on a deserted highway... in the dead of night... without a trace. Like one moment he existed, then the next... he didn't.'*

'Melodrama from you... I'm a little disappointed.'

Nasi audibly sneers.

'You seem to have forgotten... you paid for my services in advance. So please... don't attempt to patronize me. You will be expending time and effort in an entirely fruitless exercise. I'm

simply recommending you properly risk assess this threat. You should assume this Colonel knows more about your operation than you know about his, because there's way too much dust on the battlefield. And, if you elect to manoeuvre with your vision impaired... the chances you will bump into something with the potential to cause you significant harm is almost guaranteed. It's a maxim my country has come to understand better than most.'

'Are you thinking to quit on me?'

'I have not yet decided.'

'Is it a matter of remuneration?'

After a pause, Nasi says, *'Not at all.'*

'What then...?'

There's another short pause.

'Let's just say, right now, I retain a high enough level of professional curiosity to keep me from walking away. But that doesn't mean I have any inclination to sail blindly into ever more turbulent waters.'

'So can we agree a path forward that skirts the maelstrom?'

'I'm listening,' Nasi says.

Devlin has always considered himself a master of calculus. The obscene level of his secret personal wealth, testament to this innate proficiency to orchestrate and deceive those who thought themselves his superior. Consummate in his ability to gain the upper hand amid the endless power games played inside the capital beltway. Thirty years of providing access for information resulting in a huge and high-performing stock portfolio. And a hunger for wealth that had never been sated. And now, here he is, on the very cusp of achieving his life-long goal. Acquiring a tantalising slice of equity in one of only two financial organisations in the world that really mattered; whose tentacles flexed into every economic artery across the globe. North, south, east and west. Communist, capitalist, democratic, despotic. Oil-rich, gas-rich, over-run with cheap labour; prosperous in any way that could be exploited. First-world, third-world—*all around the goddam world*. Just the thought of the opportunities to come made him giddy.

He says, 'Stick with me until I call you back.'

Nasi says, *'Give me one good reason.'*

'I'll see to it your current fee is doubled... trebled, if that's what it takes.'

'Funny... I could swear I asked for a good reason.'

'Okay,' Devlin says. 'So, how does access to a client base with power and influence that makes our erstwhile antagonist look like the dockside cockroach he started out as sound to you? I can guarantee, your future employment prospects will be greatly enhanced. Plus I could arrange for the little disagreement you currently have with your government to... *disappear*.'

The connection goes quiet.

'Do I still have your attention?'

'When am I likely to receive this call?'

'How about after this unexpected visitor to our New Mexico facility is, shall we say... *neutralised*. Is that something you'd be willing to handle?'

'While it can be done. In my opinion... it's unlikely this Colonel is working alone.'

'Not your concern,' Devlin says. 'Trust me... where military matters are concerned, we're more than capable of nullifying any residual threats from this interloper. Mopping up the middle ranks is something we can handle from our end.'

'In such matters, I don't usually rely on the abilities of parties I've not been introduced to.'

'Trust me... or don't trust me. It's your choice.'

Again, the connection goes quiet.

Nasi says. *'I'm still listening.'*

'As soon as I receive independent confirmation this Colonel has been dealt with, and if you choose to keep this number active... the next time it rings, that will be your exit signal. I'm sure you have your escape route pre-planned. Any additional fees will be wired immediately. After that, lay low for seventy-two hours... after which, you'll be sanctioned to head home. Or not. You'll be free to choose.'

Devlin pauses.

'So, Mr. Abelman... are we aligned?'

After a moment, Nasi replies.

'I guess you could say, we are... for now a least.'

LUBBOCK, TEXAS

Zalizo takes his third shower of the day. As cool as the faucet would run. Dresses in freshly laundered clothes for the second time. Orders a room-service meal and a litre bottle of water. During which a multi-routed mail comes through informing him an audience with the energy commissioner has been arranged. The message includes instructions to meet with Holberton's head of security in the hotel lobby. With a caveat that an audience will only be forthcoming if security clearance is granted.

Zalizo chooses not to commit the appointment to memory. Instead, he simply ignores the summons. Rides the elevator to the tenth floor. Fist-pumps the door to Suite 1401.

After a moment or two, the door opens. Which, all by itself, vindicates his decision to by-pass the commissioner's less than stellar personal security apparatus.

'Colonel Zalizo... we presume.'

The aide looks to be in his mid-twenties and painfully thin. Sallow skinned. Sickeningly perfect teeth, if a little too long for his thin-lipped mouth. Tailored, crisp white shirt. Grey check slacks—*worn a little too short and way too tight for a male not parading up and down a Parisian catwalk*—and a pair of poser deck shoes without socks. Even in the middle of a heatwave, it was a brave look for a town this far from the ocean.

'That would be... *I*,' Zalizo says.

The aide stammers, 'Beg your pardon...?'

'There's only one of you. So the pro-noun you're looking for is... *I*. And it happens to be *Lieutenant*-Colonel.'

Zalizo steps past the stalled peacock and enters the suite. Taking in the pseudo-Scandinavian décor. Beaucoup hardwood and glass. Enough ornaments and soft furnishing to fill a decent-sized family home.

Sommerhayes Holberton is seated sideways on an over-cushioned grey lounger. Scrolling his index finger over a tablet screen balanced on his knees. He's wearing jogger pants and a Laker's T-shirt. Looking short and equally slight of stature. Even allowing for the fact that he doesn't bother getting to his feet.

'That was quick... Zac's vetting is usually an arduous affair.'

Zalizo says, 'I declined his invitation.'

'You... *declined*.'

'Yves-Saint Laurent here opened your door, just because he heard someone knocking. That should tell you all you need to know about where I assess the competence of your security management.'

To his credit, Holberton's eye contact doesn't waver.

'As much as it pains me, Colonel... forgive me, what was it again?'

'Zalizo.'

'Yes, of course... anyway, like I was saying. Hard as it is for a planet-sized ego to admit.... you're absolutely right. And, since my default is to deal in absolutes, if I'm not mistaken, you're here to offer advice as it pertains to my personal security... going forward, that is?'

'Commissioner... that depends entirely on whether you're going to take threats to your future health and well-being seriously. Because, if at any point... *going forward*, you're tempted to behave like a privileged jerk, you'll get the sum total of zip from me. Truth is, I'm far enough down the line that I can progress this operation, whether or not you end up on Salem Avenue.'

Holberton shoots a puzzled glance.

'A straight talker... I admire that. However, I'm afraid the Salem Avenue reference is lost on me?'

'It's where you'll find the County Coroner's Office.'

'*Oh*... I see.'

'Right now, Commissioner... I'm not sure you do.'

For an extended moment, Sommerhays Holberton looks for all the world like he's going to let loose his life-long assumption of superiority. Then, he visibly buttons it down, swinging his legs off the lounger.

He rises, offering his hand.

Turns out, he's a good bit taller than he first appeared. Mostly due to the fact he has an unusually long neck. And a somewhat oversized head. Both of which afford him a couple of inches more in height than he's strictly entitled to, had his anatomy been uniformly proportional.

'Well... I can see there's going to be no messing with you. And, believe it or not, I'm not so far up my own rear end that I don't recognize when someone's gone out of their way to cover it...'

He breathes out hard.

'...so, I can only offer my apologies, and accept you wouldn't be here unless the threat was credible.'

'It is,' Zalizo says, 'And imminent.'

'In that case... the apology stands. Minus my jerk-off attitude.'

Zalizo reins back his initial disdain. Decides to allow a degree of latitude for the life-time of deference the man stood before him has, no doubt, prospered under.

'Apology accepted.'

Holberton gestures an offer to sit. Zalizo declines, heading back to the door and snicking the lock, then returning to the centre of the suite.

'Zac can go check out some employment ads.'

The renewable energy tzar smiles, tilting his head.

'That's entirely possible, Colonel. Meantime... can I offer you refreshment? We've some excellent organic Guatemalan coffee I can personally recommend... Tomaz here, can do the honours.'

'I'll take a pass. I like *it*... *it* doesn't like me. Spikes my adrenalin.'

'Something stronger perhaps?'

'I'll pass on that too.'

'Sure,' Holberton says, 'Though there's one thing I'm a little curious about.'

Zalizo says, 'I'm listening.'

Holberton nods to the badge clipped on Zalizo's belt.

'I didn't know Lieutenant-Colonel was a rank within the Marshal's Service.'

'It's a temporary arrangement... for jurisdictional expediency.'

'I see... so am I permitted to know who it is you actually work for?'

‘Generally speaking... the Department of Defense.’

‘And are you able to be more specific?’

‘No... but, I’m prepared to give you access to the individual I report to. Although, word to the wise... he’s considerably less engaging than I am. So I strongly recommend you do more listening than talking. It happens to be the only way you can verify my credentials. Not because you need to. But because you should. Right now, I’d lay odds you have a large target on your back. And I shouldn’t have to remind you that, in a commercial sense, you’ve already been attacked. To my knowledge, on three separate occasions. And your construction crews have already been threatened... possibly, your lawyers too. So, however much you might not want to acknowledge the true nature of such threats... facts are facts. And it’s the reason your name is on a list with zero other candidates.’

Holberton ambles over to the window. Thrusts his hands into his pockets. Head slightly bowed.

‘Rough estimate... forty million and counting.’

Zalizo says, ‘I’d feel happier if you moved back from the window.’

‘*J-e-s-u-s*... of course.’

He returns, sharpish, to the lounger. Picks up his tablet. Stares at the screen for a few moments, before setting it down again.

‘I guess this is going to feel weird for a while.’

‘More than likely,’ Zalizo says. ‘But, you were saying something about forty million.’

‘*Ah,* yes... and that’s a minimum. Once the trouble started at our New Mexico installations, especially Dell City, our security costs went through the roof. Not to mention insurance premiums. Plus a bunch of delay penalties up and down the supply chain. And you’re right about the threats... on both counts.’

'So who's heading up the investigations right now?'

'It was all bumped up to State a while back. Here and in New Mexico. But they appear to be doing little more than sitting on their hands. Sure, we have assigned liaisons. But they're not spilling any sweat. And they sure as hell aren't sharing anything worth a damn with me or my office. All we're getting is your standard... *investigations are ongoing*, brush off.'

'You're politically appointed. You could kick up a stink. Insist on calling in Homeland Security... or the Bureau.'

'We've tried... believe me. But, up to now, all we're hearing is it would need to be pushed up the line through the governor's office. And, so far, she's shown zero willingness to punt the ball. Right now, local and state police are insisting there's no evidence pointing in any direction other than rogue employees with an axe to grind.'

'That strikes me as more than a little odd,' Zalizo says. 'Because it just so happens I was called in to advise Dallas PD on a similar spate of attacks, a little while back. And, at that time, I can assure you we treated those incidents extremely seriously.'

'And I can tell you, categorically... we've never been informed of anything of that nature.'

Zalizo pulls an expression that says—*interesting*.

'As to intimidation,' he says. 'Rogue individuals in no way fit that *MO*. That's a resource-heavy activity.'

Holberton says, 'All I know is, as of right now, as far as anyone that matters is concerned... it's still being called as circumstantial and hearsay. No-one's interested in claims of bearded men, sporting Raybans, blocking driveways with their black Escalades. Following my people around out of hours. Issuing threats to one of our attorney's, through his wife... while she was shopping in Macy's of all places...'

The commissioner returns to the lounger.

'But, if we can wind things back a little here, I'd appreciate knowing how you discovered I was being directly targeted. Because, a while back, we engaged our own private investigators... who came highly recommended. They were specifically tasked to look into any personal animosities against me being in play...'

'And, did they find anything?'

'I wouldn't know. They backed out within a month. Returned a generous retainer. Refused, point blank, to hand over anything they'd uncovered. So I'm sure you understand why I'm a little curious how you managed to put two-and-two together.'

Zalizo says, 'Let's just say... we happen to share commonality with some folk who were showing an unhealthy interest in both our itineraries.'

'Colonel... if you don't mind me saying. That's a heck of a lot of words to tell me nothing.'

'I ran into a couple of unscrupulous individuals who were persuaded to reveal their schedule... and its less than benign intent. It didn't take *Columbo* to figure out your appearance at Texas Tech was second on said schedule. I happened to be first.'

'Did they reveal who they worked for?'

'They couldn't say.'

'Couldn't... or wouldn't?'

'Trust me... if they could have, they would have.'

'Care to venture a guess?'

'Let's just say, I have a candidate on my likely suspect list. But there's a good chance they're only minding the store. As of right now, the enterprise owner is somewhat elusive.'

'Well... you might like to dial some additional numbers into your likely suspect algorithms.'

Zalizo says, 'Such as?'

Holberton hesitates.

'Well... you could start with the main beneficiaries of all that tax revenue. That's three-point-nine billion last year alone. Off of fifty-five billion in annual profits... and that's just from the top six oil producers. That's two-point-four trillion since the early-*Nineties*. And who d'you think's sucking on that big old sow's tit?'

For effect, he parodies a famous *Rodin* sculpture.

'A whole army of hedge fund managers, for sure. Wholesalers and distributors. Infrastructure supply chain... and on, and on down the line. Not to mention an estimated one-hundred and twenty million annual spend on reportable donations... both philanthropic and political. And that's not even dusting for Department of Defense prints on the tiller.'

Zalizo says, 'What's that supposed to mean, exactly?'

Holberton raises an eyebrow.

'*Oh,* come on, Colonel... you can quit playing dumb with me. Conservatively, your employer purchases a quarter million barrels of oil a day. That's equivalent to twelve-point-six million gallons of refined fuel just to keep you guys mobile for twenty-four hours. The US Army's annual dollar spend alone exceeds three billion. Factor in the Navy. The Air Force... you do the multiples. And you may think that's a hunk of purchasing leverage... but you'd be wrong. It's the other way round. Leverage lies in the risk to supply. And critical mitigation at those levels demand a high premium. Not to mention a vested interest in maintaining that supply infrastructure. And here, we're talking world-wide. So you see, for the military, it's not so much supply and demand. It's more a case of, supply or be damned...'

Zalizo keeps his counsel. It was obvious the Commissioner wasn't finished.

'...and, you can take my word. There are no tactics your employer wouldn't engage in to ensure their mainline addiction remains satisfied. Ultimately, every branch but the Navy, because they at least operate nuclear-powered assets, are one-hundred per cent tied in to the extraction of crude oil... and to hell with whoever owns the land it lies under.'

Zalizo holds out his satellite phone.

'You want to make that call?'

Again, Holberton hesitates.

'If you don't mind, Colonel... I'm going to straight-up trust you on this one. But don't ask me to extend that courtesy beyond these four walls. Because, to put it bluntly... that isn't going to happen. Not until the people you work for curb their dependency.'

'You could be waiting quite some time.'

'Could be... especially since there's a long and somewhat chequered history of stifled innovation when it comes to reducing carbon-base fuel consumption. And not all of it enacted through purely commercial mechanisms.'

Zalizo says, 'There will always be conspiracy theories.'

'Indeed, that's true. And it may surprise you to hear, back during my days as a fund manager, I used to think the same way.'

Holberton picks up his tablet. Begins jabbing at the screen with his fingers.

'But, here's an example for you. Hybridisation...'

He pronounces the word like he was delivering the opening address at a TED seminar.

'...for over five years now, the Secretaries for the Army and Navy have been sitting on a proposal that would reduce fuel consumption by thirty-to-forty percent. Reductions at that level would remove the need for this beacon of democracy and freedom to interfere in the affairs of sovereign territories, or at least those with predominantly sand-based topography, with its current recidivistic tendency.'

Zalizo feels something he can't quite put a name to stir in his gut.

'You study science to any level, Colonel?'

'I dabbled a little at college.'

Holberton raises his eyebrows.

'The question was rhetorical... You think me incapable of doing a little digging of my own?'

Zalizo says, 'It's a habit of mine not to judge.'

'That's very reassuring, Colonel. So take a perch somewhere. It shouldn't take you long to run a critical eye over this... if you're inclined to being open-minded.'

Holberton offers his tablet. Zalizo wavers, then reaches forward.

'I just might be,' he says.

MARKS CENTRE, WASHINGTON DC

In addition to being jittery, the footage playing on her laptop is out of focus and heavily pixelated. And, for any individual—*other than the one she's looking at right now*—close to useless for the purposes of positive identification.

The capture is of a lone figure. Moving in the direction of the camera. Along a narrow airport concourse. After a few seconds, the recording switches to the same individual passing through a doorway barely wide enough or high enough for someone of such evidently mammoth proportions to fit through with ease.

In any event, even without the security tape, Lafayette

Regional had offered a name the moment they'd received a description. Flight logs, manifests and a US passport number identified the person—*labelled only as a subject of interest*—as surely as if they'd been finger-printed. So now she has a name.

Runellie smiles to herself.

Victor Labette.

La Bête...

...the beast.

She'd also confirmed their antagonist to be a former high-flying CIA operator. A one-time darling of its Directorate of Operations. And the first ever new recruit inducted into its ultra-classified and much vaunted Z-Group. A covert, wet-work sub-cell that had, for years, remained faceless and untouchable. Operating with impunity. Until the day it had strayed way outside its boundaries. At a time when the Iran-Contra debacle had been at its height. Disbanded and disgraced for attempting to hold a blade to the very throats of those Langley mandarins responsible for the group's creation. And, when heads had started to role, Labette's had rolled first and furthest. After which a large swathe of the nation's most sensitive Black Ops programmes had been brought back under direct Executive Branch oversight.

She smiles to herself a second time. Pondering if her own unit's activities were subject to a similar level of scrutiny.

Meanwhile, over the preceding hours, she'd gotten a good way into their subject's bio. Digging, as far as she'd been able, into his history prior to his arrival at Langley. Back to the time he'd spent at Cornell University. Where he'd majored in languages and captained the basketball squad—*unsurprisingly*.

A little further into his past, and things became even more opaque. His language scholarship at Ithaca mired in rumour and intrigue. Mostly around the absence of any family support before his arrival in up-state New York. On the other hand, there had been one interesting recommendation, upon which his acceptance had proved pivotal. A personal endorsement from a noted dealer in antiquities. An Austrian immigrant from the post-war era. And a major private donor and fund-raiser, until he joined the worms, under the earth in New Orleans, a couple of days preceding Victor Labette becoming a freshman.

New Orleans PD investigations into the art dealer's demise had raised unresolved concerns at the time. Because the old man had been discovered naked and bound. Asphyxiated. An unmasticated fig, of all things, lodged in his oesophagus. Like something from the plot of an Agatha Christie novel. And, more than likely the reason a diligent ME at the time had not ruled out forced placement—*post-mortem*. Added to which, there had been no prints worth a damn found in the apartment. Not even the old man's. So, for sure, any assumption NOPD might have had, suggesting an auto-erotic encounter having gone tragically wrong, didn't entirely hang together. Witnesses, neighbours mostly, had made statements. Fingering a tall male caller. How tall they couldn't say—*the building's ceilings and doorways being so high an'all.* Whatever, the suspect was claimed to have been a regular caller at the old exile's apartment. And a frequent stay-over—*to boot*. Always dressed in a hoody. Most likely a New Orleans Saints fan, judging by the cap he'd always worn low over his face. Likely *Caucasian* too, because of his pale hands.

It went without saying, eyebrows had been raised. Tongues had most definitely wagged; in the manner of folk with a good amount of idle time on their hands. Whispers had echoed up and down the ornate stairwells of the exclusive colonial apartment block. But the old émigré's mysterious visitor was never positively identified, on account of the abundance of athletic young men he'd—*entertained*. After which NOPD's interest had waned. The no prints thing eventually waved aside. The old man was rumoured to have been notoriously fussy. Employing a middle-aged Latino woman to come in twice a day. The cleaner was also never traced. Presumed to have been the nine-one-one caller and assumed to have been an illegal. And by the time the dust had finally settled, the art dealer's estate had gone into a blind trust.

At which point the investigation had hit the buffers and consigned to NOPD's substantial cold case archive.

But—*and it was a significant, but*—years later, Victor Labette had set himself up as a dealer in antiquities. Made donations, albeit of smaller value, to the language faculty at Cornell.

So now, Runellie has yearbook photos of a much younger man. Classified as Caucasian, but with a decidedly evident olive tan. Thick head of hair. Soulless grey eyes. And, even back then, it was obvious he'd been built like a mountain.

She smiles to herself a third time. Finds herself speculating how much resource would have been allocated to an investigation into the suspicious death of a wealthy old white guy—*especially in Mississippi during the eighties*—if the frequent male guest had been fingered as black.

'Girl...' she tells herself. *'...just file the damn report.'*

PAULO ALTO HILLS, TEXAS

Turner's cell phone is ringing.

Seigo fetches if from the Bronco. Activates the call and holds the device up close to the Brit's good ear. Keeping the blade of his infantry knife pressed to the merc's throat.

'Where are you?' asks a disembodied voice from the speaker.

Turner says, 'Who's doing the asking?'

An icy pause slices its way up the line.

'Your newly-appointed lead contact.'

The voice barking through the speaker has a sharp accent that's hard to place.

'What happened to the other guy...?' Turner says,

The voice says, *'That's not your concern.'*

'From your point of view... maybe,' Turner says. 'But we don't take orders from any Tom, Dick or Harry who happens to call.'

'Well... Invictus is a little pre-occupied right now. So I strongly recommend against pestering him with your petty inquiries. Which means, the fact I have both your numbers will have to suffice.'

Turner stalls just long enough to suggest a plausible—*wait while I process this*—pause.

'Fine... so we're exactly where we were ordered to be.'

'And still no contact?'

'Don't you think one of us would have reported in by now if we had?'

There's another pause.

'You sound a little stressed... is what I think. Which means I need assurance your status is being reported accurately?'

Turner breathes out heavily.

'And you sound like even more of an arrogant prick than your predecessor. You need to remember we're the ones out here getting boiled. So, say your piece... then leave us the fuck alone to do our jobs. We didn't sign up to have some stiff-arsed Yid breathing down our necks. And, in case you're wondering... I've always been good with accents.'

'So it would seem,' the caller says. *'Regardless, you'll be receiving a location soon. You're to go there and wait for the individual we're sending to show. They will enter the address, and you've been tasked to neutralise whoever exits.'*

Turner says, 'And what about our Lubbock assignment?'

'It's been... re-allocated.'

'To who?'

'Again... not your concern. But be assured... they can manage every bit as well as you.'

Turner looks up at Seigo, cautious against the pressure from the blade pressed to his throat. Trying and failing to keep the realization they were quickly becoming irrelevant—*everywhere*—from his eyes.

'We'd still prefer to hear about this kind of deviation from the plan, direct from the organ grinder.'

'And you need to appreciate... not everyone in the free world understands your quaint British Empire colloquialisms.'

'From the *fuckin'* boss,' Turner growls. 'Because I'm guessing you're nothing more than hired help... just like us. So, we may just decide we ain't acting on any instructions from you, until we hear from *The Man* himself. Now, go stick that in your land-grabbing kibbutz and smoke it.'

Seigo cuts the call.

Throughout, the one named Hatton has lain unconscious. Foetal position. Breathing shallow and ragged.

Seigo rises, turning to look out over the bluff. Contemplating the grudging respect he's just gained for Turner's sense of loyalty. The outrageous insults he'd used to signal his distress. Letting his handler know to quit revealing information. Convinced his captor would put his insolence down to nothing more than the dying vestiges of colonial arrogance. The self-same conceit that had no doubt persuaded him, a Native American would likely never have been schooled in the subtle arts of deception.

Seigo turns back, decision made. Because he figures—*despite Leg having some kind of bug up his ass, over something which remained unspoken*—he knows his long-time friend would approve. The uncompromising brutality he'd witnessed all those years before was still there; albeit tempered somehow. Not constrained exactly. More like his decision-making process had acquired one more item to be checked.

Staying true to his warrior code, Seigo takes a moment to look directly into Turner's rapidly dilating pupils

He grabs hold of Turner's hair with his left hand—*real tight*. Stabs him in the neck with his right. Jerks the blade left and right. Quick and neat, and none too deep; so his blade wouldn't snag on the Brit's spinal column. Pinning him against the Bronco's grill with his knee. Releasing him only when he quits all his thrashing. Leaving him to topple over onto his side and finish bleeding out.

Then he steps over to where the one named Hatton lies inert.

CAPITOL HILL, WASHINGTON DC

Senator Clarence Hellermann III strides down the marble hallway. One of many thousands of times he's done so, during an illustrious career in both state and national politics. As he had from the very beginning, feeling right at home. Coddled and emboldened, in equal measure, by the Senate building's august history and dignified edifice. Without fear of contradiction, still one of the capital's major league players. And, for damn sure, a fully paid-up member of its intellectual elite. Although, even he had to admit—*to the delight of many*—a somewhat lesser colossus than in times gone by.

Which likely explains why, even after all these many years, he now only receives a couple of coy glances from a duet of swan-like female aides who pass him by. Looking unusually harassed and ill-at-ease. Making space for him as they scurry on. Unconsciously deferential to his passage. Their slim arms cradling binders. Gripping their cell phones with their brightly varnished nails. Blushing wannabees. Blonde enough and shapely enough to audition for cable news anchor roles—*likely before either of them reaches thirty*—fronting up some glossy early-morning news show, spewing the usual bought-and-paid-for, fully sanitized, over-scripted Beltway babble. Your archetypal purveyors of twenty-four-seven verbal fodder. All neatly packaged into endless, polarized soundbites for the mentally-challenged chattering class.

He punches his access code into the keypad next to the oak-panelled door—*suddenly weary of just how obscene and meaningless his life in national politics had become*—checking left and right, before pushing down on the ornate handle, to verify he'll have a few precious moments of isolation within the protective embrace of his private retreat. Wondering how much time he would get to sit alone, with his eyes closed. Able, at last, to shut himself off from the cluster-fuck he's foolishly allowed to spin way outside his control.

He pushes the door open.

There's a figure, leaning cross-legged against his desk. Midway to stowing a cell phone into his inside jacket pocket. Grey haired. Grey suited. Neither big nor small. Craggy-faced. Smallish, bridgeless nose that looked like it had been knuckle-busted a couple times somewhere down the line. And for someone just about to get a weighty senatorial boot up their rear, staring back without a trace of concern from beneath his fleshy eyelids.

The figure folds his arms. Waiting.

Hellermann keeps the door held open. Involuntarily stiffening his back. Puffing his chest out.

'And who, in God's name, are you...?'

His eyes dart around the room, nerve ends jangling.

'More to the point... what imbecile let you in here?'

The figure makes no move to get off the desk. Doesn't twitch a muscle in point of fact, if you discount the way he subtly moistens his thin, pale lips before he speaks.

'I'm someone with security clearance all the way to *hoodoo*.'

Hellermann says, 'I have no idea what that's supposed to mean.'

'That's because, unlike me, Senator... you don't hail from Wyoming.'

'Whoever you are... you're making no sense. And, without an appointment... you sure as hell don't belong in my office. Now... or any other time. So if you don't mind.'

Hellermann sweeps his hand back toward the brightly-lit marble hallway. Politely indicating his uninvited guest should leave.

The figure remains stubbornly immobile.

'Well, *Senator*... unfortunately for you, I operate under a long-standing special executive order. Re-issued by the last four commanders-in-chief. Or maybe it's five. To be perfectly honest, since I officially retired some time ago... I occasionally lose track.'

The figure pushes himself off the desk.

'Whichever... when it comes to securing this nation's most critical resource. Namely control of, and access to, the oil reserves its military assets require to function effectively. It means I get to go wherever I want... whenever I choose... for whatever reason I deem merits my attention. And, right now, that scrutiny is pointed squarely at you, Senator Hellermann. As well as a number of other individuals in your orbit. So I recommend you step inside, while I remind you of the ephemeral nature of political supremacy in this town. Because it's the best and only advice you're likely to receive from me, this side of your funeral.'

Hellermann feels his bowels loosen.

'For whatever reason... you and your minions have caused my otherwise meticulously-conceived operation to spiral out of control.'

Hellermann hears himself mutter weakly, '*Your* ... operation?'

'Yes, Senator... *my* operation. From the very beginning... right through to now. Every concept... every thought... every notion any of you people ever had... all of them designed or implanted by me. Right up to the point when you sanctioned that desperate bitch's attempt to cling to power.'

Hellermann swallows hard.

'None of that was my doing. I didn't sanction...'

The figure raises his hand.

'And you should have kept that germophobic viper of yours on a much shorter chain.'

The figure extends his arm, indicating the senator should move away from the door.

'As far as who I am... for the time being, I suggest we limit it to... *General*.'

He allows the door swing closed, moving slowly past the figure to stand behind his desk.

For a brief moment he contemplates standing his ground. After all, he's not short of powerful allies. Both in the Senate and the Justice Department. The thought of surrendering weakly close to unthinkable. But he's also aware the level of access and influence the figure standing before him would have needed to gain access to his office had to be off the scale.

He eases himself into his elegant high-backed leather chair.

'What reputational safeguards can I expect in exchange for my co-operation?'

The figure eyes him with cold indifference.

'None whatsoever.'

Clarence Hellermann III breathes out long and slow. Slumping back heavily and closing his eyes.

'Then I have no choice but to resign.'

'Wise decision,' the figure says.

LUBBOCK, TEXAS

A message had been left for him at the Overton's reception desk. Which is odd. Because, other than Seigo, Zalizo hadn't told anyone where he was staying. And Seigo wasn't inclined to leave messages, that was for damn sure.

He makes it barely half way across the lobby when an auburn-haired woman calls to him from behind a long, polished wood-panelled counter, topped with a bank of monitors.

'Excuse me, sir... *excuse me*. Would your name be Zalenzo?'

'Not exactly,' he says, 'But close enough.'

He veers in her direction as she continues loudly. Smiling through her lip gloss. Ignorant of her volume and the red smudge-line dotted across her teeth.

'We've received a message for you... from the Sheriff's office up in Plainview.'

She pauses and continues to beam in his direction. Enough that he feels an unaccustomed obligation to continue the conversation.

'And what message might that be... ma'am?'

The woman broadens her smile. Seems determined to keep it fixed there.

'Sheriff Tillings' secretary called. She said the Sheriff had some important information for you.'

'I'm guessing she didn't pass on the details?'

'Oh heck... *no*. I imagine it might well be confidential in nature.'

He leans in close.

'I imagine it might,' he says quietly.

'Oh, deary me,' she says, dialling her voice down to a whisper. 'Quite so... Sorry.'

The woman blushes. Strokes an illusory strand of hair back into place behind her ear.

'She said the sheriff's on his way down to meet with you.'

'Meet with me... where exactly?'

'Well... she said the Sheriff assured her you would likely know the Smokehouse on I-27.'

He says, 'Happens, I do.'

'Excellent... because she said the Sheriff is offering to stand you lunch.'

'That's uncommonly generous.'

'Well, yes Marshal. I guess it is at that... most unusual, to be sure. Tillings is well remembered in this town. But certainly not for his generosity.'

'Good to know.'

'You're welcome... So you'all have a nice day.'

'We'll do our level best. Though, to be completely candid... there may be a better chance of that happening if the sheriff's secretary had given you a hint when this tryst might take place.'

'Oh, goodness. Of course... silly me.'

The woman flushes bright as a flare.

'She said anytime around midday would be good for the Sheriff.'

'Thank you ma'am... that's also good to know.'

He turns to leave before she melts.

Thirty minutes later, he's watching Tillings as he struggles to manoeuvre his rear end from a plenty broad enough steel-framed chair. For some reason—*presumably known only to the proprietor*—there are half-a-dozen peacocks strutting around the outside dining area. Tails fully fanned; shrieking a well-timed soundtrack as Plainview's senior law officer un-wedges himself from his seat.

A few tables back, a sizable group of equally large, scrimmage-line frat-types noisily drink their lunch. Laughing like hyenas. Jostling each other for no discernible reason. Throwing play punches—*with some not so playful.*

Tillings nods his head in the direction of the raucous troupe.

'You want me to shoot them... or ask them to leave?'

Zalizo says, 'No great loss to the future of humanity, either way.'

Tillings says, *'A-men.'*

'So what have you got for me, Sheriff?'

'I see we're still enrolled in those... social engagement, self-help sessions.'

Zalizo suppresses a smile. 'Is lunch mandatory?'

Tillings says, 'Not on my account.'

'I feel the same way about banalities,' Zalizo says.

'Okay, Colonel... have it your way. I sure as hell didn't drive all the way down here to listen to juvenile cackle and have you piss on my neck. In point of fact, I'm only here because I was patrolling this town when your parents were butchered.'

Zalizo maintains a dead pan expression. Inside, he registers an all too familiar pain stabbing through his chest. That burning sensation he always feels, of old scar tissue being laid open, whenever the death of his parents became a topic of conversation.

Tillings is eyeing him closely.

Zalizo re-evaluates. Could be the guy was something more than your typical country numbskull after all.

'You think me so dumb I wouldn't recall a name as unusual as yours.'

'Not at all,' Zalizo says. 'I figured you knew something about me when you told the Overton's receptionist I'd be sure to know this place.'

'Well here's something you likely didn't figure...'

Tillings eases himself back into his seat, gesturing for Zalizo to sit.

'The Zalizo murders caused quite a stir at the time... as you can imagine. It was an unusually brutal attack for this town back then. And it wasn't beyond the realms of the possible that you were somehow involved. You know how it goes... always look to the family first.'

Tillings shrugs.

'Anyhow, you were under surveillance for a while. College kid or not. And guess what we observed?'

Zalizo says, 'I don't play guessing games.'

'Fair enough,' Tillings says. 'So I'll tell you. We observed you being observed. We traced your watchers to a Russian immigrant outfit, or some-such... running some dubious cab operation out of Albuquerque. Which turned out to be your parents' previous place of residence...'

Tillings pauses.

'...shall I go on?'

'You have your First Amendment rights, Sheriff... same as the next man.'

'Well, it wasn't my case. I was still a beat cop back then. But I do recall hearing something about a jurisdictional dispute. Along the lines of Lubbock PD being strong-armed into passing the case over to the Feds. Then, low and behold... the entire investigation is dropped. Something about a major organized crimes ruckus, out in the New Mexico desert someplace... where exactly, I don't recall. But I do remember hearing that the guys who'd been watching you had been taken out in some kind of territorial feud.'

Tillings casually waves a hand.

'So like I say... not a name I'd easily forget.'

'Fascinating,' Zalizo says.

At that moment, one of the frats yells out across the terrace.

'Hey... since y'all got tax-payer time on your hands. Either you two... *O-F-F-I-C-E-R-S* wanna come share a... *D-R-I-N-K* with us?'

Zalizo rises from his seat. Moves in a leisurely fashion toward the crowd.

He comes to a stop, face-to-face with a kid close on four inches taller. The rest of the troupe knot around, like a run-the-clock-out scrimmage. The kid starts to lift his beer in salute. Zalizo taps him in the groin with the back of his left hand—*real fast and real hard*. He ghosts a step to the side as the kid drops his plastic beer mug, doubling forward as his knees give way. Zalizo grabs a fist full of hair—*real tight*—to stop him from collapsing as he pukes. Drags the kid after him as he heads toward the parking lot. Along the way, he stomps his heavy boots—*real solid like*—onto a gauntlet of open-toed sliders. Ramming his elbow, equally hard, into beer-softened guts. Gives his drag-along a palm slap to keep him in line.

The troupe's confidence drains away faster than camel piss in a desert.

Zalizo comes to a stop at the entrance to a hedge-lined, gravel parking lot. Leaning in close to the kid's ear. Speaking loud enough for everyone to hear.

'Yesterday, not long after sun up, I got to look at a girl's lifeless body. I'm guessing she'd have been about your age. She'd been shot through the chest. Which left a hole way bigger than your mouth where her spine used to be. And, after they'd shot her… for no other reason than she happened to be there, someone slashed each of her legs wide open with a long-bladed knife. Groin to ankle. Cuts as deep as your butt crack…'

He releases the kid's hair. Knees him hard in the chest, sitting him on his ass.

'I don't think anyone would disagree… she was a lot prettier than any of you. And likely a lot more civil too, I'll bet. And, I'm guessing, a damn sight more pleasant to be around.'

He turns to the suddenly less rowdy troupe.

'Just like all of you… she was young, dumb and pretty as they come. But, unlike you… she won't ever get to drink cold beer on a hot afternoon. Or walk home to her mother's embrace.'

He points to the next biggest in the troupe.

'So here's how the rest of your day goes. Stay or leave, I've no particular preference either way. Drink or don't drink. I couldn't care less. But here's the kicker, fellas. One more word in my direction, from any of you… you'll be crawling home to momma stinking of stomach acid and warm beer.'

He clenches his fists. Wide-angles the troop with his eyes. Waits for them to drift past in turn. Then he slow-walks back to Tillings. Sits down. Gestures toward the menu lying on the ironwork table.

‘I’d be content with steak and eggs,’ he says. ‘And any vegetables not shaped like fries.’

‘Sure,’ Tillings says.

Zalizo says, ‘While we’re waiting to order... you can tell me what you’ve got. Then I’ll tell you if we are going to get re-acquainted better than when we last met.’

Tillings says, ‘I can do that.’

Zalizo says, ‘When a man stops jabbering, for no other reason than he likes the sound of his own voice... you’ll find I’m a pretty good listener.’

‘And a plain talker.’

‘Generally speaking.’

‘Okay... So, late yesterday, I got handed an APB out of Albuquerque. FBI and DEA posted. Possible domestic terrorist on the loose... though why they hit on that status beats me. Whatever, their perp was assumed to have crossed state lines. Possibly riding a stolen RAM 1500...’

Tillings settles back in his seat.

‘A vehicle matching that description was found this morning. Burnt out in some kind of arson attack, out back of an air strip off Highway 84.’

‘And you figured what, exactly?’

‘Well... I have to admit, the threat you mentioned struck me as fanciful at the time. But then, I got to thinking. What if...? So I called in a favour from a State Trooper buddy of mine. Asked him if there were any security cameras facing out from the airfield.’

The Sheriff grins long and wide.

‘We hit paydirt about four hours ago. A couple of shadowy images... at distance. But enough to get a general description.’

‘Don’t tell me,’ Zalizo says. ‘Bearded male... bald... aviator shades. Humping a canvas carry bag.’

'The very same... 'cept he must have ditched the shades. Mind telling me where you got your information?'

Zalizo ignores the question.

'How did you track me down?'

Tillings re-fixes his grin.

'Like I said, Colonel. I'm from around here... man and boy. Started out with Lubbock PD. Just like my old man before me. And his daddy was a Texas Ranger, back before World War Two. I made it to sergeant... then a short stint in homicide. So let's just say, I called in some more favours. My secretary did the leg-work. She's a very protective lady. Not to mention, extremely tenacious.'

'Sheriff, you've just gone up in my estimation.'

'Coming from you, I'm inclined to think that's a thin endorsement when it comes to flattery.'

'Not at all,' Zalizo says. 'Consider yourself entirely misjudged. And I have a feeling that row of citations on your wall is about to get longer.'

Tillings says, 'Not as important to me as you might think... but thanks.'

'Likewise...' Zalizo says, dialling in a more conciliatory tone. '...and you might consider doing me a couple more courtesies.'

'Shoot...' Tillings says.

'Call in as many favours as you can. Put the word out at motels... gas stations and the like. White male... slim... short of six foot... driving on isolated back roads, most likely. Chances are he's smart enough to change the way he looks. So forget the security footage description. Keep it to lone males. It'll be worth any police harassment claims. This one's as mean as they come. I'd appreciate a call if anything flags up.'

'That's a pretty big ask, Colonel... considering we haven't

exactly hit it off...'

Tillings goes quiet for a beat.

'But okay... let's say I'm prepared to let bye-gones be bye-gones. You mentioned a couple of courtesies.'

'Indeed, I did.'

Tillings angles his head.

'*So...?*'

'Keep a close eye on that sidekick of yours.'

'Abbott...?'

'The same.'

Tillings says, 'And why would I do that?'

'He puts one step wrong... especially around the subject of financial indiscretion. Don't fire his ass... put it in jail. Because it's going to happen. Sooner or later... guaranteed.'

'I'll take it on advisement.'

'You do that.'

Tillings says, 'Can we order now?'

Zalizo says, 'I see no good reason not to.'

LUBBOCK, TEXAS

He'd always dreamed of being a pilot. A fanciful aspiration to be sure. But it's the reason he remembers he'd watched a documentary one time. On Discovery Channel, or something of the kind. He can't quite recall when or where. More than likely in some motel someplace. A military thing from way back in the nineteen-forties. About how the Brits had seen off invasion in the early years of the war with Hitler. The Battle of Britain. All about how its puny air force had seen off swarms of Nazi bombers and their deadly fighter escorts. Engaging with the enemy, day and night. Month after month. Flying exhausted. Never backing down. The monochrome film of the aerial duels, grainy and flickering. With no soundtrack. All the same, the brutality plain to see. Relentless kill-or-be-killed pursuits, over a landscape of quaint patchwork fields. And sometimes out over the sea.

For no reason he could put words to, it had stuck in his mind.

In particular, he recalled the name of one airfield the Brits had flown out of. Where pilots had slept exhausted on the grass, next to their planes. Scrambling off to protect their capital city whenever the sirens wailed. *RAF Biggin Hill*. Little more than open pasture and corrugated sheds. Located somewhere rural, outside London.

So Perry thought it extra spooky the agri airstrip—*where he'd taken pleasure torching the kid's ride*—went by the exact same name. Biggin Hill Airport. Neighbouring Highway 84. Ten miles north-west of Lubbock.

He'd scorched the fancy pick-up out back of a long wooden hanger. Close enough to ensure it would set the building alight. Guaranteeing a pretty big distraction.

And, sure enough, it had.

He'd changed his disguise a good way down the road—*watching as the fire trucks raced back the way he'd come*—exchanging his mullah's beard and shades for a John Denver-styled hair piece and clear-lensed, frameless spectacles. The flimsy, scholarly type. Spent barely a minute, with his thumb out, before getting picked by up a slow-moving ride, rubber-necking the blaze from their a beat-up kid-carrier.

They'd dropped him off on the outskirts of town, still jabbering on about the fire—*and how fucking migrants were turning the whole goddam neighbourhood to shit*. Wishing him luck with his studies as they'd waved him off. Convinced they'd just done a wholesome Texas Tech student a small favour.

But then, he'd always looked a good deal younger with semi-long hair.

Now, he's cutting a decent-sized hole in the sheetrock ceiling of the budget motel he's booked into. Directly above the threshold. Making sure it was a decent size. Because, when the time came, he needs to be sure his movements are unhindered. Especially since he has to assume he might only get one shot at executing his plan. After all, he isn't particularly tall. Nor particularly heavy. But then, he doesn't anticipate he'll need to be. The thick plastic sheath he's bought—*in a discount hardware store half-a-mile down the commercial strip from the motel*—would see to that.

If'un he gets his timing just right.

The idea came to him as he'd waited for the fire to take hold. From the moment he'd caught sight of an orange windsock, billowing on the other side of a turf runway. The battle plan popping into his head fully formed.

Surprise and immobilize.

Just like those plucky Brits.

He has no idea how long he'll be forced to wait until his quarry arrives. Perched, as he is, just inside the roof space. The plastic sheath in position. Knotted at one end. The other end held open by a piece of garden cane, soaked in the bathtub; making it subtle enough to bend without splitting. Zip-ties and duct tape lined up against the skirting board. The debris from all the cutting, swept up and dumped in the bathtub; out of sight behind a discoloured shower curtain.

He'd watched enough orb weavers at work—*out in the back yard when he was a kid*—to know how this will go. Wrapping their prey in silk cocoons with the strength of steel wire. The grubby floor rug—*rolled up and arranged with a pillow*—stuffed beneath the bedspread, a good enough likeness to a body at rest.

Despite his best efforts, his mind races ahead to the hours of fun he'll be sure to have. As certain as he could be that he'll likely remain undisturbed while he bags his prize.

He pictures his victim entering the room. Convinced they were the predator. No doubt supremely confident in their size and power. More than likely toting a silenced weapon of some kind. And for these reasons—*and possibly more*—this would-be hunter won't think to look up at the ceiling. Because why would they? Their professional pride ensuring they'd be less likely to shout and scream once the trap was sprung.

Sure, they were bound to panic some. Maybe thrash about until exhausted. Then, for a moment or two, they'll likely settle down. Desperately searching for some way to turn their situation around.

But by then, it will be way too late.

Within a minute, whoever walks through the door—*no matter their size and strength*—they will be out of air to breathe. The bottom end of the sheath knotted tight. The other end zip-tied and duct taped. Their fate sealed—*literally*.

Perry hauls himself up through the ceiling, trailing the plastic sheath.

Not long now.

AUSTIN, TEXAS

Victor has the passenger seat of Nasi's rental pushed back to the stops, and the backrest raked past forty-five degrees.

Regardless, he still feels hemmed in.

They are parked up where West 35th Street terminates. A stone's throw from where the lesser of the nation's two Colorado Rivers turns into the upwardly mobile, suburban playgrounds of Lake Travis, before resuming its leisurely progress, onward towards the Gulf of Mexico. Occupying a space at the far end of a parking lot servicing a waterfront tennis club. Surrounded by a corral of hard courts. The thwack of balls on catgut echoing non-stop. No matter they have the windows up and the air-con blasting.

Right now, Victor is one snide comment away from putting a fist through the Israeli's implacable face.

'I'm not saying it's not plausible... I'm asking you to run it by me one more time... We're operating under a chain of command here, Nasi. I would advise you keep that at the forefront of your mind when you speak to me. I appreciate you are not inclined to toadyism *à la* Mr. Miller. Nonetheless, your assertion sounds somewhat speculative... So, if I can make time to fly back here at your request... I'm going to insist you humour me.'

Nasi shrugs.

'I'm saying... your man was overly aggressive. Like he was sending some kind of message. Excessively provocative. A situation-not-normal signal. I may not rate them, but one thing they are not is wantonly insubordinate. Brits rarely are. Their training is too regimented. They don't antagonize. They soak up bullshit orders and move forward. Especially Paras. It's in their unit's DNA. It's what makes them dependable. Plus, I had a feeling I was on speaker during the call.'

Victor breathes out heavily through his nose, trying to reduce the tension he feels spreading across his temple.

'So let's say they're compromised. And let's assume our

Colonel's the provocateur.'

'That's if he's still operating alone,' Nasi says.

'We have no evidence to the contrary.'

'As of a day ago, we had no evidence he was a spook...'

Victor grunts as Nasi continues.

'...yet more proof our field of view is narrow. Which means we can either sit tight and hope for updates, or I can go to Lubbock and make sure the core mission is fulfilled... no matter Hatton and Turner's status.'

'That wouldn't leave enough time for you to deal with our other sidebar.'

'What other... *sidebar?*'

'Perry and Carl's scheduled encounter.'

Nasi stares straight ahead. Stays silent for a good few beats longer than strictly necessary.

'You're free to take what I'm about to say any way you choose... Or you can accept this is how it's going to be.'

'Okay,' Victor says. 'I'm listening.'

'Whatever future you have in mind for those two, I want no part of it. I do surgical. As such I have no interest in socio-genetic engineering.

Victor laughs out loud.

'*Bravo*, Mr. Ableman... *bravo*.'

Nasi says, 'I mean no offence.'

'None taken,' Victor says. 'Ordinarily, I don't appreciate having my decisions countermanded. But, on this occasion, I'm prepared to respect your position. However... I still think we should continue reaching out to Hatton and Turner.'

'I have,' Nasi says, 'And they are not answering.'

Inside, Victor's sense of humour quickly drains away. It's been close on fifty years since he's been screwed by anyone without his explicit consent. He recalls he didn't like it then.

And, for certain, he doesn't much care for it now.

'Okay... let's fire a message to Turner's cell with Perry's location. If they're compromised, this Zalizo character will almost certainly start poking around. And should the fates be on our side, maybe he'll run into Perry or Miller... or both. If it turns out the *Brits* are still active, we lose nothing. They were due to move into position in Lubbock in any event. Could be we catch ourselves a lucky break.'

'In my opinion, it will take far more competent individuals than a killer of unarmed civilians and a washed-up Ranger to take such a man down. And, trust me... I've completed far more complex missions... against far more proficient adversaries... and in far less time... than the likes of Miller has ever accomplished.'

'I don't doubt it,' Victor says, 'But I wouldn't underestimate Miller's capabilities if I were you. In my experience, the *75th* are plenty tough. But, if you're assumptions are correct, and it turns out our Colonel has loosened the Brit's tongues, it might just work to our advantage if we begin to create a little chaos of our own.'

'Agreed,' Nasi says. 'Besides, there's nothing the Brits can reveal about who's been tasked to finish their mission. The only thing I told them was, replacement assets had been assigned.'

'*Assets*,' Victor says, 'Plural.'

'Correct...' Nasi says.

'Well, aren't you the sneaky non-gentile.'

Nasi sets his jaw.

'I may well be,' he says.

'Even so,' Victor says. 'We underestimate him at our peril.'

'I never underrate opponents,' Nasi says. 'But, as of right now, I'm invisible to your Colonel. So, if I get out there... this could be our first solid opportunity to out manoeuvre him.'

Victor nods in agreement.

'When it comes to warfare, Mr. Abelman... creating confusion in your enemy's mind is the next best thing to overwhelming force.'

'Akhen,' Nasi says.

CAPITOL HILL, WASHINGTON DC

Martin Devlin is sitting at his desk. Anticipating a call that hadn't come. Now the better part of two hours has passed and his office feels as frigid as its decor. In truth, the room disgusts him. In his own estimation, it's a mean, unfit space for someone with his scope of influence. Little more than a windowless hovel, lit by a single fluorescent strip, spilling its meagre wash of light across sepia walls and the odd piece of inelegant hardwood furniture. He's always felt it represented a kind of unspoken mockery. No doubt some petty facilities bureaucrat retaliating—*in the only manner they could*—against the unease his mere presence usually generated in a room. Which is why, over these many years, he'd spent a minimum amount of time there as possible. And the reason he deeply resents having to hang around this late into the afternoon.

After all, he was long past playing lackey to anyone.

To hell with that.

He scoops the cell phones off his desk. Stuffs them into the side pocket of his carry case.

As he begins shutting down his laptop, one of the phones issues an avian chirp. Which makes it the *red* one. Which means it's the call he's been waiting for.

'Yes . . .?'

The caller says, *'Are you alone?'*

The voice is gravelly, as always. Perfunctory to the point of being intensely irritating.

'The answer lies somewhere in the fact I picked up.'

The caller chooses to ignore the reproach.

'Is your asset prepped?'

'Of course.'

'And exactly how much does he know?'

'As much as he needs to.'

'That's far too vague,' the caller says.

'He knows Victor has violated the rules,' Devlin says. 'Knows he's been engaged to re-establish the status quo. And, without doubt, he knows whatever Victor has seen fit to reveal. Even so, he has no visibility beyond me. Or, worst case, the Senator. That said, he's never once enquired after sub-text. He's operating as a warhead, not a guidance system. And he knows his primary task is to wipe the board clean as soon as I give the go-ahead.'

'And, will he?'

'I believe so.'

'Convince me. It's important I'm persuaded he's everything you claim him to be... and that you have him on a very short leash.'

'He's... formidable, is all I can say. He has an aura. And he now has significant additional incentives. Including doubling his fee... and a promise to make it possible for him to return home.'

Devlin feels an chill spike its way down the line. Knows he's exceeded his boundaries.

'If he's been declared persona non grata in Tel Aviv, any officially sanctioned re-assimilation lies a good way above your pay grade.'

'Agreed... but I assume it's well within yours.'

There's a pause.

'I'll think about it.'

'I've already given my assurance.'

'Then you've misjudged your authority. I'm not in the habit of allowing myself to be backed onto the ropes... and I've no reason to change that practice anytime soon.'

'So perhaps you can advise where I can find someone else for this kind of wet work, at this stage of the game? Of all people, you know such assets don't come ten-a-penny. And their demands are not always exclusively fiscal in nature.' Besides, I'd be prepared to go all in that my guy is a match for yours.

There's another pause.

'I've said I'll think about it,' the voice says. *'And, ordinarily, I would caution anyone against getting into a pissing contest with the Colonel. He has a unique capacity for overcoming obstacles... and, without exception, the most tenacious individual I've ever encountered. He's also not averse to threatening his superiors with sanctions. Up to and including terminal. Added to which, I'm more than a little concerned he may have acquired some independent force strength. Some of whom I am aware... and some not. But I guarantee you they'll all be extremely capable. Certainly I've never known him to tolerate the company of fools. So our next moves require a high degree of finesse. And we'd both better hope the confidence you have in your asset is not... misplaced.'*

'I can assure you, my selection process was rigorous. He's former Shayetet 13... which, I've been assured, means his credentials are beyond impeccable.'

'I'm well aware of his credentials, Mr. Devlin... because I'm the person responsible for Segen Abelman entering your field of view.'

Devlin feels his saliva turn to ash.

He manages to mutter, 'Is that so...?'

'Indeed it is,' the voice says.

Then the line is cut.

LUBBOCK, TEXAS

Carl Jordan Miller knows...

...from the moment his head slams against the floor, feet swept from under him, vision sparking from the impact, arms pinned to his side by some kind of thick plastic sheath...

...he is doomed.

He tries to manoeuvre his handgun up to his chest. Use its silenced barrel to break free—*somehow*—from this suffocating cocoon. But a series of vicious blows begins pummelling his ribcage. Hammering against his skull. Busting his nose. Breaking his teeth.

He tenses against the onslaught. Because he knows, somewhere deep down—*in the dim and distant remnants of his primordial subconscious*—his only hope is to remain conscious.

And to keep fighting.

He comes round to a crushing pressure inside his head. Registers the fact he's flat on his back. Arms bound to his sides. Still cocooned inside the sheath. Figures he's duct-taped from neck to ankle. Unable to discern little more than milky shadows. Labouring to breathe under the weight of something heavy pressing down on his chest. The metallic taste of blood in his throat. *A lot of blood*. As certain as he can be that he's lost all track of time. Struggling to contemplate any future beyond the next few seconds.

He attempts to blink away the pain searing across his eyes. Seeking any tiny amount of relief he can get. But his efforts fail completely. Reflexively, he tries a second time, before the futility hits him like a hammer blow.

His eyelids have been removed.

Then, one-by-one, the inventory of torture smashes home with the impact of hollow-points finding their mark...

...busted legs for sure; because, when he tries to move, the bolt of pain makes it all the way to his chest... fingers severed; confirmed when he attempts to make a fist against his fury... flames lancing through the lower half of his gut; sickening proof his groin has received its fair share of attention...

...and no matter his years of military training, waves of panic surge through his mind. His heart pounding—*like it's about to explode*. His breathing, heavy and ragged.

He forces himself to wind back his memory reel. Searching for something—*anything*—to replace this agony and fear with rage. Desperate for any kind of mechanism he can employ to regain a semblance of self-control. Before his mind gives in to blind panic and the inevitable, unrestrained screaming.

He remembers now, he'd waited for the dot—*blinking red at the centre of the screen on the tracking device he'd been given*—to stop moving. Proximity readings confirming he would find his target at the centre of the chalet with the number twelve stencilled on its door. Waiting thirty-minutes longer than strictly necessary after the lights had gone out. Taking time to spray oil into the tumbler and over the door hinges. Silently picking the lock. Entering without a sound. Because he was nothing if not a details man. Good at what he did. Better than good. *75th* Ranger good. Which meant it was an absolute certainty he'd been betrayed. Confirmation—*though none were needed*—that nothing he attempted from here on in was going to make the slightest difference.

Only a couple months earlier he'd turned forty-two. Twenty years of which he'd spent shedding skin for the US Army. Including two fucked-up tours in Afghanistan. Chasing down a breed of men who seemed to place scant value on their own lives. And even less for those they hid amongst. In homes and hospitals, mosques and schools. Terrorising anyone—*man, woman or child*—who stood between them and a chance to take out just one Yankee infidel. Worst of all, he'd come to realise, it wasn't even a matter of hatred driving their deadly ambitions—*day and night*. For them, it was more akin to some kind of feral sport. One driven by a fervour none but the most committed disciple could ever comprehend.

Now this private contractor express he's been riding, to escape all the war-on-terror bullshit he'd been force-fed—*year after fucking year*—is about to terminate.

Which means all he can do was wait...

...just like always.

Then his tormentor begins to speak.

'Welcome back... Mister.'

Perry settles all his weight onto Miller's chest, still buzzing from all the exertion. At one point, he'd begun to think he was never going to get the job done. But he'd sure nailed that last brutal stomp. Landing it just below the guy's left ear. In all likelihood cracking his skull and busting a few blood vessels into the bargain. After which he'd gotten the big lump taped up real good. *Real fast.* Because, if his father was anything to go by, even those who thought themselves some kind of tough guy, usually ended up thrashing about like a netted catfish.

After which, he'd really gone to work.

'How you feelin' right now...? I'm guessin' not so good. Or could be a little bit of hurtin' gets you goin'...'

He leans in close to the chump's ear.

'...makes you feel alive, I'm bettin'. Takes your mind to that cold place where it gets to process nothin' but pain... and the certainty there ain't no way to escape. Exhilarating, ain't it?'

He's a little disappointed—*irritated even*—that he's getting no response. Begins to think he's pushed things too hard—*too fast*.

He stabs the tip of his knife into the guy's forehead. Feels nothing—*neither elation, nor triumph, and certainly not sympathy*—as his victim flinches. Impervious to the wide-eyed terror he sees in the blood-soaked, lidless eyes staring back at him.

'Reckon you're feelin' like I used to feel when I was a kid... every time my old man visited my bunk. Even with my eyes closed, *real tight*, I could still feel his presence. Way before his sour stink filled my nostrils. No matter how sick I felt in my stomach. No matter what I did to make myself unappealin'... I remember how alive I felt. How it amplified my senses. That's the word ain't it, mister...? *Amplified*. 'Cause, I ain't so good with words. But, yeah... I reckon I got it right.'

He grabs his captive's chin. Shakes his head from side to side.

'I would say... not long now 'till you'all meet with whoever it is you pray to... if'un you do... but, guess what, Bubba...?'

Perry stretches his lips into a broad grin.

'I'd be lyin'.'

TULIA, TEXAS

Seigo cuts a healthy slice from his order of steak. Dips it in the lake of pepper sauce that came with his order. Ignoring the hill of fried potatoes loaded onto his plate; for the time being at least. Sets about chewing the barely cooked piece of meat, like a steer working its cud.

'Just so I've got this straight...'

He jabs his fork in the direction of Zalizo's head.

'...you ain't gonna be pissing down my back over this, somewhere down the line.'

Zalizo shrugs.

'I left you out there, with no standing orders, because I trust your judgement. Besides, they pretty much sealed their fate the moment they crossed the Atlantic. From my standpoint, outside a war zone... no-one gets a pass hunting someone down for no other reason than to draw an inflated pay check.'

'*A-men*, brother.'

'All the same... it would be good to know how long they're going to stay undiscovered.'

'That, my friend, would be hard to say.'

Seigo ships another slice of steak.

'The Bronco had a jerrycan of fuel in the trunk. So, I set them alight in the front seats and rolled them into the ravine. I left their munitions in the footwell. Waited until it finished cooking off. Then I climbed down... re-doused them and set them alight again.'

'Thorough...' Zalizo says.

'I thought so,' Seigo says.

'Anything else I should know?'

'*Yeah*... Their handler was an *Israeli*.'

Zalizo gives it a beat.

'Now that is interesting.'

They'd made a stop, to intake calories, in a cattle town named Tulia. Midway between the Palo Dura hills and Plainview. It had a twenty-foot high white-washed plinth at its central intersection, with the town's name carved at its base. And a half-decent Tex-Mex steakhouse mid-way along the main retail strip; more than likely due to the proprietors not having any difficulty sourcing their primary ingredient.

'You were sayin' this town's got a dubious history.'

Zalizo says, 'I said... it had notoriety.'

Seigo swallows a mouthful of food.

'Well excuse me, I'm sure...'

He waves his fork in decreasing circles on its way back to the plate.

'...so, you gonna keep me guessing?'

Zalizo shovels his own mouthful of food.

'Story goes that, some time back in the nineties, close to one-third of the town's black males got themselves arrested on trumped up drug charges. Based solely on the word of some rogue undercover cop. No forensics, or witnesses even. Just a bunch of vague or inaccurate descriptions of those he'd allegedly bought narcotics from. One suspect had his charges dropped when he was able to show he'd been working twenty miles away at the time an alleged exchange had taken place. Another produced bank and phone records proving they'd been in another state...'

He scoops up a last forkful of eggs and beans.

'...even so, nearly all the remainder were convicted, purely on the bent cop's testimony, by local folk keen to uphold their civic duty. A few of the accused pled in exchange for lighter sentences. Though they never stopped protesting their innocence.'

'Nice neighbourhood,' Seigo says. 'Maybe we should think about staying over... just for the hell of it. See if we can't bump into one or two of those jurors.'

'I imagine that opportunity passed us by some time ago. Besides, a bunch of civil rights lawyers eventually got the accused a multi-million-dollar settlement.'

Seigo thrusts his fork forward.

'Now that's what I call a decent level of karma.'

'Even if most of them had already served the majority of their sentence?' Zalizo says.

'Bad break... good break.'

Seigo moves on to his fried potatoes.

'To a simple soul like me, sounds something close to a world in balance.'

He continues waving his fork.

'Anything good ever happen to the cop?'

'He was convicted sometime later, on a perjury charge.'

'Sounds fair.'

Zalizo grunts.

'He got probation and a thousand dollar fine.'

Seigo shrugs.

'Can't say I'm surprised.'

Zalizo pushes his plate aside.

'Me neither... and, because I can sense your own highly developed sense of civic devotion is mortally offended, you could redress the balance by sticking with me a while longer.'

Seigo continues chewing, staring at his plate of food. So Zalizo heads for the washroom.

When he returns, the table has been cleared and Seigo has settled back to stare out the window. Onto a street short on redeeming features. Unless empty sidewalks and a preference for shuttered, low-rise, red brick stores happened to be your thing.

'How much blood's yet to be spilt, Leg?'

'Hard to say.'

'So hazard a guess.'

'I made a promise to the little old crow... so I'll be looking to minimize where I can. But only to the extent I don't have to compromise some core objectives.'

'I figured something in you had changed... because, back there in the hills, you were contemplating letting those fuckers go. So, before I commit... I'd like to know why.'

'You and I both know they were doomed,' Zalizo says. 'No way they could have made it out of those hills unaided... let alone get their injuries treated hereabouts without attracting the attention of local law enforcement.'

'True,' Seigo says.

'So, even if they'd survived... their future was fraught with peril. As such, I wouldn't describe my approach as overly charitable.'

'Regardless...' Seigo says.

'You want to know what happened to my unforgiving nature?'

'You could say.'

'It's been a long-standing curse,' Zalizo says. 'But you know that already.'

'I sure do. Though, for a white boy... I guess you had it pretty tough.'

'That may be. But, until very recently, I've never considered... let alone admitted, even to myself... I have an unhealthy taste for it.'

'Buy, *it*... you mean the danger?'

'*No*, Seigo... the brutality.'

'Isn't that the natural order of things for people like us.'

'I suspect not,' Zalizo says. 'Because for the majority of the time, even for someone like you... the beast lays dormant. Stirring only in the moment... or when you summon it. It's not something you have to consciously supress.'

Seigo shrugs.

Zalizo lays his palms on the table.

'That's not how it is for me. It's not a *part* of who I am... It *is* who I am. All day... every day. And then, against all the odds, I found someone capable of lancing that abscess.'

For a moment or two, Seigo says nothing.

Then he says, 'You started running with us Scorpions way before your kin were butchered. Which means this *thing* you became... it was always there.'

'I can't deny it,' Zalizo says.

'So... this woman who found you. She have a name?'

'*Alicia*... Alicia Corazón.'

Zalizo lowers his gaze.

'She was thirty-one. Salvadorian by birth. Studied hard, worked hard. Became a corporate lawyer. Charged hourly fees that would either curl your hair, or make it fall out. Kept her moral compass steady taking on *pro bono* gigs. And I guarantee she never caused any measurable harm to anyone her entire life.'

For a moment, they both fall silent.

'I don't know what to say, brother.'

Zalizo eases back in his seat.

'And now, crazy as it sounds, I may have just been found... again.'

'The hell you say...! Are we talking recently?'

'*Yeah*... a couple days ago. And before you ask... one-hundred percent, I wasn't looking. It kind of just happened... out of the blue.'

'And, with your history... how is this in any way a good thing?'

'That's a fair question. And, truth is... it's probably not a good thing. Least ways not until I decide to quit doing what I do.'

'And what are the chances that's gonna happen any time soon.'

Zalizo shrugs.

'You know what your real problem is, *ak'is?*'

'Not precisely... but I suspect I'm about to find out.'

Seigo eases himself forward.

'You long ago lost your ability to know where you belong.'

'Could be,' Zalizo says.

Seigo shakes his head.

'Could be you don't have the faintest idea what I'm talking about.'

Zalizo doesn't respond.

'How you ever gonna centre yourself anywhere... with anyone, if all you're going to do is spend the rest of your life looking for the next trail of bad deeds and blood to follow?'

Zalizo leans forward, bearing his teeth.

'They set him free...'

Seigo eases back, folding his arms. His face adopting its usual passive mask.

'Who's... *they*, Leg? Who's... *him?*'

'It's a long story,' Zalizo says.

Seigo says, 'Same as it ever was.'

LUBBOCK, TEXAS

Zalizo sits alone in the GMC. Seigo having stepped out to re-supply himself with smokes.

During their drive back to Plainview, he'd persuaded himself not to call her—*for the time being at least*—despite the fact she'd given him the number for her cell phone. Telling him it would be fine with her should he decide to keep in touch. If he happened to find the time—*or the inclination.*

Yet here he is, less than an hour later, keying her number.

He fully expects she'll choose to ignore a *caller withheld*.

But, as it happens, she picks up.

And on only the second ring.

'Vanessa Clarke...'

'Hello, Miss Clarke...'

For a moment, all he can hear is her breathing—*slow and even*—on the other end of the line.

'...it's Leg... Leg Zalizo.'

'Now let me think... where have I heard that name before?'

He decides to play along.

'We met a while back. Tiffeney's I think it was... somewhere south of El Capitan.'

'Well I'll be... hello, stranger.'

He hesitates, then says, 'Is now an okay time to call?'

'To my eternal shame, Leg Zalizo... I distinctly recall letting you know anytime would be an okay time for me. But I can't lie... you getting in touch right now is a little spooky.'

'Spooky sounds... *intriguing*.'

'It's just... I happen to have a mutual friend over for dinner.'

'Mutual is... *interesting*.'

'Somehow, I get the feeling this is going to go one of two ways.'

'In my experience, that's usually how things tend to fall.'

'It's just... I happen to be sharing some surplus enchiladas with Doug.'

'Listen V, you're under no obligation to explain who you hang with... or why. Besides, I've never identified with the whole jealous guy thing.'

'Well now,' she says. *'V is a first for me... but I kinda like the way it sounds.'*

There's a slight hesitation.

Then she says, *'The thing is, Leg... he's saying he knows you. Or, to be a little more accurate... knows of you.'*

'A random retired medic? It seems a little implausible.'

'Yeah... I know. But when I mentioned your name, he recognised it straight off.'

'Was he a Marine?'

'No,' she says. *'He's Air Force. STS apparently... whatever that is.'*

'24th Special Tactics Squadron.'

'Sure,' she says. *'If you say so.'*

He takes a moment to consider what he's hearing. Comes to no particular conclusion.

'Anyway... he's signalling he'd like to speak with you.'

He decides—*whatever this thing is*—he's going to let it play out.

He says. 'Okay... put him on.'

The line goes quiet for a beat.

'Hello... major.'

'Time's moved on, Doug. It's Lieutenant-Colonel these days... but don't let that put you off.'

'It wouldn't... and it doesn't.'

Zalizo says, 'I should have figured as much.'

'Yeah well, I ain't gonna lie... the moment I pegged your name, you tripped some circuits I thought I'd powered down a good few years back.'

'Is that so?'

'Sure is... but, listen. You've got nothing to worry about. You were... likely still are... a legend throughout JSOC. As for me... I was pretty much standard meat and gravy.'

'Out of curiosity... which groups were you attached to?'

'Special Recon... mostly,' Doug says. *'Though I sometimes ran with SEAL Team Five... There was a time, if you needed someone*

to vector in something noisy... and in dire need of extraction... I was the guy who got in close and got it done.'

'Happens I've worked with you guys on occasion,' Zalizo says. 'Though I'm pretty sure we never met... Either way, I never once heard of anyone running with the Green Eyes referred to as standard...'

He lets his words hang for a moment.

'...and I should probably mention, I'm fairly decent with names. Unless *Doug's* a convenient sobriquet.'

'No, it's Doug... Johanssen... and you're right. Our paths never synced. But I distinctly recall, one time, you caused quite a buzz throughout my billet in Santa Rita. It was a while back now, but we were both on our way through Guam. And I heard there was a book on you... with short odds on you trading camos for neoprene. I take it that never happened.'

'Can't say I didn't seriously consider it, once or twice. Happens I like water.'

'You and me both, Colonel.'

Zalizo senses that, while they'd likely exhausted each other's verbal handshake, the tone in Doug's voice suggested something was going unsaid. So he decides to give it a second or two longer.

'This is going to sound lame...'

'Try me... You never know.'

'Fair enough. But I don't want you burning Nessa's ear over what I'm about to say... okay?'

Zalizo says, 'Wouldn't dream of it. Besides, I'm betting she thought she was revealing the bare minimum to convince you she hadn't chambered a squib.'

'Right on the money, Colonel.'

'So what have you surmised from what she couldn't tell you, because she doesn't know?'

'Nothing specific... but something's tickling my trip wires. Making me think there's a chance you're operating lights out.'

'And how, exactly, did you figure that?'

Doug says, *'I can't vouch safe this device... so let's just say, it has something to do with jurisdictional oddities and acquired intuition.'*

Zalizo says, 'Fair enough.'

'I will say one thing though. You need a helping hand with whatever it is you've got going on... you be sure and let me know. Anytime... day or night. You can reach me through Ness. Or I could give you a number I can vouch for.'

Zalizo couldn't say why exactly, but he decides to do something he's never once considered doing during the whole of his military service.

'When you ran with SEAL Team Five... you ever hook up with a pint-sized Sasquatch. Call-sign *RED-Five*?'

There's a snicker on the other end of the line.

'I sure did.'

'If I recall,' Zalizo says, 'He had a particular taste in personal weapon.'

'That's my recollection also, Colonel. I only ever saw him bumping a shotgun. Benelli M4 Super... if memory serves.'

Zalizo arrives at his next decision as quickly as any he's ever made.

He says, 'I'd be honoured to have you aboard.'

'You're kidding me...?'

'Never more serious.'

'It doesn't bother you none I've been out of the game a while... or how old I am. It's pretty much always number one on most people's take-a-hike list.'

Zalizo says, 'My old man could open a tin of beans with his teeth well into his fifties. And father me into the bargain.'

'Well, I'm not quite that old... but I can probably give you ten years.'

'How long can you hold your breath, Doug?'

'Between two and four minutes... depending on depth.'

'Run...?'

'Before my knees start complaining... twelve miles.'

'Rifle or pistol?'

'Either or neither. Makes no difference to me. I have to... I can weaponize a diaper.'

'So... that's everything I need to know, right there. Now do me another favour.'

Doug says, *'Name it.'*

'Put V back on... she may have something to say about this.'

'Colonel... you do know she's not really my little sis. Besides, even if she was, I'm all grow'd up. And I've still got all my kit... and some other stuff besides.'

'I'm sure you have... but it'll still be her decision.'

'Okay, I hear you. But just so you know how I hang where Ness is concerned... you've been on speaker the whole time.'

Zalizo says, 'I can see why she likes you.'

MORGAN CITY, LOUISIANA

To say the venerable UH60 Black Hawk, a twin-engine, medium-lift workhorse, is a familiar bird to Sergeant First Class Ellie Rundell would be somewhat of an understatement. Brought into military service, way back in the early seventies, it has a combat radius a shade over four-hundred nautical miles. Unladen, its straight-line operational range extends to just under fourteen hundred. Which means the ride down from

Columbus, Georgia to the designated jump point had been a non-stop affair.

Of course, it could be YARD DOG-Three-Seven would need to re-fuel on its way back to base. But once she'd deployed, that would be of no concern to her.

She'd embarked at Fort Benning; somewhat incongruously named after a Confederate Brigadier General who had proudly defended, then—*if history were to be believed*—continued to advocate the virtues of slavery for some time after the Civil War had ended. So, to say she had mixed feelings about the base—*where she'd honed the majority of her Ranger skills*—being named for such an individual, would have been to deny the appropriacy of the word ironic. And something her senior officers, back in the day, had repeatedly warned would impede her career if she chose to continue running her goddam mouth about it; her sub-Saharan genealogy and inalienable rights under the First Amendment be damned. And possibly the reason her ride, and subsequent flight plan, had both required the General's muscle to ensure the base commander complied with her request.

In full and without undue delay.

So, for the first time in her military career, Runellie has the revered old hauler's entire load bay—*designed to accommodate a dozen fully equipped troops*—all to herself.

Right now, they are approaching the jump point. Holding steady, to the east of Morgan City, a fraction below the craft's recommended ceiling. Wind speed at altitude between twelve to eighteen knots, and out of the south-east. Five to eight knots lower down. Ground temperature, sixty-eight degrees—*positively temperate for Louisiana*—with cloud cover pretty solid and unusually low-formed cirrostratus, topping out at eleven-thousand feet, down to an estimated fifteen-hundred.

So, despite the Lieutenant-Colonel's misguided beliefs to the contrary, tonight at least, it seems the *Lord* was on their side.

One thing she knows for sure, it was a bonus her descent would be masked from the ground once she'd deployed. Even if someone were inclined to look. And since she's jumping HALO, she estimates the chances she'll be detected at slim to none pretty much all the way down. Unless she was unlucky enough to land on someone's head. Which brought into focus her one remaining concern.

The LZ itself.

She'll be dropping onto a finger of land, comprised of nothing but forest and dirt, roughly ten miles long. A couple hundred metres at its narrowest, maxing out at two miles at its widest point—*the Shaffer Bayou and Atchafalaya River on one side, Avoca Island Cut-off on the other*—where her only option involved touching down somewhere along a thin, unsurfaced access strip, bounded either side by parallel dry stone walls. And, since the moon will be blanketed, and urban light pollution close to zero, hitting anything solid she might have missed during her study of satellite imagery—*at better than ten miles an hour*—was something she was keen to avoid.

Her one-hundred and twenty pounds worth of kit, currently slung forward of her knees, she'll tether-off a few yards out. Her broken down M110A1 rifle, spare Glock, Havoc cross-bow and compact IRS surveillance drone—*including spare batteries*—she most definitely won't. They will remain in the non-standard, specially compartmented padded utility pack she has strapped to her chest. And, while she'd never once landed on her face—*or her not insubstantial ass for that matter*—there was a first time for everything. Not to mention her long-standing respect for Murphy's Law; a certified imbalance in the universe she recalls British Special Forces routinely fretting over. Which, in rough translation and omitting profanities, went along the lines of—*if it can go wrong, it will go wrong*.

A couple of miles below, somewhere beneath the clouds, she knows there is a serviceable pontoon, canted out a short distance from the shoreline, alongside a narrow slipway. But she'd quickly dismissed a waterborne approach. For sure, it would have given her the option to provision a lot more kit—*especially ammo and anti-personnel ordinance*—but the odds of detection, accidental or otherwise, were far greater. And capsizing an unacceptable risk. Added to which, security details, no matter how proficient, almost always chose to concentrate assets around positions deemed the most likely points of attack. And while the shoreline was extensive, it would be easy enough to cover with a few, well-placed security cameras. And since she was going in blind to opposition strength, it hadn't been a difficult choice to stick with her primary skill set.

The one she's shed skin and spit blood to perfect.

Just then, the ready light, located on the bulkhead, blooms red above her shoulder.

So she stows her last-minute qualms and prepares to jump.

Years of training, and numerous active duty tours, has taught her to never leap from an aircraft—*of any kind, whatever the altitude*—unless every piece of kit is securely stowed away. So, for about the tenth time during the flight, she re-checks her night vision goggles are clipped and strapped to her helmet real tight. Double-checks the harness on her ram-air chute. Pulls her gloves taught. Confirms her wrist-mounted dual altimeter-compass is fully functional. And that her kit-release ring won't snag during the drop.

The crew chief gives her shoulder a solid slap, signalling an exaggerated thumbs up.

Runellie shuffles forward. Leaning down as best she can to

take a firm grip on the tailored harness—*with its own primary chute attached*—positioned at the threshold of the open cargo door. Fully aware her words will be lost amid the din of the engines, she still mutters...

'E-a-s-y there, boy,'

Then she launches herself and her canine partner into the void.

PLAINVIEW, TEXAS

'So what's your thinking on Johanssen?'

Seigo doesn't answer.

Instead, he blows the smoke from his cheroot out through the passenger-side window.

Zalizo has relayed the bare bones of his impromptu call to El Paso. Asked his friend if he was okay bringing on board someone neither of them had met.

Seigo had done nothing other than listen.

Which had come as no surprise. After all, it was a pretty big ask. And, if he were standing in Seigo's boots, more than likely he would be saying—*no*. Or, if he felt strongly enough, he would have simply packed his bed-roll and left.

And the reason was simple enough. One they'd both adhered to throughout their military service.

The good old twenty-sixty-twenty rule.

The one that said: no matter the profession and regardless the level of training. Irrespective of gender, intelligence, creed, or any other aspect of human behaviour—*anthropologically speaking, or otherwise*—twenty per cent of any group were as good as useless when measured against whatever standard was being applied. Sixty percent did just enough to get by. Routinely a little less. Leaving no more than twenty percent who could be relied on to give their all—*day in and day out*—because that's just how they were wired. It was what it was. Under most circumstances, until the shit made contact with the blades, there was no way to judge which percentage lane any given individual was running in.

One thing he did know, however, were the inner workings of Seigo's mind; better than almost anyone. Which likely means, as far as the big Indian is concerned, Johanssen's capabilities were an unknown when set against such a stringent yardstick.

At that moment, one of the two cell phones they'd retained from the Brit's possessions chirps an SMS notification.

Seigo grabs the device. Spends a moment staring at the screen.

'Looks like we've got ourselves the location they were told to stake out. A motel called...'

Zalizo says, 'We need to be cautious.'

'Which means what, exactly?'

Zalizo says, 'The way they told it, it sounded like a critical tasking.'

'Affirmative,' Seigo says.

'So why use a message app?'

Seigo shrugs.

'How about free end-to-end encryption.'

Zalizo raises an eyebrow.

'That's less than convincing.'

Seigo tosses the phone onto the rear seat.

They'd headed back to Lubbock after their meal stop in Tulia. Made the decision to set out for Morgan City, Louisiana at daybreak. Opting to catch some shut-eye in the GMC rather than booking a second night at the *Overton*. Partly so they could react and be on the move at a moment's notice. Mostly because of Seigo's aversion to sleeping in hotels, motels or hostels. Or any place where he couldn't see the horizon. He'd turned down promotion, and a pretty substantial US Army pension hike, to avoid spending any more time inside government buildings. That and an overwhelming impulse to return to the dry earth of his Navajo roots he'd no longer been able to resist. And most of all, his horses. On account of a long-standing opinion that they possessed more intelligence than most of the operators he'd run with over the years.

So they'd stopped off at his loaner on Davidson. Spent a while packing up the few items he'd stowed there and transferred them to the GMC. After which they'd checked the property was as sterile as he'd found it, then locked it up good and tight.

'I need you to make a call on Johanssen.'

'And if I say, *no*?'

'Then *no* it will be. Though I'm not suggesting he come aboard to change the mission dynamics. It's simply an opportunity to increase our odds.'

Seigo stays silent for a beat.

Then he says, 'I kinda liked our odds the way they were.'

Zalizo says, 'You know what I mean.'

'Seems like you're saying... we should simply trust your girlfriend's judgement.'

Zalizo says, 'Not at all.'

'What then...?'

'Seigo... he ran with SEAL Team 5. Alone, that would be plenty good enough for most people. But I was thinking, we could set him a task... one tough enough to prove him out.'

'Like what... and when?'

'I've already sent my sergeant to hunker down in Louisiana.'

'And this *hastiin* of yours... do they have a name?'

'Indeed they do. Ellie Rundell. Sergeant First Class. *75th* Recon. Runellie to you and me. And I can vouch, she's a real piece of work. In ways I couldn't begin to describe. I could task Johanssen to rendezvous with her. Get her to report how he operates... give us a yay or nay.'

'And how do you intend they find each other?'

Zalizo says, 'I figure a guy like Johanssen should have no problem triangulating off Runellie's satellite phone.'

Seigo shrugs.

'And if this lady Ranger of yours gives a thumbs down?'

'Then that's what I'll tell Johanssen. But it's my guess a guy like that will know if he's screwed up without me tapping his shoulder.'

'I don't know, Leg... it's starting to feel overly complex to me.'

Zalizo elects to let the subject drop—*for the time being*.

'So, getting back to this message. Anyone could type a bogus acknowledgement. Which makes texting critical elements of an operation fundamentally unsound... especially an uncoded location. At a motel of all places. Which makes it feel like a set-up... more than a little in fact.'

Seigo says, 'Maybe they were instructed to use a coded response.'

'Which we can't send,' Zalizo says. 'Besides, we both know codes can be broken... or given up under duress.'

Seigo leans over to retrieve Turner's phone from the rear seat.

'So... how about we give Lubbock PD a concerned citizen call. Get them to go give this motel a look-see. Then all we have to do is swing by and put that shiny tin star of yours to good use. Make like you're taking me in... stopping just to have a snoop around.'

Zalizo fires up the GMC's engine.

'Now that, my friend... is something I can run with.'

Seigo sets to finding a Lubbock Police Department number to call.

'By the way, if it stops your whining... I'm cool with Johanssen.'

Zalizo says, 'My whining apart, care to share why the sudden change of heart?'

'Because I seem to recall,' Seigo says. 'Those P-J flat-heads know their shit.'

'That's for damn sure,' Zalizo says.

ATCHAFALAYA DELTA, LOUISIANA

Runellie has lain in the same position for approaching four hours straight. Watching the same two-man patrol come and go. Both heavily armed. And smart enough to vary their route and timing pattern. Each sporting what looked like some pretty high-end military-grade equipment. Night vision goggles strapped unused on their heads now the dawn had risen. Heckler & Koch MP5Ks in preference to holstered sidearms. Remington combat shotguns slung across their backs. Hip-mounted knives in long sheaths. KA-BARs more than likely—*in the event things got up close and personal*.

One thing she knows from experience, private security goofers generally fell into three distinct categories. Muscle-bound morons who liked to play at being Rambo. Mercs motivated purely by financial reward. And last—*but far from least*—your everyday psychos, weeded out of military service during basic training; that breed of young men yearning to get their finger on a trigger and a better than average chance to pull it with impunity. So she watches them closely. Assessing their stature. The way they move and handle their weapons. Mannerisms as unique as a fingerprint, if you knew what to look for. And, for now, she's as certain as she can be, this pair fall into the middle classification.

A short while before, during their last patrol, they'd passed within ten strides of her position. Plenty close enough to persuade her it was time to bug out.

Besides which, she needed to get some shut-eye—*while she still had the opportunity.*

But, before that happened, she had an animal to feed. And an abundance of fauna to choose from. Rabbit, fox and grey squirrel were plentiful. Ditto the waterfowl—*though they had a tendency to make way too much of a ruckus while they were dying.* Raccoon and white-tail deer less so. But patience brought its own reward when it came to hunting. And Moko is every bit as patient as she is.

Possibly more so.

So deer it would be.

She waits a while longer, without a sound from the hide she's prepped, fifty-yards from the single-storey accommodation block running perpendicular to the grand three-storey, balconied main residence, before making a barely audible clicking noise with her tongue.

Moko shimmies out beside her as she preps her crossbow.

'O-k-a-y, boy... let's go find your supper.'

AUSTIN, TEXAS

'Having fun,' Victor says.

'Had,' the voice says. *'But I'm guessin' that little dot you're trackin' has moved far enough that you didn't need to ask.'*

Victor says, 'You sound deflated.'

The voice says, *'No... disappointed is what I am.'*

'Okay, Perry... so what exactly is your beef right now.'

'My beef...?' Perry says. *'Like you don't already know.'*

Victor says, 'I'm not into guessing games... so why don't you just spit it out.'

'You sent cops,' Perry spits back. *'I'm watching them right now. Which ain't that hard, bein' there's a small army of them right across the street.'*

'And why would I do that?'

'I ain't got no idea... but a whole bunch of cops is, for damn sure, what I'm starin' at.'

'Well, I would suggest you need to ask yourself why I would send anyone outside the mission team? Even you should be able to figure that would make absolutely no sense.'

Victor waits a moment for the proposition to rattle around Perry's less than capacious head.

'You are officially deceased, Perry. Why would I risk that being proven otherwise?'

'Don't know... don't care.'

'Well, you should. Because it may just stop you from doing something really stupid.'

'Stupid is, as stupid does.'

'Precisely,' Victor says. 'So if you think screwing me over has suddenly become your number one priority... for whatever reason. I can assure you to the contrary.'

'Y'know what, Victor... I've had my fill of y'all usin' fancy words. Sick and tired. So if'un you ain't gonna speak normal, I ain't gonna listen. My daddy never stopped tellin' me how stupid I was. But I learned from the shrink they forced on me during my pre-sentencing... that was all just a little thing called projection. On account of him bein' too goddam stupid to keep hold of a woman who had no place to go but somewhere worse. So, I guess you ain't the only one who knows fancy words.'

'So it would appear,' Victor says. 'But I can assure you, we think we know what's happened. You can choose to believe it, or you can choose not to. If not... we're done. And then you'll never make it to the place you so badly want to be.'

'Nice try, Boss Man... but I ain't buyin' what you're sellin'. 'Cause what I figure is... y'all thought I'd still be partyin' with your goon when the cops showed up.'

Victor doesn't answer. Mostly because it was obvious Perry had lost his head. Partly because appealing to his better judgement was pointless. After all, it wasn't like the guy had set out with much in the way of good judgement to begin with. Disappointing, for sure. But there it was. Some circuits just couldn't be re-wired, regardless the level of instruction and conditioning. No matter the time and effort. Besides, one thing at least had just been confirmed. Hatton and Turner were compromised. Right about now, they'd either be spilling everything they knew—*which, by design, was not a great deal*—or they'd turn up in a ditch somewhere, their brains seeping through double-tap exit wounds.

'But... I'll tell you what,' Perry is saying. *'I'm gonna listen to your blabbin'... not 'cause I have to. But 'cause I choose to. So go ahead... say your piece.'*

Victor begins grinding his teeth. Feeling like his head is about to explode, at having to tolerate this skinny little prick speaking to him like he was some kind of equal.

'It seems we've had some kind of infiltration, or breach... if you prefer, in our security.'

'No shit,' Perry sneers.

'We're in the process of fixing it, but it requires certain elements of the mission are put on hold... for the time being, at least. Nothing you need concern yourself with. However, it does mean I need you to...'

'Y'know what, Victor?... Screw you. I'm tired of all your, do-this-do-that, bullshit... So fucking tired. So how about we spin this round... because here's what I intend contemplatin'. Now, is that fancy enough talkin' for y'all?'

Victor can hear in the way Perry's breathing, the little prick is becoming agitated. Or possibly excited. At times it was hard to tell. Because, at heart, Perry Morgan Blake has remained little more than a child. A dangerous and tragically beautiful one, to be sure, but a child nonetheless. A lifetime of abuse and isolation having created, in reality, what the likes of Mary Shelley only ever achieved in the abstract.

'I'm gonna make my way to that big old house you'all keep in the woods. And by the time I get there, you ain't gonna be able to track no little red dot. 'Cause I'm gonna find a way to get your little bug outta my shitter. Now, I might have to hurt some folk here and there to get it done. But get it done I will... you can count on it.'

'You really need to listen, Perry...'

'Uh-uh... not happenin'. You want to speak with me... your gonna need to get your ass back to Louisiana. And if'un you get to me beforehand... so what? That's exactly what I want, you big dumb-ass.'

Victor feels a spike of rage burst like an aneurism behind his eyes. Recalling again what it feels like to be out of control. To suffocate under the dead weight of helplessness. With no tools within reach to strike out against his violators. To punish. *To eviscerate*. Leaving them to suffer a slow, agonising demise.

'So come get me, Boss Man... I'll be waitin'.'

Victor forces his voice to remain low and even.

'Oh, I will... I can promise you that.'

'That-a-boy...' Perry says.

In the brief moment before Victor drops the cell phone from his ear, he's almost certain he hears Perry say...

'...not long now.'

LUBBOCK, TEXAS

They locate the motel on the northern outskirts of town. On the south-bound side of Highway 84. A mile or so from Preston Smith Airport.

Although, in truth, it was a hard place to miss. On account of the giant tree-house out front. With a spiral of rudimentary wooden steps winding around its trunk.

The rest of the establishment is good deal more generic and made up of standard mixed-level accommodation. Some flat-roofed, some pitched. Arranged around three sides of a half-full parking lot, fronting the highway. Looking like it mostly catered for folk with thin pay cheques and their minds set on blowing their hard-earned cash in the numerous clubs and bars the neighbourhood had to offer.

And, right now, the parking lot itself is all lit up like an *al fresco* nightclub.

Seigo says, 'Looks like they've gone and called in everyone but the coastguard.'

‘I’ll say,’ Zalizo says.

‘So go do your thing, *ke-mo sah-bee*. I’ll sit tight and play captured Indian brave.’

‘You’re not funny, Seigo... so how about you stick to what you’re good at.’

Seigo affects indignation.

‘I can be... sometimes.’

Zalizo steps from the GMC. Checks his marshal’s badge is sitting front and centre on his belt as a Lubbock PD uniform strides forward with purpose. One hand on the grip of her gun—*pretty much the default pose for law enforcement everywhere*—her other hand held high.

‘This entire area is restricted to official personnel...’

The officer’s voice is a good deal more agitated than commanding. Possibly due to the nature of the scene lying beyond the incident tape and the glaring wash of lights flashing blue and red.

Zalizo says, ‘Constitutionally speaking... I doubt that statement is factually accurate.’

The uniform pauses, scanning her challenger up and down. Then waves her arm back in the direction she’s come.

‘All this not bright enough for you?’

‘US Marshal...’ Zalizo says.

He pulls the badge off his belt. Holds it at arm’s length. The uniform rearranges her hands. Hooking her thumbs under her body armour.

Default pose number two.

‘That’s as may be,’ she says, just a little too loud. ‘But that still doesn’t get you beyond the tape.’

Zalizo reads the name plate pinned above her Lubbock PD badge.

‘You sure about that, Officer... *Sandez?*’

'Pretty much,' Sandez says.

'Does it at least afford me the courtesy of speaking to whoever's in charge?'

Officer Sandez stares long and hard. Then she looks back over her shoulder to the huddle of uniforms and suits crowded beyond the tape. She turns back, raising her hand a second time.

'Wait here,' she says.

A tall and angular puritanical-looking LPD veteran, Chief of Detectives Frank Boullard, turns out to be the guy in charge. His gaunt face fixed in a surly expression; suggesting he's never been motivated to acquire anything so superfluous as a willing disposition. Sporting a pair of steel-framed, dark-lensed spectacles pushed to the top of a sharply-hooked nose.

He wears his ill-fitting tan suit, off-white shirt and thin, brown neck-tie with what appears to be unconscious indifference. And keeps his sandy-coloured hair cropped short and his hands stuffed deep in the pockets of his creased pants.

All things considered, Zalizo figures it safe to assume the city's chief of detectives is not prone to wear shades this late into the evening due to any degree of vanity. Far more likely he was colour-blind.

'Officer Sandez informs me, you may have a passing interest in what's happened here.'

Zalizo says, 'I'm curious... certainly.'

'Well, I guess that makes two of us,' Boullard says. 'But, other than curiosity... is there a pressing reason why I should interrupt my investigation to speak with you.'

'There's a flag out on a perp,' Zalizo says. 'They likely shot and cut up a kid outside Clovis.'

'Yeah... I heard about that earlier today.'

'The vehicle the victim was travelling in was a burn-out at

an airstrip not far from here.'

'Uh-huh... I heard that too,' Boullard says. 'And it makes this particular incident your business, how?'

'I was pulled in not long after the kid was found,' Zalizo says. 'The local ME attending the scene is a long-time acquaintance. Happens I was passing through the area at the time. She flagged me down... asked for my assistance.'

'All very interesting, Marshal... but you still haven't answered my question.'

Zalizo gets a feeling this wasn't going to go well.

'At this stage, the possibility our perp might be a fugitive hasn't been ruled out. As you can imagine... there's a fair few illegals, not to mention a host of local slimeballs, running around outside the terms of their bail bond, in the great state of New Mexico. And, that being the case, since it looks nailed down our perp has crossed state lines, I'd say it falls under my *raison d'être*. So, if you want to call the local ME... or check in with New Mexico State Police... or the FBI's field office in Albuquerque... I can give you a number.'

Boullard visibly relaxes, raising a conciliatory hand.

'No, Marshal... we're good. You've got your work to do, I guess... so I can't rightly blame you for being inquisitive. Though this can't be your regular patch...'

He slants his head.

'... you have a face I don't recall seeing around.'

Zalizo hooks his thumb in the direction of his GMC.

'I mostly work out of El Paso. Sometimes a little further north of the border. Happens I tracked a runner to the Palo Duro a few days back. I was on my way to snag his hefty ass when the kid was found... so I got delayed some. But it turns out it was no big deal... This one's as docile as he is inept.'

Boullard turns without further preamble, heading toward

the huddle of CSI tecs dressed in white coveralls and blue plastic over-shoes, the plain-clothes and uniforms having drifted further apart. No doubt to wag their tongues out of earshot.

'You got any kind of ID on your perp?'

'Not as such,' Zalizo says.

'Well, the individual whose room our victim was found in, booked in with ID that's currently pulling blanks.'

'Any CCTV?'

'Some... though sadly, it's a little grainy. But, I have to say, our suspect looks more like a college kid from the seventies than a brutal killer on the rampage.'

Zalizo says, 'You mean like Jeffery Dahmer?'

Boullard shrugs.

'Got me there... I guess it takes all sorts.'

Zalizo says, 'That's why I'd appreciate taking a look at anything you've got. There's always the possibility our guy was using some kind of disguise.'

Boullard raises his eyebrows.

'Sure,' he says. 'Can't do any harm.'

Zalizo says, 'What about the victim?'

'Badly cut up,' Boullard says. 'And that's putting it mildly. But he's been provisionally ID'd as a Stuart Sandersford, from a flight ticket out of Preston Smith to DFW... in the morning, as it happens. And the contents of a wallet, found in the only vehicle whose tags are not accounted for in the guest log. And one that happens to be an airport rental in the same name.'

Boullard acquires an unconscious swagger. No doubt pleased with himself on account of a damn nifty piece of police work.

The techs step aside as they approach.

'Our victim's a decent size unit,' Boullard continues as he

crosses the threshold. 'Though it didn't help him any. I guess he must have been caught off guard.'

He turns. Places a hand on Zalizo's chest.

'I hope you've got a strong stomach.'

Zalizo says, 'I get by.'

The body is lying on its back. Banged up every bit as bad as some blast victims Zalizo can recall. Clothing shredded. Fingers amputated. Patches of hair scorched down to the scalp. Eviscerated gut to groin. Lidless eyes staring blindly at the ceiling. Laid out on a clear plastic sheet striped with duct tape. Tied in a thick knot at one end. Duct tape banded where it might have been secured at the other—*like some kind of makeshift cocoon*. Blood pooled every place. Though it looked like none of it was from arterial rupture. Which was a pretty smart move on someone's part. As was the cut-out in the ceiling, positioned just inside the doorway.

Boullard seems unaffected by the carnage. Not indifferent exactly, but not far off. But, when all was said and done, Lubbock was much the same as any decent sized city anywhere else, so Zalizo guesses its detectives had more than likely encountered their fair share of wanton brutality. The town's roots lay in the mass production of cattle and cotton after all. So, deep down, its people had pretty much the same hard-nosed—*take us as you find us*—mentality common to most frontier cities. Nowadays, a little smarter and a good deal more gentrified than Midland or Odessa, for sure. Still, though, not exactly genteel.

'Any similarity in MOs?'

'Some,' Zalizo says.

'Well, it looks like our perp was in the process of bagging his guy when the first cruiser rolled up. And, on that front... we're still trying to trace who it was made the heads-up call.'

Boullard points to the cut-out in the ceiling.

'Looks like he intended to hide him up there.'

'So, your thinking is... they made their escape out back?'

'The washroom window was open,' Boullard says. 'So that's the current best guess.'

Zalizo says, 'Did you find any blood in there?'

Boullard says, 'Come to think of it... no.'

'Only it seems like a big ask.'

'What does?'

Zalizo says, 'Hauling two-hundred-plus pounds of dead weight, up eight foot, through a hole in the ceiling.'

Boullard stares down at the body over the top of his glasses.

'Could be our perp assumed they had all night to get it done.'

'Could be,' Zalizo says. 'But, at the very least, they'd have needed a ladder of some kind. More likely, a block and tackle.'

Boullard grunts.

'Maybe they were in the process of chopping our victim into smaller pieces when they got disturbed.'

Zalizo continues scanning the room.

'Yet they had time to pack away their butcher's kit, then clean it and themselves, so as to leave no trace of blood on their way out through a small window... Sound plausible to you?'

Boullard looks suddenly crest-fallen.

'Okay, Marshal... what's your thinking?'

Zalizo grid-scans the floor and walls.

'No indications of a violent struggle... and no evidence firearms were involved, even though his holster suggests he was carrying. And, since you say he flew in, presumably he booked his weapon in and out with the airline. Also, there's no blood splatter on any of the walls suggesting blunt force trauma prior to your man getting jumped. And, for damn sure, whoever did this was never going to get this much blood out of the carpets, even if they had a week.'

Boullard's posture acquires the look of someone who'd checked their lottery ticket and drawn a dud.

'So,' Zalizo says, 'My thinking would be, this plastic is from some kind of sheath that's been cut open. Which would explain how your perp was able to get the jump on a guy this big... literally.'

He looks at the hole in the ceiling.

'Chances are they jumped their man from up there. Which means your victim was expected... and within a certain time-frame. Plus, I think anyone cunning enough to pull off a play like that, is plenty smart enough to dress in coveralls of some kind. And use bin-liners to stow them in when he'd finished...'

He looks back to the body.

'...and use that length of cane to keep the sheath open nice and wide.'

'Well, I'll be damned,' Boullard says. 'I was wondering about that. Still, you ask me, that's a ballsy move... not to mention high tariff.'

'Sneaky, for sure,' Zalizo says. 'But no more original than getting the jump on someone from up a tree. Though, if I were in your shoes, I'd be keen to know who was looking to get their hands on this popular individual. And why.'

Boullard offers an expression that says—*fair point.*

'Okay, Marshal... you need to see more?'

To his credit, Lubbock's chief of detectives shows no indication he's taken offence at being schooled.

'No... not really,' Zalizo says, 'But my guess is you'll find a hardware store around here some place, where someone fitting your perp's description made purchases similar to the items used here.'

Boullard takes a long look around the room, puffing out his cheeks and shaking his head.

'Okay... let's go take a look at the security footage. Get you back on the road before you make my being here an irrelevance.'

Zalizo says. 'Sure... let's do that.'

Back outside, highway traffic has slowed to little more than a crawl in both directions.

'Goddam rubberneckers...'

Boullard has the weary tone of someone running close to the end of a long shift.

'...ten'll get you twenty, we'll be dealing with a bunch of rear-enders before the night's out.'

They make their way across the motel's parking lot through a phalanx of quizzical stares, arriving at the motel's reception moments later.

Boullard holds the door open.

'And there's one more thing that may interest you...'

He waves Zalizo through.

'...there's a fair chance our victim was ex-military.'

Zalizo pulls up.

'And we know this because...?'

Boullard reaches inside his jacket, pulling out a dog-eared photo, no bigger than a credit card.

'We found this in a wallet inside the rental.'

He holds it up for a couple of seconds—*like he'd just performed a slight-of-hand card trick*—then hands it over.

'I'm going to need it back.'

Zalizo takes out his phone, activating its camera. Waits for the image to come into focus. Takes the shot he needs, then takes the photo from Boullard's outstretched hand, giving it a closer look.

It wasn't easy to tell which one of the four soldiers Stuart Sandersford had once been. The image had been taken from distance. And no doubt some time back. The figures huddled close together. Posing next to a fully-rigged Humvee. All wearing desert camos and FAST-SF combat helmets. Olive-coloured net chokers around their necks. All but one of them sporting Ray-Bans. All but one cradling desert-camo'd M14 rifles. A mission-ready team of Airborne Rangers. One hundred percent. *No question*. Because the soldier not wearing Ray Bans—*holding an M110A1 rifle like a newborn baby*—with a dog sat dutifully at their side, just happened to be Sergeant First Class Eleanor Rundell.

They ease their way behind a waist-high reception counter, into a back room doing a creditable job passing itself off as a junkyard. Three of its four walls covered with shelving bowed close to breaking with overflowing binders. A wide-screen computer monitor and greasy-looking keyboard occupying the only portion of a workbench not littered with empty carry-out cartons and bottled water.

Boullard says, 'Run those segments again for us will you, Travis.'

It was hard to tell whether the long-haired figure, slouched back in a worn out vinyl seat, is even awake. After a moment he hunches himself forward. Begins pushing a grimy wireless mouse over an equally grubby mouse-pad.

The cursor moves. Files scroll. And, after a couple double-clicks, Travis leans back without speaking.

Two digital captures begin playing side-by-side on the monitor. One from a feed angled south-east across the motel's parking lot. The other from the camera looking down over the reception desk.

Zalizo watches in silence as a grainy figure with shoulder-length, sandy-coloured hair, sporting frameless spectacles, drifts into the cameras fields of view.

'There,' he says. 'A couple frames back...'

He leans forward, pointing at the screen.

'...freeze it would you?'

Zalizo holds his expression neutral as he watches. Staring at a face momentarily angled toward the camera covering the reception area.

'Okay... thanks,' he says. 'Let it run.'

The captures play for another thirty seconds or so.

Lubbock's chief of detectives turns. Eyeing him now, with what looks to be an uneven mix of admiration and suppressed resentment.

'Okay, Marshal... have we seen enough to satisfy our curiosity?'

Zalizo takes a moment to consider what he's seen.

Then he says, 'I guess so.'

Day Four

'What will be... will be.'

COAL ISLAND, GUADALUPE MOUNTAINS

Dawn creeps its way across a ten-mile wide basin of rocks and dry earth. A blanket of dark grey shadows—*cast from a wide arc of brooding limestone peaks*—spreading westward across the broad expanse of valley floor, as daybreak nudges its way over the eastern side of the Guadalupe Mountains.

Out of the gloom, two Apache AH-64 attack helicopters come in low and fast from the north west. Racing over the barren Permian landscape at close on three miles a minute. Spooling their engines hard. Taking up position on the far side of Coal Island's runway apron. Thirty-millimetre chain guns and AGM-114 Hellfire missile pods trained squarely at the flight-line terminal.

Moments later, two V-22 Ospreys roar over the white-washed building, tilting their twin Rolls Royce turboshaft engines to vertical as they throttle back. One outside the perimeter fence, the other inside. Each scouring up a maelstrom of sun-baked earth and loose stone. Lowering their cargo ramps before their landing gear makes contact with the ground.

Two six-man teams—*pulled straight from the Delta Force selection pipeline*—emerge from each craft. Levelling their weapons the instant their boots hit the dirt. Two squads breaking left. Two breaking right. Forming up in less time than it takes to spit, either side of Coal Island's two guard towers.

A mile out from the landing zone, a lone CH-47 Chinook delays its approach.

Inside the heavy-lift, twin-engine bird, a JLTV sits tethered to the load deck. And, whereas every member of the hastily-formed assault unit—*deployed way outside standard rapid deployment command authority*—has been briefed that they're on a proof-of-concept training mission, the single passenger waiting for a thumbs-up to climb aboard the three-hundred thousand dollar, eleven-ton all-terrain vehicle, knows otherwise.

Up ahead, the Apache formed up on the terminal's southern quarter opens up its *M230* chain gun—*its one-point-five kilowatt electric motor pouring twenty-five one-point-two inch diameter armour-piercing rounds from its rotating barrel*—strafing the terminal's radar and comms array. Tearing everything to shreds in seconds.

Almost before the debris has time to settle on the ground, four figures stumble through the terminal's windowless steel door. Falling to their knees. Placing their hands behind their heads. Eyes fixed on the asphalt.

Despite feeling like he's been kicked in the ribs by a mule, Montgomery Ray is determined to restore at least some of his usual sense of superiority.

Goddam it—he's a Yale law graduate after all. So there's no way he's willing to tolerate any horseshit from the craggy-looking individual who'd just barged into his office like he owned half the goddam universe.

Or soon would.

'My staff inform me, I'm to address you as... *General*. Which is all very interesting, except for the small fact that this is a highly classified, tier-one private sector facility. Operating... where matters of security risk and response are concerned, under an autonomous Department of State contract sanctioned at the highest level.'

The figure appears not to be listening.

‘So, *General*... let me be crystal clear. Despite your overtly provocative arrival, and your refusal to comply with our protocols and operational policies, at the very least I’m going to insist you provide some formal identification. Or, at a minimum... some proof of authority. I have a highly-trained force at my disposal. And, trust me, I will not hesitate to...’

‘And *you*, Director Ray, are speaking to the United States Department of Defense. And I have a Presidential Executive Order that means you will instruct your highly-trained force to stand down. Or suffer the consequence of having lethal force applied. And, *trust me*... that would be overwhelming and, until I order otherwise, unremitting lethal force...’

The visitor examines his finger nails.

‘...think Waco on steroids.’

He issues his ultimatum in a quiet mid-west accent. Like he’s expressing a preference for one flavour of ice cream over another. Sounding distinctly more confident than Mongomery Ray feels. And certainly not in any way cowed.

‘That will include a large, heavily-armed and tactically proficient ground contingent... and four Predator drones currently laser-assigned and awaiting Go-codes. You are further advised an *AC-130* is also running top cover with its one-O-five vectored on your position. The upshot... you have precisely one hour to get your inmates secured. After which, I expect your cage monkeys to muster on the helipad, minus all weapons, and with their hands held high. And be in no doubt, I mean that literally. You force my men to clear and detain, I can promise you... the penalties I can impose will be punitive in the extreme. You are now on the clock, Mr. Ray... so I strongly advise you get moving.’

Despite the wave of nausea rising in his throat—*issuing an instant secondary warning to his bowels*—Mongomery Ray gives a lifetime’s inclination towards belligerence one more run down the slope.

'General, even you have to agree this is all highly irregular...'

The General's expression changes. Clearly indicating he was fast approaching the limit of his patience.

'So, can I at least have sight of this executive order?'

For the first time since he'd entered the room, the General looks at him bayonet straight.

'No, Director Ray... you may not. And after you're done marshalling your staff as directed, you will get your low-slung rear-end back here without delay.'

'Can I at least ask why?'

'To discuss the circumstances surrounding the recently deceased Perry Morgan Blake... and the whereabouts of one Jacque Victor Labette.'

Montgomery Ray feels his saliva turn to ash.

'Okay, General... at this point, I think I'll be invoking my Sixth Amendment right to legal counsel.'

The General turns and opens the door.

'Director... you need to get your head around the fact that this facility, and everything in it, is now under my sole jurisdiction. Which means you, and everyone inside or outside the fence, have just forfeited every one of your civilian rights.'

'You can't...'

'Oh... but I assure you, Director. I can... and I have. So, I strongly recommend you quit jerking me around.'

AUSTIN, TEXAS

Throughout the fifty-four years since she'd left her mother's womb, she has always been able to justify the morally dubious things she's done. The kind of heavy baggage that might cause someone of a weaker disposition sleepless nights. Difficult things. *Necessary things*. Things her mother had sanctioned with a single, over-riding admonition:

'Young miss... just you remember whose daughter you are. And... no matter the cost, no matter the threats, no matter what level of intimidation you encounter.... you can never... ever, back down.'

For the whole of her sometimes tempestuous life, Lady Roselyn had bestowed upon her only child an unwavering belief that new dawns brought with them new opportunities. And that the solution to every knock-back, as often as not, lay on the other side of a setting sun.

'Play with a few dicks if you must. Massage a few egos if you have to. Just make sure you leave them wanting you, more than you want them. Keep someone far more menacing than you are as your closest confidant. Throw a few bodies down a deep well. Then quietly let those who inhabit your world know... it was you who ordered it done.'

Susan Brandt had done it all. And for close on thirty years her mother's advice had served her better than any that had followed.

The years she'd spent networking before she'd stepped into politics. The pre-emptive moves she'd made. Either laying or clearing the ground. The countless allies she'd either bought or promoted. Or blackmailed. On occasion even seduced. Impervious to shame, she'd made hard sex and the promise of access to power, a particular brand of persuasion of her own making.

But now it all counted for nothing.

All because she'd made the fatal mistake of loving her *Pequeño—and the lives of her precious grandchildren*—more than the heady mix of access to unlimited wealth and the wielding of power and influence.

So much more than her own mother ever had.

More than life itself.

For so long, it had been her abiding secret. Something Rosalynn Morrison-Banks would have ever countenanced. And now, finally, she understood why.

She reaches out for the grip of her Baretta. Opens her mouth. Presses the stubby barrel onto the roof of her pallet and pulls the trigger.

The blackness is instant.

And because she's taken the time to close all her windows—*rendering her inner sanctum close to silent*—the first person to enter the room, after the gunshot rings out, is able to register the fact that, albeit shallow and ragged, Susan Meredith Brandt—*fourth female governor of the great state of Texas*—is still breathing.

LAFAYETTE, LOUISIANA

Their route has taken them through Sweetwater and Abilene, then on to I-20, through Dallas-Fort Worth to Shreveport via I-49. And, having limited themselves to fuel stops, they've made it to the US Marine Corp Reserve Centre in Lafayette by mid-afternoon. Where, in light of a classified national security threat, the *2nd* Battalion, *14th* Marine Regiment unit commander had stowed his natural inclination to exercise the utmost caution and signed off their not insubstantial requisition from the base's well-stocked armoury.

They'd just been waved through the exit barrier when Zalizo's satellite phone rings.

Seigo adopts his usual expression of indifference.

'General...'

'Are you alone?

'Yes... but I have MIKE-*One* in situ.'

'That much I know. On the other hand... your current whereabouts, not so much.'

'En route to Morgan City.'

'Are you equipped?'

'I am now.'

'Okay, good... and, just so you know. Coal Island is no longer under private sector management. For reasons I may explain later, I chose to ignore your advice and paid them an unannounced visit. So, as you might guess, I'm surrounded by a fair few hard-ons nursing sore egos.'

'I can well imagine.'

'I won't deny, I was highly sceptical when it came to this Perry Morgan Blake character being set free... and that's somewhat of an understatement. But it's now been confirmed as materially factual. So it would transpire we're dealing with a contractor gone rogue to a degree even I'm struggling to get my head around.'

Zalizo chooses not to respond.

'And, despite your annoying habit of always managing to stay a few steps ahead of me, I do have at least one item you're not aware of.'

'And that would be...?'

'I allowed a certain Montgomery Ray to assume he'd outsmarted me by not confiscating his cell phone.'

'Coal Island's director?'

'The very same... and I can confirm the little jerk sent a sit-rep to at least two of his co-conspirators.'

'And, do we know which ones?'

'We know Governor Brandt was one of them for sure.'

He can't say why exactly, but the general's tone seems different somehow. Could be he was under a little more pressure than usual. Could be it was nothing more than sketchy reception. For sure, Coal Island has thick walls. But, for no reason he can get a solid fix on, Zalizo detects something about the man's cadence that sounds a little off. Not anything he would hang his hat on—*but there all the same.*

'I take it you haven't been listening to any radio stations over the past few hours.'

'No, as it happens.'

'Well, if you had, you wouldn't have missed the breaking news.'

'Which is?'

'The governor taking a bullet to the head.'

'Interesting,' Zalizo says. 'And what's being called.'

'Word is, she was alone at the time. So, there's a good chance her office will fall back on the tried and trusted... tragic gun-cleaning accident. For sure, they'll be no mention that she put a pistol in her mouth minutes after she received a call confirmed to have come from Director Ray's cell-phone.'

'Curiouser and curiouser.'

'Indeed... as is Mr. Ray's speculation that your deceased mass shooter is likely on his way to Louisiana. On account of some prior agreement he had with this character, Labette.'

'So, I take it the director's singing right now.'

'Like a diva.'

'And what sort of prior agreement are we talking?'

'The Director wasn't able to provide specifics. And, as you're prone to say, I'm sure if he could have... he would have. My guess is, right about now, he'll spill everything to avoid the serious jailtime he's facing. But, for what it's worth, at some point during the planning stage, he'd heard it had something to do with a hunting trip.'

'Sounds like some sort of death pact... which makes little sense, considering a Dallas court had already given him that guarantee.'

'Search me,' the General says. *'Regardless, I want this character Labette detained... and his Israeli side-kick. Without delay, if you wouldn't mind. And Colonel...'*

'Sir...?'

'...that's a direct order.'

Zalizo offers no response. Somewhere in the back of his head, a hammer had just been cocked. He'd heard it. *And felt it.* Something visceral. But nothing he can put a tag on right now.

'As for Perry Morgan Blake... I'm content to leave his immediate future to your discretion. And if you decide to play it the way I suspect you will, I'll still need his body... one way or another. I'll not get into the finer detail right now... but I need him re-interred at Coal Island A-sap.'

'Sir...'

'I need containment, Colonel. Which means your standing orders are to lock this down. That means, as of precisely this moment, you are to cease and desist with this vendetta of yours. And be under no illusion... these conditions are non-negotiable. You hit trouble, you are hereby ordered to seek authorisation to proceed. I'm in the throes of diverting my Task Force. When they arrive you are to relinquish command of this operation and accommodate as directed...'

'Relinquish command?'

'That's what I said.'

'Relinquish to whom?'

'You'll know as soon as I do. And, to all intents and purposes, this is an Executive Order, Colonel. As such, you are to receive them as if they'd been issued from the Big House. So, if you've taken steps to engage outside assistance, you are to stand them

down, forthwith... and send them back to wherever it is they came from. For now, MIKE-One is permitted to remain deployed. But her role is limited to reconnaissance. She may be your protégé but, for as long as the government pays her salary, she will operate under my direct command... I want her back on open comms... pronto.'

The line goes quiet.

'Colonel... are we clear?'

'Crystal,' Zalizo says.

'For your sake... I hope so. And for once in your life, you'd do well to heed a warning offered in good faith. Because, if you try playing me on this one, you'll end up so far over your skis you may not survive the landing. And, for perspective, your debrief will be carried out in my office back in DC. Which, as you're fully aware, doubles as a SCIF. The fact I'm insisting on a secure compartmentalised information facility should tell you all you need to know regarding how seriously I view the current situation. So, Colonel... regardless your reluctance to respond, I'm going to insist you acknowledge your orders. And that you intend to comply.'

Zalizo stares unblinking through the windshield.

'Colonel...?'

Then he kills the call.

Seigo fixes him a dead-eyed stare.

'You two lovebirds seem to be drifting toward a somewhat troubled future relationship.'

'So it seems,' Zalizo says.

'And what would be your best guess on you two deciding to kiss and make up?'

Zalizo shrugs.

'What will be, will be,' he says. 'But you know that itch you get on the back of your neck, when something the top brass is peddling smells as sour as horse piss?'

Seigo grunts, 'I sure as hell do.'

'Well... you can multiply it by ten.'

'Yeah... I figured,' Seigo says. 'And, I take it this MIKE-*One* he spoke of is your lone Ranger?'

Zalizo nods.

'So, what happens to Johanssen?'

'I've already briefed him his deployment will likely be a non-lethal arrangement... He said he'll top up his supply of promethazine.'

For a moment, Seigo falls back into silence.

Then he says, 'Strikes me, my friend... either this little old crow has made herself a nest inside that notoriously impenetrable skull of yours. Or you got yourself a major issue when it comes to having faith in your chain-of-command.'

Zalizo says, 'The general's chosen to ignore an explicit request to hold back breaching a specific location.'

'Isn't he paid the big bucks to make the big calls?'

'Maybe,' Zalizo says. 'But I tend toward holding a very low opinion of anyone who puts my personal well-being... and the safety of my people at risk, for no clear advantage.'

'Conceit,' Seigo says, 'Or stubbornness will do that to a guy... all day, every day.'

Zalizo grunts.

They've been on the road for ten hours. Which means he isn't in the mood for debate. Least ways, not until they had both gotten some rest. Before he can suggest they find someplace to take a break, Seigo lights the cheroot he'd been rolling between his fingers throughout the call. Proceeds to puff out a ring of smoke.

Zalizo drops the passenger window.

Seigo takes another long pull. Exhales slowly. Makes no

attempt to direct his smoke outside the cabin.

'Leg... of all the people I know, you were always the one least capable of constraint.'

'*Yeah*... I know.'

He flicks his lite through the passenger window.

Zalizo says, 'Everything hereabouts is tinder dry. Best you get out and douse that.'

Seigo opens the passenger door. Slides out. Unzips his fly and pisses on the stub. Delaying for a while longer than strictly necessary before easing himself back on board.

'Seems pretty clear to me, I'm gonna have to reassess. I have people I care for who rely on me.'

'You and me both,' Zalizo says.

'So perhaps its best you drop me off at the next ramp.'

Zalizo puts the GMC into drive. Points the hood in the direction of Highway 90.

'Roger that,' he says.

'Sorry, *ak'is,*' Seigo says. 'But I'd say services have been fully rendered.'

Zalizo says, 'I guess so.'

CAPITOL HILL, WASHINGTON DC

The instant a chirpy—*have-a-nice-day*—voice at CityTech Bank and Trust informs him his investment accounts have been frozen—*temporarily of course*—under explicit orders from the head of CIFRA, Martin Devlin knows the game is up. Every goddam thing he'd ever strived to achieve wiped from the board.

Just like that.

He continues making his way across Delaware Avenue. Heading for the promise of finding a little seclusion in Upper Senate Park.

The chirpy voice continues.

'If you wish to hold the line, Mr. Devlin... I can put you through to our head of compliance.'

Fucking... Goddam... CIFRA.

He feels his heart rate snap into overdrive. Hears the roar of his own blood bursting in his ears. His skin tightening like dried-out hide across the top of his scalp. Because, under normal circumstances, the Cayman Islands Financial Regulations Authority usually applied only the lightest touch, allied to a highly customer-centric approach, when it came to foreign investment protocols. But he's also well aware, every banking system has its limits. Especially when it came to complying with demands handed down from the United States Department of Justice.

So he cuts the call. Begins clenching and unclenching his fists to stop his hands from shaking; while a universe of doubt and raw fear spirals inside his head. Outside of a gym, he hadn't broken sweat since he was in his teens. And yet here he stands. Temples pounding. His shirt clinging to his back and under his arms, despite the chill wind.

Within minutes, he discovers all communications with Clarence Hellermann III have been shut down. By any method. On every goddam device. Proof positive a final nail is being driven into the cross he is, without question, about to be hung from. Because comms-down between himself and the Senator was something that simply wouldn't ever happen if everything hadn't already turned to shit in a basket.

In a moment of blind panic and desperation, he re-enters the Russell Senate Building. Wasting *God* only knows how much precious time berating interns for the kind of information they would never be privy to in a million years.

Finally, he hooks into the security cameras covering the Senator's home. Sees that the entire neighbourhood is locked down and under guard.

Yet more time wasted.

Time he now knows he doesn't have.

In the here and now, he is sitting behind the wheel of his Lexus hybrid. Parked in his luxury residence's secure underground garage. In one of the two spaces reserved for apartment forty-four. Trying to anticipate who might—*at this very moment*—be braking into his refuge. Despoiling his furnishings. Breathing their vile germs into his filtered air. Maybe they would simply block his access to the elevators. Or cover off the stairwells. Could be they could afford to be brazen. Make their move to detain him in the foyer. Subject him to the ignominy of a public perp walk. He wonders what odds he'd get that the concierge would remain loyal to an exclusive apartment dweller as valued as he undoubtedly is. After all, the Navy veteran has been pounding his immaculately-shined, military surplus boots up and down the apartment's broad front steps for close on fifteen years—*come rain or shine*. So maybe the weathered old guy would consider it his unspoken duty to find some way to signal to a resident they were walking into danger.

If he even made it as far as the entrance.

As it was, the only person he's seen since he'd arrived, had been a lone female. Someone he'd initially thought he recognised—*though just as likely not*. Wearing a dark, snug-fitting trouser suit. Maybe blue. Maybe black. One hand cradling a cell phone to her ear, the other clutching some kind of impracticably large fashion bag to her chest. Glossy auburn hair, cut short and neat above the nape of her neck. Looking harassed and in a hurry. But, with his mind in such a state of turmoil, he finds it impossible to make a judgement on such banal details.

In any event, she passes by without a sideways glance. Quickly disappearing from view. And just as quickly slipping from his jumbled thoughts.

He lifts the tube of sanitiser gel he keeps stored in the centre console. Squeezes a pearl-sized drop onto his free hand. Flips the lid secure and slots it back, next to his key fob. Thoroughly massaging the liquid into his skin, as he always does. The stink of sweat, permeating up from under his arms making him feel soiled beyond anything he's ever had to tolerate since he was a child.

Out of nowhere, he wretches into the footwell. His airways tightening as a fresh wave of panic clamps across his chest. Threatening to overwhelm him. His eyes watering, blurring his vision. Getting away from the smell of acid bile his only thought. So he fails to scan the space outside his vehicle—*just to be safe*—like he's done on practically every other occasion over the thirty plus years he's lived in DC. Because the nation's capital was nothing like an episode of The West Wing. For one thing, the hum-drum had routinely outweighed the glamorous by a factor he'd always resented. And, for damned sure, it was a city as casually violent as any place, anywhere. Intolerant of timidity; at least in those places not gated and under guard.

But, right now, all he knows is he has to breathe fresh air into his poisoned lungs. So he pokes blindly at the deadlock release button on the dash. Hears a click after a couple of frantic stabs.

He cracks the door open.

Manages to get his left foot planted firmly on the ground.

The driver's door crashes back against his shin. Followed by something bone hard slamming into his face. Detonating an explosion of pain above the bridge of his nose...

...blinding plasma flashes scorching white-hot behind his eyes.

He collapses back into the driver's seat, the upper half of his body flailing over the centre console. His shattered leg kicked viciously back into the footwell, sending shards of ice lancing deep into his groin.

A river of blood and mucus begins to stream from his nose into his open mouth, mixing with a thick cocktail of gore spraying up over his face as he chokes.

His assailant leans in through the driver-side door. Forcing their knee into his groin. Casual and unhurried. Like brutality and violence were just some everyday thing. Pushing something blunt, hard up against his temple. Raising an over-sized fashion bag like some kind of shield.

In that moment, as he feels his senses begin to shut down, he's certain he can detect a whiff of something bitter-sweet. It could be his shattered mind is determined to play one last trick. Nonetheless, he could have sworn he can smell perfume. And the sound of a woman's voice—*sharp and unyielding*.

Saying something like, *'Jesus Christ... keep still, goddammit.'*

The loud spit of a nine-millimetre parabellum, exiting a four-and-a-half inch suppressed barrel, goes unheard.

Day Five

'Package secure...'

ATCHAFALAYA DELTA, LOUISIANA

Moko stands twenty-six inches from the ground to the top of his shoulders. A little above average for a Belgian Malinois. Elegant despite his heavily-muscled bulk. Displaying all the characteristics of a breed known for its unwavering loyalty and unrelenting stamina. Effortlessly noble. Constantly alert. And, apart from the occasional billet in the pound at Fort McNair, never more than a couple feet from his handler's side from age six months.

In all their years together, Runellie has never heard her faithful companion so much as bark. Or growl, come to that. But whenever his black-tipped ears swivel sharply forward, or he raises his snout to sniff the air, she takes his signals for what they are.

A warning that shouldn't ever be ignored.

She reaches out to stroke her canine partner's mud-covered flank as Moko drops to his haunches without a sound. Ready to move, with or without command.

They are both lying prone. Both sighted in the same direction.

The familiar dry rattle of an eastern diamondback announces its presence over the incessant chirruping and buzzing of insects. No more than fifty yards away. Forward and slightly left of their position. Not that she considers the presence of a seriously venomous snake to be her primary concern. The fact this species only ever uses its distinctive alarm to warn off anything it has no inclination to eat, most assuredly is.

She senses Moko's tension ratchet up a notch. So she whispers a barely audible...

'E-a-s-y, boy.'

Then she registers a pin-point of blue light. Distance, hard to discern. But she recognises—*almost instantly*—the short and long intervals associated with morse code. Manages to decipher the brief signal on its second cycle.

V-I-K-I-N-G.

She whispers, *'A-w-a-y.'*

Moko's tension eases back a fraction before he melts into the darkness without a sound. Seconds later, a black, irregular form materialises from the foliage, barely forty yards ahead. No heat signature. No sound whatsoever. Visible only for the fact it made a sizable hole in the shadowy background of undergrowth.

Runellie mutters, *'Impressive...'*

Like all well-trained operators identifying friend-not-foe, the figure raises his gun-hand. Keeps it raised until he makes for the spot Moko has just vacated.

'You've got yourself a keen pair of ears, Sergeant.'

Runellie says, 'As a matter of fact... I have two pair.'

On what seems like base instinct, Doug Johanssen spins round to his open flank. Raising his suppressed SCAR-H rifle, fast and smooth. Runellie reaches across, placing her hand on the barrel, gently forcing it down, as Moko emerges spectral from the shadows, inches from Johanssen's head.

She keeps her voice barely above a whisper. Moko keeps his ears pinned halfway back and his nose a couple degrees above horizontal.

She says, 'You got in pretty close.'

Johanssen gives a small shrug.

'It's what I was trained to do.'

'Even so...'

'*Yea*h, well... I was part of the steering group that developed a whole bunch of stealth materials. My bag was camo and SCUBA applications. And, you could say I acquired a somewhat flexible attitude toward ownership over the years. Especially when it came to getting my hands on gear I might just find a use for somewhere down the line.'

Runellie says, 'I'll bear that in mind.'

Johanssen removes his full-face mask. Somewhere behind a wholesome, grey-flecked beard and jet-black teeth guards, she senses the man is grinning.

One thing's for sure, when it came to infiltration, this guy was plainly next level.

'The Colonel told me your original plan was to HALO in.'

Runellie says, 'We did.'

Johanssen gives Moko a short, sideways glance.

'I know it's a thing where the LZ's open and flat,' he says. 'So, for a lo-cal as shitty as this... pretty darn neat, if you ask me.'

Runellie makes a noise with her tongue.

Moko moves around to settle at her side.

'What about you?' she says.

Johanssen says, 'I high-tailed it up from a place I have on the Pecos River. Came in via the Shaffer Bayou. Landed at an inlet off the Atchafalaya River going by the name East Bend. Stowed my RHI just under a click due north of here. Vectored in on your sat-comms. Which, if you don't mind me saying... was a little high risk for my tastes.'

'Not so much as you'd think. I only fired it up a couple hours ago. Positioned it a little ways from where you signalled. Figured if you were only halfway competent, you'd avoid me if I kept it too close. And speaking of high risk... where'd you get a ribbed-hull inflatable so quick?'

'Brought it right along with me. On account it's baffled quieter than a respectful fart at a funeral. Ordinarily, I use it for lake fishing and the like. Or whenever I feel sweet solitude calling.'

'I heard you were retired.'

'And you heard right.'

'So, if you don't mind me saying... your levels of readiness seem pretty intense.'

'I happen to live in the great State of Texas, Sergeant. Depending on the weather... the whims of local law enforcement... or politicians with dubious impulses, it kinda always feels like we're slippin' towards end-of-days territory. Then there's my naturally cautious tendencies. Speaking of which, is your *CO* bringing anyone else along?'

Runellie hesitates for a beat.

Then she says, 'A few days back, he made a trip to the Navajo Nation. So I figure he's called in a favour from a guy he used to run with back when he was a kid.'

'Someone you know?'

Again, she hesitates.

'Not personally... *no*. But I looked him up a while back.'

'And...?'

'He's ex-Delta.'

Johanssen issues a long-drawn-out, 'O-k-a-y...'

Runellie says, 'Rumour is, they weren't all that distraught to let him go.'

Johanssen goes quiet.

At length, he says, 'Among all of us, those guys are the least inclined to dick around... so I figure, bottom line, that's gotta be good for us.'

'Could be,' Runellie says.

'Besides,' Johanssen says. 'The only *rumour* I ever listen to, has Stevie Nicks on lead vocals.'

Runellie chortles silently.

'Moko, meet Johanssen... Johanssen, meet Moko.'

AUSTIN, TEXAS

Victor knows it was nothing more than plain-old dumb luck. One of an increasingly regular series of power outages the Lone Star State had suffered during a month-long, particularly punishing—*and increasingly frequent*—early season heatwave. Inevitably followed by a series of severe storm cells dumping fire and brimstone upon earth baked hard as concrete.

And that had been that.

Huge lightning strikes had cut all mainline power to Austin-Bergstrom International Airport. That and a biblical-level deluge, in tandem with a leaky roof, which had conspired to take out the back-up power plant. Mobile generators were slow to come on line and limited to the tower and main terminal. So all flights had been cancelled—*in and out*. Scheduled and non-scheduled. Commercial and private. For the foreseeable, nothing was moving; with everything inbound having been diverted. Some as far away as Dallas-Fort Worth.

So far, he'd made a dozen or more calls to outlying airstrips. Pleading, cajoling, even threatening a series of numb-skulls for a private charter flight to Lafayette—*and gotten precisely nowhere.*

Inside, his emotions are raging.

Across the board, flight crews and passengers had been ordered back to the terminal by harassed facilities engineers and ground staff, citing mandatory compliance with emergency protocols. He'd tried his darndest to argue that remaining aboard his plane would cause less hassle for all concerned, until the threat of imminent armed arrest had persuaded him, no way he was going to prevail.

So, for the last two hours, he'd tried and failed to block out the ceaseless ribbon of strap-lines marching, in bold red font, across every one of the terminal's numerous TV monitors. No matter which way he turned, the same headlines scrolled non-stop beneath muted, sombre-looking cable news anchors.

GOVERNOR BRANDT IN DESPERATE STRUGGLE FOR LIFE FOLLOWING TRAGIC SHOOTING ACCIDENT

TEXAS SENATOR CLARENCE HELLERMANN III RESIGNS

LONG-TIME SENATORIAL AIDE, MARTIN DEVLIN, FOUND DEAD IN WASHINGTON DC

As it is, his immediate attention was centred on a far larger bombshell. One that had detonated a little over five-hundred miles due west. And even though Montgomery Ray's message had been terse—*containing but a single word of text*—it's thrown his hitherto ordered world into an uncontrolled tailspin.

BACKLASH

Their pre-arranged code for—*facility compromised.*

He swipes his cell phone's screen to the dial-pad. Punches the number for Nasi's burner. Waits a good number of rings. But there was no pick-up.

He hangs up. Waits a few minutes. Then re-dials. This time, the call connects.

'I need you to turn around.'

'And go where?' Nasi says.

Victor says, 'Lafayette Regional.'

'Why...?'

'So... I assume you haven't heard the news.'

'I landed less than five minutes ago,' Nasi says. *'I've just this second got my signal back.'*

'Well, the governor has been found in her mansion, with a bullet in her head. And, despite our contact reporting there's zero chance of recovery, as a precaution, I want you out of Texas without delay... Besides Perry has it in his head to infiltrate my Morgan City estate ahead of schedule.'

'If I'm to start chartering flights, I'll need access to funds.'

'I'll reimburse... that's all you need to know.'

'And you're certain there's nothing else I need to know?'

'Nothing that would make any sense to you.'

'If you want me by your side in Morgan City, holding out on me is not something I'd recommend.'

'It's not a case of holding out. It's simply the fact that the other elements will mean nothing to you.'

'Try me...'

'Listen, Nasi...'

'I will give you five seconds,' Nasi says.

Deep within his massive frame, Victor feels his rage spike way beyond its notoriously low threshold. Twice now, within the space of twelve hours, his authority was being challenged. A circumstance that for so many years had been unthinkable. And, come what may, once the ground was back in his favour, he's determined he'll resolve both issues—*with prejudice*.

'Okay, Nasi... let's play this your way. For now.'

Victor momentarily puts a seal on his fury.

'So... besides this situation with the governor, a certain Senator for the State of Texas, with direct involvement in our project, has announced his resignation. With immediate effect.'

'Is there a traceable connection?'

'Nasi, we live in the digital age... so everything's connected. Nothing is untraceable. Of greater concern, however, is the fact the Senator's aide was shot and killed yesterday. And, before you ask... it's almost inconceivable we are looking at a coincidence.'

'And the name of this... aide?'

'Not that it'll mean a damn thing to you,' Victor says. 'He's a smarmy little shit going by the name, Devlin... Martin Devlin.'

An extended moment of silence spools down the line.

'Okay,' Nasi says. *'Let's see where this goes.'*

For the first time in a while, Victor feels himself smile.

'My sentiments exactly.'

ATCHAFALAYA DELTA, LOUISIANA

As a general principle, Zalizo made it a habit to receive good news in the same manner he received the not so good.

On the upside, the weather was dry and relatively calm, which meant Johanssen had no issues rigging his remote surveillance package. A mix of fixed cameras and drones. With a LF-data link secured to a camouflaged balloon, tethered a few feet above the forest canopy. To all intents and purposes, impossible to detect. Extending their short-range comms and video feed transmissions out to better than ten clicks. As a precaution, he's also set an array of lasers, pointing at an exposed section of the access road. Which meant anyone caught out in the open would be convinced they were being sighted by a sizeable ground force. As deceptions go, it more than hit the mark.

On the downside, there was no sign of the three individuals he's driven the better part of ten hours to lock horns with.

Johanssen had ferried him in from Morgan City two hours ago. Now the three of them were gathered next to the chief's RHI, beneath a dense canopy at the head of a narrow creek, with Moko on patrol somewhere out in the woods.

'Stuart Sandersford...' Runellie is saying. '...is the name of a guy I heard was lost on patrol. Helmand Province, if I recall... and definitely a good while back. The guy in the photo you sent... that's Carl Miller. Though he mostly answered to Jordi, on account of his middle name.'

'Well... I'm afraid he'll be sharing celestial MREs with Sandersford right about now,' Zalizo says. 'He got himself chopped up in a motel outside Lubbock.'

For a moment, Runellie looks contemplative.

'We served a tour together... in the early days chasing ISIS cells. Suburban warrior nut-jobs, for the most part. They were mostly joint operation gigs... with some pretty solid elements of the Kurds YPG mixed in. We never kept in touch... but I do recall him being a pretty solid guy.'

Zalizo picks up a handful of loamy dirt.

'Did he go through sniper school?'

Runellie nods.

'Sure... A little ahead of me. He didn't shine, but he was no slouch as far as I could tell.'

Zalizo allows the dirt to run through his fingers.

'Interesting...' he says.

He rubs the remainder into his hands before pulling on a pair of well-worn Mechanix gloves.

'Okay... I'm going to need both of you to stand back on this one.'

Johanssen says, 'Stand back...?'

Zalizo says, 'I need eyes covering the access road. And use of your little light show, should the need arise.'

Runellie says, 'Is that the only reason?'

'Whether it is or not, Sergeant... it's the reason I'm giving.'

She is part way through checking her rifle.

'Sounds like a bullshit move to me...'

Johanssen looks up from his monitor.

Runellie continues.

'We've confirmed only two hostiles in the zone. And you're saying we let another three in and just sit on our hands?'

'No, Sergeant... that's not what I'm saying. I'm saying I need eyes looking out...'

Zalizo dials back his irritation.

'We have no data on what force strength this asshole Labette can muster. For all we know he may have a sizeable reserve he can call in at a moment's notice... with a level of firepower we're not equipped to repel.'

Johanssen looks back to his screen.

'I have a couple M-32s... and a half-dozen M-33s.'

'Thank you, Chief... but we'll not be using Claymores and RPGs to shred citizens... foreign or domestic, into pet food. No matter how appealing the proposition might be.'

Johanssen shrugs, 'So we're sticking to the non-lethal approach?'

Zalizo nods.

'As of right now... to the furthest extent possible, it's how it has to be.'

Runellie looks set to step across the invisible line that has always defined the limits that existed between them. They were both headstrong. Each as uncompromising as the other in their own way, albeit with polar opposite *MOs*.

She says, 'And if we get overrun...?'

'In that particular scenario, Sergeant... I trust you to know when to withdraw.'

'Count on it,' Johanssen says.

Zalizo decides to change tack.

'Besides, there are a number of other items we need to consider here.'

Runellie rolls her eyes.

'Here we go.'

Zalizo ploughs on.

'One... The General said he was aiming to deploy a ground contingent... a-sap. And we can't guarantee he's bluffing... but you can take it from me, he knows I won't relinquish command to anyone he sends. So, my guess is, for whatever reason, he's shovelling a layer of bullshit to force a delay... or maybe playing some sort of double blind to push me to act recklessly. Either way, no one is spending time in Leavenworth on my account. I've locked horns, with way too many Pentagon heavy-hitters, way too many times, to risk some over-promoted desk jockey hell-bent on getting some long-overdue payback using either of you to get to me.'

'Colonel, I HALO'd in. With a dog... in a harness. Using a general's muscle to requisition a very expensive ride down here. So I reckon plausible deniability, on my part, is pretty much spent.'

'Nice try, Sergeant... but, as of right now, you're officially under the General's direct command. And, last I checked... he reports straight to the Oval Office. Whereas, my orders are limited to removing three players from the field. And those individuals were named. So there's no way this becomes another Oregon. And there's no way you and I are getting away with faking blue-on-blue a second time. Two... I've got a weird feeling I'm still missing something here. And I'm damned if I can figure out precisely what it is. So until I get a solid bead on whatever it is that's giving me an itch, you ladies will follow orders and hang back.'

Johanssen says, 'I remember those kinda feelings. I used to get them right before things turned into a shitty handshake.'

Runellie gives Johanssen a sideways glance.

'Chief... you smell so bad, I'm shocked you could recognise a shitty anything...'

Johanssen flashes a broad grin.

'...but I'm with the Colonel about something else smelling off.'

'Okay, Sergeant,' Zalizo says. 'If something's bugging you... let's have it.'

'It's pretty simple really,' Runellie says. 'Because you say you were given three names. Victor Labette and Perry Morgan Blake I can guess. Question is... what's the third?'

Zalizo hesitates. It seemed an odd thing for her to ask to ask.

'Our Israeli friend,' he says. 'Benjamen Nasi Abelman.'

Runellie creases a smile. 'So there it is...'

She issues a trilling whistle. A few moments later, Moko breaks from the foliage, settling at her side.

'A couple days ago, I told you I'd identified four possible shooters for the DC hits. I gave the General the same four names... but I never confirmed the Israeli to him or anyone else.'

Zalizo says, 'And you're one-hundred percent sure on that?'

'Colonel... it was you who made the call on Abelman... Go with the heavier intel, you said. And I didn't see any point pushing speculation up the line... Besides, I never got much further than confirming his entry through Fort Myers a few months back. Mostly because I assumed he would have travelled under any number of aliases since then... And there's one more thing that didn't quite hang together.'

'I'm listening,' Zalizo says.

'Victor Labette's CIA bio... Digging it up felt way too easy. People like that... if the Agency wants to keep its secrets buried, it should have taken weeks to unearth... Instead it took two hours.'

'So, you're saying someone wanted it found?'

'It's not for me to say,' Runellie says. 'I'm just putting it out there that everything has begun to feel way too easy.'

Zalizo feels his blood run cold. Not because he was being played. Or who was doing the playing. Because—*when it came to it*—betrayal was nothing new. Certainly nothing he couldn't handle. Given time. More because his judgement had been so fatally flawed—*on so many levels*—and for so long. Casting doubt over everything that had gone before. Making him little more than a joystick-operated robot. Nothing more than a tool to be use at someone else's whim. Guided by blind loyalty masquerading as duty and honour. In reality, no better than the kind of mindless guns-for-hire he's always despised.

Johanssen is eyeing him warily.

'Care to fill me in on this general you'all keep talking about?'

Zalizo says, 'It's better you don't know. In fact, you need to reconsider whether you want to be here at all. Because, right about now, bugging out with no hard feelings might be a smart move.'

'I have a couple traits you need to be aware of, Colonel... Number one. I'm stubborn as a mule... Number two. I refer you to trait number one.'

Meanwhile, Runellie crouches next to Moko on the damp earth.

'What I can't figure,' she says. 'Is why Ableman would come ashore using his true identity. Unless it was to signal to someone he'd made landfall.'

'Risky,' Zalizo says. 'But it's as good a read as any... given what little we know.'

Runellie shakes her head.

'Well, if you ask me, that's some next-level stuff when it comes to shit-gone-rogue conspiracies...'

She pulls Moko in close to her side.

'But I guess there's a simple way to confirm our suspicions.'

'And what might that be?' Zalizo says.

She slides her hands into a pocket in her tunic. Pulls out a capsule, about half-an-inch long and no thicker than a pencil, thrusting it forward between her thumb and forefinger.

'Moko insisted I remove his tracker before we set out. He figured we could maybe drop it somewhere... accidently of course. See if it attracts any unwanted attention.'

Zalizo kneels down. Ruffles Moko's fur.

'Who's a smart boy?'

'I'll say,' Johanssen says. 'All we need is a good place to leave it.'

'We could use my drone,' Runellie says. 'There's a jetty we could put it on. Perfect distance away to keep anyone from getting vaporised if someone decides to do a little... airborne house-keeping.'

'I'm tellin' you,' Doug says. 'This gal's way too smart for anyone's Army.'

Runellie says, 'Rangers lead the way.'

After a moment, Zalizo says, 'I have in mind, somewhere a little more... *intimate*.'

ATCHAFALAYA DELTA, LOUISIANA

Zalizo knows the mechanical principles of a dart-gun are pretty rudimentary. Two chambers; one holding the agent, one imparting enough air pressure to force the sedative into the target's bloodstream. But, unlike a standard syringe, a tranquilizer dart is designed to puncture its victim without getting blocked by material—*or dermis*—releasing its contents through a hole set back from the tip of the needle.

Simple, but effective.

The difficult part lay in getting the dose just right. Too little and a target might continue to function. Too much and the consequences could prove fatal. As it was, volumes had to be based entirely on Runellie's estimate of each guard's body weight. After which, Johanssen made his calculations on dosage strength with all the confidence of someone familiar with the extraction of those disinclined to cooperate. Only confiding he'd erred on the high side once the darts had been primed.

Which had suited everyone just fine.

Zalizo waits for the two guards to return from their patrol. Watching them now, as they approach the line of connected cabins. Giving them credit for swinging their night vision goggles around the perimeter of the clearing one more time before lowering their weapons. Taking it back as they enter the third door in a row of six with no thought of posting a lookout. Which was sloppy at best. Over-confidence, born of arrogance, much more likely. As it happens, he's more than happy to accept any advantage he can get—*big or small*—any time he can get it.

He pulls an M84 stun grenade from his webbing with one hand. Gripping his .45 in the other. Braking from the treeline at full speed. Shooting a single round through the cabin's only window. Pitching the fist-sized canister as hard as he could through the shattered glass. Trusting his aim and the strength of his arm.

He hears a ruckus kick off beyond the door as he slides to a crouch, like a runner stealing second base, against the cabin's wood-slatted wall.

One-thousand... Two Thousand...

The blast shatters what's left of the glass. Smoke and

shredded drapes exploding from the cabin's window. Followed by silence, folding back in from the forest.

He estimates the room can't be more than twelve-foot by twelve. A single percussion grenade pretty much guaranteed to have done it's work. Even so, when it came to incapacitation, he'd always believed in a belt-and-braces approach. So he crawls past the door and lobs a second grenade through the window, staying crouched.

One-thousand... Two Thousand...

The flash lights up a small patch of forest. The bang cracking like a lightning strike.

Zalizo rises and spins through one-eighty degrees. Slamming the heel of his boot at a point just below the *Chubb*-branded lock. The frame splinters, but refuses to yield. So he gives it another meaty kick, but again it holds.

He aims his gun. Shoots three rounds at the doorframe next to the lock and kicks again. And, this time, the door crashes open.

Inside the cabin, both guards are lying on the floor. One face up. The other face down. So he holsters his .45, pulling the dart gun.

Face-down gets a four inch syringe in his ass. He flips the cover on the stock. Pulls a fresh dart from the compartment, re-charges and reloads. Face-up gets his in the meat of his thigh.

Both get zip-tied and taped.

ATCHAFALAYA DELTA, LOUISIANA

Perry Morgan Blake hears a muffled explosion.

Then a second. Followed by the sound of gunshots.

He stops swimming. Keeping his head low to the surface of

the mud-brown water.

He'd set his rowboat adrift fifty yards out from the forested shoreline. Figures he wouldn't be needing it anytime in the future. Because he has no expectations of making it back off the spit of land he's headed towards. After all, he'd riled the big dude pretty bad. Issuing the type of challenge that all but guaranteed an overwhelming response.

Exactly as he'd intended.

Right now, he is relaxed. So he gives it a moment before resuming his languid stroke. He knows the path of the river's powerful currents as well as any man could. Allows it's sweeping eddies to push him toward the shoreline with a minimum of effort. Because, the last thing he needs is to come ashore exhausted.

Confident he's judged his angles just right, he allows his mind to drift back to the scene that had set him on his path to self-destruction...

...back to that sultry day, when he'd heard coyotes snarling just off the miles-long track leading from the shack he'd called home. A good hour-and-a-half, step-it-out walk through the woods to the nearest gravel road. Moving in cautiously to check out the ruckus. Barefoot and scrawny, and scarcely taller than a stunted sapling. Shinning up a half-fallen black willow. Leaning out through its plentiful foliage. Catching a glimpse of pale blue. A shade of blue so familiar he could have recognised it from a mile away. Sunday best blue. The colour of the dress he'd seen his momma wearing as she'd walked away, into the heavy mist, that same morning.

He clambers from the water on his hands and knees. Waits a moment, scanning the tree-line, before crawling his way across the clawing mud to the forest. Rolling over a couple times, making sure he was covered head to toe in the viscous sediment.

Twenty yards inside the treeline, he sits cross-legged, waiting while the mud dries to a crust. Then he pulls his Smith & Wesson and a box of spare ammo from the waterproof satchel slung over his back. One hundred rounds of three-fifty-seven high-load hollow-points. Each with the stopping power to down an adult bear at better than fifty yards.

More than adequate for his purposes.

As to the gunshots and explosions, they could have meant anything. Could be someone had gotten themselves spooked. Perhaps a couple of booby traps set off accidently by deer. Either way, he isn't the least concerned. Because he has no intention of making this easy for whoever he'll be facing out there. *No siree.* He'd long ago acquired all the skills he needs to move through the dense woods of the Atchafalaya wetland forests undetected. And the fact he'd never grown too big or heavy means, if he needs to, he can still access the canopy with ease. And it's the reason, in their rare private moments alone, his Momma had always called him her beautiful little squirrel.

As he sets off, Perry speaks to her for what he knows will likely be the last time. Picturing her—*whole again*—while he still can. Feeling her presence quiver through him. Trying to keep the image of her ravaged flesh from his mind. The frenzied cloud of blow-fly shrouding her lifeless remains. Her once beautiful face little more than pulp. Auburn hair matted with the blood and gore of blunt trauma.

Even as a child, he'd known there weren't no creature out on the delta, but a man with a lump hammer, able to put a fist-sized hole into a human's skull.

So, as he moves deeper into the trees, he whispers the same promise he'd made every day since he left her there on the dirt...

...too scared to climb down to the ground. Too pathetic and weak and snivelling to even try and dig a grave. Too cowardly to place her body into the embrace of the soft, damp earth. To offer

her some small amount of dignity, in exchange for all the pain she'd suffered at the hands of that foul-smelling monster, for the simple crime of loving the only child she'd managed to carry to full term inside her half-starved belly. Choosing, instead, to honour her passing by hunting and torturing every breed of beast he'd seen scavenging her soul on that fateful day.

'...not long now.'

ATCHAFALAYA DELTA, LOUISIANA

They spotted the vehicles from two clicks out. Running with high beams. Hemmed in on both sides of the dirt and gravel track by shoulder-high dry stone walls.

Johanssen calls in four civilian-spec four-by-fours. Land-Rover Defenders. High riding, rugged and capable. Fitted with locking differential drivetrains, all-terrain tyres and go-anywhere suspension. And slender enough to manoeuvre down tracks impassible by the likes of military-spec Humvees. All the same, they were soft-skinned; as a good number of wounded British war-on-terror veterans could readily attest. Certainly no match for well-placed Claymores and well-aimed RPGs. And certainly not a vehicle any active contingent of the United States Army would choose to ride.

So they both agree they'd be up against contractors. And overconfident ones for sure. Or maybe—*with a little luck*—just plain dumb.

Close-by, somewhere out over the Atchafalaya River, the sound of a rotor-powered aircraft at full throttle screams westward.

Runellie calls—*showtime.*

Ahead of her position, the first radio-detonated Claymore takes out the lead vehicle. Bucking its front end up off the deck. Knocking out both its engine block and front axle. Blowing its radiator and front lights. Veering it hard into the wall. Flipping it onto its side. The second vehicle ploughs into the stricken SUV's rear quarter, ripping its near-side front wheel clean off.

Vehicles three and four slew to a stop.

The doors on the two trailing SUVs crack open.

Carbines appear.

Runellie launches a forty-millimetre grenade round into the up-turned chassis of vehicle one. Setting it instantly alight. Swinging the M-32 behind her back as she levels Johanssen's compact five-point-five-six AR-15 loaner. Sending two six-round bursts from the SIG Rattler into the flames. Strafing where she judges the meat of the drive-train to be.

Because orders were orders.

Then she vaults the wall, sprinting to her second station as the occupants of the wrecked lead vehicles spill out, moving dazed and a good deal banged up.

Fifty yards away, Johanssen vaults in the opposite direction, from the adjacent side of the track. Performing a rinse and repeat on the rear-most vehicle. Launching his own M-32 low. Giving the occupants a better than average chance at surviving the high explosive round than they likely deserved. Even so, as leaking diesel fuel quickly feeds the flames, he sends his own hail of bullets biting into stone, tracing a path of sparks to within feet of the black clad figures scrambling over to his side of the wall.

Then he activates the light show he'd set up inside the tree line. Looking for all the world like a full company of laser-sighted barrels are aimed squarely on the stricken SUVs.

‘W-E-A-P-O-N-S... D-O-W-N.’

Johanssen’s voice booms louder than a bullhorn.

‘W-E-A-P-O-N-S... D-O-W-N... N-O-W.’

Runellie counts six bodies throwing themselves on her side of the wall. She puts two rounds into her closest target. Square in the chest. Punching the figure backwards like they’d been hit by an angry bison.

She puts her third and fourth rounds into her farthest target’s ribcage. Missing muscle and bone because the figure has his rifle raised, frantically seeking something to shoot back at. The rounds slam home just below the armpit, dropping the figure to their knees.

A muffled shot spits out from the other side of the track. Followed, a few seconds later, by Johanssen’s bellowed sit rep.

‘EIGHT DOWN... ONE OUT.’

Runellie does the math.

Meanwhile, on her side of the track, those left standing had their backs lit up by a bank of lasers angled to clear the wall. Enough to persuade the entire assembly to drop their weapons as one; back over the wall onto the track. Then lock their fingers behind their heads..

She rises from under Johanssen’s camo. Re-sights the figure she’d put on their knees. Puts another round centre mass. Laying them flat on their back. She’s in no doubt her targets will wake up plenty sore, with good odds on a busted rib or three. But, unless they were particularly scrawny and lucked out with internal haemorrhaging, they would all likely survive.

She hollers over to Johanssen.

‘SIX DOWN... TWO OUT.’

Johanssen booms back.

‘COPY THAT, SERGEANT...

...NOW, THE REST OF YOU FUCKS... HIT THE DIRT’

On her side of the wall, Runellie—*AR still raised and sighted*—bellows equally loud.

'...YOU HEARD THE MAN.'

ATCHAFALAYA DELTA, LOUISIANA

'Those were explosions.'

'Thank you, Nasi... I have eyes to.'

They'd come in low from the west. Barrelling towards the dawn at better than a hundred and twenty knots; practically skimming the surface of the river. Witnessing the bright flash of explosions, a short way off to the north, blooming to an orange glow beyond the canopy.

'I warned you... and you should have listened.'

'Nasi... I'm a little concerned you seem overly agitated?'

'I would rather be agitated than pig-headed.'

Victor stares at the side of Nasi's head.

'When this is over, Mr. Ableman... you and I will play our hands. See who's pushing pairs and who's drawing a full house.'

The Israeli's focus is on the tree-line. Expression implacable. His voice calm, like he was ordering a take-out.

'You were one-hundred per cent sure we had more than enough time to prepare our ground... and you were wrong. So the time for grandstanding and fancy words has passed. Once I make cover, I will be no more visible to you than a ghost... and that is how I will remain.'

Victor says, 'You need to relax... unless, of course, you possess a unique ability to determine events happening beyond your sight.'

Nasi moves from under the settling rotors. He drops and re-slots a thirty-round magazine into his magnesium-railed AR15. Fitted with a light-weight, custom-made lower receiver. Flared mag-well for re-load efficiency. Converted to ambi-release just in case his dominant hand got injured. Titanium bolt carrier to cut more weight and lessen the recoil. And a trusty H1 night optic; mostly because it was bomb-proof when it came to holding zero when the going got tough. He takes another look at the wash of orange above the canopy.

'This bullshit ends today.'

Victor says, 'I couldn't agree more.'

Nasi sets off for the forest. Turning as he moves away.

'As of now, Monsieur Jacque... whether you agree or disagree is no longer of any concern to me.'

Victor stands frozen. Stunned by Nasi's words. Paralysed by the sudden knowledge his extreme vanity had allowed him to be played—*by everyone*. Knowing exactly what he needed to do. But, for the first time in his adult life, he finds himself unable to respond. And, by the time he snaps free from his torpor, Nasi has slipped beyond the treeline.

Disappearing...

...like a ghost.

ARLINGTON, WASHINGTON DC

If he were ever to find himself part of an identity parade, the recently appointed Chairman of the Joint Chiefs of Staff could easily be mistaken for a man lacking stature.

For one thing, he would barely reach the line marked five-foot-six. On the other hand, the moment anyone met him face-to-face, they never failed to register just how powerfully he was built. Genetics, and a good deal of humping weights during his college years, having bestowed all the attributes required by a champion wrestler. Albeit one who'd long since reached the threshold where calorie consumption had overtaken calorie burn. A short, impossibly thick neck. Chest like a barrel. Arms like the hind legs of a Komodo dragon. Feet that splayed out like a penguin when he walked—*an activity he indulged infrequently these days, to avoid the inevitable chaffing*—on account of possessing a pair of thighs as thick as some men's waists. A physique that had meant, throughout a forty-year career, he'd been forced to spend a small fortune on expensively tailored dress uniforms that had never once made him look a dime better for the effort. Or the expense.

'Okay, *General*... what in hell's name is going on here?'

The grey-suited figure stood before him shrugs.

'I guess you could call it... an operational adjustment.'

The head of the United States military glances at the slim binder—*marked Top Secret, SCI*—he's brought with him into the room.

'You're making a serious mistake if you think you can play me for a fool... *General*. For one thing, you happen to be short one gold star. For another, you lack my one-to-one access with the only folk that really matter in this town. And, while I'm reliably informed you operate under some kind of Special Executive Order... which, I'll confess, is something I've yet to get a proper handle on... don't expect me to soil my breeches, just because you get to wear a suit and tie doing your day job.'

'I wouldn't dream of it, Chairman.'

'Really, General... because, I'm seriously beginning to wonder.'

'Right now, I'll admit things are a little fluid. But I can assure you, everything will be back under control within the next twelve hours.'

'If your casual assurances were all I needed... we wouldn't be communicating inside this private *SCIF* set-up of yours.'

'I figured not.'

'Yet it didn't occur to you that Senator Hellermann would have powerful allies?'

'By *allies*, I take it you mean... *donors*?'

'I'll stick with allies... and, word is, they are more than a little concerned that one of their own has been unceremoniously eviscerated. Without their specific endorsement.'

'I can't do what I do through committee... nor would I.'

'That's understood... But while I'm told this Executive Order, along with your Whitehouse Special Advisor status, affords you a high degree of autonomy... I can't allow anyone under my command to publicly neuter one of this town's longest-served and most respected one-man institutions. Not least because this nation's military has a long-cherished history of not involving themselves in civilian affairs.'

'Well, Chairman... it happens, I'm not under your command. And I can assure you, nothing about my discussions with the Senator were in any way... *public*.'

'You were the last person to meet with Senator Hellermann before he resigned. And this is DC... so, it might as well have been a fucking town hall event.'

'He shouldn't have dropped the ball.'

'God Almighty... will you listen to yourself? Making like someone ordained you judge and jury. I'll concede the Senator is guilty of a good deal more than simply allowing himself to be played. And don't for one minute think I haven't figured out who by. So you better listen, and listen good. In isolation, Martin Devlin's demise could have been covered off without too many eyebrows being raised. To say he won't be missed...

well, I'm a mid-Floridian by birth, and I've seen plenty of gators in Lake George with more appealing personalities than that particular slimeball. But that's not the real issue here. What's at issue is the implied lethality of your threats to a sitting United States Senator... *J-e-s-u-s H Christ.*'

'I take it, Chairman... you intended to say alleged threats?'

'I'd advise you not to test the limits of my good nature, General... As of right now, I may not be in possession of the finer details. But you can take it from me... I will be soon enough. And if you think I'm going to risk any of this hair-brained scheme of yours becoming a strapline on CNN, you are gravely mistaken. What's been set in play here, is nothing short of domestic terrorism. And your part in it, not far short of *treason*. And, if I have anything to do with it, no amount of... *I was only executing orders*, is going to save your scrawny neck.'

'Scrawny it may well be. But I can assure you... I act as an official executive functionary. Tasked with ensuring the operational capabilities of the organisation you sit atop of are never compromised. In any respect... *anywhere*... at any time.'

'And you, General, can spare me the fake hubris.'

'I can assure you, Chairman... it's not fake. And a long way from misplaced confidence.'

'Either way, the only reason I don't have a squad of MPs outside right now, waiting to haul your rear end off to Leavenworth, is down to my advice being overruled... for the time being at least. Because, if it were up to me, I'd put a bullet in your head, here and now. And you can take it from me, I wouldn't lose a wink of sleep.'

'That's good to know... *Chairman*.'

'I'm glad you think so, General. In the meantime, you are to call off your attack dog and get this fucking shit-show squared away. I may not know the details of the dirty work you have him engaged in right now... but I know who he is. And I've been fully briefed on his reputation. And, to say the least... I'm not impressed.'

'Well, you should be. Because I can assure you, if you'd been properly appraised, you'd already know there's no chance in hell anyone will be able to... *call him off*. He happens to be an individual of singular focus. And, unfortunately for everyone involved, he has what might be loosely called... a dog in the game.'

The general pushing four gold stars feels his blood pressure begin to spike.

'Do you think I blew in on the last goddam hurricane? Six months in post or not, do you honestly believe I'm not entirely familiar with the labyrinthine nature of this nation's military industrial complex. You think I'm ignorant of all the nefarious connections transcending the tenure of mere political administrations. Or maybe you think I've had my head up my ass for the past thirty years?'

'Nothing could be further from the truth.'

'Don't patronise me... you conceited son-of-a-bitch.'

'Chairman, I can assure you, that was not my intention.'

'Do you know what? I don't give a rat's ass either way. And, forthwith, I strongly advise you to cease thinking of yourself as beyond my oversight. Whatever machinations you've engaged the Lieutenant-Colonel in, he's currently a serving military officer... As such, you are hereby ordered to get him back on a very short leash. Pronto. And, even though it's against my better judgement, I'm prepared to give you four hours... and not a second longer.'

'On whose authority?'

'I beg your pardon...?'

'My remit has never extended quite that far... *Chairman*.'

'Who the hell do you think you're addressing?'

The General pushing three gold stars offers a demure smile.

'Your question is somewhat retrogressive.'

'Only somewhat. Well golly-gee... that's a relief.'

'I can assure you, Chairman... despite your surfeit of gold stars, this is one rabbit hole you don't want to poke your head into.'

'Am I to understand you're refusing to recognise my authority?'

'I'm saying, until my orders are rescinded verbally... direct from the Oval Office. My response holds.'

'And if I choose to stand you down... here and now?'

'Like it or not, Chairman... this nation's non-nuclear delivery systems are entirely carbon fuel dependent. And, right now, the majority of that fuel begins life black and sticky, and either gets pumped from the ground or flushed from it by some means I don't care to understand. Let's face facts... even those silos out there in the Midwest use diesel to run their back-up generators. It ain't rocket science. It's geo-economics one-o-one. Not so long ago, if we couldn't drill enough of our own, my job... all our jobs... was to ensure we had the capability to go get what we need. Wherever it happened to be. More recently, my orders... specifically and with prejudice, are to reduce, to the greatest extent possible, our dependence on said external supplies. And, in spite of a little not unexpected hinderance from our middle eastern partners... and the usual bunch of unenlightened eco-warriors, that is precisely what I've done. And, with or without your help, permission or agreement, it's what I intend to carry on doing.'

Inside his broad frame, the four star General fights to contain his fury.

'This conversation is as ridiculous as it is preposterous.'

'Respectfully, Chairman... every wind farm and every photovoltaic array, every damn LNG terminal, stand as direct threats to the existence of the few remaining refineries this nation's military depends on. Do you really expect us to allow the global balance of power to rest in the fickle hands of these sanctimonious, blue-collar terrorists? I don't fucking think so. So, if you're intent on making this your own personal Alamo... I suggest you buckle up. Because, this operation was conceived for a singular purpose. And that purpose was to clear the field, by any and all means, of anyone with ideologies that don't align with long-standing critical supply chain doctrines. So, while it's unfortunate some of those tasked with its execution, have proved somewhat... over-zealous. The moment you attempt to stand me down, you'll likely find yourself announcing an immediate intension to spend more quality time with your family.'

The General short one gold star reaches into his inside pocket, pulling out a wallet made from the finest Tuscan leather.

'My Special Executive Order, Wesley... Ordinarily, it sits in my personal safe. But I figured a man with your imposing reputation, might just require a little additional persuasion to remain in your designated lane...'

Wesley B. Stoner adopts the posture of a man preparing to lunge forward.

'Why, you insubordinate son-of-a...'

The general pushing three gold stars stands his ground.

'So... before you engage in something you're sure to regret, I suggest you read it and commit it to memory for as long as you remain in post. Beyond that, my advice regarding the Lieutenant-Colonel is simple, but expedient...'

'Really... and what might that be?'

'Leave bringing this particular breed of bloodhound to heel, to its designated handler.'

'And if I choose not to?'

'I can assure you... the consequences will be somewhat extreme.'

Stoner balls his hands into fists.

'Well... it shouldn't surprise you that I'm no stranger to dealing with hotheads. So I'd strongly advise you inform your hound... I don't scare easily.'

Before he turns to leave, the senior officer wearing civilian attire offers a tight-lipped grin.

'That's because you don't hail from Wyoming, Chairman... so you've yet to meet a wolf face-to-face.'

ATCHAFALAYA DELTA, LOUISIANA

Nasi moves forward in a fast, self-levelling stoop. Sighting the figure moving parallel, as it crashes past a succession of thin trunks and thick vegetation.

He fires off what he assesses to be four near misses. But, to his surprise, the figure slows. Staggering forward into a small clearing. Flashlight flaring. Then suddenly pitching over. Disappearing into a patch of low foliage.

Hit or fall. In the gloom of half-light, it's hard to tell.

Whichever, Nasi knows he has the upper hand. He is on his feet. Has the advantage of elevation and approach angle. So he takes a few extra seconds to be sure he's zeroed in, feeling the familiar amount of trigger resistance.

Zalizo lights up his ultra-high beam, allowing it to fall free as he dives to the ground. Rolling a couple times as he tumbles. Quietly falling into the three-foot trench he'd finished hewing from the soft earth barely minutes before he'd heard the rotors passing overhead.

A second later the flashlight explodes. Its batteries and hard plastic casing showering the shallow trench.

Two more shots ring out.

The first passes barely inches to the right of his position. The next missing a similar distance to his left. A split-second apart. Both splitting the air, with a loud crack, punching the earth a fraction beyond the pit.

He lets out a deliberately audible grunt. Pulling his double-stack .45 free of its holster as he rolls onto his back. Head towards the direction of fire. Aiming two-handed...

...waiting.

He's loaded with one-sixty-five grain ACP hollow points. Enough close-in muzzle energy that even grazing a small patch of exposed flesh would cause it to instantly compress, then violently expand, ripping away tissue down to the bone. Generating a shockwave such that even a glancing shot would cause debilitating injury.

With the onset of dawn penetrating barely half-way through the canopy, he knows night optics would light him up from somewhere close to twenty yards out. Because he'd walked it through after he'd dug his hole. So when the sound of slow, watchful footfalls comes to his ears—*slightly right of his centre-line*—cautiously crossing the dry vegetation he'd lain in a wide, two meter deep arc, he sets himself.

Then he fires off a seven-round burst, unsighted...

...low to high.

Nasi hears the dry vegetation crunch under his feet. Instantly registering his error. He thinks about diving forward just as the first round tares a gouge through his upper thigh. For an instant, his only pain-free thought is to acknowledge the field had been prepared by someone who knew their trade.

He begins returning fire—*full automatic*—though he knows his rounds are hitting nothing but dirt. Even so, he keeps his finger pulling hard against the trigger. *Because what choice does he have?*

From barely inches above ground level, bright pops of muzzle-flash blink in rapid succession less than twenty yards ahead. He feels two crippling punches through his Kevlar, staggering him backwards as a third bullet rips through the top of his right shoulder.

The fact three rounds have missed their target, doesn't register as consolation. Because, by the time a seventh round ploughs a broad gouge through the top of his head—*hair, flesh and bone torn away*—he is already unconscious.

Roll and rise. Two seconds flat. Aim...

...rinse and repeat.

Zalizo fires off three rounds. Mid-level sight-line, over the lip of the trench. All going high. Because the figure is down. Slumped on his knees. Head bowed in what looks like prayer. Arms hanging limp. Fancy-looking AR-15 laying a couple of feet behind. His fourth round tares through the figures throat. The next two striking centre mass. Jack-knifing the figure back onto the earth.

He rises and strides across to the folded over corpse, lowering his gun. Eases back on the four-pound trigger. Puts a quarter-sized hole through the middle of Benjamin Nasi Abelman's forehead.

ATCHAFALAYA DELTA, LOUISIANA

Perry had heard the explosions, rolling in from somewhere to the west. Watched as a wash of orange light flared bright, then dim back below the canopy.

Right now, he's close on twenty feet above the ground. Having just watched—*enthralled*—as a gunfight had played out beneath him. Albeit with little or no interest in figuring out what the hell was going down. All that mattered was that by the time the victor had risen from a shallow trench, cautiously approaching the folded up corpse, he is able to shin down from his perch—*silent and unseen*—as a final shot rang out into the shadows.

He steps out from behind the trunk. Raises his Colt.

Then, as the figure turns, he hears a sound. Like someone making a clicking noise with their tongue.

Perry smiles.

He'd counted way more than a dozen shots fired. And the figure before him was packing a hefty calibre of some kind. So, even with an extended magazine, the chump was likely clean out of ammo. And clean out of luck—*whoever he was*. Even so, there's something weird about the lack of emotion on the face of the man standing before him. Not one flicker of concern. And certainly not a trace of fear. More like mild curiosity, as far as it's possible to tell—*the light bein' so crap an'all.*

Whatever.

He pulls back the hammer on his revolver, not bothering to take careful aim. He's standing well back. So no way anyone's getting the jump on him. Because he knows the drill well enough. His recent training, pretty much burnt-in instinct by now.

Ready for any eventuality.

Then he registers a different kind of sound. One that comes out of nowhere and everywhere—*all at once.* Like the distant rhythm of hooves from a wild mustang eating up the ground.

He half turns, part way through focussing his aim. Watches—*mesmerised*—as a phantom shape lunges out of the gloom. Fangs glinting white in the sallow light. Its jaws clamping like a bear-trap onto his extended arm.

He watches his pistol slow-motion-fall onto the dirt as he hollers—*long and loud.* Teeth ripping into his bare flesh. Shredding through muscle and ligament like wire through cheese. A bone-crushing force clamping down...

...*twisting and tearing.*

He stumbles and shrieks, losing his footing. Starts thrashing as his face hits the loose earth. But that only makes things a thousand times worse; a pulse of blood spraying into his open mouth, already clogged with loam. Choking as he flails. Shock and blind panic freezing his mind as he's dragged—*kicking and screaming*—through thick vegetation.

Then something that feels like a bowling ball slams into the side of his head.

Zalizo stares down at the inert form—*lying naked, bald as a coot and caked in dried mud from head to toe*—sighting his gun on the centre of Perry Morgan Blake's forehead. Resting his finger against the trigger guard. Assuming he would feel nothing but raw hatred and undiluted rage; its twin poisons having coursed through his blood for so long. Sure the impulse to pull the trigger, slow and even, would be irresistible.

But in the end, the abomination lying at his feet has become little more than a footnote. Something to pity—*almost.* No doubt the product of some heinous abuse or other. And the simple fact that he was here, stood as confirmation; Perry Morgan Blake had been trained and manipulated by Victor Labette. For a purpose no sane person could even contemplate, let alone envisage. Indoctrinated or endorsed to go right ahead and violate those who had—*at no point*—caused either man the slightest harm. Demons of their own choosing, with a litany of reasons polluting their under-developed minds to legitimise the evil choices they had made.

And there it was. *The truth of it all.* The self-same vestiges, of violence suffered equals violence inflicted, that would describe—*to the exact same degree*—his own motivations and behaviour had he been the one being judged.

Choices.

Pulling the trigger would be little more than second nature to the kind of man he'd become.

Self-appointed judge and executioner.

The all-conquering righter of wrongs.

He pictures Anne-Marie Hollenbeck—*smiling, sunlight bathing her face, a warm breeze or a boyfriend's first touch, stroking her unblemished skin*—wondering if there would have ever been a scintilla of encouragement uttered from her mouth, for him to do what came so naturally. Endlessly following Seigo's prophecy of bloodlust. Forever exacting relentless and unchecked retribution. With so many imagined blessings—*from beyond the grave*—to seek and destroy.

He doubts it.

But it was too late now.

His kick to the scrawny pricks shaven head had carried every ounce of his pain. His guilt. His desperation. The sense of betrayal he carries like a shaman's curse.

Perry Morgan Blake's neck had broken with the snap of a dried out twig. To an extent, even Moko had backed away; head bowed to the earth. Any choice he might have had, now lost to uncontrolled rage and anatomical fragility.

He loads a fresh magazine. Slides his gun back into its holster. Then sets to securing Blake's bloodied limbs hard behind his back. Rolling him over and forcing his mouth wide open. Pulling Moko's tracker from its pouch. Pushing it home, past all the dirt, as far as it will go.

Job done, he activates his comms.

'MIKE-*One*... ITEM-*One*, over.'

'*MIKE-One... go ahead.*'

'Package secure,' Zalizo says. 'Make the call.'

Then he gets to work.

ATCHAFALAYA DELTA, LOUISIANA

Victor hears a series of shots. A quarter mile off, at a guess. Fired in quick succession. Six or seven—*he can't be sure*. Followed by a short burst of what had to be rifle fire on full automatic.

It persuades him he'd been right choosing a route closer to the shoreline. Albeit it had taken him farther from the place he needs to be, it had been a necessary trade-off. Because he'd already decided, he has no intention of getting drawn into whatever was going on out there.

At least not yet.

Not until he has his weapon of choice nestled firmly in his giant hands.

Up to now, he's always fought his battles on his own terms. And he'll be damned if he'll allow some upstart, fucking *jarhead* to force him away from the strategies he's developed over a lifetime of dominating whatever space he chose to occupy. Especially any place where he elected to make a stand.

He'd owned this parcel of land for close on quarter of a century. And yet, despite the big old house's undoubted splendour—*with its elegant shuttered windows and graceful ironwork balconies*—he'd never truly considered it a home. Instead, it had remained what it had always been; nothing but an infantile indulgence. Built in the ornate fashion he'd carried in his head as a child. The kind of signature residence—*given some benevolent shift in the universe*—he should have been born into. Populated with the sort of folk who would have given true meaning to his poise and stature. And his intellect—*of course*. But the one thing his wealth could never provide was the exclusivity of a *bona fide* lineage he'd always yearned for. Because, no matter the vast array of expensive possessions he'd acquired, that special birthright worn so casually by those whose privileged ancestry could be traced—*whose place within an elite required no endorsement*—would forever remain a prize he would never hold. Which is why this facsimile, this mere folly of an ancestral home, had never become anything more than an asset listed on his investment property portfolio. The place where he'd moulded every one of his many deadly acolytes over the years. Remote enough to hide a private army. But not so isolated restless men couldn't find somewhere nearby to slake their hard-ons. A place where secret plans and intense training programs had remained obscured from prying eyes. Out of sight from medalling eco-busybodies or over-zealous park rangers.

Another round of gunfire rings out. At least six shots. Maybe seven. Again, he doesn't bother counting. Rapid, for sure, but not full-auto. And still far enough he's nowhere close to becoming concerned. One thing's for sure, they were being fired from a meaty calibre barrel.

Regardless, he keeps pushing forward through the dense

foliage, his mind ablaze with the depth of betrayal. Still reeling from the ignominy of having—*once again*—been played for a fool.

He hears a single shot boom out.

So he pushes his burning resentment aside. Shifting his focus to the XM214 sitting loaded in his well-stocked armoury. Certain—*amid all his doubts*—of one sure-fire inevitability. There wasn't anyone surviving an encounter with him, once he got his meaty hands on his mini-gun.

Somewhere to the north, a series of long-drawn-out screams echoes through the forest. But again, he pays it no heed. He would join the fray when he was good and ready—*not a moment before*.

He brakes clear of the forest a short while later. Scans the gravel driveway leading from his private riverside pontoon, three-quarters-of-a-mile through the forest, back up to the *Big House*. Pausing for a moment while he gathers his thoughts. Hearing nothing but his own heavy breathing. He re-checks his Mk48 is locked and loaded and melts back into the woods. Finding a narrow deer track leading away from the river, snaking parallel to the drive.

Back towards his arsenal.

ARLINGTON, WASHINGTON DC

It has always struck him as a capricious irony that Arlington National Cemetery lay unchallenged among the nation's most revered slices of real-estate. A suitably dignified, pristine landscape. Home to row-upon-row of impossibly precise white marble headstones. A parcel of land confiscated from the wife of a defeated Civil War general; for no other reason than to satisfy the yet to be forgiven bitterness and malice of a nation attempting to stitch its wounds after four years of partisan blood-letting. And as good a place as any to take a call. A place where an elderly man could stand with his head bowed for as long as he liked without raising even the slightest curiosity. In fact, he could have driven over in the middle of the night, if he chosen to. He was a three-star general after all. No-one in their right mind would have refused him entry.

The satellite phone nestling in his inside pocket begins vibrating. He fishes it out and pokes the pick-up icon.

'General... this is MIKE-*One.'*

For the first time in years, he feels his heart begin to race.

'Go ahead...'

There's a momentary pause.

'Sir... the package is secure.'

'Good... and is ITEM-*One* still with you?'

'Affirmative...'

'Okay... so lock it down. Then wait for extraction. And Sergeant...'

'Sir...?'

'The pair of you stay together.'

'Affirmative,' Runellie says. *'Do you want that I put him on?'*

'No, Sergeant... that won't be necessary.'

ATCHAFALAYA DELTA, LOUISIANA

Fifty yards back from the house, just inside the treeline, Victor sweeps at a patch of earth with his boots. Kicking aside a weave of thin branches and vegetation matted to a square of olive-green netting. Revealing a six-foot by four-foot heavy steel door. A large iron pull-ring at one end. No hinges visible at the other.

He enters a four-digit code into the integrated, hermetically-sealed keypad. Hauls on the iron ring. Standing aside as an internal counter-balance raises the three-hundred pound, blast-proof door to vertical. Activating his cell phone's torch as he enters the tunnel. Pulling the hatch closed as he descends a flight of concrete steps. Crouching low. Having to stoop as he shuffles sideways along the narrow walkway.

At the end of the passage, he enters the same four-digit code into an identical key-pad, next to an identical heavily-framed steel door. Pulling it wide open as he rises from his crouch, stepping into his armoury.

He flicks on the overhead fluorescent light. Stands for a few seconds, admiring the array of weaponry covering the walls on either side. Dumping his *Mk48* onto the steel table standing in the centre of the vault before pulling his mini-gun free of its mount. Dry-cycling it twice. Fixing its ammo box in place.

Then he strides across to a third steel door, killing the lights. Gritting his teeth. Speaking, aloud, the thought that entered his head the moment he'd made it to the tunnel's entrance.

'Okay, Iron Man... Let's see exactly how tough you are.'

Victor waits for his sight to adjust before taking the flight of steps, leading up from the armoury to his state-of-the-art kitchen, two-at-a-time. After all, this was no Hollywood movie. There would be no creeping around in the dark. Nervously swinging his weapon back and forth.

Screw that.

He would be commanding the field—*just like he always had.* And as he always would.

He grips his mini-gun a little tighter. Strides from the kitchen into a large entrance hall, with stairs running to the upper floor on either side. Joined together by a balconied landing curving out over the polished limestone floor below.

From the centre of the balustrade, Perry Morgan Blake's body hangs at the end of a length of rope. Swinging in and out from a well of shadows thrown by the balcony. Dripping blood as it sways back and forth.

Victor lowers his gaze. Tracking a trail of severed fingers and what—*if he was forced to guess*—looked like a piece of someone's tongue, arranged like some macabre homage to Hansel and Gretel, trailing out toward the wide-open main entrance.

'Mon dieu... n'es-tu pas le petit artiste?'

He steps into the foyer. Hauls his weapon up level with his hip. Bellows out toward the forest.

'SO HERE I AM... LEG ZALIZO.'

He prepares to move forward.

'YOU READY TO GET THIS THING OVER WITH...?'

Out in the gloom beyond the doorway, just past mid-distance, an indistinct shape ghosts between the trees.

Victor sets his weapon spinning. Spews an avalanche of three-O-eight rounds through the open doorway. Blasting chunks from the spread of trees, then ripping half the door frame to shreds. Stitching a line of holes along the foyer wall.

He eases his finger off the trigger. Waits until the high-pressure whirr of barrels spinning slows to a stop. Listens to the silence of the forest seeping back into the foyer.

Then his hearing registers a different kind of high-pitched whine. A sound he recognises all too well. The noise of an incoming projectile. Propelled—*he's almost certain*—by a single-stage solid-fuel rocket. He recalls, instantly, the last time he'd heard such a sound. Only on that occasion, the trajectory had been far enough away, he'd barely given it any thought. Hadn't even considered abandoning his sickly-sweet Lebanese coffee.

A shiver of ice spikes its way down his spine—*a sensation he barely recalls*—warning him this was going to be a whole different experience to the one he'd encountered in Beirut.

His mind starts racing. His eyes darting back the way he'd come. To the stairwell leading to the safety of his armoury. His muscles turning to lead as he wills his feet to move. Toward his only hope of finding cover before the crushing impact he knows is only seconds away hits its mark.

Towards his one chance at survival.

He is barely half way to the kitchen doorway when the explosion hits. Slamming home like a freight train. A wall of heat blow-torching his flesh, as a pressure wave lifts him bodily; like he weighed next to nothing at all. Propelling him across the length of the kitchen. Smashing him into chunks of quartz and razor-sharp stainless steel. Blasting him on through hardwood and glass at a rate even his enormous frame is unable to withstand.

He continues on with a hail of debris, large and small. Almost all of it travelling much faster than he was. Tearing at his flesh from every angle.

He lands shredded and broken. Scarcely conscious. Barely alive. His spine severed. Limbs shattered or gone. Breathing ragged and shallow. His world suddenly opaque behind a wall of deafening silence. Slowly drowning as his lungs begin to fill with blood. Anything he feels dislocated from any sense of place. *Or purpose*. Able to feel little more than vague impulses. Every one of his nerve endings burned. Every synapse devastated or malfunctioning. Every neuron unburdened from its core biological function. Close on forty trillion cells waiting for one last heartbeat before shutting down for good, on their slow passage to dust.

A last vestige of defiance forces his scorched eyelids to flutter open. And, for a brief moment, his optic nerve defies molecular mechanics. Registering a shadowy form loom out of a milky haze. A faceless, shapeless aberration, sending tendrils of something sub-zero through the remnants of his frontal cortex. Freezing whatever remained of his consciousness. Pulling him down in an iron grip.

Beyond crush-depth.

His final conscious reflex, little more than a shiver.

Unable to hear three quietly-spoken words.

'I guess so...'

ATCHAFALAYA DELTA, LOUISIANA

'MIKE-*One,* this is ITEM-*One*... we're coming in.'

Runellie says, 'Roger that.'

Zalizo breaks from the treeline to see Johanssen loading his ribbed inflatable with bags of gear.

'I'm guessing you guys had yourselves some fun holding off the cavalry?'

Johanssen says, 'It was a blast.'

'Permanently silenced or subdued?'

Runellie says, 'Subdued, as far as we know. But time and trauma keep their own tally... and we came close to running out of darts.'

'So, how long do we have before they recover from their slumber?'

'We figure four hours,' Johanssen says. 'Give or take.'

'And will they all make it out unaided?'

'There's a few could wake up a little sore. But my guess is, they'll all make it out under their own steam... eventually. Though you can probably add on another couple of hours for the hike they'll be making.'

'Excellent,' Zalizo says.

Runellie is on her haunches. Pouring water from her canteen over Moko's blood-stained jaws.

Zalizo gets to stripping down his own gear.

'Chief... if you'd be so kind and drop us back at Morgan City, I'll be sure to come visit you sometime down the line.'

'I'll look forward to it,' Johanssen says.

Runellie says, 'And after Morgan City?'

Zalizo says, 'I recommend you stay clear of DC for a while. Maybe head on back to Atlanta for a few days... or Florida.'

'MacDill or Disneyland?'

'I'll leave that decision in your hands, Sergeant. But if it's MacDill... you know who to call.'

'Sure,' she says. 'And where will you be heading, Colonel?'

Zalizo stalls his reply.

Johanssen makes like he isn't listening. Slaps the gunnel of his boat, encouraging Moko to jump aboard.

Runellie doesn't quit waiting for an answer.

'Colonel...?'

Zalizo says, 'I have a little house-keeping to attend to back at Marks Centre. After that... hard to say.'

Day Six

'Yes, Sir... No, Sir'

MARKS CENTRE, WASHINGTON DC

The General rises slowly when Zalizo enters the fifteen square-foot space fronting as a private office. If he feels an ounce of surprise, he certainly isn't letting on. Instead, he casually lifts a crystal tumbler—*half-full of something amber*—as he moves from behind his desk. Giving it an absent-minded swirl. Raising the glass and taking a decent-sized swig. Making an exaggerated show of savouring the taste.

'Colonel... so glad you could make it.'

Zalizo holds off replying. Closing the door behind him. Waiting for the snick of automatic locks to confirm they will remain undisturbed.

'Very well,' the General says. 'Since you appear somewhat peeved... maybe we should put off our debrief until you're a little less tetchy.'

'Our... *debrief*,' Zalizo says. 'Now that would make for an interesting proposition.'

'And, what makes you say that, Colonel?'

Zalizo moves a little further into the room.

'I would have thought you'd have learnt by now, once you exceed my bullshit intake limit, you're pretty much scrubbed from my good books.'

The general offers his customary thin smile.

'And this should bother me, why?'

'You can make like you're wearing big-boy pants all you like. Bottom line, General... you screwed up. Thinking you could use my vengeful nature to sanitise your little operation once it began to spiral out of control. Turning a straightforward hit job to a major-league shit-show, from the moment you outsourced to a CIA-trained psychopath. Someone so fucked up, even those old-school neo-cons in Langley disavowed him decades ago. And all because you were sure of two things...'

The General scoffs.

'Only two? But, okay... let's indulge this little fantasy of yours.'

'*Oh*, it's far from fantasy, General... and you can stick you're indulgence where the sun don't shine...'

He eases forward another stride.

'I bet you thought you'd really hit paydirt when Perry Morgan Blake was transferred out of Huntsville. Because you knew that was a bone I'd never quit gnawing at. And I'd wager you figured, once you served us Victor Labette on a plate, one way or another, your number one problem would be resolved...'

The general shrugs.

'As theories go... it's a little implausible.'

'Yes, it is. But there's one thing you didn't factor...'

'Please... do tell.'

'Runellie was never falling for your bullshit.'

'Your precocious lapdog.'

'Bravo, General. Misogyny, myopia and arrogance in one three-word sentence. That's pretty impressive...'

The General raises his glass, taking another long swig.

'Would it interest you to know what tipped her off?'

'Not particularly,' the General says. 'But I'm guessing that's not going to keep you from postulating.'

'Chain of command...'

For a second or two, the general looks genuinely perplexed.

'The moment you came to see her, she asked herself... *why me?*

You're a three-star lifer. Oval Office appointed. With easy access to a level of resource capable of getting you anything you want. Anytime. And pretty much anywhere. The kind of authority that's able to raise a SOF detachment to assault a heavily-armed facility in under eighteen hours. So, for damn sure, she wasn't buying all that '*...do you want to help the Colonel?*' horseshit.'

'Good for her.'

'Like I told you, she's one of a kind. And, just so you know... she's the reason I wasn't alone in Oregon.'

Zalizo watches a brief flash of shock spike across the general's face.

'So, you're not the first slack-skinned sack of bile to try, and fail, to nail her ass to a post.'

'*Sack of bile...* wow, Colonel. Even for you, that's a whole new level of insubordination. Which leads me to suspect you think you're in some kind of position to expose me?'

'As far as I'm concerned, you're just like any other supremacist. White, political, religious, militaristic... you're all the same to me. Just a bunch of diseased mis-fits, all slithering around the same cesspool. Which means, right now, my plans for your future are pretty fluid.'

'Are they indeed? Well, I can't imagine how you've arrived at that conclusion, Colonel. Especially since you have very little, if any, evidence of wrongdoing on my part. I'll grant you're extremely competent doing what it is you do... and that you've always demonstrated an extraordinary talent for unrestrained brutality. But if you think, for one minute, you're the one in control right now... because you're somehow special, you are not only gravely mistaken. You're also a pathetic idealist... not to mention, the kind of fool I've never previously taken you for.'

The General places his glass back on his standard, military issue steel-framed desk.

'In so far as they align with my purposes... have I valued your contributions when it came to solving my little squabbles? Yes... absolutely. But only in the manner of a hound, content to endlessly chase rodent's. Beyond this very narrow parameter, just like any other subordinate, you've always been... *expendable*. And, you appear to have forgotten... I don't answer to anyone you can expose me to. I'd always pegged you as a reasonably intelligent man... so I'm a little surprised I have to spell it out.'

Zalizo makes like he hadn't listened to a single word.

'You want to know something, General...?'

'If I must,' the General says.

'For the whole of my life,' Zalizo continues. 'I've never truly struggled at anything. From as early as I can remember, I've always flown through pretty much every challenge anyone ever threw at me...'

'Colonel... it would be good to know if this self-aggrandisement is of any particular relevance to me.'

Again, Zalizo bats his mentor's insults aside.

'But when it came to understanding the properties of light, if I'm honest, I never really got there.'

'Light...?'

'Yes, General... *light*. You see, I never really got a handle on how it manifests as both a particle and a wave... and sometimes both... simultaneously. Most specifically, the way it chooses to reveal what it is and where it is, only at the point it's observed...'

The General picks up his glass. Takes another slow slug.

'Fascinating, I'm sure.'

'And that, left to its own devices, it travels through time and space, unhindered by any need to identify itself as one thing or another. Blissfully indistinct, you might say. And, given the unresolved nature of the Fermi Paradox, my guess is, it does so largely unobserved.'

'Believe it or not, Colonel, I truly wish there was a small part of me that cared, even a little bit, about whatever point it is you're trying to make.'

'The point... you want to know my point?'

'Like a lot of folk occupying your orbit, Colonel... I realise you've never lacked for intellectual pomposity. So, if it moves this along, yes... I'd really appreciate it.'

Zalizo takes another stride forward. His expression passive. Like he was stepping up to snap a salute.

'Well, General... I've come to the conclusion, it almost exactly represents what you've become.'

'What in God's name are you talking about? Please, don't tell me you still believe I give a shit what you think of me.'

Zalizo spends a few seconds scanning the room.

'You're just a little unobserved parcel of something amorphous. Existing largely undisturbed... because no-one wants to examine, in any great detail, the particularly sordid duality you inhabit. Preferring to remain ignorant of what it is you actually do. Or where and why you do it.'

'If you say so, Colonel.'

'And, do you know what I am, General?'

'Not exactly... but, no doubt, you're just about to enlighten me.'

'I'm the split aperture that's just opened up in your little Special Executive Order experiment...'

'Good for you, Colonel.'

'Which allows me to perceive both the before, and the after. It means I'm able to distinguish wave from particle. Enables me to determine what you really are... and the position I need to adopt to extinguish your light.'

The General curls his mouth into a sneer.

'Eloquence and extended metaphor. Now it's you excelling

yourself, *Colonel.*'

'I'm guessing you thought you had all your angles covered. Knowing Runellie would never consider deploying without her dog. Going out of your way to confirm the animal was chipped. Insisting she stayed glued to my hip.'

'Each one an action with a perfectly plausible explanation. Because, believe it or not, Zalizo... I'm the one running this goddam unit. And, I can assure you, the individual I answer to won't have the slightest interest in spurious accusations against me. Or any wild conspiracies for that matter.'

'Innocent people have died...'

Zalizo takes a final half-stride forward.

'...living and unborn,' he spits through his teeth.

'I had a job to do, Colonel. And it required power-hungry fools to help get it done. That unfortunate incident in Dallas aside... I've done nothing I wouldn't do again in a heartbeat. And do you honestly think this is the first occasion I've protected this nation's interests by any and all means at my disposal? *Jesus*... you really need to get a grip on reality. And, if you're contemplating causing me physical harm... you'd better consider this. Your own less than saintly exploits, at that meth lab outside Farmington, are on a file that I hold. Those men you butchered... they were legal US residents. And particularly diligent when it came to security. They had a camera rolling. Transmitting back to their office in Albuquerque. And, even after all these years, that gets you fifty-to-life in a New Mexico State Pen... at a minimum.'

The General sets his jaw.

'It may surprise you to learn, Elizabeth Holt and I met at *Yale.* When she was tutoring while she worked towards her doctorate. And, for reasons neither of us fully understood, we hit it off. Entirely platonic, I might add. Which ensured we remained friends. Followed each other's careers. And it's the reason she brought the tape to me. Persuaded me those unfortunate Ukrainians you slaughtered were no great loss to society. Convinced me, after what had happened to your parents... you deserved a break.'

The General's eyes radiate defiance.

'So maybe you still don't get it. Still haven't figured you're the runt in this particular dogfight. And, even if you hadn't volunteered for military service, with your indomitable capabilities, I would have found a way to draw you into my domain. So, Oleg Constantine... I suggest you process that little... *item*... before you...'

Zalizo turns his back.

'You know what, General... you talk too much.'

The General picks up his glass.

'Sounds like the pot's calling out the kettle to me, Colonel. Besides, doesn't every mastermind get to make a speech...'

He raises his drink in mock salute.

'...*Lieutenant*-Colonel?'

Zalizo spins. Left fist clenched. Slamming it home a fraction below the solar plexus. A blow short on travel. Heavy on torque. Delivered upwards, with the force of a two-hundred and five pound steel piston. Nigh-on lifting the surprisingly frail old man off his feet. Snapping his head forward like he'd just wrecked his ancient Plymouth sedan, head-on into a tree. Slack jaw hitting his chest. Eyes blank and devoid of light before his rear end has time to thump squarely onto the metal chair, arranged beside his desk.

Zalizo stares at the body of the man he'd come close to considering a surrogate father. A man he'd thought infallible. Someone he'd been convinced had always covered his back.

He lifts the inert corpse from the chair. Supporting it easily. Spinning it round and lining it up. Pushing it real hard onto the corner of the solid steel desk.

Then he snags the rug where the General must have tripped

at the moment of his fatal coronary. Assesses the crystal tumbler smashed across the concrete floor as plausible. Knows the room's design makes it a perfect place to guard its secrets. No cameras. No audio. No cell phones. No recording devices of any kind permitted. Not even a notepad. Because that's the way the *General* had insisted his office be set up.

Secure and compartmented.

After a quick search of the General's body, Zalizo finds himself staring down at a figure that looks suddenly puny. Nonetheless, he snaps a sharp salute. Because—*when all was said and done*—for the time being at least, he remains an officer of the United States Marine Corp.

'General,' he says quietly.

Then he turns. Walks to the lock-release pad. Presses the green button and pushes through the door.

ARLINGTON, WASHINGTON DC

General Wesley B. Stoner taps a quiet rhythm onto his plain beechwood desk, staring at the West Point class ring sitting—*as it had since he'd graduated*—on the pinkie finger of his left hand. These days, a little too gaudy and, for damn sure, at least one size too snug.

In his other hand, a by-gone-era red telephone receiver is pressed tight to his ear.

Despite the low-tech audio, the voice on the other end of the call is as grey and graceless as a New Jersey boardwalk. Heavy on bark. Short on bite. Devoid of *gravitas.* Or, for that matter, even a modicum of intellect.

The caller fires their first question over the line without preamble.

Stoner sets himself to respond in kind. Because, if this call is headed the way he suspects it is, he's already decided—*fuck it.*

As he begins to speak, he recalls—*with a wry smile*—his mother's oft-used, earthy old-world invocation.

Just remember, son... faint hearts never lay with fair maidens.

'Yes, Sir... it landed on my desk not fifteen minutes ago.'

...

'No, Sir... It's currently being called as natural causes.'

...

'There was a good amount of alcohol in his bloodstream... yes. But right now, beyond some preliminaries, I'd rather not speculate.'

...

'No, Sir... not at this time. And my feeling is, under present circumstances... and considering his somewhat renowned skill sets, a large-scale manhunt would be ill-advised.'

...

'That's correct. He was more than likely the last person to see General Maddock alive. But even that's unconfirmed. And, as of right now, there's no suggestion he was directly involved... and no evidence the General wasn't alive after he left.'

...

'No, Sir... it's set up as a SCIF. So it might as well have happened on the Moon.'

...

'I fully expect he'll come in of his own accord. And, if he's not directly involved, it's possible he hasn't heard the news yet.'

...

'Like I said, Sir... it's possible.'

...

'That would be my fervent hope. I don't know him

personally... but I'm told he's one of a kind. With a past reputation for issuing strong... let's call it, *advice*... to certain of his senior officers. But I believe he'll recognise it's in his best interest to report in A-sap, once the news reaches him.'

...

'Yes, Sir... that's correct, but his request was never actioned. So, as of right now, he's a United States Marine Lieutenant-Colonel. And, until my inquiries are concluded, that's precisely what he'll remain.'

...

'Respectfully, Sir... since I haven't had an opportunity to identify all those involved, let alone personally debrief anyone... I was hoping *you* could tell me.'

...

'Again... respectfully. It was not intended, in any way, to be an accusation.'

...

'Well, Sir... I don't consider those particular aspects of my preliminary report represent unreasonable assumptions, given the Special Executive Order I had waved under my nose not twelve hours ago.'

...

'Yes, Sir... he did.'

...

'As I've already indicated... my enquiries are ongoing.'

...

'No, Sir... I will not.'

...

'Generally speaking, Sir... that's what *no* means when I say it. And, if you thought it would be otherwise, you can take it from me... you made the wrong appointment.'

...

'Good day to you to... *Mr. President.*'

Epilogue

'...heading east.'

LUBBOCK, TEXAS

According to his calculations, it was day nine since Vanessa Jean Clarke had taken his second order of eggs on rye.

Out to the west, the last vestige of a giant, blood-orange sun is sinking fast. Setting Lubbock's angular downtown skyline aglow. Sunlight reflecting like crimson lasers off the windows of a half-dozen or so modest towers huddled at the heart of a city that looked to be on fire.

Seventy-two hours on, and no news had broken on the events outside Morgan City. Or those in DC for that matter. Not a single headline on any media outlet—*local or national*—reporting unexplained explosions out on the Atchafalaya Delta. Or the mysterious death of a retired three-star general.

Runellie was back at Marks Centre—*much sooner than he'd advised*. Zalizo knows this because he'd spent a good amount of time watching. Far enough away to cover front and rear access. Close enough to scope anything other than the usual comings and goings at his former place of work. But, as it happened, he'd seen nothing out of the ordinary. No contingents of MPs. Or any suspicious activity from the Feds or Secret Service. Certainly no abnormal influx of top brass. And there would have been for sure, if any link with Morgan City had been made.

He was certain of it.

So he'd been satisfied his former boss had kept his final deeds close to his chest. And—*more importantly*—that his Sergeant was in the clear.

And yet, despite the radio silence, he knows the same clean-break status will not apply to him. Because, by now, someone had to know he'd been the last person to see the general alive.

It might be all they knew. But it would likely be enough.

However, if it transpired he wasn't under direct suspicion for the General's demise, they would have no reason to assume he'd found the Italian leather wallet. And the Special Executive Order it contained. With words, albeit few in number and far from explicit, confirming his mentor had possessed something close to absolute immunity. A mandate to eliminate or manipulate everyone. *Any time. Anywhere.* Including, he'd since confirmed, a certain former Green Beret. Offering the newly appointed Dallas PD captain his unit's services. But not before swearing him to secrecy. A deception that had left a cold and bitter taste in both their mouths.

So he'd decided, since he couldn't risk going anywhere near the apartment he rented in Lincolnia Heights, he'd begin his journey south by destroying what remained of his DCS comms. Hurling half-a-dozen stripped-down devices into the water as he'd driven past Lake Bancroft. Hitting the 395 to Springfield at 04.00 hours. Heading south. Joining the I-95 to Richmond. Then on through Nashville to Oklahoma City. A motel room, and the little nourishment he could stomach, paid for in cash.

Then on through Amarillo to Plainview.

Because he'd decided Clyde Jeramiah Tillings deserved to receive his thanks in person. Sure, the man had no trouble masquerading as an oversized jerk. But, against all the odds, the guy turned out to be as solid as they come. Proof of which lay in the singular fact that Deputy Sheriff D. H. Abbott was nowhere to be seen.

After which he'd driven on to Lubbock. Dropping off the GMC. Retrieving his AMX.

Next, he'd made a calorie stop at a place he used to frequent on 50th Street; unsurprised the business was still a going concern. He'd ordered kimchi, fried chicken and red rice cakes. And a pitcher of ice cold water. Receiving a few raised eyebrows and a couple of warm smiles when he'd ordered his meal and offered his thanks in Korean. Back in the day, it had been—*by a decent margin*—his favourite place to eat. And a good amount of time before he'd paid his bill, his opinion hadn't changed.

Now he was back behind the wheel of his AMX. Stalled at the parking lot's exit. His emotions crushed up against a wall of doubt. Feeling trapped. Like he was pinned to the jagged rock-face of a bottomless chasm. Trying to escape without the aid of ropes. One wrong move, he falls—*further into darkness.* Crashing back to his life of brutality. His only way out—*his one shot at redemption*—fraught with hidden and unknowable risks.

So, once again, he finds himself straddling the void.

Make the call... *or don't make the call.*

Choices.

He knows she's waiting for him. He can feel her beckoning. As strong as any pull he's ever felt. So all he has to do, is reach out. Allow her to draw him in close. Let the touch of her fingers soothe away his doubts. Trust the strength and compassion he'd seen in her eyes will help him break free. Offer him what he knows deep down might be his last chance at finding salvation.

But he also knows the odds he'll be permitted to simply walk away into some halcyon sunset, no questions asked, no strings attached—*to pursue a different life, a life free of violence*—lies somewhere between slim and a million-to-one.

So he has to face yet another cold reality. The bitter legacy of all the things he's seen and done. The immovable, fossilised imprint of the person he'd become, that would forever remain sealed inside his bones. The harsh truth lying beyond that line he'd crossed all those years before.

That place from which few men ever return.

Choices.

An alternate future lies six hours away in El Paso—*out to the west*—toward the warm glow of a setting sun. A present, as yet unresolved, lay twenty-four hours distant, back in DC—*far to the east*—in the direction of the fast-rising darkness.

Inside his head, the decision he knows he has to make begins to take on the feel of a Shakespearian tragedy. And, it strikes him suddenly, the comparison was entirely apt.

So many reasons to go to her.

So many reasons to stay away.

A dichotomy of hope over expectation. A Damoclean exercise in risk and reward.

From behind, a guy sporting a scarlet baseball cap and a sour glare leans on his horn—*long and hard.*

Zalizo raises his hand. Waves a half-hearted apology to the burly figure gesturing in the rear view mirror. Hears Seigo's voice—*dry as wind-blown grit*—whispering in his ear.

'You gonna lose everything you touch...

...for the whole of your life.'

He turns the steering wheel, pulling his cell phone from the centre console. Taps the call icon next to her number as he eases his AMX out onto 50th Street...

...heading east.

Acknowledgments

By its very nature, you might assume writing a novel would be a solitary pursuit. And yet here I am, compelled to express my heartfelt gratitude to everyone who has contributed to this otherwise entirely self-obsessed endeavour.

You know who you are... *as do I.*

Vanessa, I thank you from the bottom of my heart for rescuing me and for your unwavering belief, boundless patience and constant encouragement.

To *Jill Williams* (without whom my beginning would have never made sense); *Eleanor Murphy* (for so many things, not least giving birth, so to speak, to Runellie); and last—*but by no means least*—to my dearest niece, *Mariah Sullivan,* aka: real mom to Moko the Belgian Malinois and the novel's stand-out hero (for insisting the ending should do justice unto itself).

I owe you all a special level of gratitude.

And to others of you—*Mark Van Walwyk in particular*—who took the time to plough through any one of my numerous draughts... I thank you, one and all. Your [real-world reader] feedback was of immeasurable value. Please believe me when I say: *Every step toward seeing this project through to its end, has been inextricably linked to your generosity and insight.'*

My sincere thanks are also owed to James Essinger and James Sadlier; because, to their credit [and my good fortune], these guys know what they're doing.

Blessings to you all.

Barefoot with Scorpions is the debut novel from someone who started out in life as a Windrush generation orphan. After spending a good portion of his adult life raising a family in Cornwall – and following numerous career incarnations – he began writing in earnest while working as a crisis management consultant throughout Europe. He now lives with his partner and their collection of rambunctious animals, on the Essex-Suffolk border in East Anglia.